Matters of the Heart

Corinna M. Dominy

**ISBN-13:
978-1481210485
ISBN-10:
1481210483**

For my David

CONTENTS

ACKNOWLEDGMENTS

This is my first attempt at writing a novel. This I owe to my Creator and my God. I can only hope I have made Him proud. He also bestowed on me a very understanding husband!

Thank you, David, for your love and support as I ventured out into the unknown in the world of writing. Your encouragement on the sidelines helped immensely as I questioned the sanity of what I was doing! You pushed me when I didn't think I had anything left and you must have gained a wealth of patience as you waited for me to finish this, my first novel. Thanks, babe, you're incredible!

Thank you to my grandma, Joan Scofield, as I hesitantly put my manuscript in your hands to hemorrhage all over with your red pen. The advice and corrections of my errors were taken to heart. Your insight was very much valued and appreciated. (Any errors in this novel are my full and complete responsibility.)

And thank you to April Elder for lending me your time in teaching me the ways to get my manuscript published. Your willingness to help, even though we don't know each other very well, humbled me greatly.

And now, dear reader, I hope you enjoy the story of Jacob and Emily Matthews and Joshua and Ashley Tyler.....

Chapter 1: An Unexpected Event

Emily Matthews finally got to the door, just before the person on the other side broke it down with their incessant knocking. She had been in the back of the house sweeping rooms when she first heard it. She was sure it had been a few moments before she even heard that, lending to the possibility that whoever was there was growing impatient.

The children were outside, possibly down at the creek, so they wouldn't have alerted her to the unexpected visitor.

Opening the door, Emily was surprised to see Ashley Tyler.

"Well, Ashley, won't you come in? Silly girl, you shoulda just stepped in. You know you're always welcome to do so." Mentally, Emily puzzled. Why *would* Ashley knock on the door? There were only a handful of instances in the past twelve years that had caused Ashley to knock on their door. They were all during the time the Matthews and Tyler families were still getting to know one another and still merely "neighbors." Now, the Tylers were counted among the Matthews' nearest and dearest friends. And not just because theirs was the closest house around.

"Hello, Em," Ashley began, "I'm sorry to inconvenience you, but I must suddenly go to town. Something urgent has come up…and I need to go there," Ashley finished somewhat vaguely. She stared down at her shoes.

"Ashley," Emily started, concern etching her voice, "is something the matter? Did something happen to Josh?"

Joshua Tyler was Ashley's husband. The mill he worked at was purported to be dangerous, one of the most dangerous around. It was always Ashley's worry that something bad would happen to him.

"No, nothing like that." Ashley looked up and gave Emily a weak smile.

Emily was still puzzling over Ashley's strange behavior. "Well, is there something I can do to help?"

Ashley's face did light up then. And it almost seemed as if relief flooded through her. "Yes, yes, there is! That's why I came by. I just wondered, if it wouldn't be too much of an inconvenience, to have the children stay here with you and Jacob for the evening. At least until Josh gets home. Right now, I think they are all down at the creek."

"You've never inconvenienced me, Ashley!" Emily assured her.

'Inconvenience me! Why would she even think that?' One thing was for sure, Ashley was acting strangely.

"You're sure everything's okay?" Emily tried again.

"Yes, Em, I'm sure." Ashley suddenly grasped her friend's hand and gave her a warm, reassuring smile. "Everything is as it should be. Thank you for watching the children. I do need to be on my way so I'll be going now. Good-bye, dear friend!" With that, Ashley turned and calmly walked out of the house.

Emily, still puzzling, went back to finish her household chores.

"Hey, let's go see if Mama has supper ready yet," Alyssa Tyler suggested.

"Yeah, I'm starved!" agreed Brianna Matthews.

The two girls, separated by only one year, were included in a gang of Matthews/Tyler children who spent as many waking hours together as possible. There were eight in this "gang."

The oldest of them was the only boy, unfortunately for him. Christopher Matthews only tolerated his three sisters and the four Tyler girls if they were doing something he deemed "manly", like catching frogs or tadpoles in the creek. Which, fortunately for him, they did practically all summer long. And, since it was almost the beginning of summer, he was in luck.

Christopher was five feet, four inches and appeared to be slight in build, but was really quite solid. His eyes were round pools of deep, dark green set off by the tan of his skin. His skin held the tan year round, but was made darker by the summer sun. The sun also altered his wispy hair from a dark blond in the dreary winter months, to a pale yellow as summer approached.

He loved nature, being in nature, anything nature-related, including stray animals, which he helped as much as he could.

He was older than Madison Tyler by only one month, but

loved holding it over her as "being the oldest."

Madison Tyler was a few inches shorter than Christopher, also a point he liked to torment her about. She was also slight of build and fragile-looking. Her large, luminous eyes were jade green with yellow and darker green flecks. They accentuated the paleness of her skin. The mass of curls that cascaded down her back were a marvelous shade of copper with threads of gold entwined throughout them.

She had a stubborn streak that her fragile appearance masked.

Next in the group came the Tyler twins, Alexis and Alyssa, who were eleven. They were small for their age, appearing to be younger than they really were. The twins had been born early and never seemed to catch up to their peers. Their eyes were set close together, giving them a smart, owlish look. Their black eyes spread to an inky indigo at the irises. They had a healthy, sun-kissed glow to their skin. Yet, their hair exactly matched their older sister's.

Their looks were all that was identical about them for they had very different personalities.

Alexis was strong-willed and had lots of gumption, but could turn on the charm and be all sweetness and light if she felt like it. She was also known to be a little impulsive at times. Both girls shared a very close and special relationship and Alexis's loyalty to Alyssa was fierce. Since she was older by three minutes, she was very protective of her twin.

Alyssa was extremely studious and enjoyed school. She was quiet, but was known to open up if she was around people she was comfortable with. Those people were usually only her family and the Matthews.

Next in line, age wise, was Brianna Matthews who, like Kayla Tyler, was ten. She was older by only a mere week; to the day, in fact.

Brianna was short and plump, but in a way that gave her a baby doll look, as did her teal green eyes. The effect was completed with her skin, which was like bone china. Her blond, straight hair hung to the middle of her back. Brianna didn't let her looks fool people for everyone knew she was an adventurous tomboy. She got along well with her big brother, though he hated to admit he had a special fondness for Brianna.

Kayla Tyler was Brianna's best friend, due mostly to their closeness in age.

Kayla, the youngest Tyler, was of medium height and, like her friend, plump. Her large, round eyes were dark brown, but appeared almost translucent. They complemented her creamy skin nicely, but her flaming red hair was quite past the beautiful auburn of her three older sisters. According to her, it was the one thing that marred her looks, even though her waves also tumbled down her back.

Kayla was very exacting and proper, not doing anything she felt was wrong or ill-mannered. She was also the most sensitive of the bunch.

The two youngest of the group were Samantha and Hailey Matthews. Samantha, eight, was medium in build, though she would have preferred to be "tall and elegant." Her huge, round, sapphire eyes blazed against skin that matched her sister, Brianna's. Her hair closely matched Kayla Tyler's orange flames, but Samantha felt they both had beautiful hair. The only difference was her hair had corkscrew curls.

Samantha knew how to use her charm to her benefit, if the circumstance arose. However, she had maturity and insight beyond her years. Her parents, Emily especially, were in regular awe at how quickly she picked up on things going on around her.

The youngest, Hailey, was only six, but still kept up with the older children when they were running around.

Her height made her look bigger and older than her six years, as well as her solid build. Her big, pure jade eyes were ringed in amber. They were beautiful to behold. Besides Christopher, she was the only other child in her family that had the darker tanned skin. Curls akin to Samantha's graced Hailey's head. They were more brown than red.

Her bubbly personality was contagious and fitting with the precocious child. She could be quite mischievous as well, even more so than most six-year-olds.

Although the two youngest were sometimes left out because of their age, more often than not, they were included in the group's activities.

"I'll race ya," Madison challenged the group.

That was all it took to get the eight children moving at a rapid pace to their respective homes.

"Mama!" Brianna called as she burst through the door. "Is supper ready yet?"

Emily turned from the sink and peeling potatoes to see her brood pushing through the door. With a smirk, she noted, "Somehow you know when supper's on, don't ya?"

"Alyssa said she wanted to see if her mama had supper on. Then Madison said she'd race us, so we did!" Christopher informed her in a grown up voice that still held childish excitement.

"Shoo with you, then. Go and wash your hands for supper."

As the children left to do her bidding, she stopped Christopher.

"Uh, Chris, would you mind going over to the Tylers' and letting the girls know they'll be having supper here tonight?"

Christopher gave her a questioning look. "Shouldn't I invite Aunt Ashley, too?" The two families were so close, the children took to calling the adults uncle and aunt.

"She won't be there," Emily informed him, a little too quickly.

Giving her another questioning glance he started for the door.

Even though it had only been a couple of hours since Ashley had left, Emily was still worried. Ashley had acted so strangely. She couldn't have possibly gone to town and been back in those few short hours, but Emily couldn't shake the nagging feeling that something was wrong. As soon as she was able to talk to Jacob, her beloved husband, she knew she'd feel better. He always had a way of calming her down. That was one of the reasons she loved him so much.

Thinking of Jacob, she wondered where he was. He seemed to be a little late.

'Now I'm off worrying about him, too,' she silently rebuked herself with a sigh.

She set the last plate on the table when, as if on cue, Jacob walked into the dining room from the kitchen. The kitchen was in the back of the house, and the closest door to come in from the fields.

Emily looked up, catching her breath as always, when her handsome husband entered the room.

Jacob stood a head above Emily, which perfectly aligned her

head with his chest so she could snuggle in. His round, coal black eyes were keenly tuned in to what happened around him, keeping him alert, which helped him immensely in the fields. Kindness also radiated from his eyes, especially when he smiled and the corners crinkled. His tanned skin was the reason half his children were darker skinned than the others. He was also the reason that three-quarters of his children had varying shades of red hair, his being a dark auburn that loosely brushed his collar.

Jacob was often described as kind and fair in his business dealings. Those traits carried over into his everyday life as well. God was the center of his life, making him a devoted husband and father.

As he came into the room, he immediately went over and put his arms around his wife's waist.

She was eager for his embrace, if for no other reason than to steady her nerves. She wrapped her arms around his neck and kissed him thoroughly, the passion obviously still alive, even after thirteen years.

As they pulled apart, Jacob teased, "Getting a welcome like that almost makes it worth leaving every day."

Emily playfully swatted his chest then disentangled as the children came back from washing up. She went to the table and started putting the food out. Cheerfully she announced, "The Tyler girls are going to be joining us for supper."

She looked up and caught her husband's questioning glance and returned it with an answering gaze that only he would understand.

The three girls at the table squealed in delight as Christopher walked in, banging the door, seeming to announce the arrival of the Tylers.

The supper dishes done and kitchen tidied, the children were all cramming to finish homework they should have done earlier. Excitement over the looming last week of school made doing homework almost impossible.

Emily sat knitting a baby blanket for one of the ladies at church. Her mind, however, ran to Ashley.

'Why isn't she back yet? Where can she be?' she anxiously

and silently questioned.

Luckily, the Tyler girls were so excited about visiting, they asked few questions. Those they did ask, Emily was able to answer easily enough.

"Well," Emily remarked, "I guess it's time for y'all to be gettin' to bed."

She turned to their guests, "I'll walk ya on over to yer house in just a bit. For now, why don't ya make sure my youngsters are gettin' their night clothes on?" She gave them a wink and a smile, sounding a lot more cheerful than she felt. She needed them out of the room so she could talk to Jacob. She'd longed to all evening, but hadn't had the opportunity. As soon as the room cleared, she sprang from her seat and buried her face in his lap, not sure where to begin.

"What's going on, Em?" Jacob queried. He put down the book he was reading and laid a hand on her head.

She looked up at him, worry wreathing her face, "I'm worried about Ashley."

Jacob bent down and scooped her into his lap. Beginning to stroke her hair, he urged, "Why don't you tell me what's going on. I admit, I am curious."

The words flowed from her tongue as she unburdened her worry. Finishing, she said, "And now, I don't know what to make of her being gone so long."

"Does Josh know?"

"No, I don't think so...I don't know! Do you think she went to the mill and told him...since she *was* in town, I mean."

"Who knows? This does concern me, though. It doesn't seem like Ashley to do something like this."

Emily inwardly groaned. *'Well, most of the time he makes me feel better....'*

Aloud she said, "I'll take the girls over and put them to bed and wait for Josh. He usually gets home fairly late, but it should be soon now."

Jacob hugged her. "Don't worry, Em. She probably told Josh all about it and everything will be fine. You'll see. Now, do what you said and I'll be here waiting for you when you get back."

She looked at Jacob and tremulously told him, "She never even told me when she'd be back. Usually she's so careful of those types of details."

Jacob kissed her firmly then and soothed her saying, "Emily, we don't know the whole story. Let's wait and hear it first."

She nodded weakly. "Alright..."

"Yer young'uns are down for the night, Aunt Emily." Alexis smiled as she came into the living room from the stairs.

"Good," Emily replied. "I'll take you girls on home. Yer probably ready for a good night's sleep, huh?"

"Our ma's not back yet?" queried Kayla, concern lining her face.

By now, all four girls had made their entrance from upstairs.

"No, love, but I'm sure she will be...soon. Just wait till morning," Emily replied.

'Lord, please don't let that be a lie,' Emily pleaded silently.

Once Emily tucked her children in, she and the Tylers trooped down the lane to their house.

Once inside, she quickly got them all tucked in.

"Ya know, Mama doesn't usually tuck us in," Madison pondered aloud as Emily was about to leave the room. "But, Pa does sometimes when it's his day off or he gets to come home early."

Emily was surprised. While Ashley didn't always seem the most affectionate toward the girls, Emily knew she loved them very much.

"Well, all mamas are different. Some show love by their words, some by actions." Emily leaned over Madison for a quick kiss on the girl's forehead, then wished her a final, "Good night."

She left the room then, carefully going down the stairs so as not to waken any girl who may already be asleep. She went into the sitting room, the first door to the right from the entryway.

It was a spacious room adorned in sapphire blue and mahogany.

Emily was always comforted and found peace in this great room. She settled herself on the settee under the window to wait for Joshua or Ashley's return.

Emily was a cheerful sort, short and plump. The plumpness came after bearing four children. As a child, right up until she became pregnant with Christopher, she was thin as a reed. She did, however, keep her looks from youth.

'Pleasin' to the eye,' was how Jacob put it.

Emily's emerald green eyes were a testament to the varying shades of the color her children carried on. Her eyes were truly a window to her soul. Whatever she was thinking or feeling was rekindled through her eyes. Right now, they clearly belied her worry over her friend.

Her mass of honey-blond hair could scarcely be kept in a bun...even on a good day. Her naturally wavy hair was so thick it was a daily battle just to get it atop her head.

'A woman's hair is her glory,' Jacob often quoted to her. He loved stroking her hair and running his fingers through her glossy tresses.

She, on the other hand, just got frustrated with it. It seemed to be one voluminous mass of fluff.

Shaking her hair out...at least, the remnants that were still in the bun...she decided to lie down, suddenly feeling very tired indeed.

Startled out of her light sleep, Emily realized someone had been shaking her.

Quickly looking up, she realized it was Joshua.

"What's going on here?" he queried, looking concerned.

Slightly disoriented, Emily stumbled over her words. "Oh...oh, I thought you would be Ashley. Er...um, where is Ashley? Isn't she with you? I thought maybe she'd go by the mill to find you and tell you...well, whatever it is...."

"What do you mean? Where *is* Ashley?"

Emily's eyes opened wide as she realized Joshua knew nothing of his wife's whereabouts. Something near panic, "I don't know, Josh. She came to me earlier this afternoon and asked me to watch the girls. She said she had to go to town. Naturally, I thought she would tell you what it was all about."

Joshua paled.

"The girls are all up in bed. I better get back to Jacob and the children." Emily stood up.

Grabbing Joshua's hand, she squeezed it. "If you need... *anything*...you know all you have to do is ask."

Quietly, she let herself out.

After Emily left, Joshua stood, seemingly rooted to the spot. It wasn't like Ashley to do anything like this. What did she need to do in town that she couldn't take the girls with her? She'd always delighted in taking the girls and going to the different shops. And why hadn't she come by the mill?

Joshua's confusion quickly turned to worry, which turned to panic. He started pacing the room, unsure what to do. It was too late now to *do* anything. He was exhausted from his long shift. Thankfully, tomorrow was Saturday and his day off. He had planned on spending a relaxing day with his family. He and Ashley had even talked of having a picnic with the girls by the creek.

"Now what, Lord?" he whispered. "Where is my beloved wife?"

He slowly trudged upstairs to his room. Standing in the doorway, he suddenly felt empty. He'd had a tiny spark of hope that what Emily said was wrong. That somehow, she just missed Ashley coming home because she was sleeping, but he knew that was unlikely. Ashley would have aroused Emily, just as he'd done.

Seeing their bed empty was more proof that Ashley simply wasn't there. He sat down, hard, on the edge of their bed. It was clad in a soft yellow down comforter. He laid across the bed, staring into space. The room was just too quiet and, though normally cheerful in its soft yellow, seemed extra dark and looming to him.

He turned his head to stare at the doorknob, directly across from the bed, and willed it to turn. Minutes passed, and no Ashley came in. No warm body would curl up next to him in sleep. Suddenly, a chill shivered through his body and he slipped between the sheets, fully clothed.

Glancing over to Ashley's side of the bed, he rolled over and put his hand in the empty space. The window looking over the lane was on that side of the room. Ashley loved it because she could almost see into Jacob and Emily's upstairs. That's why she'd had her vanity placed beneath it, so she could look out the window as she completed her morning routine and brush her long, luxurious, dark hair. She also loved sitting by the window, because it was next to the fireplace and very welcome on chilly mornings.

The two damask-covered chairs by the fireplace were of the same yellow as the rest of the room. Even the walls were papered in a soft yellow with tiny blue flowers.

Rolling over to his other side, he stared unseeingly toward the armoire and writing desk that had another yellow-damask chair by it.

After an hour of tossing and turning, tears made their way down Joshua's cheeks as he felt hopelessness close in. Ashley hadn't come and he didn't know where she was.

'What has happened to Ashley? Has she been kidnapped? Has she had an accident? Where is she?' His thoughts refused to give up.

He was trying to force himself to be calm as he tried to reason. If she had been kidnapped...why? What would be the point? They lived comfortably enough, but weren't rich by any means.

If she had any serious injury that would warrant going to the nearby city, Glory's hospital, surely Doc Rowan would've sent a message or come himself to let Joshua know of his wife's whereabouts.

'What has happened to my wife?! What has happened to Ashley?' his head screamed.

Mentally, he started making a scrambled list of where he needed to start his search in the morning. Any and all shops in town, the bank, just in case anyone saw anything unusual....

"Let's see," he murmured out loud, "the doc's, the hospital...I'll just have to ride over...the stagecoach office. If she's been kidnapped, they may have forced her on the stagecoach, bound for...somewhere. Let's see...the jail? Why on earth would she be there? Hmmm... maybe Sheriff Alexander saw something. At any rate, it wouldn't hurt to check there. The hotel, I should check there, too. Their front desk faces the street...."

Joshua's brain, exhausted from mental activity, and his body, exhausted from physical labors, finally won him over to sleep, just as the sun made its first appearance over the horizon.

Chapter 2: A Cry In The Night

Joshua slept in later than he intended, but it was still considered an early hour when he finally got up. For him, it couldn't be early enough to start his search. He hustled his girls out of bed and down to breakfast.

Sleepily they wandered into the kitchen, not moving fast enough for Joshua.

Rubbing sleep from her eyes, Kayla whined, "Why are we awake so early?"

"Yeah," chimed in Madison, "it's not a school day and it's not a church day."

Joshua tried to calm his fraught nerves as he carefully tried to explain. "Girls," he began, his tone gentle, "yer Mama didn't come home last night."

There were gasps all around,

"Is Mama…d-dead?" Alyssa whispered, her lips trembling.

"No, no, I'm sure it's nothing too serious. We just need to find out where she went." Joshua wished he believed his own words.

"I wanna help," Alexis broke in.

"Well, here's what we're gonna do. We're gonna go on over to Uncle Jacob and Aunt Emily's. I'll see if Uncle Jacob can go help me look for Mama. You girls can spend the day with Aunt Emily and Chris and the girls, okay?"

Joshua noticed the lack of enthusiasm as they headed out the kitchen door, climbing the stairs that ran to the right of the living room.

Joshua could hardly blame them. Although they usually got excited about going to the Matthews', losing their Mama put a damper on things.

"Ah, well," he sighed, deciding to head up behind them. He hastened to ready himself for the long day.

Peering out the kitchen window for what seemed like the

fifteenth time in an hour, Emily sighed. She was certain she would see signs, or at least hear news, of Ashley. Perhaps she, Joshua, and the girls would come along and see them to explain that it was all just a little misunderstanding. At the very least, she figured Joshua would come to tell them...no, she wouldn't let her thoughts drift that way.

"What are you lookin' for darlin'?" Jacob asked, pressing his face into the back of her neck and wrapping his arms around her waist.

"Just seeing if the Tylers have any news," Emily answered.

"You need to quit worryin'. That's God's job."

Emily, deciding to be distracted by her good-looking husband, turned in his embrace to face him. He was so handsome, with his ruddy hair brushing his collar and swept away from his face, almost carelessly.

She had a fleeting thought that she wished she could always have his steadfast faith.

Emily didn't give herself enough credit, however, for her faith was strong and steadfast. She carried these qualities over into her relationships with friends and family as well, always fiercely loyal and ready to do anything for anyone.

Emily studied Jacob's face, then replied as pertly as possible, "He does not!"

"Does so," Jacob countered.

"He doesn't need to worry because He already knows what's going to happen –"

"Aye. And that's my point," Jacob cut her off. He smiled then and cupped her chin in his hand, kissed her lightly, then abruptly pulled away, practically shouting, "They're coming!"

Emily's eyes widened as she swiveled toward the window in anticipation. Her excitement vanished as she noticed Ashley wasn't in the company. She hurried to let Joshua and the girls in. She could hardly believe this was where she greeted Ashley less than twenty-four hours before.

"Hi, Josh, hello, you little dumplin's," Emily welcomed.

As she stepped through the door, Alyssa soberly informed her, "We didn't find our mama." Turning to Jacob, she implored him, "Please, Uncle Jacob, please help Papa find her."

Jacob already knew his answer and without preamble asked,

"Josh, where ya headed?" Then stopped, noticing the guilty look on Joshua's face.

"I, uh, hate to impose like this –"

As was Jacob's habit that morning, he cut Joshua off. "It might be easier if we start out together so we can cover more ground, if you don't mind me taggin' along."

"Al-alright. I just feel this is my problem and I should be able to fix it somehow."

"Nonsense, Josh. There's a lot of territory around here. It'll be like lookin' for a needle in a haystack if you go by yourself. We are here to help. Now, we need all the help we can get, so we should start for town to get people to help along the way. What do you say?"

Relief seemed to flood Joshua's face. He offered a small smile and nodded wearily. "That sounds fine."

Emily jumped up from the chair she had settled in. "Neither of you is goin' anywhere 'til I can get you both a canteen of coffee to aid you on your search." She jumped up to get started.

"Thank you, kindly, Em," Joshua replied gratefully. He sank down in a chair and turned to his daughters. "Why don't you gals go 'n' find the other kids?"

"Yes, Papa," Madison agreed for the group and led them out of the kitchen.

After they were gone, Joshua moaned, "I'm so worried about her. She's my life, she's my...*everything*." He finished quietly, as if to himself. "If I can't find her, I don't know what I'll do."

Emily handed the coffee over then and sat down in the chair to Joshua's left. "First, though, we need to pray before you set out."

Jacob immediately took a seat and they bowed their heads. It was quiet for a moment as they each gathered their thoughts. Finally, Jacob started. "Dear Lord, we ask that you be with Ashley right now, wherever she is. You know our hearts, Lord and how worried we are about her. Guide us with your hand, Father, so we might find her quickly."

Joshua took a turn then to plead with the Almighty. "Please, Lord, don't let me lose my wife! Please!" That was all he could get out before sobs overtook him and shook his shoulders. He buried his head in his arms, leaning over the kitchen table, giving way to the grief he'd been too exhausted to vent the night before.

"Father God," Emily picked up then, trying to keep her own tears in check, "give us all the strength to endure this time of seeking your daughter. And give special strength for our dear brother, Josh. This is his beloved wife, the one You chose for him. Lord, *please* make the search quick and fruitful so we can have Ashley home. Amen."

Jacob added a quiet, "Amen" as Joshua dried his tears on his sleeve. Emily produced a handkerchief from up her sleeve and silently handed it to him.

"Thank you, you two," Joshua murmured.

"Let's get going." Jacob stood, breaking the thick cloud of despair that had descended on the room. He helped the dejected Joshua to his feet.

"Alright," Joshua agreed. "Thanks for the coffee, Em. It looks a little bleak for an early-June day."

"Aye, it does. Well, off with you two, then."

Joshua stepped out the kitchen door leading to the backyard and, beyond that, the fields.

Jacob lagged behind a little to bid his wife a proper farewell.

"If it gets to be too late, don't fret," Jacob admonished gently, making Emily look at him. "This could take a while."

"I won't," Emily reluctantly promised. "Hopefully it won't be a long search."

Jacob gave Emily one last kiss and a smile, then was gone.

"I'd like to ride on over to Glory first, to check the hospital, and sort of get it, uh, out of the way," Joshua announced after they'd ridden awhile. They were almost halfway to town.

"I'll stay in town and ask around about Ashley," Jacob offered.

"Thank you, Jacob. I appreciate it."

They rode the rest of the way to town making small talk. They both knew it was a means to distract them from the unpleasant task at hand.

Once they got to town, Joshua turned in his horse's saddle toward Jacob. "I'll be back in a couple of hours. I hope I *don't* find her there."

"And I hope I *do* find her here," Jacob returned. "Be safe."

"Thanks, you, too." Joshua rode off through the middle of town, bound for Glory.

Glory was quite a bit bigger than their small town, Lorraine. It was twelve miles away, just ten more than it took Joshua to get from his homestead to the middle of Lorraine.

Lorraine had been named for a traveling gypsy's daughter. It was rumored that more than a hundred years ago, Lorraine had been wooed and won by a farmer's son. They wed, despite the displeasure from both families. After the wedding, they vanished, never to be heard from again.

Joshua lost no time in seeking out the Glory Hospital. He jumped down, tied his horse to the post and hurried inside, unconsciously holding his breath.

The inside of the hospital blinded him by its sheer whiteness. Everything looked stark and clean. Joshua spied a very neat and orderly desk against the far right wall and noticed a very proper-looking nurse seated behind it.

He walked up to the nurse, licking his lips, and began. "Uh, hello, I'm looking for…someone."

The professional-looking lady stared up at him with impatience written all over her face. "Yes?" she prompted, severely.

"Has there, uh…" he hesitated, not wanting to ask the question, but needing to know the answer.

"Yes?" the nurse barked again.

"There hasn't been a patient by the name of Ashley Tyler admitted here, has there?" Joshua asked in a rush, wanting to get it all out before he lost his nerve.

"Hmmmm…the name doesn't sound familiar. When did you say she came in?" she queried.

Joshua, a little more than edgy by this time, practically shouted, "I didn't!" Softening his tone, he went on, "It could've been any time from late yesterday afternoon to early this morning."

"That's not much help," she huffed. She pulled a large book forward from the corner of her neat desk. She opened it and turned back a page to the previous day's entries, running a finger down the column of names.

17

Joshua leaned over, too, looking for Ashley's name, lest this Miss Fussy Pot missed it.

Miss Fussy Pot glanced up at him, "*I* don't see it here. *I'*ll just look in today's entries." She flipped the page and again her finger made a trail down the column of names. "Nope," she snapped the book shut with the single word.

'Take the good with the bad,' his father's words from his boyhood came to him then.

At least Ashley wasn't here laid up in bed with injuries. That was the good. The bad was, he still had to find her. Where should he start? Maybe Jacob had heard something.

"Well, thank you, Miss Fuss...er, I mean, *thank you.*" Joshua doffed his hat and left.

Joshua rode into Lorraine just as the sun showed that it was getting past the noon hour. His stomach also reminded him that he ate hardly any breakfast. Maybe he could catch up to Jacob and they could compare notes over lunch.

He rode to the only restaurant in town, that of the hotel. Figuring he might as well ask while he was there, Joshua tied his horse to the hitching post and went into the hotel lobby.

"Hello, Mr. Tyler," greeted the proprietor, Mr. Rushford.

"Hey, Rush," Joshua called back, using the town's familiar name for the man.

"I was wondering if you've seen Ashley?" Joshua wasn't sure if he felt like divulging the whole story.

"I saw her last week," Rush chuckled then, and said, "but, I bet yer talkin' 'bout today. Nope, haven't seen her since she came in town last week with yer young'uns."

"So, last week was the last time you saw her?" Joshua worked to keep his voice even and hoped the tears that were threatening weren't traceable in his voice. It was ridiculous he was getting so discouraged so soon, but he wanted this nightmare to be over.

Mr. Rushford had a wealth of knowledge about people around town and beyond because of his position. He liked to use that to his advantage and didn't seem to be too sorrowful about sharing his gossip, although he referred to it as "knowledge." Joshua did not want to be the next victim of any such thing.

"Yep, last week. Ya lost her, huh?" Rush chuckled again.

Joshua shared nothing, just nodded his thanks and went out the door to see if he could spot Jacob. He was in luck because he barely had stepped outside when Jacob spotted him and hailed him over. Joshua crossed the street to meet him.

"Any luck?" were the first words out of Joshua's mouth.

'Well, so much for comparing notes over lunch,' he thought.

"Sorry, Josh," Jacob looked very discouraged. "Maybe we should take a break and get a bite?"

Listening to his belly, Joshua had to admit he needed sustenance. Especially since there seemed to be no end in sight. "Alright," he agreed reluctantly.

They both led their horses around back of the hotel and paid to have them fed as well.

The restaurant was dim, but welcoming. It was comfortably warm since the weather outside had been brisk.

After they ordered, Joshua shared about his trip to Glory and Miss Fussy Pot. Jacob, in turn, filled Joshua in on his progress, or lack, thereof.

"I saw John McKenzie and sent him north to scour the area. He came upon Lance Avery and Barnabas Knight and sent them west and east. They share in your worry. We all can't imagine what you're going through."

"I can't tell you how grateful I am for your help, Jacob. I wasn't sure how I'd accomplish this all by myself."

"Think nothin' of it, Josh. We are all here to help one another...at least, those of us who don't gossip."

Lorraine seemed to be made up of two types of people: those who helped each other out, and those who gossiped about it. Truth be told, when worse came to worst, everyone banded together and united against whatever was to come.

Their meal almost finished, Joshua laid out his plans. "I'm going to go around town to all the shops and inquire after Ashley. Then, I'll move over to the bank, Doc Rowan's, the stage coach office, the jail....I'll chat with Sheriff Alexander...."

"Whoa, whoa, whoa, Josh," Jacob put his hand up. "I'm here to help, remember? Why don't I tackle the shops? You can handle the rest. You couldn't possibly check every place by yourself before they close."

Joshua sighed in relief. "Okay. That'll be good. Thanks." He closed his eyes for a minute.

"Are you alright?" Jacob queried.

"Just tired and a little overwhelmed, is all."

"We *will* find her, Josh. Do you hear me? We will!"

They both got up then, paid the bill, and left.

Joshua began his asking around town as he made his way to the bank. He was beginning to feel more and more like this was happening to someone else. As though this were someone else's life. It was all too surreal.

Honestly, where could Ashley have gotten to? It was a relatively small town. She couldn't have gotten far without anyone noticing.

At the bank, he went right over to Mr. Ripley, the bank manager. The manager looked up from his desk as Joshua neared.

"Well, hello, Mr. Tyler, what can I do ya fer?" His eyes twinkled.

"I'm lookin' for my wife, Mr. Ripley. Have you seen her? Or, has she been here, withdrawing a large amount of money?"

Joshua couldn't believe he had let that last part slip! He had been trying to be discreet, but now, here he was, looking very foolish asking about large withdrawals of money. He was just so tired and overwrought with worry about his wife, it made him give up any last shred of subtlety.

Mr. Ripley gave Joshua a look of surprise, confusion, then almost panic. "Why, no, Mr. Tyler. I haven't seen her. Is there anything…er…wrong? I'm sure if she came in here for a big withdrawal, I would've been called."

"No," Joshua said, disheartened. "Just let me know if you do see her." He turned and trudged out the door, more discouraged by the minute.

At Doc Rowan's, Joshua heard, "Nope, haven't seen her. But, from what I gather from your face, that's not good news."

"It's both, I suppose. Good she isn't hurt, bad that I can't seem to find her."

Joshua knew that, by now, whether he liked it or not, news would spread of his missing wife. Some would pick up on this bit of information and join in the search. In fact, that had already been the case. Unfortunately, others would simply gossip and spread rumors. And not very nice ones at that, he figured.

Joshua rode over to the stage coach office then and checked with the ticket master. "Can I see the list for any departures for today and yesterday's stage coach?"

"Sorry, son, that isn't public information. We've been havin' too many robberies lately. Can I look a name up for ya, though?"

Joshua had never ridden on the stage coach; he had nowhere to go. "Well, I would like to know if an Ashley Tyler took a stage coach either yesterday or today."

"Now, let's see." The man scanned the ledger. "Doesn't appear to be. We usually have 'em sign their names, so some of 'em's hard to read. Also, not all passengers sign. Usually only the ones who bought the tickets, so most likely the men do the signin'. She was travelin' alone?" He gave Joshua a pointed look.

'Who would she be traveling with?' Joshua mused.

Aloud, and ignoring the man's look, Joshua said, "No, she wouldn't have been traveling with anyone. Thank you for your time." Joshua strode away, more determined than ever to solve this mystery.

As he made his way to the jail and Sheriff Alexander, Joshua felt he had to physically fight away the panic that was threatening to overtake him.

'Stay calm,' he ordered himself. *'It won't do to have you lose your head! Think clearly.'*

"Afternoon, Sheriff," Joshua managed as he stepped into the sheriff's tiny office.

Though the building looked big from the outside, almost all of it contained jail cells, leaving Sheriff Alexander with very little room.

"Josh, good to see ya. Need to report somethin'?"

"No, not just yet. I wondered if you have seen my wife hangin' about?" It sounded foolish, even to his own ears, and definitely more nonchalant than he felt.

Sheriff Alexander gave a short laugh. "What'cha think she'd be in for? Pretty looks?"

Joshua felt the color come to his cheeks. It wasn't often he found himself in an embarrassing situation. He forced a tight-lipped smile. "No, I guess not. Just haven't seen her since yesterday mornin'." There, now it really *was* out.

Sheriff Alexander grew serious then. "Really? Gee, I'm sorry. I didn't realize it was so serious."

"Don't mention it. Just keep an eye out for her, will ya?"

"Yeah, sure thing, Josh. Just let me know if you want me to send that report."

"Sure thing, Sheriff. Thank you."

Joshua left feeling mentally and physically exhausted. He felt he'd better make one last attempt in town before heading back home. He turned toward the post office.

"Hello," a young girl greeted as Joshua stepped in, making the bell over the door tinkle.

Joshua returned the greeting. He puzzled, trying to place the vaguely familiar face. He recognized her as one of his neighbors' daughters.

"I'm Joshua Tyler," he introduced, coming up to stand in front of her and the long counter.

"Oh, yes, Mr. Tyler, you live about two miles east of our place."

Fabian. It dawned on him then. She belonged to the Fabians. "Yes, so I do."

"I'm Herbert and Yetta's daughter, Veda."

"Pleased to meet ya...?" His question hung in the air because he couldn't remember if they had ever been properly introduced.

"Yes, likewise," she smiled.

"Do you know my wife?"

"Ummm...yes, I believe I do."

"You wouldn't happen to remember seeing her yesterday, would you?"

"Oh, no, this is my first day here. Mr. Dandin, the post master, well, you know him, I'm sure, needed extra help. He says summer's real busy, and such...."

Veda rambled on and Joshua, normally easy-going and patient, could hardly control his patience now as he waited for a break in her ramblings to inquire anything further.

Finally, Veda finished with, "So, that's why I'm here. Oh, you probably want your mail, too."

Before he could tell her he seldom got any, she slipped to the back. Coming back up, she handed him a letter.

Surprised, he took a step back, then accepted the letter, not even glancing at it.

'Probably from Mother,' he mused. She wrote every few months and, he guessed, she was due. Although, it didn't seem like it had been too long since she last wrote. *'Oh, well. I'll open it later. It certainly can wait for now. I have more important matters to figure out.'* He shoved the letter in his pocket as he turned to go, nodding his thanks to Veda.

'Ashley,' his soul longed as he mounted his horse and headed home.

The first thing he noticed when he rode up to the Matthews' to fetch the girls, were the savory scents wafting from within. He was surprised he could feel anything past his sorrow after such an unsuccessful day.

"Hello," he called out, entering the mud room at the back of the kitchen. Going through, he stepped into the kitchen and was met by giggling girls covered in flour, as they were helping Emily finish cutting biscuits to put in the oven.

"Any luck?" Emily asked quietly as she met Joshua's gaze.

He slumped into a chair at the work table. "No. Jacob not back yet?"

"Not yet. He'll probably be right on your heels, though. Why don't you go wash for supper?"

"Em, we can't impose anymore," Joshua protested. "We've practically lived at your house for the past two days. At least, the girls have."

"Josh, you're being as silly as your wife was yesterday – you're not imposing!"

"What do you mean, Em? How was Ashley acting?" Joshua straightened up in his chair.

"Well...um...just strange...kinda. She, uh, *knocked* at our door! Like she hasn't just walked in this house almost every day for the last ten years." Emily tried a laugh, but it came out sounding hollow.

"Emily, that's *not* like Ashley *at all*." Slumping back in his chair he sighed. "I am so worried about her."

The girls finished the task with the biscuits. One by one, the Tyler girls came to greet their father.

"No luck with Mama, huh?" Kayla asked.

Joshua raked his hand through his already mussed brown hair. Naturally wavy, it only made his hair stand on end. His usually dark eyes grew even darker at the acknowledgment.

Joshua's usual child-like faith seemed to be faltering before Emily's eyes. He was usually more wise than to give in to this kind of worry. He was one of the smartest, most knowledgeable people Emily knew. He knew subjects ranging from the world outdoors, to the sanctity of the Bible. And he usually possessed strong self-esteem and radiated confidence in every situation. Not much could shake him, for he was known as the rock and foundation to many close friends and family when they went through trials and needed someone to depend on. No, this Joshua before her was one Emily did not recognize.

"If you ask me, she's being just plain selfish," Alyssa chimed in.

Emily gasped at the same time Joshua exploded from his seat to his full five feet, nine inches. "WHAT!" he demanded. His usually ruddy skin couldn't hide the red fury that crept to his face and down his neck.

Alyssa shrank back. "It just seems she shoulda left a note or somethin'. She coulda let us know where she was goin'," she finished in a small voice.

He understood then and folded his lithe, lean frame back into the chair. Opening his arms, he wrapped Alyssa into him for an embrace.

"I'm sorry, honey. I'm really worried about yer ma. Sometimes worry has a way of makin' people act differently than they usually do." He sighed and closed his eyes, nuzzling his nose into Alyssa's sweet smelling hair.

Alyssa lifted her face and replied with a small, "It's okay, Daddy."

Soon after, Jacob returned and the two families joined together for their evening meal.

Joshua padded down the hall, back towards his room from the four girls' rooms. He was weary and didn't know what his next step should be in his search for Ashley.

24

"Lord," he began aloud, "only You know where Ashley is. Please guide my path to her. Help me know what to do next in trying to find her."

After preparing himself for bed, he folded his trousers over a chair. And the letter from earlier slipped from his pocket to the floor. Bending over, he retrieved it and turned it over in his hand, freezing. *It was addressed to him in his wife's hand!* Shaking, he opened the letter, fumbling with the pages as he pulled them out. Willing his eyes to focus and his breathing to slow, he read:

Friday, June 2, 18_

Lorraine

Dear Joshua,

I know that as you read this letter, you will probably be worried sick about me. I'm sorry for that. One thing I could always count on you for was that you always cared so much for me and always had my best interests in mind. That's why this next part pains me a great deal. I know how much you love, and even adore, me. However, I just can't say the same...not anymore. I'm so sorry, but I don't know if I ever was in love with you. I think it was more the *thought* of you. At least, the thought of me being *married,* with children to raise.

I guess I should tell you when I started thinking this way and questioning myself. So, here goes! I only ask that you try to forgive me...someday.

A man came along a few months ago and told me about another man, Joseph Smith, Jr. who has started a new church. Not many have heard of it yet. Some are even skeptical about this man's teachings. He's had to move a few times, apparently.

Anyway, the man that approached me is a cousin of some sort to this Joseph Smith. Incidentally, his name is Joseph also...Joseph Danielson.

I met Joseph Danielson, like I said, a few months back. His family is in the business of raising horses and he was on his way through Lorraine to look at some horses.

This happened at church one Sunday. While you talked with Jacob and Emily, I saw

25

Joseph sitting there. Deciding to be hospitable, I went over and introduced myself. I will never forget the peculiar look he gave me as he said, "You have it all wrong here." (I later learned he meant our church and some of our teaching.) He then told me of the new church Joseph Smith, Jr. has started...something about visions of some kind. Joseph Danielson asked, "Would you like to know about our church?" I admit, I was skeptical, yet intrigued, at the same time. So, he postponed his trip for a couple of days to meet with me—when you were at the mill and when the girls were at school—and he finally asked me to think about leaving with him. He said he would stop back in Lorraine on his way home after he took care of his horse business—he had several places he needed to go.

I *did* think about it...long and hard, in fact. I weighed out the pros and cons and decided that his proposition intrigued me, as does this new church. You know I've had a hard time sitting through Reverend Chadrick's dry sermons lately.

It was while pondering all of this, that I realized my love for you had grown dim. Last week, I saw Joseph Danielson again. He came back and I came to the conclusion that I wanted to go with him. I need answers for myself and I think I will get this from the new church.

We arranged for this to be the day we leave. I will leave the girls at the Matthews' and this letter at the post office for you before leaving with Joseph Danielson. We are headed for Ohio.

I hope that with time, you can find it in your heart to forgive me for running off like this. I pray you don't hate me. I know that eventually you will realize it was for the best.

With much sorrow,

Ashley

Trembling, Joshua rushed down the stairs as quietly as he could, careful not to wake the girls. He ran all the way to the creek, knowing the way even without light. Only then did he allow himself full reign of his emotions. He let out the sobs that had choked him, as he reeled from the shock of what he'd just read. He found himself alternating between cries of pain and sobs of sorrow.

He wasn't sure how long he'd lain prostrate next to the creek, sobbing with his whole heart, when he felt he could finally control himself. He had no idea what time it was, but he knew that no matter what, Jacob and Emily would welcome him in. He needed to talk to someone.

He started the walk back, numb the whole way, until he burst into the Matthews' house. He went straight to the living room, knowing that's where they spent their evenings. The hour must not have been too late, for he noticed the glow of the lamps as he entered.

"Joshua! What is it?" Emily gasped as she looked up from her knitting and took in Joshua's pale face.

Joshua couldn't say anything, just thrust the letter into her hands. Seeing he was trembling, she took it from him and read the letter, perching herself on Jacob's lap so he could read, too, as Joshua paced the room.

The further Emily got in the letter, the more she shook in rage. *'How could she?'* Emily fumed. *'What a dirty, rotten thing for someone to do to her husband! How could she?!'*

"Well," Jacob calmly stated, as he folded the letter and handed it back to Joshua, "at least we know where she is…sort of."

'Jacob is furious as well,' Emily noted. *'He's too calm.'*

Jacob Matthews was a man of action, not reaction. When he was upset or angry, and action needed taking, he waited until it was just the right time…and not a moment before.

"I'm so sorry, Josh." Emily's voice was carefully controlled as she expressed her sympathy. She truly felt heartbroken for Joshua, so she didn't want any of her fury to resonate in her voice.

"Is there anything we can do?" Emily asked.

Joshua spoke as one who is defeated. "Honestly, I don't know. I thought our life was grand. And then, THIS! *This* gets thrown at me. I guess you two just bein' here is enough for me for now."

"Okay, Josh," Jacob acquiesced.

"I just don't know what to tell the girls in the morning."

"Probably the best thing is the truth," advised Emily. "Maybe just the necessities, though. No use confusin' 'em with this new church talk. This is a difficult situation, Josh. We'll both be prayin' for ya."

"Thank you, Em."

27

"Would you like the girls to stay here for a few days while you sort through things?" Emily offered.

"Thanks for the offer, but I expect they'll be pretty broken up about this. We should take some time as a family. Maybe later I'll take ya up on the offer. We'll see how it turns out."

"Okay," Emily agreed.

Jacob and Emily stood then and sent Joshua home with a prayer in their hearts.

Chapter 3: The Best Friends A Man Can Have

A month had passed since Ashley left and Joshua felt the emptiness of her absence. Sometimes he would be overcome with bitter anger, while other times, he would feel depressed, lonely, and rejected.

The girls had all had different reactions.

Madison, on the brink of being a teenager, had reacted with strong hate toward her mother. "I'm never going to forgive her! She abandoned us and I will forget about her. I hate her!"

Alyssa was full of sorrow. Always having been a sensitive girl, she took it as a personal attack. "Why did she leave us, Daddy? I was good...wasn't I?"

This had broken Joshua's heart. He did his best to reassure Alyssa that, indeed, she was very good. It was their mother's decision to leave, but it had nothing to do with Alyssa.

Alexis cried every day. Sometimes it was quiet weeping, other days it was a gut wrenching keening.

The youngest, Kayla, hadn't uttered a word since the day Joshua broke the sad news.

Now, a month later, Joshua was getting desperate for her to talk.

He had heeded the advice of Emily and hadn't told the girls of the new church. They were confused enough. Instead, he told them that Ashley had met a man whom she thought would be able to answer the questions she had about God. So, she went on a trip with him to, hopefully, find some answers.

"Why didn't she ask you or Reverend Chadrick her questions?" Alyssa had innocently asked.

"I'm not sure, sweetheart. I guess she thought she'd be better off finding her own answers."

Joshua wearily dragged his mind from the difficult conversation and back to the present. He was still having difficulty with anger. Some days, he wished she was there simply so he could rail against her and tell her exactly what her abandonment was doing to him and their girls.

And other times, he wanted to break down and weep. It almost felt as if Ashley were dead, so great was the pain of the void she left. There were nights he would lie in bed and secretly wish she *were* dead. At least he wouldn't feel so rejected.

Alexis broke into his thoughts then to ask, "Do you think Mama will come home when her questions are answered?"

She took a bite of her supper as she waited for his answer.

"Probably not," Madison interjected. "She doesn't want us anymore."

"That's not true, Madison!" Joshua sharply reprimanded. Probably too sharply, being that she had struck too close to his own fears.

Madison couldn't keep quiet, however. "Quite frankly, I don't want her to come back, anyhow!"

"Enough!" Joshua thundered.

Calming, he then turned to Alyssa and answered her earlier question. "I really hope so. I miss her."

"So do I," Alyssa sighed.

"Well, I don't," Madison persisted.

Joshua quietly, but sternly, told Madison, "You may go to your room. Your supper is over."

Madison stomped out of the room as the others quietly finished their meal.

The next few weeks were difficult as Joshua tried to move on, as well as cope with all of his girls' emotions and feelings.

He'd been touched by people's generosity and sensitivity to the situation.

The Matthews had them over a lot more for meals.

Joshua's boss, Landon DeMorris, had generously given him the whole month off. The whole incident had gotten around town and the time off was much needed and appreciated by Joshua. In fact, he had checked his savings and seriously considered asking for the entire summer off, and starting back when the girls went back to school. He wasn't sure how far Landon's generosity would reach, but figured it was worth a try.

Entering Landon's office one morning, after gathering all of his courage, he had asked just that. Surprisingly, Landon's answer was quick and full of sympathy.

"Whenever you're ready."

He knew school would help occupy the girls' minds, but he wished his mind could be as easily occupied. Every time he looked at his girls, he was reminded of Ashley. All four of them had a good bit of Ashley in their looks, personality, or both.

Madison's eyes *were* Ashley's. Her huge green eyes belied whatever she was feeling, just as her mother's did. Her stubbornness was also definitely inherited from her mother.

Alexis and Alyssa's petite stature was a legacy from Ashley.

Alexis' sweet nature was borne from her mother. Joshua just wasn't sure where that sweet nature had gone in Ashley. He never would have thought Ashley would have left him. And so abruptly.

Alyssa had the smarts about the world and things around her that she picked up on. She learned things quickly and was eager to put to use what she'd learned. Joshua had only ever seen that kind of child-like fascination in one other person…Ashley.

Akin to her big sister, Alyssa, Kayla's similar trait of her mother's was her deep sensitivity to others.

This quality was what had first drawn Joshua to Ashley.

'Where has that sweet nature and good spirit gone?' Joshua wondered again. *'And how long will she haunt me? Will I ever be able to forgive her?'*

They were still legally married, but they definitely weren't living a married life. He didn't even know if he would see her again. He was trying to pick up the pieces of his life and was, so far, failing miserably.

At least the girls had the annual town picnic to look forward to. It was usually held two Saturdays before school started and he had definitely noticed a lightening in their mood whenever the picnic was mentioned. He was surprised and pleased to see even Kayla's eyes brighten. At least it was one good thing to look forward to and hopefully, temporarily, take their minds off their mother.

Saturday, August 27, dawned bright and sunny, which lent to the festive feel of the day. The picnic was to start at noon in the field behind the church. It would start out with picnic lunches brought by families, with games planned for afterwards, followed by a potluck-style supper and then baked goods from the ladies of the town, for dessert.

'How am I going to get through this?' Joshua thought.

There were pointed stares and sympathetic gazes; he didn't know which was worse.

"Hi, Josh," Jacob greeted, coming up to Joshua from across the field.

Joshua was so grateful for Jacob and Emily. They had lent enormous support to him and his family.

"Hi, back," Joshua returned. He was relieved Jacob and Emily had arrived. Besides church, he'd rarely been away from home since the day his world had fallen apart.

'And been made a fool of,' he silently added to his own thoughts. Mentally, he gave himself a little chastisement and tried for a more cheerful demeanor.

"What's going on over here?" Jacob queried. "You're all alone."

"Yeah, just didn't feel brave enough to deal with...*them*." Joshua indicated the crowd with a sweep of his hand. Giving Jacob a sheepish look, he continued, "Pretty cowardly, huh?"

"Not really. I'm sure it's hard, bein' yer first official time out in public. You don't know who knows what or what they think."

"That's the thing. I shouldn't care what they think."

"You're human. After awhile, I'm sure it'll get easier to slough off some of the comments and stares. This bein' yer first real outing, it's bound to be a little nerve wracking. Just stay close to Em and me–"

"Em and me, what?" Emily teased, coming up to them.

"Nothin'. Josh's just gonna stick close to us today."

"Then you can help me keep an eye on that John Carlin. He's been eyein' Brianna these last few weeks." Emily sucked in a breath of air, then puffed it out in annoyance.

"Her, too?" Joshua asked. "He's been chasin' Madison every Sunday after church...shoot."

"He's sixteen! Way too old for our Brianna," Emily indignantly commented. "And even Madison won't be thirteen until December."

"I hear he's a charmer, though," Jacob interjected.

"We'll have to keep a close eye on that one," Joshua vowed.

The picnic went along fairly well, considering all the fears Joshua had built up. However, he wasn't ready for the shock he received while watching the sack races. He'd actually been getting involved in the cheering when someone came up next to him. It was Lillibeth Claudin.

"That Kayla of yours sure can handle her own, can't she?" Lillibeth commented on the game.

Relieved that this seemed to be leading to a safe subject, he'd answered, "Yeah, she likes playing games."

"Seems to be a good outlet for her." Lillibeth's tone was sympathetic.

Joshua grew thoughtful. "I guess you're right. I'm just glad she's participatin'."

"I'm sorry to hear she can't talk."

For some reason, Lillibeth's comment irked Joshua. "Lillibeth, she can talk jest fine. She's simply choosin' not to right now."

"So sad, so sad," Lillibeth clucked. "Too bad her mama ain't here."

Joshua stiffened. Lillibeth was getting a little too personal. "Well, she ain't," came his curt reply.

"Those girls really ought to have a mama."

"They have one!" Joshua snapped, feeling himself getting mighty riled.

Seeming not to hear him, Lillibeth turned to Joshua with dewy eyes and huskily said, "And their pa should have a mate."

Joshua felt as though she had slapped him in the face. *'I'm still married! I still have a wife!'* Joshua thought wildly.

"Widow Claudin, your husband may be dead, but my wife is still very much alive."

She got up and stood right in front of him, hands on her hips and a look of defiance on her face. Her brown eyes blazing, she pertly delivered her final blow. "She may as well have died. You can't wait around forever. She should've known better than to leave such a handsome husband." With that, she tossed her head, making wisps of auburn hair fall out of her neatly pinned bun.

Joshua's mouth was left hanging open. *'Brazen hussy!'*

On the heels of that thought, another, more sobering one, formed. Did Lillibeth represent all the unmarried ladies of the town? Did they see him as an option? How could he be an option when his wife was alive and divorce had never entered his head? Surely they didn't think he would divorce Ashley!

Emily and Jacob walked up then.

"We saw Lillibeth Claudin leaving you gaping like a fish. Everything okay?" Jacob questioned.

Joshua, still reeling, answered in a somewhat strangled voice, "I...don't...know." He then related the whole, sordid exchange he'd had with Lillibeth.

"The nerve!" Emily spat. "Don't let her get to you. I'm sure she's the only one who would dare think, much less speak, such a thing. Everyone knows you're still married to Ashley. Lillibeth Claudin has been tryin' to attract anything with two legs since a month after her husband's funeral. No mournin' black fer her, no sir! And especially not for a whole year, oh no! She has hussy written all over her, that's for certain!"

"Emily Sarah Matthews!" Jacob cut off Emily's tirade, trying to be stern but losing the effect as he tried hard not to smile.

Sheepishly, Emily looked at Jacob. "Sorry."

Joshua grinned and said, "My thoughts exactly...hussy!"

Mockingly stern, Jacob cut in. "Alright, you two."

Laughing, the three went off to help get the last of the preparations underway for the picnic.

September brought the beginning of a new school year and Emily's and Hailey's birthdays. And at Hailey's birthday party, Brianna forgot that she was trying to act more grown up as she excitedly babbled about her own upcoming birthday...a mere six weeks away.

"My eleventh one!" she excitedly told her audience

Following five days behind Brianna's birthday was her big brother, Christopher's thirteenth birthday. And only two days after that, Kayla quietly celebrated her eleventh birthday.

Joshua hoped her birthday would've perked her up and gotten her to say *something*. For Joshua, Kayla's birthday was bittersweet. He was sure she was excited but, apparently, not excited enough to talk.

The fall flew by and soon plans were underway for the holiday season.

Thanksgiving was a somewhat laid back affair, since not everyone celebrated it and because it was the Tylers' first big holiday without Ashley. Joshua hoped it wouldn't be a somber occasion. He needn't have worried had he known how the day would end.

The girls all chipped in with helping Emily prepare the dinner and the pies for afterwards. Even Kayla seemed to be enjoying herself.

After the Thanksgiving feast was consumed and everyone was nursing their pies, chatter began as how best to celebrate Christmas.

"So y'all could come here around two o'clock on Christmas?" Emily asked Joshua.

"That sounds fine. Girls, what do you think?"

There seemed to be agreement all around.

Emily tried including Kayla in the conversation going on. "Kayla, would you like to help with the pies again?"

Kayla, startled, looked up at Emily from her plate, nodded slightly, then looked back down.

"We still need to play our thankful game before talking about Christmas!" little Samantha Matthews insisted.

Emily looked a little uncertain as she glanced back at Kayla.

"Yes, let's!" Alexis agreed. She was familiar with the tradition that the Matthews started from the first Thanksgiving they ever spent with them.

Joshua, too, had his misgivings. However, his were centered more around Madison and what she would say.

"Adults go first, then us kids, oldest to youngest," Hailey reminded the group.

"Alright, here goes," Jacob started. "I'm thankful for this delicious meal all you women made." His gaze was especially aimed at Kayla and was pleased to see a small smile playing around her lips.

"And I'm thankful I had such good helpers to prepare the

supper with me," Emily shared. She wanted to keep things light. She looked over at Jacob in time to catch his wink and warm smile that made his eyes crinkle. She returned his affectionate gaze.

"You go now, Daddy, even though Aunt Emily skipped you, cause I *know* you're *way* older than she is." Alyssa urged her father.

Chuckling, Joshua took his turn. "I'm thankful to have the four most wonderful and beautiful daughters in the world."

"That's corny, Pa," Madison inserted. "But, I *am* thankful for you." She had looked him in the eye as she said it, and he could tell she was being sincere.

Joshua was caught off guard. He'd never expected such a comment from her. Maybe she was coming around after all.

"Hey, no fair! I shoulda been next!" Christopher complained.

Madison relented. "Okay, sorry, but my thankful still stands."

Christopher straightened up, looked Madison square in the eye, and without blinking, said, "I'm thankful I'm thirteen, and you're not!"

"Well, I will be in less than two weeks!" Madison shot back.

Emily stepped in then, "Alright, you two, I believe it's Alexis' turn."

"Thank you, Aunt Emily. I'm thankful for Kayla. She's really the only little sister I've got. You can't count Alyssa cuz she's only younger by minutes."

Kayla's smile was a beam.

Then Alexis winked at her and added, " 'Sides, I can't boss no one else around. Even Alyssa won't let me do that!"

The adults then witnessed Kayla putting both hands to her mouth, as if to hide a laugh.

It warmed Emily's heart, made Jacob's chest swell, and nearly brought tears to Joshua's eyes. It was the closest any of them had seen to her making a sound. All of them wondered if Alexis knew just what she had done by gently giving Kayla attention like that. She certainly could be sweet when she wanted. It wouldn't have surprised any of them to know that Alexis knew exactly what she was doing.

The other children were oblivious to the moment as Alyssa reiterated Alexis' last statement. "That's right, you aren't my boss! Oh, and I'm thankful for my family."

Everyone laughed as Hailey raised her glass and, with gusto, agreed. "Hear, hear!"

Jacob chuckled, "Where did you learn that?"

Hailey answered very seriously, "At that weddin' last month."

"My turn," Brianna piped up. "I'm thankful for the snow that'll be fallin' soon."

Warily, the adult's eyes turned to Kayla, who was next in line. She slumped lower in her seat.

Emily tactfully passed over her. "Samantha, I bet you're thankful for that, too! You love ice skating!" The false cheer sounded hollow even to her own ears.

Nonetheless, Joshua mouthed, "Thank you" to Emily who merely smiled and nodded, catching a warm look from Jacob.

"Yes, Mama, I am, but I wanna say my own 'thankful.'"

"Well, then, let's hear it, little girl," her father prodded, relieved Emily's plan seemed to have worked.

"I'm thankful we get so many days off from school when it's Christmastime."

"Hear, hear," Hailey spoke again, this time in her most grown-up voice. "And I'm thankful it's my turn!"

Laughter broke out around the table again. It lasted until a tiny, yet determined voice broke in.

"I'm thankful…um…I'm thankful…"

All eyes turned toward the speaker. There was scarcely a whisper in the room.

Kayla's voice broke as she finished. "…for all of my family…for everyone in this room."

Silence reigned for only a moment before Joshua bolted from his chair and engulfed Kayla in his arms.

Emily and Jacob exchanged a brief glance before they got up to hug the little girl who had spent the last several months in silence.

"Thank you, Jesus," Joshua whispered, squeezing his daughter tightly once more.

"We've been prayin' you'd speak, child!" Emily gently embraced Kayla again.

Surprising everyone, Christopher got up, knelt in front of Kayla, looked her in the eye and told her, "I'm real proud of you,

Kayla."

They would all remember that Thanksgiving as the best one ever!

The next few weeks before Christmas flew by. School resumed after Thanksgiving and Madison's thirteenth birthday came at the beginning of December.

"Well, now I'm thirteen also," she liked to taunt Christopher.

Preparations for the Christmas supper came and went much in the same way the preparations for Thanksgiving had gone, all the girls helping Emily.

While they were preparing the meal, Kayla, who still only talked a little, piped up. "I remember helping Mama with the Christmas pies. Don't you remember, Madison?"

"Yeah," came the terse reply. Madison still struggled with resentment toward her mother.

Joshua had confided to Jacob and Emily, "I don't know what to do or what to tell her. Truth be told, I'm havin' a hard time bein' gracious in my thoughts toward their mother, too. I think I've forgiven Ashley one minute, and in the next minute, I keep thinkin' of all the hurt she's caused the family. Then the old anger gets all stirred up again. I'd feel like a hypocrite if I told Madison she shouldn't have those feelings. I know we're both in the wrong."

Jacob had simply told him, "It's wrong and human. Madison's hurt, but she's the one who has to decide when to forgive…just like you do. You both need the Lord's help, so that's what we'll pray for."

Kayla's statement had seemed to put a temporary damper on the festive mood. However, once it was time to leave for the Christmas Eve party, some of the cheer seemed to return.

The party started out with ice skating, followed by hot chocolate. Then, in the early evening, a sleigh ride along with a Christmas carol sing-along, accompanied by more hot chocolate. After that, the night was capped off with a late supper in the warm church.

As the sleigh was being loaded, Madison came running, breathlessly, up to Emily. Chattering from the cold and nerves,

Madison told her, "John C-C-C-arlin asked me to-to- to sit n-n-next to h-h-h-im! W-W-What should I-I-I do?"

Emily instantly went rigid, but hid it well. She did not like that charmer. "Do you *want* to sit next to him?"

A giggle squeaked out of Madison. "I don't know…he's handsome, don't you think?"

"He is that," Emily agreed.

"How should I act?"

"Like yourself."

"What should I do?"

"Sing, drink your hot chocolate, and by all means, keep yer hands in yer lap!"

"Aunt Emily!"

"Sorry, dear, it's not you I don't trust. I just know what adolescent boys are like. And, don't let him look into your eyes. He'll likely mesmerize ya." Seeing the shocked expression on Madison's face, she quickly added, "Have fun!"

Madison dazedly walked off, still caught up in the dream of sitting next to John Carlin.

"Lord, help her," Emily muttered.

The next day brought Christmas. After the Tylers arrived, in keeping with tradition, Jacob read the Christmas story from the book of Luke in his worn Bible. It gave everyone something to reflect on throughout the day.

After the Christmas dinner, the two families had their gift exchange. Then, the children went off to play with their new gadgets and toys they'd received.

This allowed some time for the adults to talk. For some reason, this day seemed to mark Ashley's absence, more so than Thanksgiving had.

"How are things at home, Josh?" Jacob asked.

Joshua gave what seemed to be a disgusted snort. "I don't wanna ruin the day with this talk."

Emily could tell their friend had heavy matters weighing on his heart. "It won't do any good to lock it all up inside, Josh," she gently prodded.

"I know you two mean well, but please, let's not talk about it.

Not on Christmas Day. Besides, it seems like all we talk about lately is me...I'm a little tired of me."

Joshua's light humor seemed to do the trick and the subject was dropped.

Later that evening, however, as Jacob and Emily lay in bed, Emily fretted. "He's shutting us out, Jacob."

"He's not shutting us out," Jacob assured her.

"Yes, he is. He used to talk to us about how he was feeling and about how the girls are doing. Now, he won't."

"Emily," Jacob cautioned, "you're borrowing worries. Like he said, he's just tired of talking about it. It's been almost seven months."

"I hope you're right. I hope he isn't closing himself off."

Jacob paused. He had to admit, he hadn't thought of that possibility until Emily had voiced it. "Would you like to pray about it together?"

"Yes."

They prayed then, asking for God's help with Joshua and that he wouldn't give up. They also prayed that Joshua would be reminded that they were there for him. And, more importantly, that God would remind him Who was in charge.

They said their "Amens," snuggled close, and fell asleep.

As winter closed and spring began to show itself in brilliant colors, life slowly returned to normal in the Tyler house. Joshua no longer had to fret and worry about Kayla's speech. He knew it was all the Lord's doing. The fact that Kayla spoke quite a bit less than she used to didn't bother Joshua. He still couldn't get over the simple fact that *she was talking!* Joshua had faith that, with time, she would slowly come back to her normal self. For now, he was content with the progress she'd already made.

"It's almost time for the twins' birthday," Kayla sweetly reminded Joshua one day.

In less than two weeks, the twins would celebrate their twelfth birthday.

Kayla, his sweet, fragile girl had been born when the twins were only ten months old. She'd been three weeks early and Doc Rowan had given no hope of her survival. The good Lord had proved him wrong.

Turning to Kayla, Joshua asked, "What shall we do?"

Kayla giggled. "I don't know. I know nothin' about doin' birthday parties."

"I guess we'll have to ask them."

As if on cue, the twin girls clattered down the stairs and into the living room.

"Well, just in time. Kayla and I were discussing a couple of girls' special twelfth birthday coming up."

Alexis and Alyssa smiled. "We've been giving this some thought, Daddy," Alexis informed him.

"Could we have a sort of garden party?" Alyssa asked.

"Well, I suppose…if the weather holds out," Joshua agreed. "There's a good chance it might still be too cold by then, though."

"It's been warm lately," Alexis pleaded.

"Unseasonably warm," Joshua agreed.

"We want to have berry pies instead of cakes," Alyssa added

"It seems you two have yer party all planned."

The two girls smiled at him. "Yes, we do," they answered in unison. "And Aunt Emily said she'd help us make the pies."

Ashley had believed each girl deserved her own unique birthday, even if they had to share the day. She started off insisting they have two parties until the girls decided they much preferred one big party that they could enjoy together. They generally had the same friends, anyway. One thing Ashley had remained firm on was that they have their own cake, or whatever they decided to celebrate with.

The girls left the room then to go arrange plans with Emily as to when they'd get together to make the pies. Emily had already told them that she had blackberries canned from the previous summer that they could use for the pies.

As Joshua watched them leave, an ache for Ashley grew in his heart. He still missed her, but was resigned to the fact that she'd never come home. He was afraid that even if she did come to her senses, she'd be too embarrassed to swallow her pride and come back home. He knew her too well.

The party was a big success. The March weather cooperated

so the girls were able to have their party in the back garden.

For Joshua, holding the party there was a little bittersweet. The few flowers that were starting to show their heads were flowers Ashley had planted. In fact, all the flowers in their two gardens, the front garden and the back, were flowers Ashley had planted their first spring in Lorraine. They'd moved into a small house that was originally a servant's house to the Matthews' grand home. When they moved in, the Matthews didn't live in their house. The house, which had apparently been abandoned, was too expensive for Joshua and Ashley to buy.

Joshua had tried his hand at cattle ranching in North Dakota. He had spent five years, two of them before he and Ashley were married, and three more after they wed, to get it started and profitable. However, it never came to real fruition. A friend of theirs had written them about that same time telling them of a mill that had opened in a small town called Lorraine that needed good workers. The mill dealt in lumber.

When Joshua and Ashley got to Lorraine, all they could afford was a little bit of land. Mr. Rushford from the bank told them of the little shack. He'd said the shack itself was worth nothing, so he let them buy the land and have the shack for free. Joshua had decided to tear the shack down. Now they had a beautiful home. The living quarters were all on the ground floor and to the left of the entryway. The stairs that led up to the bedrooms were straight in front of the entryway.

Outside there were two rather large gardens. The front garden was only slightly smaller than the back garden. It was used for more intimate gatherings, such as tea for a few friends or merely sitting and talking as the flowers and small trees listened in.

The back garden was used for parties only. In addition to the flowers spilling out of their beds at the entrance to the garden, there were pathways to walk along, lined with flowers. Also gathered along the path were hand-carved wooden benches that Joshua had made.

Beyond the gardens was a field that eventually sloped to a creek where the children loved to play every spring and summer. The field didn't really belong to anybody, so the Matthews and Tylers shared it.

The Matthews' farm, which is how Jacob made a living,

included cows who grazed in the field. Along with the cows were countless chickens and cats, as well as a few horses. The horses were used for transportation and work and were kept in the barn with the cows who were rotated out of the fields.

The Matthews' income also came from the fresh vegetables and fruits they grew with a small portion coming from selling the chickens and their eggs.

Joshua grew nostalgic as he realized Emily and Ashley would've been planning their annual produce and flower stand they usually set up together. Ashley always sold her pretty flowers and Emily their produce. Ashley's endeavor contributed a fair amount of income to the family household during the spring and summer months, helping them get through the winter months.

Emily was equally successful in helping her household. Jacob handled the big business of selling produce throughout the state, while Emily sold to the local townsfolk.

These were all happy times when Joshua's life seemed simpler. He sighed. He and Ashley really had had a good life together…or so he thought.

'*My ways are higher than your ways and My thoughts higher than your thoughts,*' immediately sprang into Joshua's mind.

'*So you're saying there's a purpose for all this?*' Joshua challenged.

Again the familiar passage sprang to Joshua's mind.

'*Alright, Lord,*' Joshua begrudged.

Yet, he couldn't understand God's will in all this. When would he be able to forgive Ashley? Would it have a hold on him forever? It seemed anytime he had memories of their life together, no matter how happy those memories started out, he always seemed to come back to that same hated bitterness he loathed. Yet, there it was, ready to suck him back in.

'*Lord, I just want to be rid of it. I don't want to hate Ashley. I don't want to keep blaming her and holding a grudge against her. She's the mother of my beautiful girls. I just want to forgive her and move on. I'm moving through each day, but emotionally I'm stuck in my bitterness. Lord, please, send her home to me. Please let me forgive her because You command it and because when she comes home, I want to love her unconditionally, just as You do.*' Joshua didn't realize he'd been crying until he felt the tears on his face.

Embarrassed, he started to walk aimlessly down one of the garden's pathways, apart from the party. Walking blindly, he let the tears run their course.

"Look at me, a grown man, crying in the middle of his daughters' birthday party," he mocked himself aloud.

"What's wrong with that?" a voice asked.

Startled, he dried his eyes and looked up to see Jacob and Emily strolling toward him, arm in arm.

"Oh," Joshua started at Jacob's question, "um, well, nothing, I guess. Never mind." He gave a self-conscious laugh.

"I think it's sweet," Emily decided. "You're so overcome with emotion that they're getting older. I cried a little after Christopher's birthday. He's thirteen now…practically a grown man!"

Jacob chuckled. "Now, let's not grow him up too fast!"

This was too much for Joshua. All he was trying to do was get a little solitude so he could be with his thoughts, when he *had* to come across this smiling couple. They were his best friends, but he felt a little bit of resentment that they had each other. Here he was, without his wife, because she chose a different way of life. A life that didn't involve him or his girls.

"It's not that at all," Joshua snapped, giving in to self-pity.

Emily stopped short. "Oh, well, what is it, then? Can we help?"

"You know, Em, you can't always fix everyone's problems!"

A little shocked, but trying to smooth things over, Emily told him, "I'm sorry, Josh."

Joshua couldn't seem to help himself and continued. "What are you doing out here, anyway, romancing with your husband?" The ridiculous accusation didn't seem to pierce Joshua's sensibilities. "Shouldn't you be helping clean up? What are you doing, strolling along, as the other women have to slave away to clean up the party?"

This did rile Emily and she answered in a none-too-quiet voice, "I figured, Joshua, that since *I* baked *your* daughters' birthday pies *and* got the party all planned, *I* could allow the other ladies to clean up without me!"

This snapped Joshua back to reality. He'd lost control of his emotions and, worse, he was lashing out at one of his best friends. The same friend who had been there for him through all the trouble with Ashley. The same friend who had been some of his strongest support.

Joshua's voice was a whisper with emotion. "You're right, Em. And you did a wonderful job. The pies were delicious." He looked both Joshua and Emily in the eye. "I'm sorry. I should never have let my emotions get out of hand like that."

Leaving them to stare after him in puzzlement, Joshua quickly walked away.

Emily turned to Jacob. "Now do you see what I mean? He's just not the same!"

"Yeah, Em, I do. I'm sorry I didn't see it before."

Chapter 4: Word

Joshua decided to swallow his pride and go to the Matthews with an apology…a real apology. Not like the one he'd offered at the party and then ran away like a coward.

As he stepped out his front door, he spotted Herbert Fabian coming up the road from his farm, heading toward town.

Herbert Fabian was a heavy set man with brown eyes in his weathered face. His longish brunette hair reached to the collar of his shirt.

Joshua saw that Yetta, Herbert's wife, was with him. She was quite a bit shorter than her husband, but just as plump. She had many laugh lines around her mouth and her chocolate brown eyes. Her honey-blond hair had waves in it, no matter how tightly she pulled it back.

Joshua knew them as his neighbors and from Herbert's position as a handyman about town. Yetta had been an acquaintance of Ashley's and had been invited over several times for tea.

"Mornin', Herbert," Joshua greeted.

To Joshua's surprise, Herbert stopped the wagon and quickly got down. He moved with such speed, despite his size, Joshua suddenly knew he had news of import.

"I was wonderin' if I could talk to you. Well, actually, my wife was wonderin'."

"Sure," Joshua answered, puzzled. He looked up to Yetta on the seat. "Ma'am?"

"Hello, Mr. Tyler."

Yetta was helped down and all three stood in the lane outside Joshua's house.

"Shall we go inside?" Joshua offered. He led them into the house and all the way through to the parlor at the back of the house. He wished he'd followed tradition and put the parlor closer to the front.

"Please make yourselves comfortable. I'll go get us some tea."

"That would be lovely, Mr. Tyler," Yetta thanked him.

He finally got the tea set up and they were exchanging pleasantries and slowly sipping their second cup when Herbert ventured the subject they were there to discuss.

"Josh, you're probably wondering why we're here," Herbert stated.

"I'm a tad curious," Joshua agreed.

Herbert took a breath then dove in. "My, uh, Yetta, er, wife here, went to visit her sister, Debra. She, uh, saw someone."

Joshua was baffled as to how any of this pertained to him.

"Josh, I saw Ashley," Yetta blurted out.

Joshua's head snapped up. He was stunned into silence.

"She was hangin' laundry with some other women when I saw her. She was out in the wilderness area. I was drivin' through it with my brother-in-law. He was taking me back to catch the stage coach home. We passed all sorts of covered wagons set up everywhere, it seemed. I asked him about it and he told me about a man named Joseph Smith –"

Joshua's eyes bulged at the familiar name as he interrupted, "Joseph Smith?"

Yetta gave him a bewildered look. Joshua quickly encouraged, "I'm sorry, go on."

Yetta continued. "Uh, Joseph Smith, he leads a group that call themselves the Saints, or something, I guess."

He could barely focus on what she was saying.

"Well, some of them are moving out, apparently," Yetta informed him.

Here, Joshua again looked puzzled. "I thought they were in Ohio."

"Oh, they were, but some of the Saints were driven from their homes so lots of 'em left Ohio. What Olaf, he's Debra's husband, told me is, there's funny business goin' on. Their doctrine isn't widely accepted, so they aren't bein' very welcomed wherever they go. That's why some of 'em's been driven from their homes."

Joshua's throat had gone dry. What had Ashley gotten herself into?

"What kinds of things don't people agree with?" Joshua ventured.

"That's kinda the sketchy part, Josh," Herbert entered into the conversation. "No one really talks about it, they just get kinda jumpy when the Saints are around or when there's ever any mention of 'em. The Saints apparently decided to start a new town or somethin', because of it."

"That's where I saw Ashley!" Yetta jumped in. She got thoughtful then. "You know, I shoulda made Olaf stop and let me talk to her. I mentioned to him, offhand-like, 'I know her'. He seemed kinda anxious to get by them, though. Josh, I think she saw me! I looked over my shoulder one last time and she was still hangin' laundry, but she looked up and straight at me. She ducked her head then, ashamed-like, and quickly walked toward a wagon. It was strange. I just *know* she recognized me."

Joshua simply sat there, shocked.

"Josh, I felt it was our duty to come to you and tell you" Herbert finally broke the silence.

"Th-thank you, Yetta, Herbert," Joshua choked out, then stood to show them out.

"I know this must be a shock. I hope you aren't upset we came." Yetta grabbed his hand and gave it a reassuring squeeze.

Joshua mumbled, "Thank you. It helped, actually." Joshua numbly walked to the door and saw the Fabians off.

He stood in the lane a long time contemplating, processing, trying to absorb what he'd just learned.

'*If Ashley saw Yetta, why didn't she acknowledge her? Wave, smile...something? What does this mean? I'm so confused, Lord!*'

His random thoughts continued to swirl around his head as he turned to go back inside. A movement caught his eye and he turned his head to see the Matthews' home. He caught Emily watching him, a peculiar look on her face.

"Are you alright?" she called to him from her part of the lane.

Joshua felt awkward, given the circumstances he'd last spoken to her. "No. Em? Would it be okay if I talked to you and Jacob?"

"Of course!" Emily brightened. "We'll be right over as soon as supper's finished this evening."

Chapter 5: Life Moves On

Later that evening, after supper, Jacob and Emily showed up on Joshua's doorstep.

"Thank you for coming," Joshua greeted quietly. He had had the foresight to send the girls to bed early, which proved difficult.

Joshua showed Jacob and Emily to the living room and invited them to sit down.

Joshua cleared his throat nervously. "I've invited you here for two very important reasons. First, I really need to apologize to you for the other day at the girls' birthday party. Actually, Em," Joshua turned to Emily, "I guess my apology needs to go to you. I'm really sorry for what I said. I know you care about my family and me." He paused and looked at Jacob, including him. "You both do. Emily, I feel terrible. And Jacob, I'm sorry for disrespecting your wife. This has really eaten at me and I'm very sorry."

"You're forgiven, Josh!" Emily readily accepted. She jumped up from her seat and gave Joshua a warm hug.

Jacob echoed Emily's sentiment. "Think no more about it, Josh."

"Thank you. I feel much better getting that cleared up. Now I can move on." There was a pause. Joshua took a few moments to gather his thoughts. "I've been, uh, struggling…a lot…um, with negative feelings…toward Ashley. *Lots* of negative feelings. More than I've even let either of you know."

Emily snuck Jacob a pointed look.

Jacob returned it with a look of his own, then said, "Josh, your thoughts and feelings are yours to share, or not. We don't have claim to them. You have the right to keep them to yourself. We only want you to share them if, and when, *you* feel ready to share."

"I would like to share with you why the Fabians were here earlier."

Emily's eyes twinkled. "I will admit, I was curious about that!"

Jacob cautioned. "Emily, this isn't gossip to be spread

about."

Emily demurely agreed. "I know."

Joshua only smiled at that. "I thought that would grab your interest. They, or rather, Yetta, seems to know where Ashley is–"

"She does?!" Emily interrupted.

"She does."

"Where is she?" Emily demanded, scarcely being able to contain her excitement.

"Let the man finish, Emily!" Jacob lightly admonished. "I mean, please, go on, Josh."

"Yetta saw her when she was visiting her sister."

Joshua then retold the whole conversation he'd had with Herbert and Yetta.

"The funny thing was, Yetta said she was *certain* Ashley saw her, but Ashley didn't do anything. No smile, no wave, no nothin'. Isn't that odd?"

"Peculiar," Emily remarked.

Joshua went on in a quiet, thoughtful tone. "After thinking about it for some time, I feel calmer, more peaceful about Ashley. I think I've even gotten to the point of forgiving her. At first, when the Fabians came, I was beyond confused and felt all the original hurt come rushing back. I even wondered, hoped, actually, that Ashley would come home. But I feel utterly sad for Ashley now. Sad that she felt she needed to go to such lengths to search for God. I do genuinely worry over Ashley's spiritual health. If that many people would go to such lengths to basically ex-communicate those Saints, then what is it that they are they doing? What, exactly, has Ashley gotten herself into? And yet, as I've sat and stewed and fretted, God finally thwacked me upside the head…figuratively, of course. I had never truly given Ashley up to God. I kept trying to figure out how to fix things on my own. I kept trying to mend my own hurt. I finally realized that I wasn't even on the same page with God, even though I *thought* I was. I thought I was giving things to God, but in actuality, I was too prideful to let it go. I guess, to me, if I really let it go to God, it meant I lost because I didn't have control anymore. I didn't even realize I wanted control! I felt that since Ashley left and I had no control over that, I had no control over anything. So, I tried to control my own thoughts and emotions instead of really giving them to God."

"Emily perceived something was wrong, but I didn't believe her. I'm so sorry. I had no idea you had so much going on," Jacob interjected.

"You have nothing to apologize about," Joshua protested. "I invited you over tonight to apologize to *you*. Besides, how could you know how I was feeling? I certainly haven't been in the mood for sharing. I guess women's intuition can be helpful, huh?"

Jacob gave Emily one of his smiles that made her tingle from head to toe as he said, "Yes...a very good thing."

The middle of April passed, along with Samantha's ninth birthday. Her birthday marked the last of the line of the Matthews/Tyler birthdays until September when her mother's would set them all in motion again.

Joshua hadn't told the girls about the Fabians' visit because, he figured, at this point, they were finally coming to grips with Ashley being gone. They'd finally been able to settle down. Yet, he could honestly say, life seemed easier now, despite the recent news of Ashley. His renewed peace with God was no doubt the factor.

Although, he had to admit, another reason that he hadn't told the girls was because he knew they'd bring up the idea of him going after Ashley. He honestly didn't know if that was something he could do. He'd forgiven her, but he didn't know if he would be able to see her.

On the one hand, he could go up there and demand, as her husband, that she come home. He knew from experience, though, that that wouldn't work with her. She was very stubborn and would take it as a personal challenge *not* to go with him, just to prove her point.

He could go seek her out just to talk and see how she's doing and where she is, spiritually. This thought scared Joshua more than anything. Not for himself, but for her. He thought about what Yetta said, about Ashley not acknowledging her presence. It unnerved Joshua. Something just didn't feel right about that. Ashley was always very friendly with people she knew. Either she didn't see Yetta or... It was the latter, the unknown, that had

Joshua scared.

Joshua and Ashley had had a very close relationship, up until right before she left, the time, he now knew, when she had started meeting with Joseph Danielson. Ashley may have left him, but Joshua still felt a close connection to her and couldn't help but feel something was very wrong with Ashley...and it unsettled him. Whatever ever his decision regarding his wife was, he had to do it on his own...without Jacob and Emily's help. And he had absolutely no idea or inclination as to what that should be.

'Father, a clear sign would be kinda nice.,' he prayed. He was feeling torn apart by his decision. *'Should I go after Ashley or should I continue to pray she comes home to me...to us? I so much want this family whole again!'*

The room was silent, empty. And nothing came to Joshua.

On the verge of sleep, one word crept into his mind and brought a peace that stole over him. The word was: WAIT.

Joshua continued to wait as spring came to a close and June started with summer's promise

On this day, he and his girls headed down to the creek. The day was a perfect early-summer day of light blue sky and wispy white clouds.

Sitting with his back against a giant old oak tree, Madison came to join him.

"It's her anniversary," Madison sighed, breaking into his thoughts as she sat down.

Not understanding, Joshua lazily mumbled, "Hmmmm?", his eyes still closed from enjoying the pleasant heat of the day.

"Mother's, uh, Mama's...it's her anniversary," Madison rushed on.

Slowly, Joshua's eyes came open to focus on his daughter. "What are you talking about, Madison?"

"The day Mama left. It's...well...today."

Today, Saturday, June 2.

"Oh, it is," he said, trying to disguise his surprise. How could he have not remembered?

"Can I talk to you about her....or would that be too painful?"

A few months ago it would've been. "Of course, darlin'."

The younger girls were wading in the creek at the moment. Perfect time for a father-daughter conversation.

"I felt really angry for long time. Over the past few weeks, as I realized it was going to be Mama's one year anniversary of being gone, I thought about how much she missed…and it's her fault she missed it. I thought I'd be angry by that, too, but instead, I realized I was actually sad for her. I know it's her doin', but she missed out on all our birthdays, on the sleigh ride, Christmas Eve, and hearing Kayla talk again. I know if she hadn't left in the first place, Kayla wouldn't have stopped talking. But still…."

Madison paused. Joshua was shocked at not only how mature she was becoming, but at how close some of her feelings mirrored his own! Fancy that, they had common ground…after all the difficulties they'd had with one another.

"I guess I'm trying to say that we all wouldn't have realized how strong we could be…individually and together as a family…if she hadn't left. I'll admit, I'm still confused as to why, but I'm accepting it better now, I think. And, Daddy," Madison paused, clearly needing few moments. Her eyes misted. "I don't think I'd be where I am today without you."

Joshua had to blink back the sudden tears that sprang to his eyes. He cradled her head against his chest.

"You make me proud, darlin', to hear you say those words. There was so much anger and bitterness in you and I didn't know what to do."

Joshua then tilted her head up so he could look her in the eye. "To be fair, I will tell you one secret."

Madison smiled. "What's that?"

"I was feeling the same way. So, even though I'm an adult, and I'm supposed to have everything figured out, I was still hurt and angry and confused, too."

Madison's eyes widened in surprise. "No, Daddy…you? Well, we couldn't tell. We all thought you still loved Mama."

"I do."

"Even after all she's done?"

"Yes. God put it in my heart to love her and cherish her no matter what, and I do. Sometimes it's hard, but God is helping me through all that."

Madison sighed. "I suppose I could do with a little of God's help, too." Smiling to herself, she confessed, "I really only thought of Him as some being in the sky who looked down and made sure we were doing the right thing."

"He's so much more, Madison. I think a lot of people feel the way you do, though. He's a big, awesome God and it's hard not to get overwhelmed by the thought of Him. You really can't contain Him into one set image."

Silently, Joshua thanked God for the conversation he'd had with Madison. It seemed they were on a road to recovery.

Joshua prayed fervently for Madison since the day of their talk. He very much wanted her to know God.

As the summer came upon them, he realized he'd have to pray harder than ever because Madison seemed to have grown sweeter on John Carlin. And, much to Joshua's surprise and chagrin, John Carlin's interest didn't seem to wane from Madison. In the past, he seemed to flit his feelings from girl to girl. Now, he definitely seemed very interested in Madison. Joshua preferred the old way; when John's affections weren't centered on *his* daughter.

After supper one evening, Madison seemed preoccupied.

Joshua tried not to worry but she didn't seem to be able to calm down or sit still.

When he was about to ask her, she nervously blurted, "Papa, may I go walking…with John?"

Joshua was shocked speechless. Walking? His daughter? Already? With a boy? Wasn't she too young? Trying to remain calm, he nonchalantly asked, "When?"

"Soon." She glanced at the clock on the mantle. "In about half an hour."

Joshua still hadn't warmed up to the boy, but could not think of a reasonable excuse to say no. He vaguely remembered that age and figured if he did, they'd sneak around behind his back. At least now, he'd know what was going on.

"Okay," he finally relented, "but you are to be gone for no more than thirty minutes, tops. Am I understood?"

"Yes, Papa!" Madison gushed as she fled the room to freshen up.

Too soon, the dreaded knock came at the door.

"Hello, Mr. Tyler. I, er, was wonderin' if, er, Madison had, um, talked to you?" John stuttered after Joshua had opened the door.

Deciding to have some fun with the boy and make him squirm, Joshua played innocent. "Talk to me? About what?"

The boy licked his lips. "Um…walking, sir."

"Walking?" Joshua asked with a straight face. He kept the boy standing outside as he continued. "Why should she talk to me about walking? I can walk just fine! Can you? Do you have problems walking, sonny? That's such a shame."

"Oh, well, uh, no, sir. Um, I mean, I can walk just fine…and you can, too, apparently…that's good, sir. Um…I was just…."

"Just what? Wondering if Madison could?"

The boy's face brightened. "Yes."

"Well, yes, she can walk perfectly fine! Funny subject to come all the way over here to find out."

John's face fell. He didn't know what else to do other than turn around and head home. He was just starting for his parents' wagon he'd driven over from his house, when he heard Madison.

"John! Where are you going?" She rushed down the steps from the porch.

Turning around in relief, he greeted, "Hello, Miss Tyler." John bowed.

Joshua took note with surprise at the boy's courtesy to his daughter by bowing!

Madison noticed a peculiar twinkle in her father's eye and correctly deduced he'd been teasing poor John.

"Good-bye, Father," Madison quickly hustled John away. "We'll be going now."

Joshua used the sternest voice he could muster. "Remember, half an hour, no longer!"

"Yes, sir!" And then John actually bowed to him! Joshua correctly put it down to nerves.

Later, as Joshua retold the story to Jacob and Emily, he said, "I was mildly surprised by him. He actually used manners. I figured he'd at least be cheeky, but he wasn't."

"That *does* surprise me," Jacob agreed. "If I may say so, I'm glad his eye has landed on Madison. She is, after all, closer to his age than Brianna."

"Still, Madison is only thirteen compared to his seventeen. That's quite a jump in age."

"I hope Brianna takes this news okay. She really seemed infatuated with him for some reason, even though he hardly gave her the time of day," Jacob contemplated aloud.

"That's exactly the attraction…a boy who seems utterly unattainable and aloof is irresistible to a girl," Emily had to explain.

"I don't see why," Joshua objected.

"Nor do I," Jacob confirmed.

"I'm shocked, sweetheart!" Emily lamented teasingly. "That's how you got me! Don't you remember?"

Jacob gave Emily a questioning look as she began to clear the supper dishes.

"Um, no, sorry, Em."

"You silly! I have one name for you…Julia Burke."

"Oh, Julia Burke!" Jacob cried.

"Who's that?" Joshua asked. "Or should I not even venture there?"

"*She*," Emily began, "was my arch nemesis. As soon as it was obvious to everyone around that *Jakey* Matthews had his cap set on Julia Burke, I was consumed with jealousy and went after him."

Joshua raised his eyebrows. "*Jakey?*"

"Oh, yes. That was his childhood nickname," Emily seemed overly enthusiastic to share that bit of information.

"Alright, alright. Everything worked out just like you wanted, didn't it?" Jacob groused, none too pleased with resurrecting his childhood name.

Emily went over to Jacob then, put her arms around his shoulders and kissed him soundly on the mouth.

Jacob turned pink, "Emily! Not in front of our guest."

Emily returned, "Oh, it's just Josh! He's used to it."

Chapter 6: The Letter

Joshua had been praying a lot and *still* didn't know if he was supposed to track Ashley down, or not. It had been nearly a month since he had started giving the subject serious prayer but he still had no clear answer. He knew Ashley would resent him for coming after her, but enough was enough! He was her husband, after all...yet, wasn't that the very attitude that had driven her away in the first place?

When the answer finally did come, it was a shock so great, Joshua had no way to prepare for the horror it would bring.

Joshua had started taking the girls to town with him once a week, unconsciously taking the place of the trips Ashley used to take with the girls. It was on one such trip when Joshua received his answer.

They had arrived in town and headed to the general store, as usual. The postmaster, Mr. Dandin, called to him from the corner of the store.

"Say, Mr. Tyler, I believe I have something for you. A letter."

Joshua had written his mother around the same time Yetta Fabian had told him of her visit to her sister's. He had updated her on the recent happenings, but she definitely wouldn't have had time to get his letter and respond already. No one else usually wrote him.

Curious, and with a hint of unexplained foreboding, Joshua walked over to Mr. Dandin to get the letter. As soon as he grasped the envelope, he knew who it was from without even looking at the writing. Looking down at the familiar writing, his heart sank.

"Thank you, Mr. Dandin," barely left his lips as he turned to hurry out to the privacy of his wagon. The girls were around town and weren't expected to meet him for lunch for another hour.

He anxiously tore the letter from the envelope and read his wife's writing:

Saturday, June 2, 18_

Dear Joshua,

By now, you probably think any letter from me will contain something unpleasant. You've probably also figured out that I am not coming back home. I suspect you would have heard from Yetta by now so I decided to write you to clear up some things. I thought the date fitting, being the anniversary of my departure.

Joshua looked back up to the top of the page and noted, with surprise, that indeed, it *was* written the day of her anniversary. He glanced back down to his spot in the letter and continued to read:

To start, I want to clear up why I didn't respond to Yetta when she saw me. We Saints have to be careful who we interact with.

There are a lot of outsiders who don't understand us and have no desire to do so. That is why we must be careful and had to move as, I am sure, Yetta shared with you. I have found out, since then, that Yetta's sister and brother-in-law are the leaders of one of the groups that strongly disagree with some of our beliefs. It is one of those beliefs that brings me to the purpose of this letter.

Within the Saints, there are men who take more than one wife. There are a lot of rules and regulations regarding this, but once the elders approve, Joseph Danielson has asked me to marry him. And I want to marry Joseph. Yes, he's the man I left with. He's a good man and I love him.

Joshua suddenly felt like someone had punched him in the stomach. All of his air whooshed out. He couldn't breathe and had to re-read the last few sentences three times before his mind would start comprehending the words.

'She's my *wife! Joseph Danielson has no claim on her! She loves him? What about me? I love her!*'

He felt sick as he hurried to finish a letter he didn't want to continue reading.

Joseph has assured me that having more than one wife is acceptable. He, himself, has four others, but he married them as spiritual wives. This helps them secure their eternity, as it will with me. He says I'll be the only wife he truly loves. Of course, he still has obligations to his other wives. He even had to ask his first wife, Louise, if he could marry me. Of course, good wives say yes. He says in rare cases, the women have more than one husband, too. I suppose I'm one of those rare cases. He says the church would be more accepting of our marriage if I weren't married at all, so I'm writing to tell you a final good-bye. Please don't contact me. It would make too much trouble for me. If you still have any feelings of love for me at all, please let this be a final good-bye. I don't think I am even supposed to be writing you now, but I thought it would only be fair to you to tell you. I knew you wouldn't come after me because you know me so well and knew I wouldn't go with you willingly. That would still hold true now, as I am about to marry the only man I've ever truly loved.

Again, Joshua had to stop and take a few deep breaths to steady himself. The letter was almost more than he could take in. He finished the letter in a quick blur.

Joseph and I don't intend to tell anyone I'm married already so it would be best if you just forget me. I want to forget my past and look forward to my future. I'm sure your life is a lot happier now that I'm not in it. I know mine is.

Best Regards,

Ashley

Joshua started to feel the old bitterness rise again. "Don't go after her, huh?" he muttered, "Well, maybe that's just what I *will* do! Maybe I should ruin what she thinks is her chance at happiness! Maybe this is the answer God has given me."

Trying to calm himself, he knew better than to go off after Ashley on a bitter whim. He would only be using God as his excuse to do what he deemed the right thing. Maybe he should go after Ashley, but only if it was truly the direction God was really leading. He couldn't do it on his own terms. If he ended up going, he knew it would turn into a power struggle. That was no way to win Ashley back...not only to himself, but especially not to God.

His daughters happened to choose just that moment to seek him out.

"Daddy, we're hungry. Can we go get lunch now?" Kayla asked.

"Sure, let's go," he agreed. He acted as normal as he could possibly muster. It must've been successful because the girls didn't seem suspicious.

Off they went to lunch at the hotel. Ironically, this was exactly how their trips to town had ended with Ashley, too, but none of them gave it a thought.

Over the next few weeks, Joshua spent an ever greater deal of time in prayer for Ashley. He had to believe it was working its way into her heart.

He had decided from the time he got the letter that he wouldn't tell the girls about it. They were all doing so well, considering, and he didn't feel the need to undo any of their progress with moving on.

At this point, he hadn't even told Jacob and Emily. He figured he would, eventually, but he still needed to process all Ashley had told him.

It was nearing the end of summer and almost time for the annual summer picnic. The thought brought a lump of dread to the pit of his stomach. He'd heard Lillibeth Claudin had been having a beau court her from a small town nearby. Maybe the picnic wouldn't be so bad after all.

Thinking to the months ahead, he suddenly started feeling very overwhelmed. The weeks after the picnic would be bringing the beginning of school and the start of the line of birthdays that seemed endless until March. The thought brought a wave of sadness. More birthdays Ashley would miss. And she didn't even seem to care!

Which led to more bitterness and resentment...and wondering. Wondering why Ashley had really left. She had said she was searching, but had she really felt she couldn't come to him with her questions and doubts? She is his wife! Why would she feel like she couldn't come to him?

Those thoughts raised questions of their own. Like, why did she feel she didn't love him anymore? Had *he* really been the reason she left? Could she not stand being around him any longer? What could he have done differently?

Still, a year later, the questions invaded his thoughts. When she had first left, it seemed he was in too much shock to ponder much of anything. Then, the anger and bitterness had taken over, not to mention the problems that arose with the girls trying to cope.

However muddled her thinking was now, he knew that wasn't the real Ashley. He *knew* the real Ashley and he loved *her*. He could never do what she asked in her letter–forget her.

And there was his conundrum. Technically, she would be having an affair, if she went through with it and married Joseph. She didn't say when they were to be married. Should he divorce her simply because she willed it? They hadn't lived as husband and wife for a year now.

No, he couldn't do it. Even if she had asked for that specifically, he couldn't divorce her. It didn't matter what her so-called religion believed. He didn't give up. By law, God's and government's, she was bound to him! And now he sounded like a controlling husband. Maybe he should expose her to the so-called leaders of her newfound religion...but he knew, deep down, that had nothing to do with it. He did love her and she was his wife and he still missed her, despite the turmoil and grief she had brought to her family. Of course, that line of thinking only served to upset and make him angry and bitter all over again.

Joshua decided that maybe he needed some sound advice to help him make sense of his torn mind and heart.

Chapter 7: What To Do

Emily went to open the door to the incessant knocking. For a split second, she recalled over a year ago, one fateful afternoon started in just such a way. Shaking her head to clear the cluttered cobwebs of the past, she pasted on a smile.

Her smile turned to genuine warmth when she saw who was on the other side of the door. "Hello, Josh, come on in. Why were you knockin'?"

For a moment, a stab of fear shot through Emily as she remembered similar words that had accompanied the knock at the door that other afternoon. Why were these thoughts suddenly, unbidden, assailing her today?

"Formality, I guess," Joshua chuckled nervously. "Our children are all down at the creek and I thought I'd stop in. I hope I'm not disturbin' yer peaceful afternoon without 'em runnin' around."

Emily laughed. "Nope. Tryin' to tidy up from 'em runnin' around! Hold on, Jacob's outside. I'll go get him and fix us some lemonade. We *should* relax and enjoy this summer weather. It won't stay around much longer."

Before long, the three were sipping lemonade on the front porch. Small talk soon turned to more serious matters when Jacob innocently remarked, "I'm surprised you haven't run off after Ashley yet."

Joshua shifted uncomfortably. "Yeah. That's why I came here today. To discuss it."

"Oh?" Jacob questioned.

"I'm not sure what to do. I keep thinkin' I should, and then I convince myself not to go. Part of me wants to know exactly what's going on with her. And part of me makes excuses why I can't go. The main one being the girls. How would they react knowing I was going after Ashley? They've finally accepted things the way they are and don't seem all that eager to have her back. I think there's definitely still some hurt left over and may never fully go away. But there's been positive progress with moving on and I don't know how me going after Ashley would affect that. And there's also the matter of Ashley. Part of me thinks she'd resent me coming. But..." he paused. Not for dramatic effect, but because he wasn't sure how to explain the letter. "She wrote me," he finally said on a sigh. "And now, part of me thinks she may be asking me, in her own way, to come get her. Although, it would seem quite contrary to what she wrote in the letter."

Joshua leaned forward in his seat and handed the letter to Jacob. Jacob took it, but didn't open it. He eyed Joshua uncertainly. "Are you sure you want us to read this? It sounds personal."

"Go ahead," Joshua prompted. "I need your advice and it'd be easier if you knew what I was talkin' about."

Jacob and Emily peered over the letter, sitting side-by-side on a settee. If it weren't such a serious matter, he would've laughed outright, the way both sets of eyebrows shot up at the exact same time.

"Wow, Josh, that's...some news," Emily began after they'd finished reading.

Jacob slowly folded the letter back up. "So..." he exhaled, "what do you need advice about?" Jacob's troubled brown eyes met Joshua's.

"Everything, I suppose." Joshua flinched as he admitted, "The marriage part, in particular."

"Okay, start talkin'," Jacob prodded.

"I've had old doubts rise to the surface after reading this letter. It's made me question myself, my marriage, everything! I've had old guilt haunt me, too."

"Guilt?" Emily questioned.

"Yeah, about Ashley. About how I treated her. About what kind of a husband I was to her."

"You were–are–a wonderful husband, Josh. She always told me so. What do you have to feel guilty about?" Emily gently questioned.

"You know about my pride issue."

Jacob and Emily exchanged uneasy glances. Slowly Jacob affirmed, "Yeeesss...."

"I think I may have drove her away."

Emily bit back a smile. "Josh, annoying as that was, I doubt that's what drove her away."

"Yes, it is. Think about it. She had questions about God. She didn't feel she could come to me. She sought answers elsewhere…from a stranger, no less!" Joshua raked a hand through his thick hair, his trademark of frustration.

"Josh, she's still the one that left, though," Jacob reminded him. "She could've–should've–stayed and talked to you. As your wife, you should've been the first one she confided in."

"Exactly! Which is why I'm questioning it. Why did she feel she couldn't come to me? I can't help feeling that if I hadn't had such a chip on my shoulder, she wouldn't have felt that way."

"You were convicted of that and forgiven already. I was one of the ones who had the unpleasant task of coming to you and talking to you about it, remember? We prayed about it, together. I was there, you were repentant and, by that, you were forgiven." Jacob did his best to make Joshua understand.

"I know, but I've slipped." Joshua confessed quietly.

"We all do. It's part of being human. We learn from it and try our best not to do it again. But, we do. And we will. That's why we're not perfect. It still doesn't excuse Ashley's behavior, and you've got to stop trying to do that. Go after her if you must. Try to reconcile with her, but don't make excuses for her. That's the worst thing any human being can do for another. We don't grow if we completely ignore weaknesses in each other. With God's strength, we're supposed to help each other try to overcome them."

Joshua took a huge breath and decided to ask the question he didn't want to ask, but needed the answer to the most. "So, do you think I should give Ashley a divorce? It might make things easier on her. Or it might make them worse for her. Especially if all those elders and people don't know she's married."

"That's a huge decision, Josh." Jacob was astonished, truth be told. "Do you *want* to give her a divorce, or are you merely thinking that's what *she* wants?"

"Of course I don't *want* to! I'm thinking of her honor and reputation. I don't want her to be an adulteress, but according to that letter, she may already be one. And, honestly, I'm kinda mad she doesn't even ask for a divorce. She could've had the respect to at least try and do the right thing before plunging into a marriage with someone else. This whole group sounds like they play by their own rules and make their own laws. And I think that maybe she really does believe all that nonsense about men having more than one wife." Joshua was silent for awhile. He didn't want to admit his feelings, even to himself, but he had to say it aloud so it felt real.

He finally broke the silence. "After all this time of lovin' Ashley, this last letter finally convinced me of something I've been strugglin' with for awhile. I know I still love Ashley but...it doesn't feel the same. It feels more like how I'm *supposed* to love others, but not so much like I love my wife as my wife anymore. I know that's a convoluted way of sayin' that. I'm unsure."

Jacob spoke then, "Alright, I will say this. I can't see how Ashley's impending marriage can be deemed legal. And, if there's any hope of her coming back around, you're the one who'll need to be there for her."

Joshua nodded. "I thought along those same lines time and again. I really don't want to divorce Ashley. She may be unfaithful, but she's still my wife and I need to fight for her! I'm gonna go after her. Whether or not she comes back with me is up to her, but at least I can live with myself knowing I tried."

Arrangements and preparations were made as Joshua set out on his quest to try and win Ashley back and have her come home.

The girls would stay with Jacob and Emily and he'd take the stagecoach.

The whole trip, Joshua's stomach was in knots. Part anticipation. Part dread. He had no idea what awaited him when he found Ashley. He wasn't even sure he could find her. He was given directions by Yetta as to the whereabouts of where she saw Ashley. Yetta's brother-in-law, Olaf, would meet him at the stagecoach when he arrived.

Late one night, he was jostled awake as the stagecoach came to a complete stop at his final destination. Bleary-eyed, Joshua took in the dim outline of a small building that housed the horses for the stagecoach and the ticket office. Stretching his legs felt good as he got out of the coach. He was handed down his bag and hefted it onto his shoulder. He'd planned on only staying long enough to find Ashley and convince her to come home. Deep down, he knew this would be easier said than done. And could quite possibly drive a further wedge between them. He banished the rest of his negative thoughts and set off to find Olaf. Yetta had described him as being tall and gangly with red hair and freckles that made him look younger than he was.

"Joshua?" came a loud, booming voice.

Joshua looked over and saw a man fitting Olaf's description, but the voice seemed to belong in another body. Olaf looked as though he could be blown over in a stiff breeze, but his voice was hearty and strong. And loud, as Joshua came to learn.

Coming over, Olaf slapped him on the back and gave him a firm handshake. "How was yer trip? I hope ya fared well." Olaf's voice could easily have carried over an entire crowd. Being that there wasn't one because of the late hour, it simply echoed back almost as loud as it had gone out.

"It was without incident, which is always a good trip to have on a stagecoach. You hear stories of robberies."

"Don't worry, my boy, no robberies around here. Mostly they happen out west. What we have to worry about around here is them Saints what yer wife got herself all tied up with."

Joshua presently found himself liking Olaf immensely and the strange way he talked. It was amusing in a good way. Joshua smiled. "So I hear."

Olaf led Joshua toward his waiting wagon. "I don't want to start no trouble, but I have some men that have been watching them Saints pretty close like. They report to me or one of the other leaders in our group. We're tryin' to dissuade our congregation from bein' too friendly with 'em. They're bad news. But, since you're here, we may as well get started on the task at hand. First thing in the morning, we'll set out. I'll go with you to the outer edge of their group. They don't even have no houses or nothin' built yet. But they're workin' on it. Anyways, you ride on in and look for Ashley. But, don't get surprised if'n you come across a little trouble. They don't like outsiders."

Joshua's stomach did a flip-flop. Tomorrow! He could see Ashley tomorrow! He hoped it'd be true. He did miss her, even if he was thinking of her less and less as his wife.

Bright and early the next morning, after a quick breakfast, Olaf led Joshua and three other men from his group out to the Saints' residence.

"I brought the extra men in case we run into trouble. Them Saints act all innocent and nice, but they has a mean streak underneath all the niceness. They is guarded."

Joshua knew Yetta had told him they'd been out in the wilderness, but he hadn't realized just how far out it was going to be. It seemed they rode all morning. "How long does it take to get out to them?"

Olaf spit off to the side then answered. "Three hours."

Joshua wiped the sweat from his brow and took a swig of water from the canteen strapped to the saddle. The day had barely started and already it was sweltering under the sun. Finally, Joshua could see what looked like a camp not far off. Tents and tables and lean-to structures were set up, scattered here and there.

In a voice quiet, for him, Olaf informed Joshua, "We've arrived. Me and the men'll stay back here. You ride on and see what you can find out."

Swallowing hard, then taking a deep breath, Joshua murmured, "Lord, give me strength." It seemed that all he did on the stagecoach besides sleep was pray about this very moment. Now that it had arrived, he didn't know how to proceed.

Olaf had lent Joshua one of his horses to ride and now he guided the horse, step-by-step, with shaking hands beyond the first tent. He'd entered Saints territory. He wandered through the maze of structures and tents and found no one. It was odd until he noticed a group of women ahead, on the other side of the camp, hanging out laundry. Eerily, the same setting Yetta had seen Ashley in.

Joshua decided it might be less intrusive and intimidating if he tied the horse somewhere and walked in on foot. He swung off the horse and tethered him to a post that was sticking out of the ground. He wasn't sure what it was for, but figured it'd work as well as anything.

He walked through to the stares of the women who had now spotted him. His eyes swept the group of women, but he didn't see Ashley. "Hello," he greeted. I'm looking for Ashley..." Tyler? Danielson? My wife? How would she be known? Clearing his throat, he tried again. "I'm looking for Ashley. She's to be married to Joseph Danielson."

One lady stepped forward. She looked to be in her early forties, short, squat, with her hair tied back in a severe brown bun streaked with gray. Suspiciously she asked, "Who's askin'?"

"Uh, Josh…" he offered tentatively. He didn't know if they'd been apprised of Ashley's situation or not. Or if they even knew Ashley. He'd never been told how many were part of this group, but it had sounded like a lot.

"No Ashley here," another stepped out and said. She was prettier and younger than the first who had spoken. She was tall and appeared of delicate health.

The group of women was silent and stared back at Joshua, offering nothing further. Seeing no other course of action, Joshua doffed his hat and turned back the way he had come.

He bent to untie his horse and turned, nearly bumping into the younger woman who had spoken.

Her voice was low and quiet as she leaned into him and spoke rapidly. "I think I know who you are and who you're looking for. When Ashley first arrived, no one knew anything about her, but she changed all that. She was quite open about her past, but some of us soon put her in her place. She could get in trouble if it was known that she was married. The elders generally frown on that. They prefer all sister wives to have only one husband. Besides, what kind of woman leaves a family she already has to come out here to this?" The woman spread her arm to gesture, a disgusted expression clear on her face. Seeming to forget about Joshua, she muttered, "Who did she think she was, anyway? Thinking she could marry Joseph? I was supposed to marry him. And then his baby brother takes a fancy to me, and next thing you know, I'm married to Joel Danielson and poppin' out four of his babies." Starting, she came out of her tirade and almost seemed surprised to find Joshua still there. "Sorry, she's married to you, I take it. Anyway, last I knew, she'd gone over to the other camp on the other side of this one. The east side."

Again, Joshua doffed his hat. "Thank you, ma'am." And he was off.

He got to the outskirts of the camp without incident and relayed to Olaf what the mystery woman had told him.

"Hmmm…seems they're growin'. I didn't know the other camp was set up already. I knew they was aimin' to expand this one. I think that's about another four hours from here. We might wanna think about goin' on a ways and settin' up a camp of our own. We ain't gonna make it out there before nightfall. Sorry, Josh."

Joshua wasn't sure what he'd expected, but getting any information as to Ashley's whereabouts was more than he had dared hope for.

By the time Joshua and the other men had bunked down for the night, he realized just how exhausted he was. He didn't think he'd get any sleep with the discomfort of his bedroll and thinking about Ashley, but it seemed like only a moment he was thinking about her, and the next, Olaf was rousting him out. They sat around the dying campfire to eat their quick breakfast and then doused the fire and set out on their way.

Joshua was surprised to find he was a bundle of nerves. Ashley was close, he knew it! He hoped it would be today that he could finally see her.

They followed the same routine as the day before. Except Joshua left his horse outside the camp this time, with Olaf, and walked in. He felt less conspicuous that way and it seemed this camp was a little busier. He stepped inside the boundaries and was immediately spotted by a man on a horse. "What d'ya want? Are you a spy from that gang that's tryin' to get rid of us?"

Joshua thought of Ashley's letter. Should he reveal all? How much would hurt or be harmful to Ashley? He tried out the same answer he'd given the day before. "I'm lookin' for Ashley. She's marryin' Joseph Danielson."

That information seemed to register with the man. "Yeah. So? What's she to you?"

Joshua hoped the next bit didn't get Ashley into trouble. "She wrote me to tell me she was gettin' married and I wanted to come see her myself."

Suspicion lay heavy in the man's eyes. "She knows she's not supposed to be writin' letters to outsiders. You kin or somethin'?"

Joshua breathed a sigh of thanks to God for the man framing the question in such a way that he didn't lie. "Yes, sir, I am."

The man eased up some then. "Well, I guess that's alright." Pointing, he asked, "See that structure over there with the flag?"

"Yep."

"She'll be in there. That's the mess hall and the ladies who are on kitchen duty today will be over there about now, gettin' lunch ready. Word of caution, if you see any men, duck and hide. That's your only hope of seein' your sister. Usually the others aren't as lax as I am about outsiders. You're liable to get shot. Hurry now. Git!"

Joshua was a little scared, a lot nervous, and a lot thankful. He kept thanking God over and over that he'd found the one man who wasn't as vigilant about his post. And thought Ashley was his sister, no less! That was a happy accident that the man had assumed that.

Joshua got to the door of the mess hall and took a few deep breaths. He was going to see his wife! A thrill ran through him as he pushed the door open. The activity ceased as the women were shocked to see a strange man enter the building. One that didn't belong there. "I'm, um, I'm—"Joshua stopped as he saw a woman step out from behind the counter that ran along the far wall. Slowly, she walked forward, looking very upset. "Joshua!" she hissed. "Outside! Now!"

Joshua and Ashley stepped out the doors, but Ashley didn't walk far. "Go home, Josh! I can't believe you're here! I told you not to come and yet you disregard my wishes! I knew you probably didn't love me, but this borders on hate. Do you know how dangerous this is going to be for me now? Everyone in there saw you and some only need a reason to get rid of me. I'm the outsider here still, and I'm not well-liked."

"Then come home, Ash. We all want you home."

"No, Josh! I won't! I can't! I've made my bed and now I have to lie in it."

Joshua contemplated her words and insisted, "No, you don't. It sounds like you don't really need an excuse to leave. Sounds as if you don't like it here. You should come home with me." Joshua looked at her with pleading eyes. "You don't have to marry Joseph. You can still come home with me. The girls miss you." He knew there were times they did.

"Don't, Josh," Ashley stopped him.

But Joshua didn't know how, or want, to stop. "Emily and Jacob miss you."

"Don't, please, Josh!" Ashley begged now. "Don't say their names! I can't bear to hear them."

"Why is it so hard for you to give in? I'll take care of you. Please come home!" Joshua slowly stepped forward and enveloped Ashley. Holding her in his arms, he kissed her hair, her forehead, her cheeks. And then she broke away.

"I can't, Josh! I told you! You need to leave! Leave me be!" Ashley started walking away, but Joshua grabbed her arm.

"Please, Ash, why can't you leave with me? You seem miserable! Come home," he urged.

Ashley jerked away. With deadly calm and eyes heavy with dread, she hissed, "I married him." And then she stormed inside and slammed the door, leaving Joshua's heart in tattered ruins.

Joshua frowned. In a resigned voice, he said, "I mostly feel bad for the girls. They need a mother around. They need normalcy in their lives. A routine would help. It would be nice to find someone they can stay with for the nights I work late at the mill."

It had been a few months since Joshua's confrontation with Ashley. As expected, it had created quite an upheaval for the weeks following it. What he hadn't expected was how quickly his girls seemed to move past it. Yes, they'd been upset she didn't want to come home. He hadn't told them all of the details why. Just that she felt she couldn't leave and had refused. He didn't think it'd help to tell them she'd married another man illegally...in God's sight, as well as the state's.

"Why, Joshua Tyler!" brought him back to the present. "I've been doin' that for the last year. Why can't I continue?" Emily protested.

"I really would prefer someone who lives in town. That way I can ride by and get them on my way home from the mill. On days they get out of school and I get off early, I can go by and pick them up and take them home. Otherwise, I was going to see if they could spend the night at the person's house for the nights I get off late."

"You go right by our house already! This is nonsense you're talkin',"

"Please, Emily, I feel bad enough having taken advantage of you two so much over the past year-and-a-half."

"You're not takin' advantage! We've loved helping out. Those girls are like daughters to us."

"Please, Emily, my mind's made up. This way, I can pay someone and not feel so bad. You guys won't accept my money."

"Dang straight!"

"Hey, watch yer mouth," Jacob teased his wife.

"Make him change his mind. He's your friend."

"I'm afraid I can't, Emily, love. His mind's made up."

"I don't know who to ask, though," Joshua admitted.

After a few moments of silent defeat, Emily timidly suggested, "Reverend Chadrick and his wife, Elise?"

"Well, they are in town, which is closer to the mill. They have a family, though. I'd rather not have the girls be an added burden to somebody."

"And yet, you let me contend with them this whole time?" Emily teased, deciding to be a little petulant.

Joshua shot an amused look at Emily, then continued. "Maybe someone who's lonely, someone to whom the girls may be able to bring a little cheer and company."

"What about Mrs. Ulrich?" Jacob contributed, mentioning an elderly widow who lived alone on the outskirts of town.

"Hmmm…maybe. But what about when I have to work late and they would have to, possibly, stay the night? Mrs. Ulrich needn't be bothered to get four very active girls ready and off to school."

"Josh!" Emily suddenly exclaimed. "I think the answer's right under your nose! What about Katherine Taylor-Ryan, the school teacher herself! The girls adore her, she seems fond of them, and lives right next to the schoolhouse. It's perfect!"

Joshua grinned. "Thanks, Em, that's a really good idea!"

He just hoped young Miss Taylor-Ryan thought so, too.

Luckily for Joshua, Katherine Taylor-Ryan felt it was a very good idea indeed. The details were worked out and everyone was happy. Especially the girls who finally had a sort-of mother figure who could give them undivided attention, something they'd been craving for a long time. Little did anyone know just how much the Tyler girls would need a mother figure, when the letter came.

Chapter 8: Grisly News

It arrived on the afternoon of Tuesday, October 2. By now, Joshua wasn't really surprised when one of Ashley's letters arrived. He figured it meant she must feel some responsibility to him as his wife to let him know what she was doing. It didn't stop him from being curious, however, when it was hand-delivered by Yetta Fabian. Her daughter, Veda, now fully employed by Mr. Dandin, the postmaster, thought her mother could deliver it, being that they were neighbors and she would be going past the Tylers' house.

"Thank you, Mrs. Fabian," Joshua acknowledged.

"Have a pleasant afternoon, Mr. Tyler," Yetta wished as she rode off with her husband in their wagon.

Joshua headed to the back garden to read it. What he read, however, made his blood run cold. And that's why Jacob later found him lying, passed out, on the ground.

The letter read:

Saturday, September 8, 1838

Far West

Dearest Joshua,

You have been such a wonderful husband to me these past fifteen years. I was a fool for leaving you. I now know how blessed I was and how wonderful my life really was with you. I'm sorry I took it for granted.

About three weeks after you came, I found out that I was number thirteen! Joseph had told me I was only his fifth and that I was the one he really loved! What's worse, some men from the church came to talk to him. They had some suspicions he had multiple wives. It turns out, he wasn't supposed to have plural wives at all! Only select men were to obtain plural wives, also

74

known as spiritual wives, and you had to get special permission and have specific qualifications. Joseph had somehow found out about this secret pact---perhaps because he is a relative of some sort to Joseph Smith, who only told a select group of men about this practice. It seems there were several other men who abused this practice, too. These men all saw it as a way to...I don't know how to put this delicately into words in a letter. They all, uh, wanted an excuse to have numerous relations with many women. It would be deemed acceptable, since they were their wives.

I am so ashamed of myself and the way I have carried on. I don't know how I could have let myself be duped like this. I should have stayed where I belonged---with you. I always knew I could count on you and knew you really loved me, despite how I felt. How I long to be able to go back and change the past.

I hardly saw Joseph after we wed. When I did, it was only for him to, uh, reap the benefits of marriage. This is so painful for me to tell you. I've never been so humiliated or felt so dirty. You never made me feel this way! If I thought it would assuage my guilt, I'd beg you to take me back. But, you deserve better than that.

There's talk of us leaving here. We've grown quite a bit and have acquired numerous new members.

Joshua, I'm beginning to feel that something isn't quite right with the church and some of its beliefs, but I can't leave. I've made a couple of attempts to come home to you, even though I know I don't deserve to. Each time, Joseph has become violent and prevented me from leaving. Now I'm scared to even try anymore. I've been wretched, evil. I can't go on like this. By the time you read this, you'll be free of me and be able to live a happier life.

I've learned that the elders of this cult, because that's what I believe it is, are very possessive of us, all of us. Mostly it's the women who are suffering. The men can do pretty much whatever they want. They aren't bound by the same chains.

My life was over the moment I met Joseph Danielson and so I will take the only way out I know. I will shortly be going to meet my Maker and may He have mercy on my soul! He alone can punish me for the anguish I have caused. Please know that I am truly and deeply sorry, Joshua. By the time you read this, I will be gone from my earthly body.

With deepest regret,

Ashley

Jacob had come to ask for his help on the farm when he found Joshua. He saw the letter lying next to Joshua and rightly assumed that something in the letter had caused Joshua's shock. He grabbed the letter and left to fetch Doc Rowan.

By the time Jacob returned with Doc Rowan, Joshua was starting to regain consciousness. The doc looked into Joshua's eyes and felt around for broken bones. He probed Joshua's head and Joshua winced when the doc felt a large bump. Finding nothing alarming, Doc Rowan started in with questioning.

"So, what seems to be the trouble, sonny?"

"Uh, he just had a bit of a shock," Jacob quickly answered for him.

Joshua gave him a puzzled look. "Uh, yeah, had…some…er…news."

"Are you going to be alright?" Doc Rowan questioned as he helped Joshua up to a sitting position. "You know, if you had been, oh, maybe three feet over, you woulda hit yer head on this here bench. Yer lucky you landed on grass."

"I feel fine, Doc, really. Thanks for comin' out. I have Jacob here, in case I need him, but I'll be fine."

Doc Rowan looked a little doubtful, but relented. Turning to Jacob, he instructed, "If he starts to feel dizzy, you make sure and come get me."

"I will, Doc. Thanks for comin' out here with me."

After Doc left, Joshua looked at Jacob and asked, "Did you see the letter?"

"I saw it, but didn't read it." Jacob produced the letter he'd thrust into his pocket for safe keeping. "I had come over here to ask for a hand on the farm. Got quite a shock when I found you here passed out cold. When you didn't wake up after a few minutes, I got scared somethin' mighta been wrong with you. I guess I overreacted, huh?"

Joshua shook his head. "It's okay. You were right, though. I got quite a shock in that letter." He gestured for Jacob to read it.

It was Jacob's turn to be shocked.

"I'm still in shock, I guess." Joshua admitted when Jacob was done reading. "And numb. It hasn't quite sunk in."

Jacob sat down next to Joshua on the ground, their backs now resting against the bench.

"I don't think I can bring myself to tell my girls about this. They have gone through so much already. It seems things start to settle down, then BAM, something else happens."

After a few moments' silence, Joshua broke in. "I'm the cause of all this, Jacob. *I'm* the reason Ashley got involved with Danielson in the first place. She left *me* for him and those Saints. If I'd have been different, a better husband, she never would've left!"

"Josh, she seemed to take full responsibility for her actions."

"My head understands that, but my heart doesn't. My heart is sorta rulin' my head, I suppose."

"Right now, I think Satan's rulin' you. He's makin' you believe your doubts and have guilt that has no place bein' there. It didn't sound like she placed any blame on you."

Joshua felt his old anger and bitterness flare as he perceived a sermon, of sorts, coming from his best friend. "This afternoon, I find that I'm a widower and you have the nerve to *preach* at me about *my* guilt?! You don't know what it feels like! You didn't push your wife away and drive her to suicide! So don't tell me how I should or shouldn't feel!"

Jacob realized his mistake. Why did he have to give voice to his opinions all the time? He should've been quiet. His heart went out to his friend and he tried to apologize. "Josh, I'm sorry—"

Joshua didn't want to hear it. "No, don't! *Don't* sit there and lecture *me* on how *I* feel! I have lost my wife! You still have yours, GO HOME TO HER!"

"Josh, I really am--"

"I SAID, LEAVE!" With that, Joshua bolted up from the ground, trying not to stumble. He felt suddenly woozy, but made his way up to bed.

Jacob sat, dumbfounded at what a mess he'd made. It was his

fault. He hadn't been able to stand seeing his best friend beat himself up like that and so he'd opened his big mouth, thinking he was being helpful. Joshua was on a destructive path and Jacob didn't want to see him go down it again. Jacob knew, however, that he should've waited for later. Much later.

Joshua laid his head on the pillow and immediately the tears began to flow. He couldn't cry out there with Jacob; he was too angry at him. Finally, he could let the guilt, remorse and utter despair have their way with him. He spent the rest of the afternoon in bed, but sleeping little. His emotions had run the gamut by the time his daughters found him.

The girls had been able to go home after school that day because of it being Joshua's day off. Little did they know of his despair that would soon be theirs, too.

They had come home from school and changed to head outdoors to spend time by the creek. The weather was mild, but not warm enough to wade in the creek, so they played on the banks. After a couple hours, it was suggested they get supper started.

"I'm hungry," Madison had announced.

"Pa's probably wonderin' where we are," Alexis put in.

"Let's go!" Kayla called as she started running for the house. "Race ya!"

They were giggling as they came in the house.

"I can't wait to go to Miss Taylor-Ryan's tomorrow," Alexis spoke up as they hung up their shawls.

"Don't let Pa catch ya talkin' like that," Kayla warned. "I think it hurts his feelin's we like goin' there so much."

"Aww...he ain't around," Alexis protested.

"It is *isn't*, he *isn't* around," Kayla corrected. "And where is he, anyway?"

They traipsed through the house, eventually heading upstairs, where they found him sound asleep in bed.

"Uh, oh, Pa must be sick," Alexis wondered.

"Shh!" Madison shushed as they backed away from the door

and headed downstairs.

"We'll wake him when supper's ready," Alexis decided.

"Hey!" She suddenly stopped short, peering out the slightly open door that led out to the garden. "What's Uncle Jacob doin' here?"

Three heads swung towards the door as Alexis pushed it open. They could see him staring listlessly ahead, back still against the bench, his horse tethered nearby.

The first voice that registered in Jacob's head was Kayla's who quietly giggled, "Should we poke him and see if he's still alive?"

Registering their approach, Jacob rolled his head to the right to eye the four as they came nearer. "I'm alive," he confirmed.

'*Although I don't feel it,*' he thought.

"What're you doing here?" Alexis asked. "I bet Aunt Emily's cookin' supper. She's probably wonderin' where you are."

"Probably," he vaguely agreed. He couldn't look them in the eye so he looked past them, as if searching for something. "You didn't happen to see yer Pa in there, did ya?"

"He's in bed, Uncle Jacob. He looks real tired." Madison informed him.

"I need to talk to him a minute. You girls best get supper started. He'll probably be hungry when he wakes up."

"I wouldn't wake him, if I were you, Uncle Jacob. He's grouchy as a bear when he gets woke up," Alyssa cautioned.

"Yeah, like a great, big grizzly,' Alexis added and the four giggled.

'*Please, Lord, don't let this break their spirits*,' Jacob silently prayed.

He made his way into the house then and quietly up the stairs, trying to decide if he should wake Joshua or simply sneak back out and go home. He knew this was something he needed to make right, so he aimed for Joshua's room at the top of the stair. As he hesitated to knock, he heard soft crying. He hesitated a moment more wondering if he should leave Joshua alone. He finally decided against it. Joshua had needed a friend earlier and he hadn't been much of one then, but he could now.

Softly, he knocked on the door.

"Girls," came Joshua's tired reply, masking the tears well,

"could you please come back later?"

"Josh," Jacob called, "it's me. Can I come in? I need to talk to you."

Silence.

Jacob pushed open the door anyway and almost gasped aloud. Joshua seemed to have aged in the time since he left the garden. His hair looked almost gray in the light and his face was ashen.

Jacob stood before Joshua, feeling very much like a repentant child. "I was thinkin' of headin' home and wondered if you needed anything."

Joshua silently shook his head, not meeting Jacob's eyes.

"Josh, I'm real sorry about earlier. This is a terrible time for you and I should've kept my opinions to myself."

Joshua simply shrugged. He mumbled "forgiven."

"Your girls are looking for you."

Joshua looked up with panicked eyes.

As if on cue, a soft knock sounded at the door. Alyssa entered after Joshua's grunt of acknowledgement.

"Aunt Emily is here. She looked real worried when I told her you an' Uncle Jacob were up here."

The two men looked at each other warily.

"Tell her--" Joshua started, but was interrupted as Emily forced her way into the room.

"Don't bother tellin' her nothin'. I'm here. What on earth is goin' on?"

"Not now, Em," Jacob replied firmly.

Emily turned to Alexis. "Why don't you girls go on over to our house and stay for supper? You can help Brianna finish gettin' it ready."

Alexis' eyes glowed. "Okay! I'll go tell the girls!" She quickly scampered down the stairs to deliver the news.

"What is goin' on?" Emily tried again.

Joshua decided to ignore her question and, instead, told her, "Em, I don't think tonight's really a good night for the girls to go over for supper–"

"Oh, nonsense," she interrupted. She mistook his slight hesitation then for agreement.

"Emily," Jacob began in his quiet, yet warning tone, "you need to heed Josh. Now's not a good time."

"And why not? What is goin' on?! I know somethin's wrong. My woman's intuition has been goin' all day and I could feel that somethin' bad was about to happen. Obviously somethin's happened, now what is it?"

Jacob's words were clipped as he broke them off, one by one. "Emily, now's not the time. Just go home."

"Josh?" Emily turned pleading eyes toward him.

He looked up with soulful eyes and simply shook his head.

"We'll talk later, Emily, when Josh's good and ready," Jacob insisted.

Something in Jacob's look at Joshua and his tone, clued her in. "It's Ashley, isn't it?"

She saw their hesitancy. "It's Ashley!" She felt panic begin to choke her. "What? What about Ashley?"

Emily's babble made it hard for Joshua to keep quiet and concentrate. He wanted to shout the truth at her. Yet, at the same time, he didn't want her to know. He didn't want to hurt anyone else. He wanted to be left alone. He could feel the tension mounting. He willed Jacob to say something, to make her go away.

"Emily Sarah Matthews, I order you, as your husband, to go home!" Jacob sternly warned.

"Where is she? What's happened? Please tell me! Is she alright?"

Joshua snapped. "She's dead, Emily! Ashley is DEAD!"

Chapter 9: "Now What, Lord?"

Luckily, both men were on either side of Emily and could catch her as she fell.

Jacob took over then, lifting his wife up into his arms.

Joshua suggested, "Why don't you lay her on our–my–the bed."

"Don't you need to lie down, too? The doc wanted you to take it easy."

"I can't lie still anymore. I feel like I should be *doing* something."

Jacob concentrated on Emily. He was glad then that he had thought to bring the smelling salts with him that Doc Rowan had used on Joshua. He put them under Emily's nose. "Emily? Emily, darlin'. Wake up, sweetheart." Jacob gently tried to revive her, concern etching his face. It seemed as though the salts weren't working. Jacob was about to give up and fetch Doc Rowan again, when Emily moaned.

"Emily!" Jacob cried in relief. "Are you alright?"

"Yesh," she slightly slurred the word, trying to regain full consciousness. "What happened?"

"You fainted, love," Jacob softly explained. "Do you, er, remember...anything?"

Emily scrunched her face in concentration. "Yeeess," she slowly admitted. Then tears filled her eyes. "Oh, Josh!" she wailed. "I'm so sorry!"

And then the three shared in their grief.

"What do you suppose they're doin' over there?" Alyssa sat at the dining room table of the Matthews' next door. Supper was nearly ready.

"When I showed Aunt Emily upstairs, she looked real worried. And Papa and Uncle Jacob looked real serious," Alexis informed them.

"Somethin' is goin' on, that's fer sure," Madison alleged. "I can feel it in my bones."

"Mama was real worried when she left here and went over lookin' fer Pa. She said Chris was to be in charge until they got back," Hailey explained.

"That's right," Christopher agreed, somewhat smugly. "Now, git me my supper, women." He smiled a self-satisfied smile until Madison tipped his chair back, nearly spilling him.

"Hey!" he shrieked, grabbing onto the edge of the table. As he did so, he pulled the tablecloth, inadvertently knocking most of the dishes to the floor.

"Oh, servant," Kayla sang out, teasing him, "we need clean dishes so we can eat our supper. It's nearly ready so you best git a move on."

At that, the girls tittered and flounced out of the dining room, leaving Christopher to glower after them.

Back at the Tyler house, gloom hung heavy.

"I suppose we should git on home and leave Josh be for a spell," Emily finally conceded. She was also worried about leaving the children alone so long.

"Are you hungry at all?" she asked Joshua then.

The answer was flat. "No."

"We'll have your girls stay the night with us. You come whenever you're ready," Jacob informed him.

"They're bound to have questions about what's been goin' on over here. How will you answer their questions?" Joshua's voice held a bitter note.

"We'll think of something," Jacob assured.

"They're supposed to go to Miss Taylor-Ryan's tomorrow. I'm supposed to go to work. How do I explain anything to them, when I haven't even told my own daughters?"

"We could simply tell the girls you aren't feeling well. I could ride over first thing in the morning and tell Landon the same thing. The fact that the girls are staying with us will back that up. For now, I think that would suffice until you are ready to talk."

Through the exchange, Emily kept quiet. She didn't trust her voice or her emotions. Numb and shock were doing a good job of masking everything else. Thankfully her husband was good at taking control when the situation arose, despite how he might be feeling. If left on her own to deal with the situation, she would have failed miserably.

Jacob noticed his wife's preoccupied state and suggested she go downstairs and pull herself together before going home.

"That m-m-might be b-b-best." Emily tried choking back the tears that sprang up and overwhelmed her.

'*Like dust in the wind*', she thought. '*For dust you are, and to dust you shall return.*' Emily didn't know why that popped into her head.

Dust was fickle when blown by the wind. Human beings were fickle, too. Life itself was fickle. No one knew when their life would end.

Jacob led Emily down to the sitting room, a room where she had waited on another fateful night.

"Are you going to be okay here?" Jacob asked, concerned.

"I think so."

He gave her a questioning look, but didn't probe further. "Okay. I'll come back and check on you later if you haven't made it home."

She simply nodded, not trusting her voice. '*How can he be so strong through all of this?*'

He kissed her forehead then was gone.

The four of them had had such fun times together, Emily reflected. Good times. Touching moments. They'd shared everything life had thrown at them. Joys. Sorrows. They'd weathered it all together. And now this. One of them was gone...for good.

Emily bowed her head and prayed through her tears. She needed guidance, she needed peace, but most of all she needed her Father. '*Father, I don't understand this. Why Ashley, why like this? Why now? Why didn't You show her the way home? Please, please comfort Josh...comfort us all, but especially Josh.*'

Emily sat there quietly. She couldn't imagine life without Jacob. They were two halves of the same whole. Kindred spirits. She knew Joshua and Ashley had shared the same bond...long ago.

By the time Emily felt she had no tears left to shed, she was physically spent and emotionally exhausted. She was aching and tired and longed for her bed. Unfortunately, the room had darkened and she could barely see her hand in front of her face, yet had to somehow find her way home.

When Jacob had originally come over earlier in the day, there had been no need of a lantern. Now, she found herself without a way to light a path home.

After Jacob and Emily left him, Joshua sank down on the edge of the bed, too exhausted to do much of anything. Much later he shook himself and realized it was dark. He lit the lamp by the bed and stared at the flame.

Slowly, thoughts started to make their way back into his head. *'Lord God, I don't know what to do. I'm at a complete loss and have no idea how to cope with this. For some reason, you keep showing me that my life is not going to settle down anytime soon. If that's Your will, so be it...but don't leave me stranded by myself. Help me to learn whatever it is you're trying to teach me, because I really need to get through it and have my life settle down, for my girls' sake. Please, God, I'm begging you!'*

Despite his best efforts, worry and fear gripped his heart and twisted his stomach. How would he explain this to his girls? How could he possibly? He hoped God gave him an answer, and quick!

He was physically and mentally exhausted, but didn't think that he'd find sleep, due to pure anxiety. He finally resigned himself to crawling between the covers and blowing out the light.

Jacob had had a hard time pulling himself together for the short walk home from Joshua's house. Since he didn't have to be the strong one anymore, the one the two most important people in his life leaned on, he could give in to his grief. He did so briefly, pulling himself together in time before stepping inside and letting the children see him.

How could their lives have suddenly turned upside down like this? One moment, hoping Ashley would come home; praying, pleading with God that she'd see the light. The next moment, she's gone...completely and forever. Jacob fervently hoped she had made her peace with God. Then reality kicked in. How could she, if she took her own life?

He shook his head to clear the dark thoughts. He had to act carefully around the children. Or, at least, less downcast.

He entered the kitchen through the back door. There was very little evidence of supper. The two towel-covered plates on the small work table were the only testament.

Nothing seemed amiss. He crossed to the small ante-room that opened into the dining room and led to the living room. He was greeted with eight expectant gazes.

"Well?" prompted Madison.

"Well, what?" Jacob forced mock cheerfulness.

"Is everything alright?" Alexis asked.

"Fine, just fine," Jacob assured.

"Where's Mama, then?" Christopher demanded, eyeing his father skeptically.

"She's still at Aunt Ashley and Uncle Josh's."

Jacob nearly choked on Ashley's name.

"She's no aunt," Alexis fumed. "We haven't seen her for a year and more. She's not even a mama!"

Jacob dropped to the floor where the group had been sitting, evidently playing a game before he came. He ignored the remark and redirected the subject. "Guess who gets to spend the night?"

"Really?" That was all it took for Kayla to get excited.

"Why?" Alyssa questioned, suspiciously.

"Well, your Pa's not feelin' too well. We thought it would be a good idea for you to stay the night." Jacob hoped he sounded convincing.

They all looked at him suspiciously.

"There's something wrong, Pa, isn't there?" Samantha asked.

"Why do you ask that?" Jacob was sweating now, fearing they would somehow find out the truth.

"Yer actin' funny," Hailey concurred.

Jacob made a big show of looking out of the window. "It's gotten dark. I need to go back and get Mama. She's stuck without a lantern and it's gotten dark outside."

Thankfully, the children were distracted by that. He was exhausted and didn't know how much longer he could've faked it.

Emily fumbled along the dark road, squinting, when she saw a light coming toward her. Jacob, she realized in relief. He had come to give her light so she could walk home.

When he got closer, Emily flashed Jacob a smile. "I was wonderin' if you'd realize I was missin'."

"Of course I did. I woulda come sooner, but I had a lot of explaining to do."

Apprehension filled Emily's face. "But, did you–"

"No," he cut her off. "I didn't tell them anything. Just that their Pa didn't feel too good.'

"When do you think he'll tell them?" Emily wondered aloud as they walked home hand in hand.

"I don't know."

Emily sighed heavily, feeling very weary.

As they walked into their home, they were met by silence. The children had obviously taken themselves off to bed. They wouldn't have to worry about more questions…at least, not tonight.

Joshua tossed and turned all night. Any time he closed his eyes and dozed, he kept picturing what Ashley's lifeless body must've looked like. His nightmare, when he'd doze, was that he kept seeing himself going toward her, intending to awaken her, then drawing his hand back at the last moment, realizing she was dead. That's when he'd jerk himself awake, trying to clear the disturbingly vivid images from his head.

Somewhere around dawn, he pulled himself up and fluffed his pillow behind his back. He didn't think he could go back to sleep again. He was tired of having the same nightmare over and over again. In the quiet, thoughts started replacing images. Questions ran through his mind. How would he be able to break this tragic news to his daughters? He knew he couldn't wait too long, they probably already knew something was horribly wrong. God bless Jacob and Emily for fielding their questions.

After a few more hours of no sleep and much contemplation, Joshua came to the conclusion that he needed to tell the girls and the sooner, the better. If the girls knew he had kept this to himself too long, they'd be extremely hurt. They would already be devastated at the news. He would not be the reason to cause them any more pain.

He finally rolled himself out of bed already dreading what the day had to bring.

Chapter 10: Beginning Of A Year

Joshua pulled himself together as much as he could. He had dressed slowly and skipped breakfast altogether. He wasn't hungry.

As he walked down the lane to the Matthews', he mentally reviewed what he would say. Nothing sounded right. He reached the Matthews' and suddenly felt his stomach doing flip-flops. He wasn't ready for this, but it had to be done. Taking deep, ragged breaths, he pushed open the front door. "Hello!" he called out.

Hearing voices coming from up the stairs directly in front of him, he followed them. At the top of the stairs was a combination sitting room and library. It was surrounded by five doors, most of which led to bedrooms. Joshua heard the chatter coming from one of the doors to his left. The only one slightly opened was the one to Brianna's bedroom, so he started for it. He was met by giggling girls.

"Hi, Papa," Alyssa greeted.

"Hello, girls," Joshua quietly returned. "Go ahead and git yer things. It's time we headed home."

There were groans accompanied by reluctant compliance.

"Hello, Josh," Emily had come upstairs behind him. "Jacob is in town. I believe he was goin' to see Landon first, then to the schoolhouse. The children were all a little curious as to why they were being held out of school today."

"They'll know soon enough, I guess," Joshua informed her gruffly.

Joshua's girls came out then with their arms full of belongings.

Curtly, Joshua nodded toward Emily. "Good day, Emily." He then walked away with his daughters trailing behind.

"Girls, sit down," Joshua started, roughly. "I've got somethin' to tell ya." He sounded gruff, even to his own ears.

Softening his tone, he tried a different approach. "Did ya get all yer things put away from yer stay next door?"

"Yes, Pa," Kayla answered.

"That's good." He took a moment to clear his throat. It was now or never.

"Uh, girls, I got another letter from yer ma."

"What does it say?" Alyssa's innocent indigo eyes brightened for a moment.

"Is she finally comin' home?" This was posed from Alexis.

"She's been away long enough to find her answers?" asked a hopeful Madison.

"Does she miss us?" asked Kayla in a wistful voice.

Joshua choked back his tears. He was about to tear their world apart, but he forced himself to continue. They needed to know. "No, girls, none of those things, I'm afraid. I think you need to hear the whole story about your mama leavin'. I know you've probably heard some of it in gossip and I've filled in bits and pieces here and there. I want you to understand your ma a little better." He told them the full truth, not leaving anything out. Not even the mistakes and faults that he contributed to her decision to leave.

"So, she wrote me a letter…to say good-bye," he concluded, trying not to give in to the tears that were threatening. Retelling the events that had occurred over the last year-and-a-half were painful to live through again.

Quietly, Madison asked, "Where, Papa? Where did she go?"

Joshua was able to answer truthfully before delivering the final blow. "Only the Lord knows, darlin'." In a stinted whisper, he changed their lives forever. "Yer mama took her own life."

There was stunned silence before the wailing began.

At least two months passed before things settled down around the Tylers'. In the meantime, news spread like wildfire, even though Joshua had barely spoken to anybody during that time.

The holidays had come and gone without fanfare. He and the girls simply hadn't been up to celebrating the festivities. Not a day had gone by that the girls didn't break down into tears. During those times, Joshua held his grief together until a private moment presented itself when he could give in to it.

It was hard for him to come to the realization that his hope of Ashley ever coming home was now obliterated.

After the holidays, the girls returned to school and Joshua obligingly went back to work.

The only times they saw Emily were when she occasionally brought them supper and on Thanksgiving and Christmas. She brought them supper from their own celebration, though it hadn't been very cheerful at their house, either.

Sometimes Jacob had accompanied Emily, but it didn't seem to matter. Joshua kept everyone at a distance.

"I feel so helpless," Emily confided to Jacob. They had been over to Joshua's earlier that evening. "My best friend is gone and I don't even know how to help her family through it."

"They still need their time to grieve, sweetheart."

"They've had to start these past two years so badly. I want to help them through their hurt. They are so secluded; they don't even go to church!"

Jacob tried to assure her. "Give them time, they'll come around."

"I know."

Emily herself was still grieving for her friend. It not only affected the two of them, but their children as well. They had a few questions, but mostly felt the pain of their friends. They had each secretly imagined their life without Emily. Sensing the gloom that seemed to settle, they kept quiet and to themselves, not wanting to put any more distress on either of their parents.

Brianna had especially looked forward to school starting again. She was still sad about Aunt Ashley, but needed to get out of the gloomy atmosphere. And she longed to see her friends again, to lend them whatever support and comfort she could.

The Monday following the Christmas break, Brianna left for school. Yet, as she walked, she couldn't seem to shake the trepidation that followed her every step.

"Madison!" Brianna called.

Brianna had seen her friend loitering in the schoolyard, looking unsure about entering the schoolhouse itself.

Madison turned. She eyed Brianna as she approached.

If Brianna had been expecting a warm welcome, she would be

sorely disappointed.

"Hello, Brianna," Madison greeted, not unkindly, but certainly without warmth.

Ignoring her tone, Brianna gave her friend a warm squeeze then, lowering her voice, said, "I'm sorry about your mother."

Madison shrugged her friend off and sulked inside.

'She's sad, don't take it personally' Brianna reminded herself.

Throughout the day, she received the same treatment from Madison as well as the other three, though in varying degrees.

Kayla seemed to relapse into her non-talking self again.

Alyssa flat refused to look at anyone, while Alexis did quite the opposite; glaring at anyone who glanced her way. It was as if she was warning, but at the same time daring, anyone to say anything to her.

Brianna and her own siblings tried their best to be patient and understanding, but it became increasingly harder throughout the day.

Emily sympathized when Brianna came home and sobbed out her story. She sat and hugged Brianna, willing her daughter's hurt, as well as her own, to go away.

"They're grieving right now," Emily tried to explain in an alteration of her husband's words from a few days before.

"I know," Brianna sniffed. "I just want my old friends back."

"I know you do, darlin'. I do, too."

"I'm sorry, Mama. I know Aunt Ashley was your friend, too." Tearing up again, Brianna finished. "And now you'll-you'll-never see-see her again...."

Emily's eyes welled up then as mother and daughter wept together.

After some time, Emily lifted her apron to wipe her eyes.

"Try and put yourself in their shoes. How would you feel if you lost me? Think about how they must feel, losin' their mama. They probably don't wanna talk to anyone right now. Uncle Josh certainly doesn't and yer pa and I are tryin' to respect that."

"I know," Brianna acknowledged. "I've already imagined losin' you." She clung to Emily then. "I would hate it! I would never wanna lose you. I love you, Mama."

"And I, you, darlin' girl." Emily kissed the top of her daughter's head. This wasn't her little girl anymore. She'd turned twelve in October and was growing up fast. She obviously was thinking on her own, having her own feelings...feeling compassion for others. Emily was proud of her in a bittersweet way.

"Let's just hold on and be patient, hmm? Pa and I are bein' patient with Uncle Josh. They'll get through it. Until then, we need to simply let them know we're here for them and leave them be."

"Kinda like God?" Brianna questioned.

"Hmm, what do you mean?"

"God's always there for us, but sometimes we're too hurt to remember where He is."

Smiling, Emily hugged her daughter tight. "That's exactly right."

The veil of gloom that had been hanging so heavily over the house seemed to have lifted, if only a little bit. It wouldn't be completely gone, however, until their friends were back under their roof once again.

Joshua walked into the kitchen the next morning. "How was your first day back yesterday?"

"Fine," was Alexis' flat reply.

"How was everything at Miss Taylor-Ryan's?" he probed. He hadn't seen them after school their first day back since he'd had to work. He'd worked a shorter shift, so was able to pick them up on his way home that night.

"Fine, Daddy," Alyssa was quick to assure him. "Everything was fine."

"Well, the good news is, you don't have to go over there after school today. I have another early shift today and I have tomorrow off!" His mock cheerfulness didn't fool anyone.

"We don't mind, Pa," Madison spoke up. "We like Miss Taylor-Ryan. We like going to her house."

"Good, I'm glad to hear that." A shadow passed his face, however. '*We can't go on like this forever. I can't keep inconveniencing people every time my life seems to fall apart.*' Joshua sighed aloud.

"Daddy, is somethin' wrong?" Alexis cut into Joshua's thoughts.

Joshua shook himself. "No, darlin'. Just wonderin' what to do with you four girls. I can't keep allowin' people to take care of you. That's my job, but I simply don't know what to do with you while I'm at work."

"We don't mind and I know Aunt Emily and Miss Taylor-Ryan don't mind, or they wouldn't have offered."

"I know, but don't you ever wish you could come home and stay there?"

Alexis considered. Carefully she replied, "Well, yes, that would be nice...to *always* come home, but we understand."

"It would be especially nice to be able to stay home now. I can't stand the way everyone stares questions at us," Madison said.

Joshua frowned. "Did something happen at school?"

"Just the curious stares that made us feel uncomfortable. Why do people have to be so nosy? They know what happened. Why can't that be enough?" Madison lamented. "Brianna, who's supposed to be my friend, wouldn't stop tryin' to make me talk to her!"

"Madison, Brianna *is* your friend. She loves you very much and cares about you." Joshua gently reminded her.

"Yeah, well then, why haven't you been talkin' to Uncle Josh and Aunt Emily when they come over and try and talk to you?"

That brought Joshua up short. "I do talk," he answered curtly. Deep down, however, he knew Madison was right.

Relieved he could change the subject, Joshua announced, "You girls need to leave for school."

After they left, it gave Joshua a chance to think back over the last few months and everything they had missed celebrating with the Matthews. Besides the holidays, there were birthdays that had been missed. Brianna's birthday had come and gone without them being there to celebrate for the first time since the friendship of the two families began. He wondered if his girls had realized they'd missed it, if it affected them, if it affected her not to have her best friends there for such an important occasion. They had also missed Christopher's birthday, as well as Jacob's. Not only had they missed their friends' birthdays, they'd let a couple of their own slide by without celebration as well. Madison had turned fourteen in December and Kayla had turned twelve in November. At least Kayla hadn't spent her birthday in silence, like the previous year, but Joshua wasn't so sure that completely ignoring it was a better option. None of them had noticed that he hadn't even gotten either of them any presents.

He knew he'd behaved abominably toward Jacob and Emily. When they had come over, he'd barely let them in the house. He'd taken the food and basically threw them out. The realization stung a bit. He could blame grief---and they probably understood---but, he knew better than to blame his feelings for treating others so badly. He hadn't stopped to think about theirs or anyone else's feelings. In fact, besides the few words he had spoken to them, he hadn't talked to anyone other than his girls.

He owed Jacob and Emily an apology yet again.

"Hello, knock, knock," Joshua called out later that evening. He'd timidly opened the Matthews' front door, calling out as he came. It felt refreshingly familiar being able to walk into their home without formalities again. "I'm here to make peace." He tried for lightness as his girls followed him through the house.

"What?" Emily answered, coming in from the kitchen beyond. She had a fine dusting of flour covering her apron.

"Here." He held out an offering of chocolate cake with icing.

"Thank you," a startled Emily graciously accepted. She gave them all a curious look. "What brings you here?"

"We missed you!" Alyssa blurted out.

Emily, taken aback, caught her breath as her eyes filled with grateful tears. She held out her arms and embraced each girl in turn. "We've missed you around here, too. It's been too quiet. The children have been quite mopey, in fact."

"We brought the cake as a peace offering. We've alienated ourselves and hurt the ones closest to us." Joshua's sincere words were spoken directly to Emily's heart.

The cake had been the girls' idea. They'd also started feeling badly about how they had treated their friends.

Emily deftly dried her eyes. "Come back to the kitchen for a cup of tea and I'll slice up this delicious cake. I was makin' biscuits to go with supper. You *are* stayin' aren't ya?" Now that it seemed things could start going back to normal, Emily found herself blabbering on and on.

"Wild horses couldn't stop us," Kayla informed her seriously, bringing a round of chuckles.

Joshua vowed that'd he'd find a private moment to express his gratitude to Emily and Jacob for being so understanding with him.

It was a noisy evening as the two families came together for their first meal in a long time.

As the night wound down and the children went off together to catch up, Joshua got his opportunity to talk openly with Jacob and Emily.

"I really want to thank you two for your friendship and support. I know I've acted in a way that left a lot to be desired and I'm sorry."

"Oh, hush, Josh," Emily stopped him. "We've all been dealt a blow that none of us could hardly be prepared to handle."

"It doesn't excuse the way I've, well, treated you. We completely shut everyone out. Including those who care for us the most. After Ashley left," Joshua took a moment to compose himself. "I immediately came to you two for help, and you didn't let me down. With her, uh…the recent, er, issue…well, it raised more questions and feelings than I was ready to face. When she had initially left, and after the guilt of my, um, hand in her leaving…at least, what I perceived was my part in her leaving, eased, I had hoped she'd return. You helped me hang onto that hope, to cling to it. I could finally seek the forgiveness I so badly needed from God and could forgive myself, too. *She* even wrote that she forgave me! When she…when I…well, with her *gone,* I mean, *really gone* there was…is…no hope left. I felt, still feel, hopeless. I lost my wife…for good. That's it. It's finished. And for awhile, it made me feel like the ultimate failure. I started questioning everything. What could I have done differently? Should I have gone after her the way I did? Should I have simply stayed home? Would she still be alive if I had?" Joshua paused. "I simply don't understand the *why* in all of this."

"I don't know if you'll ever know *why,*" Jacob replied.

"Everyone is responsible for their own choices. The same exact thing could happen to two different people and the outcome would, most assuredly, be different. It all depends on how the person reacts. With Ashley, it was *her* choice to stay away. It was *her* choice not to come home and it was *her* choice to...." Jacob faltered, unable to finish his sentence.

"My head knows that," Joshua conceded. "My heart hurts for what *could have* been, if only *I* had done something different. What it would have been, I don't know. I know I would've felt like a coward had I not gone and at least tried to get her to come home."

"Josh, do you remember why you went?" Emily asked, gently.

Joshua's face grew pensive. "Yes."

"Why? What was it that made you go?" Emily dug deeper.

"I loved...still love...her. And I *knew* God was telling me to go. Even though I knew, deep down, that going there would only make her resent me, I *had* to go."

"At least you tried. And you did what you believed you had to do. You didn't know if going would have made a difference. You didn't know if going would have prompted her to come home, after all."

"That's the point, though, Jacob! She didn't come home!"

Jacob tried choosing his next words carefully. "Josh, how do you know...she wouldn't have still...uh, ended things the same way, even if she was home? Think about how much more traumatic that would have been for your girls."

Joshua hadn't thought about that aspect. In his narrow mind, he had only seen one scenario if Ashley had come home...they'd live happily ever after. He was still unsettled and eventually voiced his apprehensions after several minutes of silent contemplation, all around, of Jacob's words.

Joshua began haltingly, "For some reason, I seem to have, uh, sort of...made peace, if you will, more quickly with Ashley's death...than I expected I would. Don't think I'm some cold cad. I am very upset still, I have many questions unanswered and I don't understand all the whys, but I seem to have had a harder time when Ashley initially left, than now. Is that...I mean, what's wrong with me?"

Emily spoke slowly as a thought took shape. "I don't know that anything is, Josh. When she first left, perhaps that felt more like her death to you, than now. You grieved harder then. You were in complete shock at her loss, not having anticipated anything like it. Now, she's already been absent so long, it's harder to make it feel more real."

Jacob added his own thoughts. "You had lost *her*, in a sense, but you hadn't lost the *hope of her* coming home. Now that hope is permanently gone, it seems you are more so grieving the loss of that hope, rather than Ashley herself. You had already come to terms with her absence."

In a strange way, this was making sense to Joshua. "At the risk of sounding completely insane and even more cold, I was thinking about trying to find a more, er, permanent mother figure for the girls. A, uh, wife. The girls, well, they need stability and...um..." he trailed off at Emily's horrified look. Gulping, he knew better than to bring it up. It was too soon to discuss it. He knew it. He tried explaining, but only succeeded in lamely saying, "You two have been great and Miss Taylor-Ryan has been wonderful, but they need...a mother." He broke off at Emily's continual look of consternation. "I guess you're not ready to hear this." Joshua couldn't seem to stop babbling. "The girls are growing up so fast and soon they'll have questions, er, *female* questions, and I don't have the right answers for them. I need someone to take care of my family instead of having to rely on others."

"I understand, Josh," Emily assured him, reluctantly.

She suddenly found herself in a silent, inward battle. '*How could he even* think *about replacing Ashley so fast?*'

On the other hand, it wasn't as if he were talking *immediately*. She knew he wouldn't go out and marry the first woman he saw.

'*And why doesn't he deserve to find someone else?*' Emily countered to herself. '*He deserves to try and find happiness. The good Lord knows how miserable and full of anguish he's been since Ashley left.*'

Emily and Jacob exchanged silent glances, not needing words to convey their feelings or say aloud that their thoughts ran along the same course.

Chapter 11: A Few Ideas

Joshua left the Matthews' feeling somewhat better, yet, at the same time, a complete and utter fool.

How could he have told them of his decision to find a wife? How crass and uncaring did he seem now? They took it alright and seemed to understand…at least, they *acted* like they did. He merely wanted some sort of normalcy again for his family. They had been existing minimally for so long, it was starting to be scary how normal it felt. His girls needed a mother and that had been all there was to it. However, the prospect of having someone to come home to wasn't an altogether unpleasing thought. He would like to know that he was capable of some sort feelings for someone else. Maybe not love, but genuine affection.

"Papa, good night, I said!" An exasperated Madison broke into his thoughts.

"Sorry, darlin'," he sheepishly apologized, thankful his daughter couldn't read his mind. He wasn't sure how his daughters would react to having a new mother.

Madison leaned over and kissed his cheek.

"Good night, Madison."

Madison, the name he and Ashley had picked out for the baby they were sure was a boy. But they loved the name so much they gave it to their firstborn daughter instead. At last, he'd had a fond memory of Ashley.

"What do you think about Josh's decision?" Jacob asked his wife as they lingered over their cups of coffee after supper the following night.

It was nearly March, but the weather was still crisp and cool by day and even more so at night.

"I hate to admit it, but the girls do need a mother-figure."

"I know. It doesn't make it less strange having him think along those lines, though."

They sat in silence for a few minutes.

Suddenly, Emily smiled. "This'll be fun!"

Jacob would've been shocked at his wife's seeming complete turn-around, but he knew her too well. Instead, he quickly cautioned, "Oh, no, Emily, don't!"

"What, Jacob?" she innocently feigned confusion.

"You have yer 'match-makin' look."

"I will merely be helpin' out a friend."

"Emily," Jacob's voice was dubious. "He didn't sound like he wanted to be matched. He wants a wife so his girls will have a mother. Nothin' romantic...he didn't mention anything about love. This is about fulfillin' a need his girls have."

"But, Jacob, that's plain wrong, marryin' without love! I'm just takin' it a step farther. Couldn't hurt! He'll thank me later, you'll see."

As Jacob watched his wife, her green eyes bright with matchmaking thoughts, he couldn't help himself. He stood up and grabbed Emily out of her chair, nearly spilling her coffee.

"What are ya doin', Jacob?" Emily sputtered.

Jacob embraced her and, looking at her lovingly, he kissed her on the nose. "Yer cute as a button, ya know that? Especially when yer schemin'." His dark eyes twinkled.

Emily pushed at his chest, but remained in his embrace. "Yer not so bad yerself," Emily added coyly. "I think it's time fer bed."

Jacob and Emily enjoyed getting back to the Sunday routine of having Joshua and the girls over for dinner after church.

It was on one such occasion, a few weeks after Joshua's decision to find a bride, that they found themselves discussing it again.

"I'm trying to decide how to go about, er, choosin' a, um, lady," Joshua commented when Emily asked how the search was going.

"It'll take time. You have to woo them and let them get to know ya. Not many women are wantin' to marry some man they don't know," Emily cautioned. She didn't add that not many women wanted to marry a previously married man with children, no matter what the circumstances were.

"There are some very nice, eligible ladies that attend the sewing circle. Surely you know some of 'em." Emily glanced up to meet Jacob's wink, and returned one of her own.

Concentrating as she bit her lip, Emily finally rattled off a list. "Deborah Harvey...oh, she's really pretty and sweet...Odelia Rycroft, she's nice and really cheerful, it can actually get a bit annoying. She's happy *all the time*...oh! And there's Marcella Angus! She's a real beauty and such a sweetie pie. She's the kindest person I've ever met. She couldn't say a mean word about anybody. Of course, there's also our dear schoolmarm, Miss Taylor-Ryan–"

"Emily," Joshua cut her off, "that's fine. Uh, quite a list. I'm sure I'll find...someone...who catches my eye–"

"And yer heart!" Emily couldn't help adding.

Joshua colored slightly. "Uh, no, I don't think so. I really just want someone to be a...mother...er, to the girls. I mean, uh," he stammered, "I wouldn't mind if I cared for her. I suppose I would be a pretty lousy husband if I didn't. But not that, not that kind of love. Er, I mean, I don't need to be in love." Joshua's discomfort was making him babble.

"Ah, but *caring* can turn *into* love," Emily lightly teased.

"I suppose all that's left now is for me to tell the girls."

"You haven't told them yet?" Emily was shocked.

"Well, n-no."

"Oh, Joshua! What are we gonna do with you? How can I find someone your girls will like if they don't even know?"

"Uh, Em, since when did you decide you were gonna be helping me find someone?"

Emily blushed.

"Sorry, Josh, she's an incurable matchmaker," Jacob warned.

Joshua chuckled, "Thanks for the warning. Actually, Em, I think I would like your help. It's been...awhile...since I had to woo someone."

Emily clapped and giggled. "Yay!"

Jacob rolled his eyes to the ceiling. "Heaven help us."

Over the next few weeks, Emily kept her eye out for eligible ladies. Being a small town, everyone knew everyone, so it was more a challenge of weeding out the desperate spinsters who wanted to get married from the true ladies of the town who would be a good fit for Joshua. Unfortunately, the spinsters seemed to be coming out of the woodwork, overshadowing any of the other ladies.

Joshua complained to Emily one day. "I don't know about this, Em. It doesn't seem to be working! None of the ladies I've tried getting to know so far have seemed to be a good fit."

Emily tried reassuring him, despite her own misgivings. "Josh, you gotta give it time. You can't expect to find the right woman right away."

"I simply wanna find someone to care for the girls. I'm not lookin' for attraction on my part…or hers."

Emily knew that as far as women were concerned, he wouldn't find one who'd marry him without some attraction on their part. Slightly piqued at Joshua's attitude, and the fact that hers was the same way, she asked sarcastically, "What's the problem, then? By those standards, we shouldn't have any problem finding someone to marry you. Why, any woman should be falling down at your feet, seeing as how they will be promised to be a mother, but not a wife. You really know how to sweep a girl off her feet, Josh!"

"Come on, Emily, you know that's not what I meant! I only mean I want someone who will be a good mother, but I don't necessarily have to get all warm and tingly. I can't help it if she does or wants that. Marriages of convenience happen all of the time." Joshua could feel himself get irritated back at Emily and spouted, "At this point, any desperate spinster would do, as long as she could be a good role model."

"That's it? Just a role model? Why not continue having them go to Miss Taylor-Ryan's then, if that's all you want? It seems to me, Joshua Tyler, that maybe you *are* trying to find a wife, too, but you aren't willing to admit it."

Joshua couldn't deny it, although he wanted to. Instead, he took the coward's way out and turned and walked away.

Watching his retreating back, Emily thought over what she had said to Joshua and it gave her an idea.

As the weeks turned to months, Joshua didn't have to try so hard to seek anymore. The secret was out and it seemed the ladies of Lorraine were now flocking to him.

"Daddy, why are all these ladies wantin' to talk to you so much?" Madison questioned one evening at supper. "They all seem to try and find reasons to come up to you after church and when you go into the general store."

Joshua hadn't yet sat down and told the girls his intentions of finding them a mother. It seemed now would be the time. Taking a deep breath, he confessed, "It seems they heard I was lookin' for a wife." He carefully tried to keep his tone conversational.

"What?" Kayla mouthed the word, but no sound came out. Her sisters mirrored her actions unconsciously, all four mouths hanging agape.

"I thought you girls might benefit from havin' a woman around the house." Joshua hoped he sounded nonchalant because he felt far from it. His brow had broken out in a sweat.

Alexis surprised them all by speaking. "As long as it isn't any of *those* ladies, daddy, okay?"

Joshua put his cup down that he'd been about to take a drink out of and stared at her. "O-okay. Why not?"

"They aren't *real*. They act like they are pretending to be all nice and sweet, but they aren't. I don't like that," she answered.

Kayla agreed. "Yeah, daddy, they're pretty, but they act all ga-ga!"

Joshua was surprised by their seeming acceptance…barring the current flock of women that had so far presented themselves. "I'll keep that in mind."

Later he settled himself in an armchair and started skimming the paper when an advertisement caught his eye. It read:

```
              WANTED:
   Good men of moral, godly character
        to marry and be good husbands
        to women of godly virtue who
   want to start a new life for themselves
             in a new setting.
```

```
All inquiries directed to
        Arthur Kenny
        197 Adams
     Harrison, Maine
```

His heart thumping fast, Joshua looked back up at the date of the newspaper. Tuesday, March 26.

With a thud, his heart stopped. This was just about the time Emily proposed to help him find an eligible lady to marry. Was it a sign? Was he supposed to contact this Mr. Kenny? Was this a sign from God?

Chapter 12: An Urgent Decision

Joshua sat down later that week to write out his response to the advertisement. He had decided that would be the best course of action for his girls. Yet, try as he might, the words simply wouldn't come. He'd sat for the better part of an hour, but nothing he tried to pen sounded quite right. He either came across sounding too arrogant or too ignorant. In frustration, he threw his pen down and stood up.

"That's enough of this business," he muttered to himself. "I must be destined to be alone. But how hard can it be? I only need a mother for my girls, that's all!"

He picked up his hat from his bed and smooshed it on his head with a "harrumph!"

He wandered aimlessly in the gardens at first, furthering his distance to include the fields. He knew the girls would be done with school soon and wondered if he could help his restlessness by riding into town and surprising them. As he turned around to head back to the house, he thought better of that idea. If he did, they were sure to pester him with questions about his response to the advertisement. *They* were all surprisingly excited by the prospect of a mail order mother–*he* decidedly wasn't... anymore. The idea left him feeling...silly.

"Josh has certainly been quiet lately," Emily observed after supper, busy with her knitting in her lap.

Jacob looked up at his wife, enamored by the way the candlelight cast its glow on her hair, turning it to spun gold. He stared at her long enough, she unconsciously asked, "What?"

Instead, he replied, "I found him quite chatty at dinner on Sunday." Jacob teased, giving her a wink.

Emily gave him a piqued look before continuing. "You know what I mean! He hasn't mentioned any women he might be interested in. He's been very quiet on that point."

Turning more serious, Jacob sighed. "Em, leave him be. If he finds someone, we'll know."

"That's the point, I sense there *is* something, but he's not telling us."

"And what would he be hiding? And why? Even if he was, a man's entitled to his own secrets."

Emily gave him a wry smile. "Not when his friends are trying to help him find true love."

Jacob simply smirked.

Dear Mr. Kenny,

I am writing in regards to the advertisement I saw in the newspaper for a mail order bride.

I am a man with the means to support a wife. I have four daughters, ages ranging from twelve to fourteen, including a set of thirteen-year-old twins. Therefore, the prospect must love children.

I would describe myself as average height and of average build. I have brown hair and eyes to match.

I have a simple faith and love of my Lord and Savior, Jesus Christ. I must insist on someone who shares the same beliefs.

If there is someone who fits the above requirements, I humbly ask that you consider me a suitable choice for her so we may start a correspondence.

Joshua added his address and signed his name. And then he sat there. He couldn't quite get himself to actually put the letter in an envelope and seal away his fate. Every day he awoke to the letter on his writing desk, staring back at him, imploring him to do something about it. And there it sat for several days.

Joshua figured his girls would be asking about the whole mail order wife ordeal. There were rumors flying about his desperation for a wife. He sometimes hated living in a small town. His business wasn't his own. Of course, he had already learned *that* the hard way regarding Ashley.

"Papa?" Madison cautiously knocked. Upon invitation, she stepped into his room.

"Hmmm?" he answered, distracted as he fished his other boot out from underneath the bed.

"We were...um, all of us, that is...were just wonderin'..." Madison hesitated.

"Out with it, Madison. I don't have all day to stand and chat," he answered as he sat and tied his boots on his feet.

Madison hurried on in a rush. "Have you found a lady yet? A lady to marry, I mean?"

Without looking up from his feet, he answered with a curt, "No."

Madison sighed in relief that startled Joshua into glancing at her. "Good."

"What? Why?" he asked.

"We thought a mail order bride would be romantic, but we've been talkin' and decided we wouldn't like it. We wouldn't even know her. And what would everybody in town think?"

"Madison, we aren't to concern ourselves with what others think about us."

"Oh, I know that. It's just...it'd be strange, is all. We really don't like the idea anymore." Madison bit her lip, for fear she'd gone too far in voicing her opinion.

"You girls don't need to worry," Joshua patted her shoulder as he walked by.

And as he passed the writing table on his way out, he knocked the letter into the trash can with a satisfied smile.

"What, exactly, did he say?" Alexis questioned Madison on the walk to school.

All the girls were dying of curiosity.

"Exactly what I said. We aren't to worry about it."

"He didn't specifically say he *wouldn't* get a mail order bride, did he?" Alexis glumly wondered aloud.

"No," Madison answered somewhat uncertainly.

"Should we tell Aunt Em and see if she can get him to change his mind?" Alyssa asked, convinced now that they were about to introduce a stranger into their lives.

"I think, for now, we should mind our own business," Madison hissed.

They were nearing the school and she didn't want anyone to hear them discussing their father's love life, or lack thereof. She had to admit, it was odd to think of her father falling in love with anyone and getting married. Personally, she didn't feel the need for him to remarry. It felt wrong somehow, like he would be forgetting their mother. Besides, they'd been fine on their own! They didn't need a mother looking after them; they had made it so far.

Madison resolved that if her father thought they needed looking after, and that was the only reason he wanted a wife, she would prove to him that she, Madison Hannah Tyler, could take care of them all.

Emily was trying to decide how to best approach the subject with Joshua concerning his pursuit of a wife. While Sunday at dinner would be the perfect *time*, she simply didn't know what she would say. After all, she *was* a caring and concerned friend…who just happened to be dying of curiosity.

As it turned out, Madison proved to be unwittingly useful.

Emily watched Joshua all through dinner, which wasn't lost on him.

'*How does she do that? How does she instinctively know?*' Joshua had known Emily long enough to know when she was trying to figure something out. And she had the look that she was trying to figure something out about him. It put him a little on edge because he didn't know just how much he wanted to divulge to his two friends.

Madison had been watching her pa, as well as watching Aunt Emily watch her pa. A plan was starting to take shape in her mind, but she was a little afraid to try it. What if it didn't work? What if she got in trouble? Yet, she and her sisters were dying to know and their father hadn't said anything of his decision to them and they were growing impatient! If he wouldn't talk to them, she'd have to force him to talk to Uncle Jacob and Aunt Emily. Taking a big, deep breath, she announced, "Daddy's decided not to pick a lady from town. He's waiting for a lady to pick him…sort of."

Madison held her breath and looked at Joshua. He'd never said they couldn't say anything. He simply hadn't said that.

Shocked at first, Joshua didn't know what to say. He glanced at Emily and Jacob to see their reactions. Shock colored Emily's face and Jacob's only showed confusion. Casually he verified, "Well, uh, apparently my carefully guarded secret is out." He tried to keep his tone light, all the while sweating under the pressure he felt. *'Well played, Madison,'* he wryly thought. Looking around the table, he announced, "Actually, I've decided not to go that way after all."

His words were purposefully directed at Jacob and Emily. He didn't know if he could keep a straight face if he talked to his daughters. Madison's daring had surprised and amused him.

"What? What are you talking about, Josh?" Emily asked. "What way?"

Joshua was suddenly sheepish. "I was, briefly, considering a mail order bride."

Emily's mouth fell open in shock. "A what?!"

"Have you heard of them?" Joshua continued on, innocently.

"Yes, but Josh, that's no way–"

"I know, Em," he cut her off. "That's why I'm not."

"But why *were* you, Josh?" Emily wanted to know.

"It was, uh, intriguing…" he trailed off, not completely sure of his answer.

He was suddenly very aware of the little ears still in the room. The more complex answer that he'd spent the last few days finding out didn't seem appropriate to discuss with children in the room. Turning to his daughters, he asked, "Will you please excuse us?"

They must have sensed Joshua's discomfort because the request was barely out of his mouth before the room cleared of anyone below the age of thirty.

Joshua watched them go then turned back to Jacob and Emily, clearly uncomfortable. He tried to begin again, but started out haltingly. "Okay, here's the, um, here's the truth. I sorta, er, kinda have been, uh, feelin' lonely. I kinda, um, discovered I'd like to have a, er, sort of companion, and well, a wife actually." Joshua hated himself for tripping over the words and not having the courage to tell his dearest friends in the world the simple truth.

"I tried telling myself I needed to find a wife for the girls' sake…so they'd have a mother. But lately I've found the idea of having someone, well, love *me* not such an appalling idea. Why can't I have both? Someone who can be a mother to my girls and whom I can love and have that love returned. Do you think that's wrong? I feel sorta unfaithful to Ashley or her memory or… something."

"It's been over six months, Josh," Jacob gently reminded him. He silently added that it wasn't as if Ashley had been much of a wife in the years directly preceding her death.

"Is that why you haven't been attracted to anyone, do you think?" Emily questioned. "Guilt?"

"I don't know," Joshua answered slowly, thoughtfully. "It could be." The words soaked in as he contemplated them, then smiled. "Either that, or I'm too picky. Subconsciously I may be trying to measure everyone against Ashley."

Emily had quiet opinions of her own. Ashley could certainly be passed up by any woman. She ended up not being good enough for Joshua, that was for sure. Emily was shocked the thought had even entered her head. Instead she voiced, "Maybe you need to start all over and give them a fair chance."

Joshua groaned. "It's too hard. There's no one good left." Smiling, he teased, "Why can't I find someone like you, Em?"

Both Jacob and Emily laughed outright.

In mock warning, Jacob asked, "You wantin' what you can't have, Tyler?"

Joshua grinned mischievously and gave Emily an exaggerated wink.

Emily fixed him with a pert stare and pretended to snub him. "I'm too perfect; there's no one else like me."

It turned out Joshua didn't have to do much at all in the pursuing. It seemed that once the eligible ladies found out Joshua was finally free and looking, he found himself being invited to teas and dinners nearly every day of the week! He had created quite the gossip.'Tyler and his women.' That's how it'd been phrased! It was embarrassing!

Sometimes Jacob and Emily were invited as well and then it wasn't so bad. Always he and the lady were properly chaperoned. Although he'd had the pleasure of their company, he still hadn't found The One.

There had been the sweet Devin Harvey first. He'd asked her to Sunday dinner, which had included the Matthews. She seemed only too pleased about that. After the supper, Joshua could only judge that she was still sweet as ever…and quiet. That was it.

A few days later, Odelia Rycroft had the chance to wear him thin with her incessant laughter. It didn't seem to matter what he said or talked about, she found it extremely amusing. He found it extremely irritating.

Three afternoons later over tea, he thought he might have found a potential in Marcella Angus. Jacob and Emily had been invited as well, so that helped to ease his anxiety. It turned out, he wasn't as nervous as he thought he'd be. Marcella was very attentive to him, but not overly so. She was the perfect hostess and had everyone at ease from the very beginning. It was a thoroughly enjoyable afternoon.

However, the following week, he'd had the complete opposite experience with Henrietta Chester. Her manner was much too forward at the supper she'd invited him and his family to. All through the horrible affair, she'd coyly try and catch his eye across the table. When she did, she flirted shamelessly with her eyes. Not only that, it seemed that while he was there, she'd found any reason she could surmise to touch him. And when she did, it was always a too-familiar caress. He couldn't think back on that dreadful night without shuddering.

Mercy Burne was the last he'd visited with. The circumstance was a bit strange, but he'd enjoyed her company just the same. She'd invited him to her house for an engagement party for her sister, Madeleine and fiance, Rhett Reynolds. The couple he only knew distantly.

Mercy had been an angel through and through. And he'd discovered a strength in her character he hadn't noticed before. It wasn't so much stubbornness as it was a steadfastness to her morals. She had been extremely easy to talk to, even when she didn't agree with his opinions. Although she had held her own, she was open to other's ideas and didn't make them feel silly for having them. The only drawback was that she was at least ten years his junior.

One young lady he had overlooked before was the spinster schoolmarm, Miss Taylor-Ryan. He wasn't completely sure he should even consider her, being what her position was and the fact that it could create an awkward relationship between his daughters and their teacher, much less gossip around the town. He'd already had enough of that. Still, the idea of giving the schoolmarm a fair chance was appealing to him. He felt he'd regarded her as too much of a resource, having helped quite a lot with his girls, than he had of seeing her as a proper lady and prospect.

He hadn't particularly liked the manner in which he had acquainted himself with the various women. It was like they were all a dish for him to sample, ready to be spat out if the taste wasn't quite right. It had never been this hard with Ashley. He'd seen her and known right off that she was for him. Of course, maybe a little more discretion might have been useful; still, she had given him four beautiful daughters and for that, he could never truly disgrace Ashley's memory.

However, he needed to stop comparing these poor, unsuspecting women to Ashley. Anymore, he was beginning to think Ashley was a poor ruler to measure them by, anyway. The thought made him cringe, but didn't revolt him the way that he thought it should.

Sighing, he relented in his mind to give Miss Taylor-Ryan a chance. He didn't hope for much because, so far, none of the prospects were overly promising, but he resolved to do it.

The annual summer picnic was approaching. It seemed like an appropriate event to ask Miss Taylor-Ryan to accompany him and his family. For some reason, it was harder asking her than it had been with anyone else. Finally, the Sunday before the picnic, he mustered up his courage.

"Howdy, Miss Taylor-Ryan," Joshua greeted her, doffing his hat.

Katherine Taylor-Ryan gave Joshua a curt nod and answered, "Mr. Tyler."

Then the stammering began. It softened Katherine as she watched the grown man before her work hard to get his request out. She even bit back a few smiles.

"I was, er, wondering…that is, if um, you'd ever, er… consider, Miss Taylor-Ryan, you might wanna, uh, go to the picnic. With me, that is…and the girls, the picnic coming up, you know, uh, the annual one." He finished in a rush.

'*Idiot, idiot, idiot!*' Joshua mentally kicked himself. He'd sounded like a complete fool.

Trying to suppress a grin, Katherine merely smiled sweetly. "Mr. Tyler, I would be honored to attend with you...and your lovely family."

"You would?!" He didn't mean to sound so surprised, it had just slipped out. "I mean, oh, you would. Well, good, that's good then, I guess." He tried to compose himself.

Katherine couldn't help resisting, "You guess? If you're not sure, maybe we should postpone this for another time." She gave him a disarming smile.

Joshua's eyes widened. "No, no, we'll pick you up at ten o'clock on Saturday morning. For certain."

Katherine did grin then. Arching her eyebrows, she replied laughingly, "I was joshing, *Joshua*."

Joshua couldn't seem to reply. He couldn't believe how nervous he was!

"I'll be waiting, Mr. Tyler. It might do well to close your mouth, though." She blessed him with her most disarming smile, causing Joshua to stumble backward and trip over his own feet before making it back to the safety of his wagon.

"What'cha lookin' so silly for, Pa?" Alexis called out to him from her perch inside.

"Hush, girl," Joshua answered as he deftly climbed up into the seat and headed his team homeward.

The weather for the picnic was bright and clear.

It was hard for Joshua to believe that it had been over two years since he had attended the one with the disaster of Lillibeth Claudin. He cleared his mind. He wanted to have a pleasant day with Miss Taylor-Ryan and his girls. Not bad memories.

They pulled up to the small white house next to the school. Joshua climbed down to fetch her and was unprepared for the vision he was met with.

"Why, Miss Taylor-Ryan, you look," he gulped, blushing slightly, "pretty."

"Thank you, Mr. Tyler," she smiled. "I think we are beyond acquaintances now, don't you? I have been keeping your girls, after all. You may call me Katherine."

Joshua nervously smiled. "Uh, oh, ok. Uh, my friends call me

Josh. You're my friend. You can call me Josh."

'Stupid, stupid man!' he inwardly groaned. *'Stop talking already! You've established your friendship, you dolt!'*

"I prefer Joshua," she decided aloud, a teasing smile playing about her lips.

He grinned at her stupidly. "Well, alright."

To Joshua's relief, Katherine and the girls did most of the talking on the way to the picnic. They hadn't seen much of each other since school had let out and there was much catching up to do.

Joshua admired the school teacher. As she talked to his girls, he couldn't help noticing her. It was a lot easier when she wasn't focused on him while he noticed different things about her. She held herself in an almost regal manner without being snobbish. Her stature was tall, even while sitting, and she carried herself like a proper lady; like one who had gone to one of those manner schools.

Joshua watched her animated eyes as she conversed. He noticed they weren't a deep blue, like an ocean, but rather a light blue, like the sky. In them he read warmth and kindness.

Light brown tendrils kissed her forehead and the nape of her neck, gently curling as they rested there. The rest of her hair was caught up in a graceful coif.

Her blue gingham dress exactly matched her eyes.

Almost too soon for Joshua's liking, they arrived at the picnic. However, it turned out to be a most extraordinary day. He had more fun and laughed more than he had in quite a long time.

Somewhere deep inside, a tiny bud of hope began to bloom. Hope that he could be happy again someday. Truly happy. And it could be with someone else. He had the fleeting thought that he may have found someone he would be happy spending his days with. But was it too soon for him to feel this way about her? True, she wasn't some stranger. Not nearly as strange as some of his recent experiences with some of the ladies of the town. Yet, he had to remind himself she may not return the feelings. But dare he hope that if he moved slowly enough and took enough time with her, that feelings for him could develop? Yes, he could allow himself to hope.

School started and Joshua was strangely thrilled by the prospect. It meant he would get to see more of Katherine. He was still floating on clouds from the picnic and decided he should find out exactly what his girls thought of Katherine. If he were to pursue this, he'd need their favor since it would affect them, too.

Shortly after school started and brought with it its steady routines, he broached the subject. "How's school going, girls?"

"It's going fine, Pa." Kayla gave him a confused look. "We've barely started."

"I know. Just making sure it's been a good start." He stalled. Then cleared his throat. "What about Miss Taylor-Ryan? You still like her? Is she still a good teacher? Are you glad she's the town's teacher?"

The girls all exchanged glances. Their father was acting strange.

"We like her, Daddy. We've always liked her." Madison was puzzled as well. "Why are you all of the sudden so interested in her and how we feel?"

"We like her, Pa, okay?" Kayla suddenly thought she had an idea as to where this was going. "I thought you were interested in all those other ladies."

Madison became alarmed. She wasn't so sure she was ready for this from her papa. And toward Miss Taylor-Ryan!

"I was...am. Uh, mind yer tongue, Kayla. I think I've allowed all of you to talk to me too freely as of late. Y'all need to mind yer place. I simply wanted to know how you felt about Miss Taylor-Ryan." Joshua harrumphed.

His daughters, except Madison, exchanged secretly amused smiles. They knew Joshua had a propensity to act gruff and irritated, even though he wasn't, really, when he was in uncomfortable situations. They knew the best course was to let him take his time getting around to whatever subject he'd rather avoid. But it didn't keep them from having some fun with it.

"Why? You wanna marry her?" Alyssa asked innocently.

Joshua scowled. By this, the girls knew they were onto something.

"No, he doesn't!" Madison interjected angrily. She got up and stormed out of the room. Moments later, they heard a door slam.

"What's the matter with her?" Joshua wondered aloud. He'd finally caught on to the merry, teasing mood of the other three.

"We don't really know," Alexis answered honestly. "She didn't start actin' funny til you decided not to order a bride, or whatever that was called."

"Hmm…" Joshua was thoughtful. Then, "You girls know I'm doin' this for you, don't you? Just so you have a mother again."

The girls exchanged uneasy glances then.

Kayla sighed "We know. We just don't understand completely. We're all doin' fine without one. We don't need a mother, so there's no point in making yourself miserable trying to find us one."

"Darlin', sometimes, as a child, you don't know what you really *need*. It's my job as your father to decide that."

Over the next couple of weeks, Joshua thought about that a lot. Was he only trying to find them a mother? Or was he also trying to find himself a wife? Could he, and should he, do both? What if he was trying so hard to convince himself his girls needed a mother so he wouldn't feel guilty for realizing his need for a wife? He truly missed having someone to share his life with. He missed having a wife to care for and someone to care for him. Did he even deserve to have that again after the way he'd messed it up the first time?

He knew he *shouldn't* feel guilty about Ashley. Her choices were hers, and hers alone, to make. But that didn't keep the guilt from creeping back over him.

No matter where they led, his thoughts always returned to his girls and what was best for them. Was he being selfish in pursuing a wife? Should he give the girls a choice in the matter? Could they dictate his happiness?

Despite his best efforts, he re-lived the day of the picnic often in his mind. Usually when his mind was so wayward, he quickly reeled it back in. He was afraid it would only hurt more to hope for something that wouldn't happen. He hadn't taken the step to formally call on Katherine and honestly didn't know if he would. Especially after the way Madison reacted.

It seemed every step of the way, every milestone, good or bad, he was constantly in unchartered territory. And he was alone in trying to figure out how best to deal with the situation. It would be nice to have someone who could be there with him, hold his hand, through it all. Unfortunately, it was that very decision he was wrestling with at that moment. Sure, Jacob and Emily could help, but they'd never experienced anything like this. And they probably never would. So, he resigned himself to the fact that he would have to be content with raising the girls by himself. Watching them grow up, by himself. Watching them marry and start families, while he remained alone. How he yearned to have someone to share those experiences with. To watch them and savor them with. He wasn't usually so melancholy and he yearned, too, for the day when he'd stop pining after something he couldn't have. Could he accept it if this was God's will for his life? As lonely as he was and as much as he wouldn't admit it to anyone but himself, could he bear it if he wasn't destined to find anyone else? And if that were so, why did Katherine keep finding her way into his thoughts on a daily basis?

Joshua and Katherine's friendship grew, but never developed into anything beyond.

Emily, of course, could see where it was headed and started inviting Katherine over for the family dinners on Sundays after church.

Soon, the whole town was buzzing about Joshua and Katherine and the spark they seemed to be igniting. Of course, they themselves didn't take notice.

Madison was in a fit about it. "I like Miss Taylor-Ryan and all, but she's all wrong for Pa. It won't work, it simply won't!"

A mere month had passed since her father and the lovely schoolmarm had started rumors circulating in the small town of Lorraine.

The girls were gathered in Madison's room, supposedly doing homework.

Alyssa spoke up tentatively. "I kinda understand, though. And I wouldn't mind, very much, her bein' our mama. Right now she's our teacher, so it makes it awkward. But once she's married, she can't be our teacher anymore, anyway."

"Do you see how our classmates look at us?" Kayla fumed. "They think we're being treated differently because our pa is sweet on the teacher!"

Always hopeful, Alyssa offered, "Chris said Aunt Em was really happy for Pa and Miss Taylor-Ryan. If Aunt Em thinks it's good, wouldn't it have to be?"

Madison groaned. "Aunt Em *would* be happy. Samantha said she's the one who put him up to finding someone."

In their own way, they all wished for a mother of some sort.

Madison did have to admit that she'd longed for a mother at certain times since her own had left, but she'd never shared it aloud. She'd already had to talk to Aunt Emily out of sheer fright about womanly matters. By the time she'd even thought to bring Emily into it, she had already made a list of her possessions and to whom they should be bestowed, upon her young and untimely demise. It had taken a full hour for Emily to calm her down enough to explain a woman's cycle and that she wasn't dying. That would've been a time that it would have been nice to have had a mother to talk to. As much as she loved her Aunt Emily, and Aunt Emily had been patient and kind and understanding, it had still been awkward.

After that, Madison made sure to keep an eye on her sisters so they wouldn't have to have the same scare she did. Not that she'd remember half of what she was supposed to tell them. But, she could direct them to Aunt Emily and it wouldn't be quite so awkward for them as her, since they wouldn't have to seek her out themselves.

Alexis simply missed being able to have cozy chats with an older woman who was wiser than she and could help explain the mysteries of life to a thirteen-year-old girl. None of these things were things she would even begin feeling comfortable talking to her father about.

Alyssa was a born romantic and couldn't wait to grow up. Of course, that would include her Prince Charming riding to rescue her on his white horse. And after that happened, she would need a loving mama fussing over her on her wedding day. Knowing that wouldn't happen made part of her fairy tale die.

Kayla's young world had already been turned upside-down. She could've used a mother's love immensely already, being that she was the most sensitive of the four. She was the same age Madison had been when Ashley had left. A mother's love would do her good in bringing her out of herself and into a more confident young lady.

Joshua only thought they needed a mother because a responsible father would want what they perceived to be the best for the children. And the best thing for any girl was to have a mother.

Chapter 13: The Accident

"I love ya, darlin'." Jacob bid Emily good-bye as he headed out to the fields.

"I love you, too." And with a kiss, she sent him on his way.

Jacob always worked too hard at harvest time, was Emily's opinion. She always worried about him until it was over.

Later, when Jacob came in for his dinner, he informed her, "I'll be a little later tonight. There is still a lot I need to get up from the ground or it's going to rot. Don't expect me for supper."

Emily was used to the routine by now, but still sighed heavily. "I'll sure be glad when harvestin's over. As always." She gave him a weary smile. "You always work too hard. And you look especially tired today."

The previous evening, Jacob hadn't come in until well after nine o'clock because he was behind in getting up the harvest. And then Jacob had woken up by four o'clock that morning to try to get another head start.

"I'll be alright, don't you worry." He got up and cleared his plate. After depositing his dishes into the sink, he grabbed Emily around the waist and kissed the top of her head then moved lower to her lips.

After a few more moments together, Jacob pulled back. "I should start back out."

Emily sighed and gently pushed him away. "Alright. I'll send Chris out to help when he gets home from school."

Jacob smiled Emily's favorite smile. The one that showed the dimple in his chin.

"Do that," he affirmed cheerfully, then was gone.

As usual, Emily watched Jacob through the window until she could no longer make out his form.

Jacob had worked on the vegetation for awhile then remembered Emily had asked about the winter firewood the other day, so he decided to start on that next. As soon as he was satisfied that the other farm hands had the harvesting under control, he switched tasks.

He was just finishing up a good supply when he saw the children coming down the lane from school. He called Christopher over. "Hey, Chris!"

Christopher immediately loped over. "Yes, sir?"

"Yer mama's gonna have you come on out and help me get the last of the vegetables up. Meet me in the far field once you get changed."

"Yes, sir, Pa," Christopher readily agreed. He loved being outdoors and it didn't matter to him what the reason was.

Christopher ran off and Jacob mounted their new horse, Jody. She was a bit skittish still, but Jacob used her to ride around the fields and check on things so she could get used to being ridden.

As Jacob plodded out to the far field, he spotted some deer that would look good in the smoke house. As he attempted to reach around to grab the rifle he always carried behind his shoulder for just such an occasion, he loosened his grip on Jody for a moment. In that same moment, a snake slithered across Jody's path, spooking her. Jacob saw the snake as he turned back around, realized what was happening, and tightened his hold, trying to calm Jody; but she'd have none of it. She reared back on her hind legs and bucked Jacob off, despite his best efforts to hang on.

Jacob had the wind knocked out of him and lay there, stunned. He tried to get his brain to cooperate and his body to move when he realized Jody was still spooked. Jacob tried to roll out of Jody's path, but it was too late. Jody bolted and trampled Jacob in her haste to get away.

Leaving his father in the woodshed, Christopher had run into the house to change his clothes. Rushing by Emily, he had called, "Ma, gonna go help Pa."

Hurrying to do his father's bidding, he changed in less than three minutes, and was running back down the stairs before Emily could fully register what he'd said. "Bye, Ma!" he called as he ran by again and out the door.

He hurriedly saddled their horse, Gypsy, to ride out to the

fields. He galloped to the edge of the far field and slowed when he saw Jacob up ahead. He was about to call out when he saw Jody rear up. Instinctively Christopher knew something bad was about to happen and he froze. He couldn't seem to move as he watched the horrifying nightmare take place. It all happened fast, but seemed to also be happening in slow motion. His brain wouldn't register what he'd just witnessed. After it was over, he remained fixed to the spot, dazed. Only Jody charging past seemed to shake him from his amazement as he had to maneuver Gypsy to get out of Jody's path. His frozen brain woke up then and he yelled, "Jody! NO! Come back!" Torn between his father and going after Jody, he quickly realized he needed to help his father. He climbed off Gypsy and ran to Jacob's side. Standing over his father, he was rooted to the spot at the sight that met him. Shock set in and he started shaking all over. Falling to his knees, he began yelling. "PA! MAMA! PA!" Even as he looked over his father's broken body, he couldn't stop yelling. Seeing all of the blood turned his yells to shrieks and screams. His voice finally gave out and he realized no one would hear him so far out. He had to ride back in. Quickly, he scrambled back on Gypsy and rode him hard, barely taking time to tether him outside the back door before bursting into his house.

Choking on dry sobs, he screeched, "Mama!" Standing in the middle of the kitchen, tears streaked down his face.

Emily had heard Christopher's commotion and had rushed into the kitchen. "Chris! Chris, what is it? What happened!" She dreaded knowing the answer.

His words came out in a rush. "There's been an accident! It's Pa! Jody...I should've stopped it!" He couldn't continue. He crumpled to the floor sobbing, his head in his hands.

Stunned, Emily reached out as he hit the floor, sinking down next to him. Her arms automatically embraced him and tears welled in her eyes. "Tell me, Chris! You need to tell me what happened." She worked at keeping her voice even. It would help nothing if she lost control, too.

In broken sobs, Christopher recounted what he had seen.

Emily could keep it in no longer. "Lord Almighty, save Jacob!" she implored. She had to physically put her fists against her mouth to keep from losing control. She forced her thoughts to be logical.

"Chris, you need to go get Doc Rowan!"

By this time, Brianna, Samantha, and Hailey had heard the commotion and come to investigate.

As Emily and Christopher prepared to leave, the other three were able to glean bits and pieces of information.

"Chris is going to fetch Doc Rowan. I'm going to Pa and waiting for them there. You girls stay here."

Emily took Gypsy and Christopher ran to hitch up another horse.

As soon as Emily reached Jacob's side, she slipped off Gypsy. One look at her husband's lifeless form made her ill. Swallowing the bile, she kneeled by Jacob's head and softly called, "Jacob, Jacob." It was the same voice she used to awaken him from slumber. Only, this time, he didn't stir and pull her to him, as he usually did when he was struggling between wakefulness and sleep. Emily didn't notice the blood as she cradled his head in her lap. Bending near so her lips grazed his ear, she called again, a little louder. "Jacob, wake up. Please!" As each attempt proved fruitless, Emily could feel her hysteria arise. "Jacob!" she screamed and called over and over until her voice was hoarse and all she could do was mouth his name.

She was fervently stroking Jacob's face and mouthing his name when Doc Rowan arrived.

Gently the doctor took Emily by the waist and eased her away from Jacob. Emily silently cried a few feet away while Doc Rowan performed his check on Jacob's lifeless body.

Quietly he turned to her and said, "He appears to be hanging on, but barely. It would be best if you leave me to my work. I'm afraid I'll have to work on him here. Moving him could prove to be futile."

"No, I'm staying here with my husband!"

"Mrs. Matthews, please, you need to go. The best way to help him is to leave me to my work."

"No!" Emily remained obstinate.

"Emily, I'm telling you, as a doctor, you need to leave. I am not speaking to you as a friend. Your husband is seriously hurt and I need to tend to him. The longer you stand here and argue, the more you are endangering your husband's situation by not letting me attend to him. Go home!"

Casting one more look at Jacob, Emily marched back to Gypsy in a huff.

'*Who does he think he is?*' Emily fumed on her way back home. '*Jacob is* my *husband! I want to be there with him! It is my* duty, *my* right, *as Jacob's wife.*'

As she neared the house, Emily's anger subsided as the realization sunk in. Jacob's wounds could be fatal. And she'd had the *audacity* to stand there and argue with the doctor? She could've wasted precious time. Her emotions ran the gamut and she began sobbing. "Jacob, please, no! Don't go! Please stay with me!"

As she entered her house, she fought to control the sobs. She was greeted with the solemn faces of her children.

"How's Pa?" Christopher asked without preamble.

"Doc's with him now. We'll know…something soon, I hope. I'll be upstairs in my room."

Emily fell onto her bed and sobbed into her pillow as she fervently prayed for her husband's life.

It seemed like hours before Emily heard a knock at the door below. With much trepidation, she got up and mutely went down to answer the door.

"Emily…Mrs. Matthews…" there was a pause as the doc took a breath.

Emily felt herself slowly sinking down as she knew what the next words would be.

"I regret to inform you…" and Emily felt the floor solidly beneath her.

Piercing shrieks filled the house. She was surprised to find they were coming from her mouth. The children came running, took one look at their mother, and burst into sobs. Their father had died.

Death notifications were something Doc Rowan hated. It was the worst part of his job. The townsfolk weren't merely his patients, they were his friends. He had lost a friend today and silently joined in the family's grief.

It was some time before the tears ebbed…for now. The

children eventually wandered off to be by themselves in their own grief. Doc Rowan delicately informed Emily, "I will need some help, er, cleaning up. Would it be alright if I, er…informed Josh?"

Numbness was coming, to dull Emily's pain. Her answer was lifeless. "Whatever suits you, Doctor Rowan."

Yet another less than desirable aspect of his job. He felt he had to be too crass at times. Yet, he knew that if he didn't move Jacob's body soon, the vultures would find it. It had been a few hours…he sighed. One more issue needed attention.

"Er, Emily, um…" he cleared his throat. "Where would you, uh, like his final resting place to be?"

'Stop makin' me decide things!' Emily wanted to scream. She knew he was simply doing his job, but why all these questions *right now*? Couldn't it wait?

Her answer was quiet. "Under the big oak tree by the creek. He loved sitting there. We would often sit there together."

Doc Rowan nodded and quietly left.

Joshua had finished his supper and was headed to his study when the knock sounded at his door.

Opening it, he was surprised to find the doc standing there. "Hello, Dr. Rowan."

"Perhaps I should come in, Mr. Tyler."

"Of course." He led him into the parlor and they each took a seat.

The doctor cleared his throat once…twice…three times. "Uh, Josh, Mr. Tyler, there's no easy way to say this. I'm, uh, here on Emily's behalf."

"Emily?" Joshua was puzzled. "Is she okay? Where's Jacob?"

Doc Rowan summoned his professional tone. "Mr. Tyler, there's been an accident." He then proceeded to fill Joshua in on all the details as he knew them. "Chris happened upon the scene and witnessed the whole thing."

Joshua simply sat there, too stunned to move.

Doc Rowan faltered then, "I'm so sorry, Josh. I know the two of you were extremely close."

"Where is he…his…Jacob…where is he?" Joshua

stammered. He suddenly had the morbid urge to see it. To make sure this was all real and not an impossible nightmare he couldn't wake up from.

"In the Matthews' far field. Emily said to move, uh...him...to the, uh, oak tree by the creek."

"Did you? Move...him...yet?" Joshua swallowed hard, choking on the words.

Summoning courage, the doctor answered. "No...I can't by myself."

Joshua abruptly stood up. He suddenly felt the need to do *something.* "I'll help. Let's go."

If Doc Rowan was surprised by Joshua's seeming urgency, he didn't show it.

Joshua could feel the numbness set in, dulling his ache. He needed to move, and soon, so it couldn't consume him. Swiftly, he moved to the door and was gone, the doc on his heels.

Emily heard Doc Rowan leave as he headed to Joshua's house. By this time, the children had wandered back in from wherever they had gone, not sure what to do with themselves.

"I'm going upstairs," she announced to the room in general.

"Me, too," Christopher announced quickly. He left the room before anyone could see him start crying again.

The three girls tearfully followed Emily up the stairs to their rooms.

In no time at all, she had flung herself onto her bed in a sobbing heap. There was no Jacob now to comfort her anguish or quiet her sobs.

Much later, Emily fell into a fitful sleep. In her sleep, she kept groping for Jacob to keep her warm and confused when she couldn't find him.

It was past midnight before Joshua and Doc Rowan were finished and he could head home.

Finally, Joshua was alone with his thoughts. Jacob was gone. The words still hadn't quite sunk in and become real.

Joshua contemplated going into the Matthews' house before

he passed it on his way home. He felt he should check on Emily. As he got closer, he realized the low window to Jacob and Emily's room was glowing with light. That decided it for him and he turned up the walk and circled around to the back door.

He knocked softly on the door, but got no response. The thought came to mind that maybe everyone was asleep and a candle was left burning, in which case, he should investigate. Pushing the door open, he stepped inside, listening. Yes, everything seemed quiet. He took a few more steps. No...wait...he faintly heard something. Walking to the stairs leading to the second floor, his ears strained. He heard faint crying. He could guess which room it was coming from.

Swallowing hard, he climbed the stairs. He was standing in front of the bedroom door now and trying to decide if he should simply go in. It was the middle of the night! Would it be appropriate for him to be alone with Emily? Even given the circumstances?

Duty set in. He needed to look after Jacob's family and make sure that Emily was going to be okay. He left the door open for propriety's sake and headed in. He shook his head, wondering why any of that even mattered right now.

He went in and pulled a chair over to the bed. Emily was still fully clothed and tears were streaking her cheeks, but she appeared to be sleeping.

"Emily? Are you sleeping?"

"Ummm, hmmm..." Sleepily, she looked up at him, her eyes glassy and completely unfocused. "What are you doin' there?"

"I wanted to see how you were...how you were holdin' up." He couldn't help the tears gathering in his own eyes.

"Holdin' up?"

Joshua delicately tried a different approach.

"I just now got finished helping' Doc Rowan...with Jacob."

"Jacob?"

By the low candlelight, Joshua finally noticed Emily's unfocused eyes.

"Emily, are you awake?"

Emily reached up and grabbed Joshua's hand and squeezed it. "I'm glad you're here, Jacob. Now you can wake me up from this nightmare I'm having."

Alarmed, Joshua tried loosening Emily's hold, but her grasp was firm.

'Lord, she's gone mad or somethin'! This is too much for her to take! What do I do? She must be delirious, thinkin' I'm Jacob.' Joshua decided it might be better to have Emily sleep it off. He told himself she likely wouldn't remember any of it in the morning and it might be best to play along for now so she could peacefully go back to sleep.

He gently loosened Emily's hand and as calmly as he could, told her "It's alright, darlin'." He used the name he knew she'd recognize as Jacob's. "I'm goin' to get a drink of water. You go back to sleep, now." Tears slipped from Joshua's eyes as Emily sleepily released her last bit of a grip on his hand. "Mmm…kay, Jacob. I love you." Her eyes were closed now, but whispered, "Don't ever leave me."

Joshua miraculously managed to choke out, "I won't", before making his escape into the night.

Emily awoke the next morning to a slight headache and a fuzzy image of Joshua having been in her room and an even fuzzier one of Jacob.

"Had to have been a dream," she whispered, rolling over. She found an empty space where Jacob usually was.

Emily frowned. "He must've gone out even earlier today. There must still be a lot to get done before harvesting is over."

Something still didn't seem quite right. Her forehead creased in puzzlement.

A soft knock sounded.

"Come in," Emily invited.

Brianna pushed the door open and stood there. Eyes red rimmed and hair unkempt, she looked a mess.

"I needed to see you, Mama."

"What's wrong, Brianna?"

Brianna came to Emily's outstretched arms and curled up next to her in bed. "Oh, Mama," she moaned.

Curiously, Emily asked, "Where's your father?"

Seeing the panicked look in Brianna's eyes, Emily felt even deeper that something wasn't right.

"What? What is it?"

Brianna anguished. "Mama, don't you remember anything about yesterday?"

Emily lay very still and glanced down, noticing her clothes. Unchanged. Then the events of the previous day came flooding back.

Brianna wrapped her arms around her mother and the two shared in each other's grief.

Chapter 14: Seeking Comfort

Jacob's memorial came sooner than Emily had expected and would have liked. Well-meaning neighbors kept bringing food and inquiring as to when the service would be. Joshua had stepped in then, noticing how overwhelmed Emily was, and took care of the preparations for Saturday, September 28th.

Until the dates became important, Emily hadn't realized that the accident had happened on Joshua's 36th birthday. Had they even had plans to get together with him that day? She couldn't remember. And why did it even matter now?

'*Inconsequential, Emily,*' she told herself. She'd found herself thinking of numerous things that were small, tiny, miniscule, compared to what had happened. She didn't know why. Perhaps it was a way for her to cope, by keeping busy, even if it was with the small and mundane that hardly mattered.

The memorial took place at the site of Jacob's burial. Emily stood next to Joshua who was solemn and silent. Their children gathered around them.

The newly dug grave served as a reminder of how precious life was. And how quickly it could be taken away.

Joshua saw movement out of the corner of his eye and turned to see Reverend Chadrick and watched as he took his place. Joshua stared straight ahead.

Reverend Chadrick began. "Here lies Jacob Michael Matthews, taken from us far too soon on September the twenty-sixth, at the young age of thirty-five. He was a well-loved and well-respected member of this congregation and our town. Look around and you can see how much of an impact he made."

Emily watched everything unfold as if from a great distance. Try as she might, she couldn't focus on the eulogy or much of anything Reverend Chadrick said. In fact, everything since the accident had gone by in a blur. If it weren't for Joshua and Katherine, she didn't know where she'd be.

Emily was certainly grateful to Joshua for the way he had

taken over the arrangements. She could only imagine how hard it was on him, too. He and Jacob had been like brothers. She finally risked a glance at Joshua, standing stoic and tall, Katherine on his other side. Yes, those two had definitely been her rock over the last two days. Katherine slightly surprised her since Emily didn't know her as well. But that had changed fast, and she immensely liked the young school teacher. Emily fervently hoped the two would be happy together. As happy as she and Jacob had been.

'Why am I thinking this now? This is hardly the time nor the place! It doesn't matter, anyway! Nothing seems to matter anymore.'

Looking around, Emily knew she couldn't escape the reality. Hot tears coursed down her face and she was unable to stop them. Sobs escaped her lips try as she might to firmly press them together. She squeezed her eyes shut so tight she began seeing stars, and swayed. Luckily, Joshua noticed and put his hand under her elbow to help steady her. Christopher, on her other side, slipped his arm around his mother's waist.

If Emily cared and had paid any attention to the gathering of people, she would've been embarrassed at her rising sobs. As it was, although the whole assembly could hear her clearly, Reverend Chadrick continued on as if nothing were happening.

"And so, I commit his soul to the Lord Almighty. Emily, if you would…"

Emily's head jerked up at the sound of her name. *'What? What am I supposed to do? WHAT AM I SUPPOSED TO DO?'* Panic choked her.

Joshua dropped his hand from her elbow and squeezed her hand. "The flowers" he said in a low voice, making sure no one heard but her.

"Oh…right," she murmured. Emily and her girls had gathered wild flowers to place on the mound of dirt that now marked Jacob.

Reverend Chadrick filled the awkward silence while Joshua and Emily's exchange took place. "Because of the nature of Jacob's accident, he has already been buried. Emily will be the first to perfume his grave with flowers."

Emily and the girls took turns placing the flowers.

Tears swam in Emily's eyes as Reverend Chadrick spoke the

words, "From dust you were taken and to dust you shall return."

    Katherine had organized the luncheon that now took place at the Matthews' house. Emily really didn't feel like attending and wanted to make her escape to her bedroom.

    Yet, she had to endure such niceties as Yetta Fabian offered. "We are *so* sorry for your loss, Emily."

    As they hugged, Emily dutifully answered, "Thank you."

    "How are you holding up, dear?" came from another neighbor.

    An automatic reply escaped her lips. "Very well, thank you." Her response got her an odd look, but she didn't care.

    "The funeral went just beautifully," Elise Chadrick, the reverend's wife, offered.

    Emily was weary of playing hostess. Curtly she replied, "You should let Mr. Tyler and Miss Taylor-Ryan know."

    Seeing she had slightly offended Mrs. Chadrick with her blunt reply, she quickly apologized. "I'm sorry. I only meant that, since they handled all the arrangements, they deserve the recognition." Even that seemed awkward. Emily didn't know how to act. How did you act at your husband's funeral that was acceptable? Especially when he'd died at such a young age? Emily felt extremely out of place and had no clue what she was doing, except listlessly wandering the room and encountering well-meaning neighbors.

    Elise gave Emily a sympathetic look and patted her arm as she said, "Of course, I understand, dear."

    '*No you don't!*' Emily wanted to protest.

    No one could possibly understand such a thing unless they had been through it.

    Emily wondered if she could slip away unnoticed yet. It seemed all the neighbors and townsfolk chose that moment to corner her, one-by-one, and offer their condolences.

    It was going to be a long day.

    "Well, that's *finally* over," Emily muttered to herself as she shut the door on the last guest.

"What, Mama?" Brianna asked.

"Oh, nothing." She turned from the door to survey the mess that needed cleaning up and groaned.

Joshua and Katherine seemed to suddenly appear then.

Katherine went over to Emily and gave her a genuine, warm hug. Emily offered a tight smile.

"What shall I do first? Put on some tea or start cleaning?" Katherine questioned, no-nonsense.

Emily's mouth fell open. After all Katherine had done, was she actually offering to stay and help clean up? But, Emily did *not* feel like cleaning up right then. Emily was about to suggest starting with a cup of tea at the very least, postponing the clean-up, when Katherine broke in.

"Close your mouth. I suspect you don't feel like doing this, so I could get you a cup of tea before I start or you go on up to bed. You look a little worn down. No wonder, with the nature of the day and all." Giving Emily closer inspection, Katherine frowned. "Hm, maybe you should head on up to bed."

Emily remained speechless. How did Katherine know what she was thinking? Finally she managed, "Oh, Katherine, you don't need to *do*...anything. I can always clean up later. I do feel a bit peaked."

"If I'm not imposing, I'll get started. Joshua needs some rest, too, so I'm sending him home with the girls. I have no other plans."

Emily suddenly had no words for the emotions she felt right then. Gratitude pushed its way forward and she offered Katherine a genuine, "Thank you!"

"Well, get on upstairs, then" Katherine encouraged, smiling warmly.

Emily reflected that Katherine must make a very good teacher, indeed. She had just the right amount of firmness...and bossy! But the more Emily got to know Katherine, the more she discovered and liked about her.

Emily turned to Joshua. "Thank you for all you've done. I can't–"

"It's been my honor to help you," Joshua cut in.

With a lump in his throat, Joshua bid Katherine and Emily good-bye.

As he left, Emily couldn't help but notice the tender way he and Katherine exchanged glances. It reminded her so much of herself and Jacob, unbidden tears sprang to her eyes. Quickly, she wiped them away with the heels of her hands.

"I think I *will* go and lie down for a bit." Emily then trudged up the stairs to her empty bedroom.

Groggy with sleep, Emily awoke to the sound of clanging dishes and the voices of her children and...who did the female voice belong to? Was Katherine still here? Her nose picked up the faint scent of cooking food. Had Katherine started supper, too? Emily glanced around the room, well past being in shadows. It was almost pitch black! Definitely past suppertime. Seven o'clock, maybe?

Emily settled back against her pillows once again, trying to decide if she wanted to get up. Surprised, she noticed her stomach let out a tiny gurgle. How could she be hungry? Her grief hadn't exactly elicited an appetite. Of course, her body still needed food and she'd only eaten toast and had tea.

Gingerly, Emily made her way downstairs. She'd had to light a lamp to find her way.

"Look who's awake," Katherine greeted cheerily. "We made fried chicken."

"I'm glad they were helpful." Emily was aloof in her reply. A little dazedly, she asked, "What time is it?"

Absentmindedly she took stock of her surroundings. The kitchen positively gleamed! She glanced through the doorway into the dining room and beyond into the living room. They appeared just as tidy.

"Seven o'clock or so," Katherine returned. "Oh, I hope you don't mind, but I had Hailey run over and invite Joshua and the girls over to join us for supper. I doubt any of them felt like cooking."

"That's perfectly fine," Emily assured her, noticing the growing mountain of food as Katherine kept setting dishes on the table.

"This all looks delicious, Katherine, but you've done too much!" Making sure Katherine didn't misunderstand and think her ungrateful, Emily met her eyes. "Thank you."

Katherine self-consciously turned away, but not before Emily saw the faint blush to her cheeks.

Emily continued. "I really appreciate all your help with the preparations for today, all this food, all this," she gestured to the impeccably clean house.

Not quite meeting her gaze, Katherine simply responded, "You're very welcome, Emily."

Katherine wasn't used to so much praise and was relieved that Joshua arrived then and could get her out of the spotlight. She did nothing more than what she used to do for her father and brothers before she came to Lorraine to be the schoolmarm.

Before long, the mountain of food slowly diminished.

"That was excellent, Katherine," Joshua praised.

Many thanks started round the table then.

Katherine chuckled and tried to be nonchalant. She surprised them all by revealing, "It was my pleasure. I love to cook."

"You do?" Emily asked.

"Oh, yes! After my mother passed away when I was twelve, I had to take over the household responsibilities. That included cooking for my father and two brothers. My mother had loved cooking, too, and I suppose I naturally followed in her footsteps."

"I didn't know you had lost your mother," Joshua sympathized.

Katherine looked away, but he continued to stare. Joshua was continually being surprised by her. She had many attributes that he admired. And she had been wonderful in helping with Jacob's funeral arrangements, seeing that he and Emily were too distraught to even know where to begin.

Katherine spoke up then. "If we're all finished, I'll get the coffee and start cleaning up."

"Can't we have coffee?" Samantha begged.

"Only adults, little lady," Katherine teased.

"Awww…" came the reply.

"Would you like to do another grown-up thing, instead, and help clean up?"

It was amazing the speed that the children used to vacate the room.

Katherine set to work immediately in the kitchen while Emily and Joshua lingered over coffee in the dining room.

Joshua peeked at Emily, trying to assess her well being. "How are you doing, Em?" The question was asked in his low, tenor voice.

Emily answered slowly, almost as if measuring her mood that very minute. "I cry a lot. I'm overwhelmed with grief...isn't that how it's supposed to go?"

"I meant how are you coping, besides all the crying? Are you able to sleep? Are you eating alright? Are you taking care of yourself? That sort of thing."

Emily regarded Joshua a moment then asked, "Are you my doctor, Josh?"

Joshua clarified. "I'm only looking after my best friend's widow. I wanna make sure you're alright." He covered her hand with his.

"I'm fine," she bit out. "As well as can be expected. Aren't those the right words?" She fiercely drew her hand away.

Joshua had noticed her giving those same glib replies earlier at the luncheon. "Why do you keep fixating on the *right response*, Emily? There is none. There is only how you feel, and that's not right or wrong...it's simply how you feel."

Emily sat there, stunned. She hadn't really thought about it like that before. Joshua was right, she *was* trying too hard to do everything right.

"I don't know," she growled, suddenly irritated with herself and with Joshua for bringing her to the obvious realization. "I suppose I want people to see that I can grieve in the proper way, no flagrant drama, no overly showy signs of desperation that my world has fallen apart. That I *can* keep it together, if only on the outside...for show..." her voice broke. She struggled to go on, almost to herself, as if to convince herself. "I *can* hold myself together, for my family. I *can* hold my family together...I *am* a fit mother, even without a husband."

Emily burst into tears and covered her face with her hands, bending over the table.

Joshua wasn't quite sure what to do. He got up and went over to try to comfort her and soothe her with low, gentle murmurings.

Katherine became an almost permanent fixture at the Matthews' household. She seemed only to leave long enough to teach school in town, and then she made her way back afterward. Her presence cast a certain peace and calm and semblance of order. She almost always brought food and completely took over the kitchen. And, more often than not, Joshua usually found his way over during the course of the evening and, more specifically, for supper, as his girls were over there, as well.

Having Joshua, her dearest friend in the world around so much, helped Emily immensely in her grieving. She suspected it helped him as well. And Katherine was getting right up there on her close friends list, not that it was so long.

Little by little, Katherine brought a calm to her soul that Emily didn't think she'd ever regain. In her own way, Katherine was a healing balm to everyone around her.

Emily and Katherine's friendship took off and flourished. Emily even found herself being able to get back to small tasks around the house. Tasks as simple as sweeping out a room. And as time passed, Emily's sense of normalcy started taking shape. Again, in large part, due to Katherine's steadfast friendship.

Over a month had passed now and Katherine started feeling close enough to Emily to start confiding in her about Joshua.

"He's so sweet!" she would prattle on, not that Emily minded. "The way he is with his girls is simply precious. He seems to anticipate their needs before they even have to say a word. Of course, I'm sure you already know that, since you've known him so long. I admire how hard a worker he is. He works at the factory *and* comes here to take care of your animals and everything else that Christopher can't get to." Joshua had started that recently. He knew the Matthews' farm was their only livelihood and he took it as his duty to help out, now that Emily was alone with her children. And Emily didn't know how she'd ever thank him.

"He's such a good man," Katherine finished.

"Aye, that he is," Emily acknowledged.

'He reminds me so much of Jacob...' At least Emily could think of Jacob now without *immediately* breaking into sobs. All the same, tears did gather in her eyes.

Noticing Emily's shimmering eyes Katherine anxiously asked, "Did I say something to offend?"

"No, I just got to thinking about Jacob."

"Another good man. Christopher and the girls always talked highly of him at school."

Emily dried her eyes with the corner of her apron. "Good to hear," she smiled.

Emily looked up and caught Katherine staring at her.

"What? What is it?"

Katherine breathed a self-conscious laugh. "I'm sorry. It's just that...your eyes are the exact same shade of green my mother's were. Especially when she'd been crying." Then she chuckled, "Of course, that was a lot. She was very sensitive. Once, she literally cried over spilled milk. I'd had a glass with some apple pie and accidentally knocked it over. And she cried because she thought *I* would be upset over ruining my favorite dress." Katherine suddenly giggled. "Oh, Mama..." Katherine seemed lost reminiscing, "she was dear, though," she added, more to herself.

"How long did it...does it..." Emily wasn't sure how to phrase her question, "take? To get over losin' someone...someone you love so much?"

Emily didn't think she'd ever be able to smile or giggle over her own memories of Jacob, even the good ones. It still hurt too much to even think of him, knowing she'd never see him again. Never feel his arms around her. Never smell his scent as he came in from the fields. She ached for him.

"Oh, I've never truly *gotten over* Mama. The hurt ebbs, certainly. And, of course, it's different with everybody. We all grieve in our own way. And my case may be different still. I've never lost a spouse. Just a mama. I imagine it must be much harder losing a spouse. You usually expect to lose a parent, just a process of life. Plus, there's usually another one left to hold you up, especially when you lose one so young. With a spouse, well, suddenly you must find yourself having to be the one who has to do the holding."

Emily stared at Katherine, bewildered. "How are you so wise? That's exactly how I feel without my Jacob. Alone, utterly and completely."

Katherine suggested quietly, "Maybe Joshua could tell you about it."

"Maybe. I hate to pry, especially about that. His situation was so much more difficult…and different."

In a quiet reverie, Katherine mused, "That it was."

By Thanksgiving, Emily felt a little more normal. As much as she could be, facing the holidays without Jacob. And the children were working on it as well.

Emily, Joshua, and Katherine were closer than ever… especially Joshua and Katherine. They weren't officially courting, but the rumor was, it wouldn't be long.

In Katherine's mind, however, it may never happen.

"He seems so aloof in that respect," Katherine had confided in Emily.

"Give him time, he's a man," Emily advised. "If there's one thing *no one* can do, it's make Josh Tyler's mind up for him."

Emily often mused how strange the circumstances were that brought her and Katherine together. While Joshua had most assuredly proved to be a faithful friend, he inadvertently had brought the one person she truly needed to help her get through some very difficult times. Katherine was another woman she could confide in, even things she wouldn't feel comfortable bringing up to Joshua, especially being that he was a man. Emily cherished Katherine's friendship and could never stop being grateful for it.

"I'm so excited to celebrate Thanksgiving. I've never done it before, nor know of anyone who has. It's not a popular holiday to celebrate," Katherine remarked.

"We always have fun with it," Emily answered and did feel a spark of excited anticipation.

Emily and Katherine threw themselves into the holiday's preparations. As they worked, Emily would regale Katherine with stories of Thanksgivings past. Of course, it included the story of when Kayla found her voice.

"I remember that time," Katherine reminisced. "She had been so quiet in class. I knew it had to do with her mother. I never did find out why she'd started talking." She gave Emily one of her heartwarming smiles. "Thank you for telling me, Emily."

"We have to do that, you know. We have to play the

'Thankful Game,'" Katherine urged.

Emily still found herself amused by Katherine's outbursts of childlike exuberance.

Emily laughed. "It's a tradition! Every year."

Despite losing a father and husband, the Matthews had bonded together even stronger.

When it came time, Emily suddenly felt a little nervous about how the 'Thankful Game' would go. But, one by one, around the table it went. Katherine had gone first, sensing it might be difficult for anyone else at the table to go first.

Katherine was on Emily's right, along the length of the table, while Emily sat at the head, where Jacob had usually sat. Joshua sat at the opposite end of Emily, her usual spot.

Katherine started then. "I'm thankful that I have had the privilege to get to know you better, Emily. And that goes for Joshua, too. If it weren't for him, we wouldn't have become such good friends."

"Thank you, Katherine. I reciprocate. That's my thankful, too," Emily tried letting her turn slip by.

"Hey, no fair! You know you can't do that, Mother," Christopher resisted. "You have to think of your *own*. No fair stealing Miss Taylor-Ryan's."

"My, my, Christopher. Aren't you the one for details?" Katherine teased.

"He always has been a rule keeper," Emily acknowledged. "Oh, alright. I'm thankful for…hm, let me think." She tapped her chin with her index finger, her eyes lighting on the subject of her sudden thought. "I'm thankful for Uncle Josh. He's been extremely helpful here even though he has his own job at the mill to attend to. He does whatever is needed, no matter the chore."

Christopher decided to pick up where Emily left off and the game proceeded. The last one surprised them all. It came from Hailey.

"I'm thankful Pa went to heaven. Even though he died and we are all sad, I'm glad we'll get to see him someday in heaven." As an afterthought, she added, "Besides, I'm sure he's much more happy with Jesus."

The room fell silent.

After the new year started, the fast approaching planting season smothered Emily's thoughts. How was she going to do it all by herself? It was their livelihood, but the few farm hands they had couldn't possibly take on all the extra tasks that needed to be done, as well as the extra planting. Why hadn't she thought about it sooner? She hadn't planned!

Not a day went by that she didn't pray that God would send her the help she needed. During prayer one day, only one name suddenly came to mind. She knew it was an answer to her prayer yet, she hesitated, not wanting to ask. The person had done so much to help already. How could she possibly ask this person to do more? A plan started forming and before she could change her mind, she quickly scurried down the lane to Joshua's house, praying that if this were the answer, he'd be at home. She had to do it before complete doubt set in and her nerves took over.

Knocking loudly to drown out any voices that might be protesting in her head, she tried to rehearse what she might say. In the end, she decided that since God had obviously led her to this decision, she'd let Him run her mouth, for once.

Feeling her nerves subtly taking over, she fervently willed, *'Come on, Josh, open the door!'*

As if by magic, her plea was promptly answered. Emily offered up a silent word of thanks.

"Hi, Em. Come on in."

"Josh," Emily began without preamble. Her throat squeezed tight as the words rushed forward. "Would you like to work for me?"

'Uh, that was rather fast and forward, Emily' she cautioned herself.

Since the silence dragged on, she thought maybe she should try again. "What I mean is, I really need help on the farm, especially with planting season fast approaching. I didn't really mean work *for* me, per se. You could take over Jacob's position. You'd be the boss, it's just you'd be working our land." Emily took Joshua's shocked silence for hesitation. She tried to make it sound promising. "It'd be your job. You'd be paid. I know there have been times that you've wanted to quit the mill, but couldn't because you need a job. If you're still of the mind to, you could quit there and work here…I mean, at our farm."

'*Emily!*' she kicked herself. '*Did you even let God get a word in edgewise?*' But she realized she felt much more calm, as if she knew a good thing had been done. Well, asked, anyway.

Joshua smiled suddenly. "Emily Matthews, you're an answer to prayer! I have been prayin' for a way out of the mill job. It's too dangerous a job to risk the girls losing their only parent. It's been getting worse, too, because they are trying to save money so they've been cutting corners that seem even more dangerous, to me. Especially over the last year. But since there's not much work around here, I've had to stick it out. Yes, Mrs. Matthews, *you* are an answer to prayer!"

Emily held out her hand to seal the agreement. As the two shook, Emily announced, "Mr. Tyler, consider yourself hired!"

Chapter 15: A New Decision

Joshua fit right in on the Matthews' farm. He did well being the overseer and boss, but also worked hard alongside the farmhands plowing and planting. Working with his hands somehow made him feel more fulfilled than his work at the factory had. At the factory, he watched machines most of the day. After working hard all day outdoors, he felt as if he'd accomplished something.

At first, Joshua wasn't quite sure how to act around Emily while he was there as an employee, so to speak; to act as her friend or merely an employee. Starting off, he thought it best to act merely as an employee. He even went so far as to bring his own dinner and ate with the other farm hands out in the fields. Even Jacob had done that from time to time, if he was too far out for it to be convenient to come in and eat. That had lasted all of three days when Emily had stormed out of her house and marched herself to the fields, fists on her hips. She was in a snit.

"Joshua Tyler, what do you think you're doin'?"

There were a few snickers from those nearby. A few quiet "oohs" and "he's gonna get it" were mumbled under breaths.

Joshua was genuinely dumbfounded. "What do you mean Em...uh, Mrs. Matthews?"

"For three days, I've cooked you dinner and you haven't even bothered coming in for it!"

A few more chortles were quickly choked back when Emily focused her glares on them.

A worker named Armstrong, better known as "Arms" because of his gangly frame of all arms and legs, rather than his name, unwisely spoke up. "Uh, oh, Josh, you made the boss lady mad."

Although he was boss over them, Josh felt more like equals to the young men he worked with and hadn't bothered with the formality of having them address him more properly.

"You hush yer mouth or ya won't have a job," Emily

snapped. "I'll tow ya out on yer ear and tell yer mama you've been lippy."

Arms ducked his head to hide the heat of shame that crept up into his already ruddy face.

Addressing Emily, Joshua turned back to her. "I'm sorry, Em…Mrs. Matthews. I didn't know you'd want–"

Emily almost smiled, but hadn't had a genuine one since Jacob. "Oh, Josh, I can't stay mad at you. I'll always be Em. Now come in for dinner."

As they sat in the dining room eating, Joshua admitted, "It didn't even cross my mind to eat with you."

"It's alright, Josh. I shoulda told you from the start. It was too foreign for me to not have someone to cook for during the day."

"Well count me in!" With that, Joshua shoveled a forkful of potatoes into his mouth, then grinned.

"This is much better than the lunches that Katherine packs for me. Don't get me wrong, I appreciate them, it's just…well, you can't beat home cooking."

Emily gave him a peculiar look.

"What?" he asked, dumbly.

"Katherine packs your dinner for you?"

"Yeah, when she comes over with the girls after school. Why do you ask?"

"Oh, you pig-headed man! *Why* does she do that, do you suppose?" Emily and Katherine had almost daily conversations about Joshua now. Katherine fretting that he'd never ask her to marry him and Emily trying to soothe Katherine's doubts, all the time wondering the same thing.

"I don't know, to be nice?" Joshua wasn't quite sure what Emily's interest in Katherine and his dinners was, but it was making him sweat under his collar. Pulling at his shirt, he hoped it would relieve the sudden heat he felt.

"No, Josh, she cares about you, but you're oblivious to her affections! Let me make one thing perfectly clear. That girl loves you."

Joshua's food suddenly turned to dust in his mouth and he felt the need to be outside so he could breathe. His face hot, he mumbled something about needing to get back to work and promptly left the house.

The conversation stuck with him for quite awhile, however. The words, "...that girl loves you..." haunted him more than anything else.

Katherine *loved* him? He knew she was fond of him, as he was of her. But, *love*? It couldn't be so! He couldn't allow himself to get that close. Katherine deserved better and he didn't deserve Katherine. Why had he been interested in Katherine in the first place? Was it really as simple as him needing to find someone for his girls' sake? Did the girls *really* need looking after? Or was that simply a ruse to justify his own longing?

Joshua watched Katherine with the girls a lot. She did exceptionally well and they adored her. And it wouldn't be as if things would change that much if he did end up marrying her. In fact, it might make things easier. Now that Joshua didn't work at the mill anymore, the girls didn't go to her house, but Katherine couldn't bear not seeing them. So, she started taking them home and staying to get supper started, then leaving once Joshua was home.

Joshua smiled then, as he always did when thoughts of Katherine crept in, which happened quite often. *'Tyler, you should court her already!'* The sudden thought startled him a little and an argument with himself ensued.

'And why should I do that? She might refuse me.'

'Why would she refuse you?'

'Because I'm old.'

'So she's a little younger...big deal! What does age have to do with anything if you're in love?'

Joshua slightly grimaced at the word. It wasn't that he was opposed to the word, he simply didn't know if that was what he felt for Katherine. To be fair, he really didn't know if that would be a word *she'd* use to describe her feelings either. He'd only heard Emily refer to it that way.

Finally, he made himself face the one reason he'd tried hard to bury. The ultimate reason of why he was afraid Katherine wouldn't want him as a future husband. She wouldn't want to be tied to an old widower with four daughters, whose first wife had killed herself. As much as he tried to relieve himself of the guilt, it still surfaced when he thought of Ashley. He still felt a responsible role in Ashley's death.

Rationally, deep down, he knew the truth. He knew there was nothing, absolutely *nothing* he could've done to change Ashley's mind. He even went after her, trying to do so, but to no avail. If he was honest, he didn't know what he would've done differently after Ashley left. It was the fact that he should've done so many things differently before, that haunted him. *He'd* been the overbearing husband Ashley couldn't turn to when she'd had questions. *He* was the one who hadn't noticed any signs that Ashley was unhappy. *He'd* been the prideful one that was embarrassed his wife was even having doubts about her faith. No, he didn't deserve to have a woman like Katherine. And why would God allow him another wife when he couldn't even handle the one he'd had?

Subdued, he realized he should stop trying to pursue her before she got hurt in the process.

Two weeks later, Katherine was, once again, taking the Tyler girls home.

Lifting up her arms, she stretched toward the sky and took a deep breath of the fresh, damp air.

"Spring is coming!" she enthused. "I can smell it. I can *feel* it! It's the mark of new beginnings."

Climbing down off the wagon, she suddenly frowned. New beginnings. It was almost March and it sure didn't seem she and Joshua were any closer to a new beginning of their own. He seemed even more distant, no matter how much more effort she put in. Not only did he remain aloof, he acted with what she could only describe as barely controlled civility.

For once, she rued propriety. If only she could get him alone and make him explain....

Her cheeks burned at the shameful thought. Gracious! What would that look like?

She had tried to forget about him, but that hadn't lasted long. It was hard to forget his curly brown hair; his warm, dark eyes that seemed to penetrate with one look; the way his muscles slightly rippled under his shirt. And the unphysical, his kindness, his patience, his very virtue. Katherine was completely lost and gone on Joshua Tyler and she couldn't deny it, as much as she wished it were possible. Besides, she knew she'd miss the girls terribly.

'*You'd miss him terribly, too,*' she silently mocked her weakness.

She was too involved in his life now to simply back away because of his confounded male stubbornness and pride! At least, that's what she suspected was the problem.

"Come on, Miss Taylor-Ryan! We wanna bake some cookies," Alyssa urged her forward toward the house.

"I'm coming!"

Her musings would have to wait, she had cookies to bake! And she would *not* think about the sweet man who had fathered the precious girls who were going to help her bake them.

Joshua found his resolve harder to keep than he thought. He had tried so many times not to think about Katherine, or tried so hard to be around her as little as possible, or tried not to talk to her too much. And it was as if she somehow knew of his intentions and made it harder for him to stick to his decision. She did things, or said things, or looked at him in a certain way, that made him unable to pretend he no longer cared for her.

At church one Sunday, she had brushed against him accidentally when passing. It had sent a shock through his entire body.

The next Saturday, as if seeing her every week day at his house wasn't enough, he saw her at the general store. She was coming in as he was going out and he'd been forced to talk to her. As usual, she'd been sweet and charming.

Katherine, for her part, had decided she'd play Joshua's little game until she could figure out what, exactly, he was going to do. And while he made his decision, she'd make it hard on him to completely refuse her.

After that, Joshua seemed to see Katherine everywhere he went.

Usually the conversation went something like, "How do you do, Mr. Tyler? Fine weather we're having, isn't it?"

Joshua would always watch her mouth, sometimes idly wondering what it would feel like to kiss it. And he'd usually pull himself back to reality in time to answer. "Yes, ma'am, it surely is."

After each encounter, he'd be irritated. Irritated with himself for having a reaction to her. Irritated at her for seeming to thwart his attempts at aloofness.

Joshua finally decided he'd pick the girls up from school or have them walk. Gently he broke the news to Katherine and she seemed fine with the decision, to his relief. He'd secretly expected a fight of some kind. Deep down, he kind of wished she had. Since she hadn't, he found himself a little frustrated. Of course, he didn't know why he'd felt that way, because he'd never admit to himself that she had such a hold on him after all.

Over the weeks, he kept pushing his feelings down, but they suddenly came to a head one day.

Joshua had come in from the fields a little later than usual. He realized the girls weren't home yet and he'd have to go fetch them. He wasn't suddenly put out because he'd have to get them, but because he'd have to be face-to-face with Katherine.

The whole way into town, he began seething, trying to convince himself it was only because he was feeling inconvenienced.

As he stepped inside the schoolroom, Katherine looked up.

Without preamble, he tersely asked his daughters, "Were you planning on coming home today?"

"Yes, Papa," Madison answered. "We stayed a little while to help Miss Taylor-Ryan with some things."

"Get out to the wagon, girls." He decided he may have some things he wanted to say to Katherine that the girls shouldn't be present for.

As soon as the room was clear, he started in. "Couldn't you have at least had the decency to bring my girls if you were gonna keep them here for so long after school?"

Katherine answered in a tone that matched his terseness. "We figured you'd be in the fields and not notice if they were a little late. We didn't know you'd come after them."

"I see."

Katherine decided now was the time to get everything out in the open so she pressed on. "It has not escaped my notice that I seem to no longer be fit company for you or your family anymore." She did her best to keep her tone firm.

Her heated words only fueled Joshua's ire.

"That's not the way of it at all." That was his only answer and he didn't seem ready to offer any more explanation.

Katherine, to his surprise, suddenly looked defeated. She didn't argue back. She hung her head and shrugged her shoulders, sighing wearily.

Joshua was immediately concerned, forgetting his wrath from moments before. "Katherine, what's wrong?" His tone was soft now.

Seeing Katherine so deflated and vulnerable unnerved him. She didn't respond, but was still and refused to look at him, staring unseeingly at her desk instead.

"Please tell me, Katherine."

He went to kneel by her and gently lifted her chin with his forefinger. Tears silently slid down her cheeks. He dropped his hand at once, as if he were burned. Her sorrowful look cut into his heart.

"It seems my feelings have been misplaced, Mr. Tyler. I was in error and it was my own stupid fault for thinking you cared about me as much as I care—cared about you."

Joshua was dumbfounded, to say the least! He had been so careful, at least he'd thought he had. This hadn't been his intention. Hurting her was what he had tried to avoid, but it seemed he had unwittingly done so anyway.

"Katherine," he started softly, dropping his head. He couldn't bear looking in her eyes and seeing the hurt he'd put there. "I'm truly sorry. You deserve to be treated better. I have—had—I've had feelings for you, but I've come to realize that you deserve much better than me and so I've been tryin' not to show my feelings so much. I didn't know you cared so much. I only did it because you deserve someone without such a…past. And someone who's never been married. Someone with whom you can start your own family, not someone with children already. Someone you can experience all the new things of marriage with."

Katherine hadn't given much thought to any of that. She'd only wanted Joshua. And besides, what did it matter? She loved Joshua's girls and cared a great deal for him. Why would any of the rest of it matter? Yet, here he was, hat in hand, trying to give her a way out already…and they hadn't even started anything yet.

She felt herself suddenly stubbornly refusing. She *wouldn't* allow herself to release him. Not yet. Not til they had tried, at least. And hopefully not ever. She had to say something.

"Joshua, I don't care about any of that. Not in the sense you think I do. If, one day, you feel like divulging further information about your past, then fine, but I don't expect it. Let it be in the past. It's you I care about." She immediately blushed at the bold confession, but continued before she lost the rest of her nerve. "I admire you, Joshua and I respect you. I *care about you!*"

Joshua could only stare deep into her eyes, surprised and humbled by her confession and then he slowly lowered his lips to hers. The kiss was brief and sweet.

Pulling away gently, Katherine had a few dizzying seconds.

Joshua took longer to awake from the dream of the kiss. When his senses were fully awake, he instantly felt shame for his bold action. "Katherine! I acted without thinking. Please accept my deepest apologies!"

Then it was Katherine's turn to not think before blurting out, "This better mean you will start courting me properly!"

Still kneeling, Joshua clasped his hands and pleaded, "Miss Katherine Taylor-Ryan, might I have the privilege of courting you?"

Katherine couldn't fully suppress her giggles at his gallantry. A wave of nerves and shyness assailed her. Willfully pushing it down, she made herself be calm. Lightly, she teased, "Goodness, Joshua, it isn't as if you're proposing marriage."

Joshua gave her a lopsided grin. "Nope, not yet."

Katherine blushed fiercely at that.

Noticing her red cheeks, Joshua couldn't let that go. "I take it I'm your first suitor." He winked.

Caught up now, Katherine answered pertly, "It just so happens I had one when I was younger."

"Oh, is that so. And should I be jealous?"

"No, it was a secret."

"A secret, huh?"

"Yep. Me and Edward Clemens."

"Hmmm. You know, for a schoolteacher, that isn't very good grammar."

Katherine playfully swatted his arm. "Oh, hush. We were

young, only about twelve, I think. Well, *I* was. He was fourteen and sweet on me. We said we would court each other in secret, given that *I* was so young and all. We stole a kiss in the schoolyard by a blossoming apple tree."

Joshua had, by now, adopted a casual stance, leaning against the desk, his arms folded across his chest. "And where is this Edward now, might I ask?"

Katherine laughed outright then. "He was sweet on a lot of girls, it turned out. They were all secrets, too. We caught on to his scheming, my friends and I. After that, anytime a new girl came to school, we warned her against him. He didn't like us much after that. He finished school and went off somewhere to apprentice for…something," she waved her hand in casual dismissal.

"I better make this official then, before he comes back lookin' for you. What day and time should I call?"

A thought suddenly struck Katherine. "Joshua, we don't have a chaperone! I live alone and that would be highly improper!"

"I'll see if Emily wouldn't mind. She'll be thrilled to hear about it."

They settled on a day and time as the two walked outside, having closed the school up for the day.

They parted and Joshua hopped into the wagon. He told the girls the good news on their way home and was rewarded with squeals of delight.

For himself, he was excited to be able to share the news with his dearest friend, Emily.

Chapter 16: Courting Katherine

It was late in the evening before they got home, so Joshua's news had to wait. The next morning, however, before heading out to the fields, Joshua stopped by Emily's house. The children had all headed off to school together, so it gave Joshua the perfect opportunity to speak to Emily alone.

"Hello!" Joshua called out as he entered. He made a beeline for the kitchen, correctly assuming that Emily was cleaning up from breakfast.

Emily turned around from the sink, drying her hands on her apron as Joshua came in. "Oh, hi, Josh! Didn't expect to see ya til noon."

"I have news that couldn't wait."

Emily arched her eyebrows, "Oh?"

Joshua's dark eyes lit up as he exulted, "I'm courting!"

Emily, taken aback, gasped, "Who?"

Joshua chuckled then. "Why, Katherine, of course! I thought it'd be obvious."

A peculiar feeling stole over Emily, although she didn't know why. And she couldn't place it, except to think it felt more like a foreboding. "Oh!" was all she could think of to say.

"And, Em, I have something of great importance to ask you."

She reiterated, "Oh?"

"You see, we need a chaperone, being that she lives alone and all. Could you do it? Would you be our chaperone? It would be Saturday afternoons at four o'clock. It would only be for an hour or two. Please?" Joshua looked like an eager little boy waiting for Christmas as he put on his best pleading face.

Emily scolded herself for not being more excited, but she couldn't shake the feeling that something felt off. It made no sense since she had been pushing for this very development to occur. In the end, she surmised she was being possessive of her dearest friend, and that was all. They both meant a great deal to her and she didn't want to lose either of their friendships as they developed a deeper relationship with each other. She convinced herself that's all it was and, with time, she'd feel the proper excitement for her two dearest friends. In the meantime, she'd simply have to fight her misgivings, as they were unwarranted. It also meant she couldn't accept Joshua's proposal since she felt she'd do a grave disservice to the excited couple.

Shaking herself mentally, she realized she needed to answer Joshua's question. Thinking quickly, she tried to find the best way to let him down easy, but couldn't even find a valid reason why she couldn't chaperone. Thinking on her feet wasn't her strong suit, but she started talking slowly, pondering as she went. "You know, Josh, I don't think I'll be able to. The children are home on Saturdays and I'd like to spend time with them. Besides, won't you need someone to keep an eye on the girls while you're gone?" There, that seemed reasonable enough…except her children were within the same age as Joshua's and they were all within the age of being able to be left alone for a few hours. As for them being home Saturdays, it was true enough they *could* spend the day together, however, they all had their own chores they caught up on, on Saturdays, so it was really of no consequence if Emily decided to leave for a few hours. But Joshua didn't need to know that.

Emily saw the look of disappointment on Joshua's face. It bothered her greatly that she had caused it, especially since the excuses she gave were very poor, and she knew it.

Joshua tried to persuade her. "Oh, Emily, they'll be fine for a few hours. They're all old enough." He tried to rally his spirits, but was becoming disheartened. He half-heartedly tried to argue his point some more, but realized she was firm in her decision. And he was bewildered at her reaction. He'd expected her to be excited. Hanging his head in defeat, he resigned. "Alright, Em, I'll see if Mrs. Chadrick would mind bein' a chaperone."

Emily felt awful, but didn't think it would be wise of her to tell Joshua of her misgivings. If she were right, Joshua would eventually realize that courting Katherine was a mistake. If she turned out to be wrong, she would have spoken up for no reason at all, and possibly could damage their friendship in the process.

She didn't know how to mend the rift she'd made and watched Joshua walk away. Watching Joshua out the window and seeing the dejected way he headed for the fields made Emily instantly reconsider. Impulsively, she ran to the door and called out, "Josh!"

Slowly, he turned around.

She ran over to catch up. Forcing a tight smile, she said, "Alright, I'll do it. I'll chaperone you two, if you really want me to."

Joshua's eyes lit up. "Really? You will?" Before Emily knew what was happening, Joshua grabbed her by the waist and twirled her around in a happy dance. "Thanks, Em! You're the only one I'd want there." Emily laughed and Joshua impulsively kissed her cheek before setting her back on the ground. Giddily he ran off to the fields.

Emily, recovering, put her hand to her cheek and muttered sullenly, "Well, he didn't have to go and do that!"

Joshua's excitement the following Saturday afternoon, Emily had to admit, was a bit contagious. Her feelings of unease were beginning to ebb. Maybe she had simply been nervous for both Joshua and Katherine, wanting everything to work out perfectly for her two closest friends.

Joshua was going to pick her up on the way into town to Katherine's house. Emily looked the part of a disapproving chaperone, as she was still wearing black. It had only been six months since Jacob's death. Still, it irked her that she was put in the position of the part that was generally for an older woman if the young lady's parents weren't available. She reminded herself she was happy for them and should be honored they'd asked her to do such an important task. Without someone chaperoning, they couldn't court each other. However, for the current occasion, she was glad she was still in her mourning. The black seemed appropriate, somehow, for her uneasy feelings hadn't been completely snuffed out.

The knock on the door came, and Emily went out to meet Joshua. "Are you ready?" he asked, offering his arm as they descended the porch stairs.

Emily looked Joshua over. He caught her looking and asked, "Do you approve?"

Emily pretended to look critical. "I suppose I do."

Joshua *did* look rather dashing. His dark brown hair was

parted to the left and slicked back except for one stubborn lock that fell forward on his brow. It really wasn't that different from the way he dressed for church, she critically noted. His trousers were a soft gray, coupled with a blue button-up shirt that complemented his dark good looks, under a gray vest that matched his pants. His shiny black Sunday boots completed his outfit.

He chuckled. "Well, thank you, Em. I suppose you'll do, too" and he gave her a teasing wink.

Joshua stood nervously on Katherine's stoop and Emily stood discreetly behind, waiting for Katherine to answer the door.

Katherine opened it and greeted them warmly, inviting them in.

Katherine's house was a small, one-story cottage, but had plenty of room for her. The residence was part of the pay as a school teacher.

After a short walk down a narrow hall, it opened into a cozy sitting room. Katherine showed her suitor and chaperone to their seats.

As was appropriate, Joshua took a seat across the room from Katherine and Emily took a chair in the corner. An awkward silence fell over the room. It had been awhile since Joshua had found himself in this position. He racked his brain for something to say, and finally came up with, "Thank you, Katherine for allowing me the privilege of courting you." He gave her an impish grin, knowing he was making a fool of himself.

Feeling a bit nervous and self-conscious herself, Katherine answered, "You're welcome. Thank you for the generous offer."

'Are they conducting business or are they courting? It's hard to tell,' Emily silently mused. She felt a bit prickly about being there, and now it seemed they were simply wasting her time. Taking a breath, she realigned her thoughts. *'Come on, Em, this isn't about you. This stage of courting is awkward. Give them a chance.'*

Emily did have to bite back a grin when, after a few more seconds of complete silence, neither seemed inclined to say more. And it did amuse her that these two close friends were acting so proper with each other.

Finally the couple settled for a half hour of small talk until Joshua finally asked Katherine, "Would you care to take a stroll around town? The weather looks fine."

The town could be easily viewed from Katherine's sitting room at the front of the small house, for there was a large window overlooking the main thoroughfare.

"Would that be acceptable to you, O Chaperone?" Joshua teased Emily with the lofty title.

Emily figured it would be a quick walk, even if they tried hard to take their time.

Emily acquiesced.

The ladies stood and Joshua offered his arm to Katherine.

"Remember, there are eyes watching," Emily tried to pull it off teasingly, but there was an underlying edge that belied the truthfulness of the statement. They didn't seem to notice her subtle warning.

"We'll be on our best behavior," Katherine assured her smilingly.

After they left, Emily settled herself back onto the chair. She supposed she should snoop out the window, but knew she could trust Joshua and Katherine and they wouldn't do anything inappropriate with the whole town watching them. For it was a small town and most assuredly the gossips and busybodies would be peeking out windows to see who was walking by. They would be better chaperones in this case than Emily could be. Aside from herself, no one else knew the two were courting. Of course, if they continued strolling arm-in-arm around town, it would get the gossip going. Emily delicately shuddered contemplating the melee that would certainly follow services the next morning. The town may be small, but the gossip was certainly big.

Idly, she stared at the bookshelf by the chair Joshua had vacated. A good book in a quiet room sounded divine, but that's not what she was there for. Restlessly, Emily got up, supposing she should take her chaperoning duties a little more seriously.

Peering out the window, Emily murmured to herself, "Well, look at that! Mr. Vantrice, that nosy grocer, has them cornered. He'll surely tell his wife now." While Mrs. Vantrice wasn't the biggest gossip in town, she wasn't the quietest either. Emily was sure that between the couple, they'd make sure the word got around about Joshua and Katherine.

Seeing them together made the peculiar feeling rise in her chest again. She was tired of the feeling surprising her whenever it felt like it. She wished the blasted feeling would go away. There was no call for it so she decided to ignore it. It was getting to the point where her happiness for her friends was being overshadowed by the unexplainable and unsettled feeling.

Emily had been in her reverie and now caught the happy couple ambling up the boardwalk and to the front door. Not wanting to be found spying so openly, she hastened back to her chair. Quickly she unseeingly grabbed a book from the bookcase she'd spied earlier and sat down, opening the book to a random page.

Joshua and Katherine entered the house then and Emily heard their footsteps coming down the hall to find her.

"We're back, Em," Joshua announced, even as they stepped through the doorway.

"Oh, hello," Emily nonchalantly closed the book and laid it down.

The gesture wasn't lost on Katherine and she grinned as she read the title. "'*The Beginning Alphabet for First Year Students*'? Why, Em, I'm surprised! I thought you knew your alphabet already."

Emily looked down at the book in bewilderment, then blushed.

"You know what I think, I think we have a real busybody on our hands," Joshua teased, guessing the situation.

Blushing furiously now, she admitted, "It seems I've been caught. I told you 'there are eyes watching.' I just didn't tell you they'd be mine." She tried to pass off something like a smile, but it faltered.

Soon after, goodbyes were said.

On the ride home, Joshua commented, "I think that went rather well, don't you?"

Fighting down the absurd feeling again, Emily agreed. "Katherine's a dear. You really are lucky, Josh. You couldn't do better."

Joshua got lost in thought then and the rest of the way home was spent in companionable silence.

Emily's suspicions of gossip proved true. There were plenty of whispers and stares the next day at church. Emily took her usual place on the same pew, only today, she sat between Joshua and Katherine.

By the time church let out, it seemed everyone in town knew, or at least guessed at what was going on between the two. Thankfully, a lot of them seemed to be well-wishers. Still, it was awkward being the center of so much gossip. Both Joshua and Emily knew it well from the past, and Katherine was getting a taste of it now.

"Well, you two make a fine lookin' couple," Marcy Burne commented.

"Thank you, Miss Burne," Joshua said. "That's awfully kind of you to say."

Joshua and Katherine stood together, though not close, in the churchyard, greeting passersby and neighbors and everyone in between who was curious about the newly developed couple.

"We'll have to invite you two over for supper soon," Yetta Fabian offered when the crowd allowed her to approach the couple.

Though not intentional, a small line had formed of curious onlookers who wished to speak to the couple and glean what information they could to pass on later. It made both Joshua and Katherine uncomfortable but, at the same time, it amused them and so they indulged.

Next was the pastor's wife, Elise Chadrick. "Mr. Chadrick and I would like to invite you over for dinner after church next Sunday."

"We'd be honored, Mrs. Chadrick, " Katherine accepted.

After Elise Chadrick walked away, Katherine's hand flew to her mouth and she blushed. "I'm so sorry, Joshua! I didn't mean to answer for us both."

"Don't worry about it. At least you didn't say something in front of her. She'd most likely make some comment about us acting like an old married couple already." Laughing he added, "I haven't even proposed...yet," then winked.

Joshua enjoyed the crimson that crept back into Katherine's

face.

"I'm only teasin'!" he laughed.

Katherine uneasily joined in, then answered tightly, "I know."

Then why did it bother her so much, she wondered. *'It only caught me off guard, that's all. We've barely started courting! Of course it would be too soon to speak of marriage. He was only teasin'.*

Yet, Katherine found herself frequently mulling over the offhand comment. Joshua had intended to tease her, but it had affected her deeply.

A month of Saturdays flew by as Joshua and Katherine deepened their relationship. Yet Joshua was bothered by the fact that there were things about his past he still needed to share with Katherine. Things about Ashley and why she'd left. He didn't feel ready, but he knew she needed to know.

This led him to reflect on how true his feelings were for her. How strong were they, really? He reminded himself that they had already gotten to know each other fairly intimately before their official courtship started. Jacob's death alone had brought them closer. Of course, he'd had to go and mess that up, too. How could he ever prove to be a better husband if he went around interfering in things because he got scared? That's all it had been, he'd realized. He was so scared of messing things up with Katherine, like he had with Ashley, it was almost as if he subconsciously went out of his way to do just that. But if he ever got to the point of proposing, she deserved to know him fully. Katherine already knew the surface stuff, but she didn't know all of the emotional scars that came with it.

"Papa," Kayla called then, "it's past three o'clock. Ya need ta scoot if yer gonna pick up Aunt Emily before your courtin' at Miss Taylor-Ryan's."

"Thank you, angel, for letting me know. I'm on my way."

He went out and hitched up the team to his wagon and left. On his way to Emily's, he reflected that she could make it easier for him to tell Katherine about his past…and Ashley. Unlike any other chaperone they might've had, she already knew everything there was to know, so he could talk about it in front of her, and even draw comfort from her, as he told Katherine. He felt it was time to get things off his chest and circumstances seemed to be working in his favor.

'Okay, it's not circumstances, Lord,' he acquiesced. *'It's you.'*

As he helped Emily into the carriage, he decided he would forewarn Emily of his decision. Mostly so she'd be ready and not taken by surprise when he broached the subject, but also so he could draw strength from her knowledge.

A few steps into the conversation mentally, Joshua was temporarily baffled when Emily simply greeted, "Hello, Josh."

He realized he hadn't spoken anything aloud. He regrouped and decided to begin again, this time aloud, so Emily could actually respond in her own words. "Em, I have something to run by you...."

"Well, here we go," Joshua determined as he reined in the horses outside Katherine's house.

"Now, are you *sure* about this Josh?" Emily was a little skeptical as to whether or not this was a good idea.

"Yes, she deserves to know. She needs to know, if she were...er...is to make, uh, any...er, decisions about a future with me...later."

When the realization struck that Joshua was talking about marriage, apprehension hit Emily in the pit of her stomach. Again, she had no logical reason for her feelings so she tried to ignore them.

Katherine was hospitable as always. "I made some lemonade and sugar cookies. Would you two care for some?"

"Yes, we would, please," Emily answered for them both. Looking at Joshua, she apologized. "Sorry. I didn't mean to speak for you."

"It's okay, sis," Joshua grinned back.

Lately Joshua had taken to calling her that. She appreciated the sentiment, as they were close, but the endearment irked her. She simply assumed it had to do with all of her weird feelings lately concerning Joshua and tried not to make too much out of it. She began thinking that perhaps it wasn't all about Joshua at all and she was simply still reacting to Jacob's death and dealing with it in a very strange way. Never having gone through the grieving process such as this before, she had no idea how she was going to react. That thought comforted her a little because she hated feeling so disconsolate regarding Katherine and Joshua.

"I'll be right back. Make yourselves comfortable." Katherine left the small parlor then.

In a whispery hiss, Emily questioned Joshua. "How are you going to broach the subject?"

"I don't know yet. An opportunity will present itself. God's in this. I know He put it in my mind to do this, He'll let me know when the time comes."

Katherine returned then carrying the lemonade and cookies. She had balanced cups on the platter with the cookies.

"Here, let me help you." Joshua got up to lend a hand.

Once they were seated with refreshments, talk turned to the mundane.

The longer it seemed to take for an opportunity to arise, the more uptight Joshua became.

Emily sensed his frustration, but couldn't think of a way to help. Joshua had kept running his fingers nervously through his hair, a sign to Emily that he was very agitated, indeed.

Oddly enough, the gesture turned out to be the opening he needed. Observing Joshua, Katherine finally asked, "Is there something the matter, Joshua? You keep running your fingers through your hair."

Stunned, Joshua hadn't realized he'd been doing it. It was an unconscious gesture. Joshua started pacing the room.

'Uh, oh', Emily observed, 'when he paces, too, it's really not good.'

"Yes, Katherine, there is, actually. I have a matter I need to discuss with you." He stopped pacing a moment and bowed his head to collect his thoughts.

Suddenly, Katherine was worried. 'He's going to propose! He can't propose here; Emily's here! Proposals are supposed to be romantic and private.' Getting control of herself, she forced reason to intervene. It was too soon, he couldn't possibly be thinking of marriage. She was getting ahead of herself. She made herself calm down and listen to reason.

Joshua forged ahead with his plan. "I believe the time has now come for me to share with you about my past." He had to believe that the direct approach was best.

Katherine smiled to herself. As serious as Joshua obviously was, he sounded like a prophet, coming to foretell future events. 'The time has now come....'

Emily, too watched the scene, slightly amused. She knew of Joshua's tendency for dramatics when he had something that he felt strongly about and needed to say. Sobering, Emily knew it for what it was; he was about to speak from his heart.

Sitting back slightly, Joshua focused and organized his thoughts. "I know you are aware of a little bit of my past, but I want you to know me fully.

"I married Ashley when I was nineteen; she was eighteen. We were madly in love and had been sweethearts practically since childhood, it seemed.

"We grew up in Virginia together, but moved here when we got married. We were young and simply wanted to have our own fresh start in our new life so we moved away from our families.

"Shortly after we moved here, Ashley became pregnant, and Madison joined our family. We thought she'd be a boy and had picked the name Madison, but she was a girl. So, we still named her Madison, intending to call her Maddie. But as she got older, Madison seemed more fitting to suit her stubborn nature. Maddie seemed too weak a name." Here Joshua smiled fondly over his eldest child. His pride in her was evident. He continued.

"Madison was still pretty young when we met Jacob and Emily, who immediately became our closest friends. We've seen each other through everything. This includes the hardest time of my life, nearly three years ago...when Ashley left.

"About the same amount of time before that, I had noticed Ashley wasn't actin' like herself, but I couldn't pinpoint the problem and sorta ignored it. I suppose I didn't really want to acknowledge there was a problem.

"So, it came as a sort of surprise when she began questioning God. It shouldn't have; I was her husband, I shoulda known, but I wasn't very attentive. She questioned everything we had been raised to believe. Everything about God, about church, about...everything! And I truly handled it terribly. I have an overbearing nature that, even now, I'm working on. I let it take hold of me. I simply couldn't wrap my mind around someone questioning God. My overbearing turned to arrogance. I felt she should know better, having been raised in the church."

Joshua's voice began to fill more and more with emotion. "I let her down. I'd kept draggin' her in to talk to Reverend Chadrick, but my motives were less than honorable. I wanted the reverend to tell her she was foolish for questioning God. I wanted her to know she was wrong...and I was right. This was so arrogant and full of pride. Who was I to demean her in such a way? God wants us to find out answers by reading the Bible, which means we will invariably have questions. It also means He's okay with us questioning. So why wasn't I okay with my wife questioning? I should have been the one to answer her questions, but most of all, I should have had the patience and understanding to want to answer her questions. Instead, I wanted her to simply trust in God merely because that's what we had been taught. That's what I had done, after all...like I said, I was arrogant. I was fairly high on my horse, focusing on myself and my shame that my wife was having doubts and questions about God.

"If only I had taken the time to really listen to her doubts and talk with her about them, I don't think she would've done what she did."

Pacing restlessly again, Joshua stopped then and, bowing his head, sighed heavily. He blew out another breath and confessed. "As you can probably tell, I still carry the guilt. Some days are better than others...if I don't let myself think about it."

Emily was a little shocked at the confession. She hadn't realized to what extent he had still been carrying the guilt. Watching him, with his head still bowed as in defeat, she had the alarming thought that he was fighting tears. She knew the signs.

Katherine had sensed the change as well. She wasn't sure if she had wanted to know all this, but it seemed important to him that she did. Why? She cared for him, greatly, and about what had happened to him. But, none of it made any difference to her because all she knew was the Joshua he had been with her. And that was the one she cared about. She realized he may be afraid the truth would change her opinion of him. Perhaps that was why it was so important to him that he share. But, she still respected him.

Maybe even more so now that he had shared. So she supposed she was glad he had shared an intimate part of himself with her. He had made himself more vulnerable, exposing insecurities. That had taken a great amount of courage. She was touched that he trusted her so much.

This man gave her strength, support, encouragement. He may even share his family with her someday. He was a good man! And yet, in between all of this, she felt faint stirrings of misgiving. Almost as if he weren't right…for her. But she knew he'd make a good husband! Her unease simply didn't make sense!

Joshua had gained control and continued. "I realize now that since she felt she couldn't talk to me, and because I had acted so formidably, she was scared of telling me the truth. She probably resented me, too."

Emily gasped involuntarily. "Josh, don't say that!" She hadn't meant to speak while he was relating his past, but his admittance was too much! Maybe it had been true, at the time, but it still gave Ashley no excuses! And yet, Joshua allowed it to be, time and again. Emily could hardly bear for him to keep carrying it around and dwelling on it after so much time. It tore at her heart.

Emily reflected on her own thoughts when she had first heard Joshua tell it. Ashley had never confided any doubts to her either; about God or any of it. It wasn't just Joshua Ashley had refused to talk to; she had stubbornly refused to seek counsel from anyone.

Joshua turned dejectedly toward Emily. "You know it's the grim truth, Em. That's why she began seeking answers elsewhere. That's why she left with *that man.*" Thoughts of Joseph Danielson still made him cringe.

"I suspect in all her searching, she must've realized she was wrong. It was hinted at in her letters; she came out and told me so in her–" he stopped and swallowed hard, "last letter. By then, I fear she felt trapped. I think she felt rejected by me so didn't know she could come home." Here, Joshua paused. Quietly he ended, "And I think you know the rest of it, Katherine."

Moved by his honest vulnerability, Katherine stood up and went to him. She steadily met his gaze and told him, "I'm honored you trusted me with your soul, Joshua." She could only imagine what it had emotionally cost him to open up to her the way he had. "You are a fine man, Joshua Tyler." She continued, "It's obvious you've learned from your past mistakes. I've never felt you to be overbearing or arrogant. I believe you are a changed man and I am concerned with the amount of guilt you still seem to be carrying." She grabbed his hand and held it. "I want you to hear me now, Joshua. People make their own decisions and only they are responsible for their actions. Even if they are reacting to something we've done, even if we've done it wrongly, we aren't responsible for their reactions to it. We can seek forgiveness for our wrongs from God. We can ask them for forgiveness. We can forgive ourselves and determine to do better. That's all we are responsible for."

Joshua was exceedingly grateful he hadn't scared Katherine off after all. Looking back at Emily, he grinned. Then he turned back to Katherine and said, "That's what a friend once told me."

Continuing in earnest, "Katherine, I think you're good for me. Thank you for listening and not turning me away. I am truly blessed and honored to be courting such a lovely woman. I feel you are the healing balm I've been needing."

Katherine blushed and looked away. *'He shouldn't say such things. Especially in the company of others.'* Nonetheless, it brought pleasure to hear such words from her suitor.

Chapter 17: Some Womanly Advice

Emily woke up the morning of September twenty-sixth, eighteen forty, feeling out of sorts.

Laying an arm across her eyes to shield out the morning sun streaming through the window, she tried to put order to her thoughts. She knew this was a day of some significance, but she didn't want to think about it—it was the one year anniversary of Jacob's death.

She suddenly felt very weary and very alone. Weathering the last year had been quite a feat. Deep down, though, she knew it had all been a front. She'd done it for her children, acting like she had it all together, before she really had. Burying her feelings had become second nature after the first couple of months had gone by. The grief was still buried beneath her façade.

Recognizing this, she felt an overwhelming sadness that after a year, she still hadn't grieved in a way that brought closure. Of course she'd been sad and cried, but after the initial emotions were dealt with, she found she had neither time nor inclination to deal with them. She had a family, after all. Her children had needed her, more than her grief had. Now on this, the anniversary, the hurt felt fresh and new and she dreaded getting out of bed.

How would the children feel today? Would they even remember the significance of the date?

Her thoughts turned toward Joshua. Would *he* remember? He was busy with Katherine now…and it was his birthday, besides. Could she still lean on him for support, if needed? How would that look, now that his intentions with Katherine were clear.

She idly wondered if she should let the children stay home from school. More so, she suddenly felt too weary to even get out of bed, not to mention getting breakfast ready and their lunch pails packed.

Sighing, Emily sat up and plumped her pillows, sagging against them. Scanning the room, she again noted how big it felt without Jacob and his belongings occupying it. Would she never get used to that?

Her eyes fell on her wardrobe then. She was free to wear color again, as far as propriety dictated. But was she really expected to stop wearing black? Just like that? She didn't want to stop wearing the black! The enormous decision seemed to overwhelm her and she panicked at the thought. How else was she to show her remembrance of Jacob? How would people know she still loved him and would never forget him? Wouldn't they think she was being callous by not wearing the black anymore?

She did stop to consider that she had let the children start wearing color months ago. And she knew it would be viewed as pathetic if she went around in black too much longer. She would definitely be considered eccentric then. People would think she was trying too hard to hold onto her dead husband's memory. Then what? She'd be the sad, broken-hearted widow who couldn't move past her husband's death.

And why should she be expected to, she stubbornly insisted. Why couldn't she cling to his memory? Jacob had been her other half. Her soul mate!

She simply wasn't ready to move on and an overwhelming urge to cry suddenly took Emily by surprise. Trying to stave off the tears, she decided the best thing to do would be to simply get up and get on with her day. Besides, the children would be up and wanting breakfast and finding it odd if she weren't down there where they expected.

Sighing heavily, Emily resignedly pushed back the covers. Feeling a bit defiant, against what, she didn't know, she didn't dress. Instead, she put on a wrapper. The thought struck that perhaps a bit more time in bed after the children left wouldn't be an entirely bad idea. So she didn't make her bed either. For some reason, her acts of defiance pleased her.

Emily descended the stairs to the sounds of a rising household.

Entering the kitchen, she was greeted by Samantha and Hailey.

"Good morning, Mama," Samantha said first.

"Mornin'," Emily returned.

Hailey's "good morning" was a hug and kiss on the cheek.

Emily didn't know if she should mention the date, so asked

brightly instead, "Lookin' forward to school today?"

"Oh, yes!" Hailey enthused. "I made a new friend already. Aubrey. She's new to town. Her pa's the new doctor, since Doc Rowan wants to retire an' all."

Emily had forgotten that. She rarely paid attention to news anymore, preferring to be wrapped up in her own little world. Lately, some days, she didn't quite know how to cope. Jacob was gone. Joshua and Katherine were wrapped up in each other. She could feel her urge to try and deepen other relationships slowly slipping away until one day, she realized it was gone altogether.

She turned to Samantha. "What about you, Samm? Lookin' forward to school today?"

"Oh, it'll be alright, I suppose."

Emily expected such an answer. School never was a favorite of her second-to-youngest.

Emily turned toward the stove then to start breakfast. And to hide the sudden and surprising tears rising to the surface. They hadn't seemed to notice the significance of the day.

Emily managed to get the children off to school and the kitchen tidied in less than an hour. She sighed with relief, suddenly exhausted. The house to herself, she could succumb to the desire of going back to bed.

None of the children had mentioned the anniversary, but she told herself that didn't mean they had forgotten. They may have merely been trying to spare her feelings.

Still, as she trudged upstairs, she couldn't help but feel the tiniest bit of regret that none of them had mentioned the date.

"Did you notice how Mama seemed to mope around this mornin'?" Christopher asked his sisters as they walked to school.

This would be Christopher's last year in school. He wanted to be a veterinarian but, since the town didn't boast one, he planned on studying under the new doctor, George Allison. That way, he could learn about medicine. At least, the general basics and how to administer. He'd have to do a lot more additional studying to incorporate animals, but he could be the town of Lorraine's only veterinarian.

"It *is* the anniversary of Papa's..." Samantha trailed off.

"That's probably why she was so sad," offered Christopher, after a few moments.

"Do you think we should have mentioned it?" Brianna queried.

"No!" Samantha vehemently opposed. "It would've just made her feel worse."

"Well, I'm going to talk to her later," Brianna made up her mind. "She needs someone to talk to."

"Aw, she can talk to Miss Taylor-Ryan. She don't wanna hear from us. We're just young'uns," Samantha contradicted.

"I'm still gonna do it," Brianna resolved. "Besides, Miss Taylor-Ryan's busy with Uncle Josh these days."

"That's true," Samantha finally conceded. "Well, whatever you say to Mama, I hope it cheers her up. I haven't seen her this sad since Pa died."

The Matthews still had times when they missed their father, and the anniversary didn't help to alleviate those feelings. Yet, they had done their grieving at the time of his death, so were better able to handle the anniversary day.

Their ma, on the other hand, was a different story.

As soon as he entered the kitchen, he knew something was amiss. It was too quiet, for one thing, and Emily wasn't in the kitchen as usual.

Looking around the few rooms downstairs, Joshua called out for Emily. When that produced no results, he climbed the stairs two at a time, a little more urgently, calling, "Em....Emily? Emily!"

Peeking in her bedroom door, he didn't expect to find her, so was alarmed when he saw her in bed.

Going over, he gently shook her. "Emily? Emily, are you okay?"

Emily slowly rolled over and opened one eye, peering up at him.

Joshua noted her eyes were red and swollen, as if she'd been crying. "Were you sleeping?" he asked instead.

"Only just."

"Are you alright?" Alarm colored his words.

Emily gave Joshua a queer look then, suddenly frustrated, asked, "Don't *you* remember what today is?" She was appalled that *no one* seemed to remember, not even her own children!

Calmly, Joshua replied. "Yes, Em, I do. Are you alright?"

"No, I'm grievin', leave me alone."

Really worried now, Joshua offered, "Should I call the doc?" He had thought Emily had done all of her grieving along with the rest of them.

"No!" Emily fiercely refused. She sat up abruptly, making her head hurt.

"Would you like to eat something? Katherine sent some food home with the girls yesterday. I could run next door and get it. I honestly didn't even know if you'd be up to cookin', bein' what today is, and all..." he trailed off, seeing Emily's desolate look.

"There's enough left for two," he encouraged.

To her horror, and his, she burst into tears. "Yer dinner! I forgot about yer dinner! I'm supposed to make ya dinner and I forgot!" She buried her face in her hands and sobbed.

If Joshua hadn't known Emily was serious, he would have laughed at the absurdity of the reason for her tears. Instead, he gently tried to take her hands away from her face. "It's alright. I can go get some food, remember? Come downstairs and I'll go get it." He carefully sat down next to her on the edge of the bed, not wanting to inadvertently make things worse.

Instead of complying to Joshua's request, Emily slumped over and fell against Joshua's chest, face still covered with her hands.

Perched precariously on the edge of the bed, the unexpected extra weight made Joshua start slipping to the floor. Unable to stop the momentum, he let gravity have its way with him and gently cradled Emily against him as they slid to the floor. She didn't seem to notice. Silently, he waited as Emily spent her grief in his arms.

A long while later, Emily was finally able to pull herself together. When she realized where she was, all at once, she disentangled herself and shot up. "I'm sorry, Josh! That was very inappropriate of me! Please forgive me."

Joshua stood up then, too. He felt...strange, suddenly realizing the intimate situation. Before, he wouldn't have given it a second thought. They were more like family, but now.... "That's what friends are for...to cry on. I'm glad I was here to comfort you," he offered, lamely.

Emily stoically perched herself on her bed. "I'm still so lonely without Jacob" she mused, mostly to herself. "I miss him so much." More directly to Joshua, by way of explanation of her outlandish behavior, "I don't think I fully allowed myself to grieve when he died. There were details to work out and children grieving themselves...I had to be the strong one and now I'm about spent doing that."

"You've been the strong one long enough." Trying to change the subject, Joshua suggested, "And now you need food. I can bring the food to the kitchen."

"No. I don't feel like leaving my room right now. You go ahead. If you leave me some, I'll eat later."

"How 'bout I bring it up here, then?" Joshua secretly didn't believe she would eat at all.

"No, Josh. You don't need to wait on me."

"And you don't need to be left alone right now. I'll be right back."

Joshua galloped down the stairs and didn't let up on the pace all the way to his house. He grabbed the food and brought it back up to Emily's room then watched to make sure she ate some, too.

"The children will be home soon," Joshua informed her. "They may be curious as to why yer still in yer wrapper."

Emily's eyes widened. She suddenly realized how absurd the whole situation was. Here she was, in her *bedroom* of all places, eating dinner in her night clothes, at nearly two o'clock in the afternoon, and with a *man,* no less! Never mind he was a close friend, it dearly lacked propriety.

Guilt washed over her. '*Lord, please forgive me. If I had acted with a little bit of decorum, we wouldn't be here.*'

Calmly, Emily inquired, "Is it really that late?"

"I came lookin' for ya at noon for dinner. It's now about two o'clock."

As if on cue, the chime on the grandfather clock above stairs in the library sounded.

Joshua grinned devilishly, raising his eyebrows. "See?"

"Will you please excuse me then, Josh? I need to get

dressed."

"Certainly. I'll get back to the fields."

"No, you'd better go on home. You've done enough for me today. The farm hands can take care of it."

"Consider it done, Boss Lady." He granted her his trademark wink and smile as he got up and left.

Emily turned towards her wardrobe with trepidation.

"Mama?" Brianna knocked on Emily's door later that evening.

Emily was sitting up in bed, reading.

"Come in," Emily answered.

Brianna came in to sit on the edge of the bed.

"It's past bedtime, sweetheart," she gently reprimanded her daughter.

"I came to see if you were sad."

Emily was touched by her daughter's concern. "I'm alright. What makes you ask?"

"You were so sad this morning. We all noticed."

Emily felt heartsick. She hadn't wanted them to know. "You noticed that, huh? I'm sorry I worried you. It's just that today is–"

"Papa's anniversary. We remembered."

Brianna took something out from under her wrapper. "I made this for you today. Miss Taylor-Ryan said I was doing so well in math, and since she was doing review, I could use the time quietly for whatever I wanted."

Emily took the piece of paper Brianna held out to her. It was a drawing of Jacob. Brianna had proved to be quite a good artist in the past, so Emily shouldn't have been surprised it was quite a good likeness. But she was. In the drawing, Brianna had caught Jacob's eyes sparkling as he smiled at something in the distance that had caught his fancy.

"He's smiling at you, Mama."

Emily's eyes filled with tears as she hugged Brianna tightly. "Thank you, darlin'. I'll treasure this always."

"Do you feel better?"

"I do."

"I could stay longer, if you like."

Emily nearly smiled. "Are you tryin' to git out of goin' to bed?"

Brianna grinned. "Maybe."

Emily shifted and Brianna stood. "Good night, Brianna."

"'Night, Mama."

In the house down the lane, Joshua was thinking of his neighbor and friend. He'd experienced strange emotions earlier when he had held Emily as she cried. She had felt so fragile, as if she might break, dare he move her. The most troublesome feeling of all was the sense of rightness when he held her, as if he belonged there. As if it would always be his job to comfort her. He explained it away by assuring himself he was merely doing his brotherly duty by his friend. He still referred to her as Sis, some of the time.

'Lord, please be with Emily. This was undoubtedly a hard day for her to get through....'

He was vaguely disturbed by the fact that he had hardly thought of Katherine all day. As he drifted off to sleep, he reminded himself that it had been a significant day and had other pressing matters on his mind instead.

The weeks passed and Emily felt herself sinking deeper into her dark depression. Try as she might, she didn't seem able to pull herself out of the downward spiral.

She couldn't get herself back into routines and she felt tired all the time. Her purpose in life seemed fuzzy, at best. Not to say she neglected the children, but they were older now and didn't need to rely so heavily on a mama.

The only time she saw people was at church because that was the only time she ventured outside of her house and the only time she made herself put on an act that everything was fine.

Only those closest to her—her children, Joshua, and Katherine—knew the truth. And they all worried about her.

Emily tried finding the strength that had served her so well in the weeks following Jacob's death, but it seemed to be failing her. Most likely because it hadn't been strength at all, but denial.

Adding to that, seeing Joshua and Katherine together only started making her bitter. They reminded her of what she no longer had, and would probably never have, again. She knew that wasn't being fair, and that somewhere deep down she knew she was happy for her friends.

However, in the broad daylight of her current emotions, she saw none of that. She simply found it trying to be in the couple's presence and see their complete happiness. It only made her feel that much more alone.

As for the rest of the town, she had them all fooled. The only two other exceptions proved to be Yetta Fabian and Elise Chadrick. They were able to pick up on her current state and befriended her the more for it. Emily appreciated them anew, despite the fact that they were older than she. They lent much knowledge and wisdom, for which Emily was extremely grateful.

To her chagrin, despite her newfound friendships, Emily still missed Joshua's close friendship immensely. The pure and simple fact was no one could replace him.

Joshua must have missed Emily, too, for one Sunday, just after the start of November, he sought her out after church services. Joshua wasn't quite sure what to say. He didn't quite know how to talk to her, ever since the anniversary, because he found himself feeling awkward in her presence.

Clearing his throat, he haltingly started, "Em, um, how are you? I've…we've…been worried about you. Are you good? Are things good?"

Emily gave her pat answer of, "I'm fine, thank you."

"Uh, Em," he tried again. "I was wondering if, um, I could come by, er, later this week, perhaps, sometime in the evening. There's an issue I could really use your counsel on." He hoped the subject of his visit would put some life back into her. Then again…it may not, being the nature of the subject he wished to discuss. He'd have to wait and see.

"Yer not just gonna try an' git me to talk about my feelin's over a cup of tea, are ya?" Emily couldn't keep the sarcasm out of her voice. Hearing it, she cringed, but said nothing. She hadn't realized just how bitter she'd become.

As of late, Emily was getting a little put out by Yetta and Elise's tea time attempts to get her to talk. She had, on one occasion, told Joshua about this annoying habit of theirs.

He'd answered as only a close friend, and brother, could "Em, you know those ladies are just tryin' to help. You've been kinda sour lately."

"Sour, huh? What do you want my company for, then? You don't even come in for dinner anymore. Ever since..." She knew he knew good and well to which day she was referring, but she didn't want to speak it aloud.

"Maybe if you'd soften up and give me back the old Emily, I'd be more obliged," he'd returned, with some heat to his words.

Emily had given him a scathing look.

Joshua brought Emily back to the present. "I need some womanly advice and you're the only one whose advice I'd trust."

Emily softened seeing Joshua's pleading face. "Oh, alright. How 'bout Thursday evenin'?"

"Can we do it after the children are in bed? Say, nine o'clock? I need complete disclosure on this, or else it wouldn't matter having them around."

"Fine," Emily conceded somewhat coldly. Truth be told, she wasn't too keen on being alone with Joshua. "Thursday at nine, then."

Promptly at nine o'clock on Thursday evening, there was a rap on the back door of the kitchen at Emily's home. Joshua hadn't wanted to go all the way around to the front.

Emily had put a kettle on for tea, so was already in the kitchen awaiting his arrival. She let him in as soon as she heard him at the door.

"It's getting nippy out there. The holidays will be here before we know it." Joshua blew on his hands to warm them.

"Don't remind me," Emily stated coldly. Then rebuked herself. She could certainly be civil to Joshua. He'd done nothing to her and didn't deserve her icy treatment.

She handed Joshua a cup of tea. "Here, drink this. It'll warm yer hands."

Joshua took note of Emily's curt manner.

"Em, if you'd rather do this another time, we can. I don't mind. It's just...the personal matter is...uh...delicate and it'll be a lot easier to discuss without the girls around. But, if you prefer, I could come back—"

"Might as well get it over with," Emily cut in. *'Come on, Emily, be nice!'* she urged.

Joshua seemed fidgety. Emily noticed.

"Ok, here goes." Joshua took a deep breath and delivered the shock of Emily's life, though it shouldn't have been.

"I want to ask Katherine to marry me. I know it has only been about seven months, but I really do believe I love her. Is it too soon? I need advice!"

"Not if you don't mind people gossipin'," Emily expressed bitterly.

Joshua was a little taken aback. And a little crestfallen. "You think so?"

There. There it was again. That stubborn feeling that wouldn't leave Emily alone when she thought of Joshua and Katherine. It was a terrible feeling and Emily had always felt guilty for it. Still, it didn't soften her tone when she said, "Isn't it customary for you to court her for at least a year before proposing?"

To Emily's ears, she sounded downright rude. Trying again, she used a gentler tone. "Well, maybe it wouldn't be that bad. It *has* been over six months. I think that's acceptable. Some might consider it a bit soon, but maybe if you set the wedding to actually take place after a year, there wouldn't be much talk."

To her, it did all seem a bit sudden, but she wasn't sure if that was truly her feelings or she was reacting to the strange emotions. "Are you sure of her feelings?"

Joshua was quiet for some time. Finally, he answered. "Is any man really sure until they ask the question?"

Emily bit her lip and thought about that, then answered slowly, mulling it over. "No, I suppose not." *'But they should be, if they both are truly in love.'* She didn't think Jacob had any doubts when he'd proposed to her.

Joshua's next question caught her completely off guard. "What do *you* think, Em?"

"What do I think about what?" She stalled. She needed time! Time to sort out the correct response. She couldn't tell him how she really felt, because even she didn't understand it! Yet, she had to come up with something; he'd know it if she lied. Besides, she dearly did *not* want to lie!

"About Katherine. About Katherine and me. About us getting married. About us in general."

Joshua felt his face flush. He was rambling like a school boy. No, worse. Like a school *girl*!

"I really love Katherine. She's become very close and special to me." Emily was glad she could at least speak honestly of Katherine. As for the rest, she had no idea what to say. Maybe if she didn't answer the rest, he wouldn't pry.

No such luck. "What about Katherine and me? Do you think we're compatible?"

Still stalling, Emily decided to answer his question with a question. "Are you unsure of something?" Surely he wouldn't be questioning her about all of this if he were certain of his own feelings, as well as Katherine's. Or at least have a hint of Katherine's being in the affirmative.

"No, but it would mean the world to me…to us…that is to say, Katherine and me…if we knew we had your blessing."

"Why do you need my blessing? You're already courting. It would stand to reason that marriage would follow. You are two grown adults capable of making your own decisions, regardless of what others think."

"There it is."

"What?"

"That note."

"What note?"

"That tone…in your voice. I can tell you're not happy about something. What is it?"

At least they could squabble like siblings.

Why did he have to know her so well? She could think of nothing to say but the truth and that wouldn't do! She couldn't tell him the truth. It would hurt him too badly. And, she may even be wrong! All because of a stupid little feeling.

"Nothing of importance…truly." There. That wasn't a lie. For all she knew, her strange feeling *wasn't* important. How could it be? It made no sense. Ha! She'd found a loophole to her problem.

"Yes, it is important. I want to hear it."

Emily stared down into her teacup. She couldn't hurt him merely because of a hunch. Yet, she heard herself say, "I'm uncertain." But, she quickly added, "If you're certain, then it doesn't matter how I feel. Only you know how you feel, and that's the most important thing."

"Uncertain? About what?"

"About you and Katherine. Please, don't ask me to explain. I don't understand it myself. It's all based on a strange feeling I've had. You know me and my feelings." Her attempt to lighten the mood with humor fell flat.

Emily saw the hurt reflected in Joshua's eyes.

"You don't think Katherine and I should be together because of some silly premonition you have? That's great, Em!" he exploded. "How long has this been going on?"

Emily cringed at the sarcasm in Joshua's voice, but knew it was borne out of hurt. She may as well tell him, he knew the worst already. "Since you started courting." Desperately, she tried to undo the damage. "It really shouldn't matter what I think! Why are you putting so much stock in that? I can't tell you how to feel or what to think. That's all you! Only you can know that. If you're uncertain about something, you have to work that out yourself. You don't need me for that. Please stop putting such serious decisions on me; it's not fair!"

Quietly, which meant he was extremely mad, Joshua evenly asked, "Since...we...what?"

Now Emily felt a little heated. He'd asked for the truth, and she'd given it.

"Now I understand why you hesitated being the chaperone. Luckily for you, we were able to find someone else to chaperone, since you decided to become all distant. By the way," he dropped to a whisper. Not a good sign. "Thanks for your vote of confidence."

"Josh, please don't be mad. Like you said, it's a silly premonition. Before you two started courting, I thought you'd fit together nicely. You seemed to fit each other's needs perfectly!"

Still sarcastic, Joshua asked emphatically, "Oh, so now we don't?"

"No, I didn't say that! I still think you make a wonderful couple. I'm happy that you're happy! I honestly don't understand this… I'm genuinely sorry I brought it up."

"Katherine and I *will* get married, Em, whether you like it or not."

"Good, I sincerely hope you do." And she meant it now. He was being quite unreasonable and the quicker someone could tame him, the better.

Momentarily, Joshua forgot he hadn't even asked his intended yet. Hadn't even heard her thoughts on the subject, for that matter.

Emily had had enough. "You know, after you get engaged, you won't be able to come over here…at least, not as much as you do. And certainly not alone…like you are now."

Still riled, he didn't understand where she was going with this off-hand statement. "Yeah, so?"

"Perhaps you should start practicing that now."

Somehow, with that new realization, Emily saw things clearly. She knew, in part, what her strange feelings meant. She was beginning to see Joshua differently. Maybe now that she knew their relationship was going to change completely, she fully understood what she'd lose. She saw him not as a friend, but as something more. Oh. No. She was momentarily numbed and stunned at the same time. How could this be? She'd had that feeling six months after Jacob had died! Something was not right, but she couldn't deny it any longer. That's what she felt. She was dismayed to feel tears slipping down her face.

Mistaking the reason for the tears, Joshua immediately softened and assured Emily, "We'll still see each other. I can still come with the girls. We can even bring Katherine with us to visit. I know you miss her."

Dear, sweet Katherine. It broke Emily's heart knowing she had already betrayed her friend. She would definitely be guarding her thoughts and feelings closely from now on. Especially when either party was present.

"I better go, Em. Morning comes too soon when you're sleepin'." He smiled and winked.

Emily strangely felt lighter with her new resolve. She had a purpose now. She would work on getting over her hang-ups and simply be happy for her friends. This was all absurd and she could now try to get over it and move on.

"Thanks for agreeing to talk with me."

"I'm glad I was able to listen, even if I didn't help much. I'm real sorry about my outburst."

Joshua draped his arm over her shoulder in a brotherly gesture as they walked to the door.

"So, does this mean you approve after all?"

"Yes, Josh, it does. I always have. I feel better having talked about it."

"Good."

After bidding Joshua goodnight, Emily breathed a sigh of relief and sent up a prayer of gratitude.

Chapter 18: Aching Arms

Emily was excited! Katherine had come to visit. Emily hadn't felt true happiness for a very long time. As she and Katherine sat down to chat, Emily felt a sense of normalcy settle over her.

The talk eventually turned to Joshua and Katherine. Katherine confessed she wished things could move forward between the two of them.

"Maybe he doesn't want to be rushed," Emily suggested, trying to sound aloof.

"I don't know…I love him, but wish he'd give me a chance to show him how much I trust him."

"Patience, Katherine, you've only been courting a little less than a year. People may talk if you announce anything too soon. He's probably thinking of that." Emily smiled to herself, knowing that he'd had those exact thoughts not too long ago.

"I suppose, but we could keep it a secret…for a little while."

"Not in this town. There are no secrets."

Katherine was happy she could finally anticipate a day when Joshua would propose. The strange misgivings had been with her for so long, she was able to ignore them now. She now had herself convinced she had simply needed more time; that she wasn't used to the idea that Joshua had been a married man. She really did love him and wanted to be Mrs. Joshua Tyler someday. Hopefully it would be sooner rather than later, but Joshua seemed to be determined that it would be later rather than sooner.

Emily had a wild thought. "If Josh gets his act together, we could have a party! We could invite the Fabians, the Chadricks… well, all our friends."

Katherine was caught off guard. "What? Why?"

"Why not? It could be to announce your engagement! And for the simple fact that winter will be coming soon and we won't be able to travel anywhere very easily for a while once it sets in."

"But, what if he doesn't propose?"

"Oh, let's do it anyway. It'll be fun! Let's do it before we all have to stay cooped up inside." One reason Emily wanted a party, one that she couldn't say aloud, was that she needed a reason to smile and laugh again. She hadn't done either since Jacob...she couldn't finish her thought.

Gladdened at seeing her friend's cheery spirits return, and warmed by the idea, Katherine agreed. "Alright, let's do it!"

The two began talking details.

Silently, Katherine added a few names to the guest list... single male names.

Unaware of her friend's silent scheming, Emily prattled on. "It'll be so much fun!" But she still couldn't quite smile. Trying not to be ruled by her misgivings, Emily timidly asked, "Maybe a smaller, intimate gathering would be best. What do you think? We could just invite the Chadricks and Fabians. The Fabians could bring their daughter, Veda...she's an adult now, hard to believe! Since the Chadricks don't have any children that would make eight for supper."

Katherine slyly suggested, "How about ten? It's more of an even number," thinking of two more people she'd like to add.

"Ten's more of an even number than eight?"

"Well...it would make things...easier."

"How does adding *two* more, make things *easier*–"

"Let me worry about that, okay?"

"Okay," Emily agreed somewhat uncertainly. Why did she suddenly feel like Katherine was scheming?

Katherine was silently plotting, trying to think of the two most eligible bachelors in town.

The next Sunday at church, Emily found herself unable to concentrate on a single word Reverend Chadrick said from the pulpit. Joshua and Katherine had been making it a habit to sit together. For some reason, today of all days, it made her miss Jacob.

What wouldn't she give to be able to simply sit with Jacob in church once again. It was a small thing, but she'd been frequently surprised by how many little moments in a day made her miss Jacob. There were many small things she longed to share with him, if only one more time. Thinking of it then made her heart ache. They'd had their own silent language, understanding each other perfectly with a simple glance. On days like this, she could feel the depression barely beneath the surface, waiting to come up and grip her again. She dreaded the coming winter months, knowing she would be facing them alone again. No warm embraces to keep her chills away on icy winter nights. Emily involuntarily shivered.

Watching her friends was bittersweet. It was painful, yet she was also truly happy for them. Finally, she thought.

"Please rise for the closing hymn," Reverend Chadrick intoned.

Goodness! She had tuned out the entire sermon! Obediently, she flew to her feet and started singing.

The time for the party had been decided and the guests had been invited. All that remained was to prepare the food. The day of the party, two hours before guests were due to arrive, Emily and Katherine were in the Matthews' kitchen doing just that. The menu had been set to ham and collard greens, biscuits with apple butter, and mashed potatoes and gravy with blackberry cobbler for dessert.

As happens when women enter the kitchen to cook, general chit chat started. And, of course, Katherine had to broach the subject of her beloved Joshua.

Emily inwardly cringed, but didn't let it show. Not because she didn't want to talk about him, but because she lately seemed to fight a daily battle to keep the depression at bay. Talking about Joshua and Katherine brought it that much closer to the surface. The result was a strange mixture of emotions.

"And Joshua told her to mind her own business." Katherine giggled. "Isn't that cute?"

Emily had completely missed the story.

"I know Alyssa would be appalled if she ever heard me calling her cute...or relating *that* story. The twins are fourteen, after all. To think she had snuck in the hall while we said good-bye...and caught us kissing! Well, I never have been so embarrassed in all my life!"

Kissing. The last time Emily'd experienced that

phenomenon was the day…never mind, she told herself. She didn't want to think of that day. Ridiculously following on the heels of that thought, Emily wondered what it would feel like to kiss Joshua, then instantly rebuked herself. What had gotten into her? She went from the extreme of being on the cusp of depression regarding Jacob, to thinking about kissing Joshua!

'Lord, I love Katherine and don't want to hurt her. You've gotta help me here! I don't want to love Josh this way. Please take it away.'

Emily knew she had awhile before the wedding, especially since Joshua hadn't even proposed yet. Hopefully by then she would be able to think of Joshua in the proper way.

"Why, Emily, you are positively distracted! Are you sure you're up for this party? You haven't been yourself lately." Katherine's words were gentle.

"Who said that?" Emily nonchalantly asked, trying not to let her emotions show.

"No one had to say it. I can tell. Joshua has noticed, too. Enough to mention it to me. We were both a little surprised you wanted to have this party. We'd hoped it meant you were, er… coming around."

Joshua had been talking about her! Stupidly, this bit of information thrilled her, but was short-lived when she mentally kicked herself for thinking it.

'You're not a schoolgirl, anymore, Emily!'

Emily answered Katherine in what she hoped to be an even tone. "I guess I decided I needed more happiness in my life. Jacob would, no doubt, be disappointed in the way I've been acting. He'd want me to move on, not mope around." Quietly Emily turned away then to tend to the stove and hide her sudden tears.

Wasn't it time she stop all this crying? It had been over a year! Still crying over Jacob bordered on pathetic, didn't it? Emily hated people seeing her cry.

Katherine wisely didn't say a word. *'Lord, please help her broken heart mend. Please remind her of Joshua's and my friendship and that we love her and that she needn't hide her tears.'*

Emily composed herself and turned from the stove. "I

suppose it's time to set the table for our guests."

Joshua was the first to arrive, of course. To Emily, it seemed he was extremely early and it was an interminably long time before the next guests arrived. The time gave Emily an opportunity to get thoroughly put out by the inappropriate, to her, behavior Katherine and Joshua were exuding. They kept casting each other glances, obviously loaded with hidden meanings, and were outrageously flirtatious.

In reality, Joshua was only half an hour early and he and Katherine behaved in the same way they always had with each other. Good natured teasing and an occasional brush of the hand or some other innocent gesture.

Trying hard to sound offhand, Katherine mentioned, "Oh, Emily, I found two extra guests. I think you'll like them."

Emily didn't miss the conspiratorial wink Katherine gave Joshua. In other circumstances, Emily would have anticipated the excitement of trying to figure out who they were. However, Emily knew Katherine too well and didn't trust that wink nor the covert tone she'd picked up in her voice. In short, Emily didn't like what Katherine was implying.

The next guests arrived then, forcing Emily to concentrate on them. It was the Fabians, followed shortly by the Reverend and his wife. No sooner had Emily closed the door against the chilly night, than the last two guests arrived. It was a coincidence they came together, but when Emily realized who they were, she suddenly felt ambushed. The two bachelors confirmed Emily's fear that Katherine had been scheming. Sudden anger welled up inside her, but she quenched it. Now was not the time and the two innocent men had nothing to do with it. Her anger was directed at Katherine and Joshua, who had been in on the scheme. She couldn't believe their nerve! Did they not know she wasn't ready for this?

Katherine came up then and greeted the guests. "Why, hello, Doc Allison, Sheriff Alexander. Won't you come in?"

The new doctor and the sheriff?! Emily managed a tight smile and, for some unknown reason, felt herself curtsy! She then escaped to the safety of the kitchen, mumbling an excuse about checking on the food, and left an amused trio in the entryway.

In the kitchen, Emily chided herself for being crazy enough to think up this party. Suddenly, she wanted everyone gone and she wanted to be alone.

Thankfully, Katherine had had the presence of mind to show the guests to the sitting room, smoothing over Emily's abrupt behavior. As for Emily, she didn't care what those two men thought of her. Maybe now they'd be discouraged in pursuing her. On second thought, they *were* men. Maybe they hadn't found her behavior odd after all. Maybe they thought it perfectly normal for her to curtsy. Men didn't usually concern themselves with female behavior, much less try to figure it out.

She did have to admit that the look on the doc's and sheriff's faces had been rather priceless. The mental picture suddenly seemed funny to her and for the first time in nearly a year, she let out a little giggle. What started out as a little giggle, turned into full blown laughter, but she tried keeping it quiet. Their look of utter astonishment, coupled with Katherine's eyebrows raising nearly to her hairline in shock, making her eyes bulge wide, almost to the point of crossing in on themselves, had Emily leaning over the sink for support, shoulders shaking in silent glee, seriously questioning her sanity. In the middle of it all, she thought wildly that perhaps she was going a little mad. Surely the incident wasn't nearly so hysterical, but she couldn't seem to stop. Her emotions hadn't exactly been stable over the past few weeks…or, even the past few months, really.

Katherine came into the kitchen, looking for Emily, and found her slumped over the sink. Mistaking the emotion, she went over and put an arm around Emily's waist. Speaking in soothing tones, she tried her best to comfort her friend over her misjudgment in inviting the two bachelors. "Emily, dear, you really are overwrought. I'm so sorry I invited the doctor and the sheriff. It showed extreme lack of judgment. Perhaps it was too soon. I'm going to send everyone home."

Emily whirled around, causing Katherine to let go. Tears of mirth ran down her face as she protested, "Oh, don't do that!" She had barely caught her breath, and a giggle escaped. Suddenly, she was seized uncontrollably again. How good it felt! She could feel herself beginning to be free of the oppression she had been under.

The laughter was contagious, and Katherine found herself

joining in not knowing why, but she was relieved to see her friend laughing again. It had been too long.

Apparently the party in the other room heard their merriment and came to investigate. For, when Emily and Katherine turned around, they found themselves with an audience!

Quickly sobered, Emily composed herself. Politely, she invited, "Won't you please follow me back out to the dining room? Supper will be served shortly."

Emily was certain now that her erratic behavior had not earned her favors and she didn't care. She also knew it had earned gossip about her, but again, she didn't care. For the rest of the evening, Emily was on her best behavior and carried on smoothly.

In retrospect, Emily knew God had intervened on her behalf for the rest of that evening. If she hadn't ended up starting the evening in such high spirits, she knew she would've silently fumed at Katherine and Joshua all night. The dears did not deserve that. Besides, she would've missed out on getting to know the new, and widowed, doctor, George Allison as well as the sheriff, Roarke Alexander. They were both delightful men...and apparently not easily scared, so that was good.

The only letdown came at the end of the evening. Everyone except Joshua and Katherine had left. Joshua was getting ready to take his leave, so he was bidding Katherine good-bye with a chaste kiss. Emily had walked through from the dining room in time to see it, and fled up the stairs to escape. She hoped she hadn't been noticed.

Unfortunately, the stairs could be viewed from the entryway. As Joshua had pulled back, he happened to glance up and had seen Emily's haste.

Katherine's back had been toward the stairs and Emily had been surprisingly quiet, so Katherine was unaware of what had transpired.

As her friend, Joshua wanted to know if Emily was alright. As a taken man, he had to let her go. So, instead, he opened the door and let himself out

Chapter 19: The Bachelors

Emily suddenly found herself with two potential suitors. She was loathe to admit that she only looked at them as a mere distraction. They were both very acceptable gentleman, but they merely helped occupy her time and kept her from thinking of Joshua.

Her little diversion, however, was soon found to have a major downfall. When it was spread around that Emily was entertaining one doctor, George Allison, and the sheriff, Roarke Alexander, she suddenly found herself flocked with suitors. It was obvious women were scarce in the area, but Emily tried her best to graciously deter them. Some turned out to be extremely stubborn – or desperate, Emily wasn't sure which – and wouldn't take no for an answer.

It was still a blur to her on how it happened, but she found herself with three suitors in one day! At eleven o'clock that morning, armed with only her charm, her children, and Mrs. Chadrick in the sitting room as chaperone, Emily opened the door to Leverett Edwards.

"Hello, Mr. Edwards, won't you come in?"

"Thank you, Mrs. Matthews." He doffed his hat.

Emily suddenly felt very uncomfortable with having her name coming out of his lips. She was still a Mrs., in name only, true, but it made her feel unfaithful all the same.

"Please, call me Emily," she quickly amended.

"Alright, Emily."

Throughout the beginning conversation, Emily noticed that a good portion of Leverett's thick brown hair was turning gray. *'He's a little old for me, I think.'* As they continued to converse, she found herself distracted by this. *'Is it as inappropriate for a man to be asked his age, as it is for a woman?'* It wasn't that she'd never seen a man near her age without gray hair, it was just that, Leverett seemed to have *a lot* of it! *'How old* is *he?'* she couldn't help wondering again.

She knew that now that she was single, and there were very few available women to choose from, men of varying ages would be wanting to call. She couldn't fathom why anyone would particularly seek her out. Except that she was still somewhat young—younger than most of the bachelors—and could take care of a house. That was all. She idly wondered if any of her potential suitors were actually interested in getting to know her.

Emily couldn't see herself as she truly was. For starters, she still possessed her youthful looks, though a bit more mature than childhood. Yet, her golden tresses still shone; her eyes still sparkled green, telling the story of her soul; her skin was smooth and her cheeks held a tinge of pink. Her figure, which had dwindled during the year following Jacob's death, was starting to fill back out. And those were only her physical merits.

Unbeknownst to her, the bachelors and widowers of Lorraine did consider Emily's character and saw in her a good, wholesome woman. Naturally, they were also looking for companionship, which Emily herself longed for. Even more, they longed for love, acceptance, and understanding from someone who could fill their days with meaning. They, unlike Emily, were able to see in her all of those things and much more.

Leverett had always been a bachelor, but it didn't mean he didn't long for a family and love any less.

Emily inwardly cringed as the time seemed to drag by. She played the part of hostess well enough, she simply didn't think she cared for the company. Politeness reigned, however.

"How're things with you, Mr. Edwards?"

"Please, if I'm to call you Emily, you must call me Leverett. And I'm fine, fine, can't complain."

Emily wished now she hadn't insisted he use her first name. It had been an impulse to appease her guilty conscience. She was afraid that now they were on a first name basis, he'd want to become too familiar too quickly.

Emily had always hated small talk, finding it painful to mask what she truly felt. Still, she tried putting her guest at ease. Leverett seemed a little shy now that it was just the two of them. He hadn't seemed so after the services Sunday and had overheard her telling Joshua that he and Katherine could come by for dinner. Somehow, Leverett mistook that to mean she would be entertaining Joshua. Still fuzzy on the turn of events, Emily had heard herself extending an invitation to Leverett to call. It was completely not the way things were done and Emily still didn't know exactly how it had happened. Only that Leverett wiggled an invitation out of her.

In truth, Leverett had been relieved he had found a way to call on Emily. He'd been wanting to approach her for quite some time, but was too self-conscious to make the first move. Admittedly, he had seized on an opportunity that presented itself, and only felt a little remorseful for playing on Emily's sympathies to get himself an invitation.

"We shore do miss Josh at the mill," he mentioned at one point.

Emily had lost track of the conversation, but realized they were past the small talk and moving onto more familiar topics.

"Yes, well…" Emily was unsure what to say to that.

"Yeah, it's just not the same. He was our comic relief, to tell the truth. Our boss would come down hard on anyone he felt particularly irritated with that day. It was usually trivial matters, too. Anyway, Josh was real well-liked by ever'one."

A tiny frown creased Emily's brow. Perhaps that was why Joshua had jumped at her offer of employment. She hadn't known what problems there were, being wrapped up in her own woes. She honestly hadn't given it much thought – neither then nor since.

Curious now, Emily asked, "Were things bad at the mill?"

Quite honestly, Emily hadn't realized Leverett was employed at the mill. Perhaps this was why Joshua had seemed enthusiastic about Leverett calling on Emily. She supposed that if Joshua hadn't seen anything to worry about with Leverett, she ought to give him a fair chance.

"Things are getting better now. We have a new boss and he's changing things around. Unsafe procedures and machines were two main points of concern." Suddenly Leverett cleared his throat. "It's nothin' I'd care to discuss with a lady, beggin' yer pardon. I don't wanna offend delicate ears." He decided to change the subject and volunteered, "Josh talked about you and yer husband…he was real concerned about you after yer husband passed away. We was all grateful to you, offerin' him a job and all. He deserved to get outta the mill the most." More to himself, he added, "He couldn't say enough good things about you."

Without a thought as to how eager she sounded, Emily breathlessly asked, "What did he say?"

Unluckily for Emily, Leverett was rather a sharp man and picked up on her tone quickly. He got a thoughtful look on his face, sat back, and simply stated, "I'm not who yer lookin' fer. I shoulda known someone else woulda snagged yer heart."

Puzzled, Emily sat back in her seat as well and carefully asked, "What do you mean?"

"I mean, I knew I wouldn't be yer first choice as a suitor. I didn't realize you already had someone in mind." He chuckled. "It never hurts to try, though. Yer a real nice lady and yer perty and sweet and kind. Any man would be lucky to have you, and would be happy to, as well."

Blushing at such compliments, Emily tried protesting, "N-no, that's not truly the way it is." Guiltily, she knew that was exactly the way it was. Except for the part of being had.

"Yer heart is set on someone else. I won't say who, to avoid causing you further embarrassment. I promise not to say anything, but you need to be careful."

Leverett rose to go, but turned at the door. He kindly left her with a word of advice. "You are a desirable woman, Emily, don't let anyone tell you different or make you think otherwise."

"Care for another cup of tea, Keary?" Emily asked. Her second suitor she had known for years, as they had grown up together. If nothing else, Emily felt he'd be a safe reason to stop all future suitors. She knew all she had to do was say the word and he'd act accordingly. Truth be told, if she needed to remarry simply for her own sake and safety, she wouldn't mind it being Keary. He had recently moved to the area from their childhood hometown.

Keary Somerville was solidly built with broad shoulders. He wore his black hair slicked back. His friendly blue eyes were open and honest, inviting anyone to confide in him.

Three years ago, Keary had become a widower. Not wanting to stay in the big city alone anymore, he'd decided to find a nice, small town to reside in and happened into Lorraine. Keary

travelled a lot for his job. He was a buyer of cattle for a local
herdsman. He, Emily, and Jacob had kept in touch. In the past, his
job had brought him through Lorraine and now it seemed the
timing was right for Keary to make Lorraine his more permanent
residence. Well, as permanent as a travelling cattle buyer could be.

Keary and Emily had already been visiting for well over an
hour and the supper hour was approaching.

"Keary, you'll have to bring your teacup and accompany me
to the kitchen. I need to get supper started. Kenneth Roan is due
promptly at seven."

"Hmm....Kenneth Roan. He's a bit pompous, if you ask
me."

"Well, I didn't ask you, now did I?" Emily teased.

Emily started supper and let the rein on her thoughts loose.
Her conversation with Leverett bothered her and, despite enjoying
her time with Keary, it would creep into the back of her mind. She
needed to explore it and what it meant. She was uncomfortable
with how obviously transparent she'd been. She hadn't meant to
hurt his feelings, but was afraid she had. And if Leverett could tell,
were others able to, also? Unhappily, she knew all the suitors were
a waste of her time and theirs. But now that she was in so deep,
how was she to get out of it? She knew she hadn't been ready for
courtship yet.

Deciding to promote Keary to confidante, since she no longer
had Joshua, Emily asked, "Keary, could I ask you something? It's
about a conversation I had with Leverett Edwards earlier."

"Good man, I like him."

Emily smiled her agreement. "He said something…
interesting earlier and I wondered if I really am transparent after
all."

Her words made no sense and Keary looked at her curiously.
"Tell me about it."

She related her whole visit with Leverett. When she finished,
a shadow momentarily crossed Keary's face and all he uttered was,
"Hmmmm…."

"What's that supposed to mean?"

"It means, I happen to agree with him." Teasing Emily,
Keary conspiratorially added, "And I, too, know who it is."

"Oh, you men think you are so mysterious," Emily

sarcastically remarked.

And, yet, Emily knew they were right. She simply couldn't believe she was so transparent. She wondered who else may have figured out her little secret. Not Joshua, surely...hopefully....

Samantha came in then, interrupting the moment. Upon seeing Keary, she started backing out of the kitchen. "Sorry, Ma, I didn't know ya still had a caller."

Emily was feeling uncomfortable with Keary's spot-on observation and welcomed Samantha's diversion. "It's okay, sweetie. Come in and sit a spell."

'*Coward*,' Emily's conscience pricked.

"I thought I smelled supper cookin' and wanted to come see if it was done."

"Nope, not yet, but almost."

Samantha sat and talked with Keary for quite awhile as Emily finished supper.

"Why don't you go wash up, Samm? And tell the others supper will be ready soon."

Samantha bounded out of the kitchen to do her mother's bidding.

"Well, I guess that's my cue to leave." Keary got up and turned toward Emily. Her back was against the sink and her arms were folded across her chest, a defiant stance.

"Em, could I call on you again?"

That was not what she had expected him to say. Especially due to the secret he now knew about her. Insanely, her heart started beating wildly. She wasn't sure if it was because he actually wanted to see her again, or if it was because she was unsure of how she felt about it and didn't know how to respond. Already she knew she had no physical attraction to the man, although the other single ladies of the town would surely think she was crazy. She simply allowed that it had to do with the fact that she and Keary had known each other so long. Perhaps that was why they definitely had a connection that pulled them together. That alone meant a lot to Emily. She felt her options were definitely limited, seeing that Joshua wasn't available and she'd need to get over him sooner or later. She felt as if she were behaving like a schoolgirl!

"Um, y-yes, Keary, that would be acceptable," she finally

conceded.

With a boyish grin and a quick "good-bye", he was gone.

"Hey, where's Mr. Somerville?" Samantha asked, disappointed, as she entered the kitchen.

"He's gone."

"He's not stayin' for supper?"

Christopher came in then. "Samm said Mr. Somerville was here. Where's he at?"

"Gone," said Samantha, downcast.

Brianna and Hailey entered in time to hear Emily say, "He just left."

"Aw!" Brianna pouted.

"Mama? Is Mr. Somerville a suitor or a friend?" Hailey asked.

"Both, dear," Emily replied, surprised to find herself blushing.

She noticed the marked silence of her children and looked at them. "What?"

Four pairs of eyes exchanged glances. Christopher spoke for the group. "It's just that…well, how come you have so many men around?"

Emily tried not to chuckle in her nervousness. Put like that, it made her sound like a common hussy. She tried to defend herself. "There have only been two, so far. And only one more is coming tonight." Sighing, she conceded, "I know it's strange, but I want to see what my options are."

"First off, there was the doctor and the sheriff and then the two from tonight, if you're going to count Mr. Somerville. That's more than two. Secondly…options for what?" Brianna demanded.

Exasperated, Emily chided, "You watch your tone, young lady. And I think you know good and well what! We've been over this before, anyway. We need a man around here. And I'm lonely for another…companion…and I'm sick of seein' people like your uncle Josh and Katherine Taylor-Ryan bein' together while I have no one." *'Well played, Em, you impudent child,'* she silently rebuked.

There was silence and Emily was mortified she had shared her feelings so openly with her children. Having Keary around would be a good thing. At least she'd have someone to talk to about all her feelings, instead of spewing them all over her children. Her face flamed and tears sprang to her eyes. "Oh, dear," she uttered, seeing her children's shocked, open-mouthed faces. Parents weren't supposed to express their feelings so openly with their children. Especially about their love lives! She turned and calmly exited the room.

    Emily had been ready for the pasty-faced, red headed Kenneth Roan to leave the moment he'd arrived. After her outburst in the kitchen, she had not felt like having visitors. Mrs. Chadrick had been gracious and had comforted her the best she could, but Emily gently dismissed her after supper. The children were there and Emily already knew she would not want anything progressing any further with Kenneth Roan.

    Here she was, half an hour after his arrival, and she'd already had to swallow a scream. The man never seemed to stop talking! He had the irritating habit of answering his own questions and repeating random words.

    The first portion of the conversation went something like this:

Kenneth: Glad it hasn't quite froze over yet, right, right?

Emily: Yes, it–

Kenneth: Oh, right, right, wouldn't be good for your crops, right?

Emily: Yes, that's–

Kenneth: I'm sure you have precautions. You deal with this every year, don't'cha, don't'cha?

Emily: Yes, we–

Kenneth: Yep, you do, you do; of course you do!

'*Just say it once, Kenneth, and be done with it*!' she wanted to scream.

    Her façade, however, showed quite the opposite. She had pasted a small, demure smile on her lips. The feigned listening position had been her pose for the last several minutes as he had rambled on about…something. And he hadn't seemed to notice that neither her expression nor her posture had changed. Nor that she had given up trying to make any comments.

    Finally, the time came that she could politely, and

surprisingly with the little grace she had left, show him to the door.

Leaning against the closed door, she sighed. Never again would she entertain three men in one day!

Joshua felt a little giddy. He had taken the stagecoach to the city a few days before and was finally getting back, carrying the trophy he had gone after, so to speak. He could hardly contain his excitement. The best part was that his daughters were in full support.

That evening, the five worked together to put their plan into action. The next evening was the big event and everything needed to be perfect.

At long last, it was time to move forward to the next phase of the plan and Joshua was a bundle of nerves. "Alright, girls, I'm off! You know what to do, but remember, I'm trusting you to finish before I get back."

"We know what to do, Pa, now go!" Alyssa urged.

Joshua hoped the plan wouldn't be spoiled as he glanced at the sky. It had been a gray October day and, although only five o'clock, the darkness was starting to surround him when he finally reached his destination.

He hopped to the ground and forced himself to calmly walk up the steps to the small house and rap on the door. It seemed an eternity before anyone answered.

"Joshua! What a surprise!"

Katherine stood silhouetted against the faint light coming from her home. Joshua's breath caught at the soft beauty it created. Her hair was golden fire and her cheeks, rosy. Her eyes shone like sapphires. The sapphires gazed at him inquisitively as he felt himself get lost in them.

"We don't have a chaperone, or I'd ask you in. I suppose there's a reason you're here," Katherine broke into his reverie.

"Tonight, we don't need a chaperone," he answered somewhat mysteriously. "Bundle up, I'm takin' you for a ride."

Giving him a puzzled look, Katherine turned around and went inside to comply.

Joshua prayed the final preparations were being taken care of at the moment. He wanted everything to go perfectly. This was only the second time he'd done this, the first not being quite as romantic. He quickly pushed that memory away.

At last, Katherine, bundled from head to toe, emerged.

"You won't get too cold, will you?" Joshua asked anxiously. Everything had to go perfectly.

"No, I have on my warmest clothes. Where are we going?"

"You'll soon find out. Here's a blanket."

Katherine giggled, "Joshua, can't you simply *tell* me what you have in mind?"

After mounting the wagon, Joshua simply leaned over and whispered in her ear, "Trust me."

Joshua thoroughly tucked Katherine into the wagon so she wouldn't be cold and drove the team as hard as he dared, unable to contain his excitement any longer. As he approached his house, he could see a faint glow coming from the front garden. That was a good sign. Everything must be in place. Turning to her, he requested, "I would like to put a blindfold on so you get the full effect of the surprise. May I?"

She suspiciously eyed him, but agreed.

He carefully helped Katherine down from the wagon, and walked her to the garden gate. "Okay, I'm going to take the blindfold off now." Together they stepped through the gate and gasped as one. Joshua hadn't been sure what to expect, but nothing this spectacular had entered his imagination.

His girls had done an amazing job of transforming the garden into a magical paradise. Candles were everywhere; hanging from trees in craftily thought up containers; covering every flat surface imaginable. Joshua knew the girls had spent weeks making the candles and he'd even helped fashion special holders so they'd be safe and protected from catching anything on fire. His daughters had certainly been creative in thinking of ways to cover the garden in candles to create a romantic atmosphere. Right in the middle of the garden, spread on a huge blanket, was a picnic. Surrounded by candles, of course.

Marveling at the wonder, Joshua and Katherine had ambled around the garden, stopping at last by the picnic. When Katherine turned to look back at Joshua, he was down on one knee. Reaching out, he clasped one of her hands in both of his own.

"I have something I need to ask," he began. He then let go of her hand and dug inside his vest pocket to pull out a small box. It was the treasure he had brought back. Opening the box, the candlelight seemed to make the contents gleam.

Katherine saw the golden ring then. A flashing blue turquoise, her birthstone, was surrounded by two smaller diamonds, one on either side. Her breath caught.

Trying to steady his nerves and his voice, Joshua quietly asked, "Katherine Taylor-Ryan, would you consider giving me the honor and privilege of being my wife?"

Tears sprang to Katherine's eyes then. She found herself on her knees in front of Joshua, embracing him and fervently whispered, "Yes."

Emily and Keary were enjoying another visit with one another, when a knock sounded at the door.

Keary teased, "Expecting *another* suitor?"

Emily chuckled as she opened the door. She was met by, "We're engaged!" proclaimed by Joshua and Katherine in unison.

Dumbfounded, Emily stumbled back. Finding her voice, she quickly pronounced, "Congratulations! Come, tell us *all* about it." In fact, it was the last thing she wanted to hear about. Of course, that would be impolite. When someone came to tell you about their engagement, the proper thing to do was to listen. Especially when it involved your two closest friends in the world.

Keary watched her with amusement. *'She's a good little actress, I'll give her that.'*

Upon entering the room, Joshua noticed Keary then. "Sorry, Em, I didn't realize you had company. We can tell you the details later." Joshua turned back towards the door.

"You most certainly *will not*, Joshua Tyler. Now, you two sit down and tell us everything."

'Very good,' Keary added with a silent chuckle.

Emily dutifully ooohed and aaahed over the ring, making a huge effort to show her support outwardly. Inwardly, she was having a serious dilemma. Of course she was happy for them; as happy as she could be, in any case. At the same time, she realized that this engagement meant a huge change for all of them. A change she knew had been coming. She only felt utterly left behind, was all, as this happy couple started a new life. How childish! Self-pity. She loathed self-pity in anyone, but it was especially hated when it came from inside.

For the rest of the evening, Emily continued listening and commenting in all the right places, as Joshua and Katherine reveled in their joyous news. Emily watched Joshua's eyes light up as he listened to Katherine regale her audience with the details of their engagement. She was stupidly and childishly envious that she wasn't the object of Joshua's affection. It was made more bitter when he caught her eye, winked, then went back to giving his undivided attention to his future bride. How dare he wink at her! was her initial, indignant reaction. But she suffered in silence as she realized he wouldn't be doing that anymore in the future. She felt silly as she realized she'd miss his winks, whether made in jest, encouragement, or just because, as that one had been. Oh, what was wrong with her? And why hadn't God taken her feelings for Joshua away? It was pretty cruel, if you asked her. Of course, God wasn't in the habit of asking. He simply acted as He saw fit for the situation. And He always had a reason. That thought made her feel uneasy. What reason would God have for not taking her feelings for Joshua away?

Chapter 20: A Missing Link

"Mama?" Brianna called.

"Yes, darlin'?" Emily called from the kitchen. Samantha and Hailey were helping her get supper on the table.

Coming into the room, Brianna inquired, "Are Uncle Josh and the girls comin' over for supper tonight?"

"No, they aren't."

"Why not?"

"I suppose they have other plans."

"It's sure been awhile since they've come over for, well, anything."

"I'm sure they're busy with weddin' plans and Miss Taylor-Ryan. I wonder if she'll let you call her aunt once they're married," Emily mused, discouraged to hear the thought spoken aloud.

"I don't think I'd like that," Hailey piped up then.

"Why not?" Emily asked.

"She's too serious for that nonsense, as she'd call it."

"Oh, I don't think so. Yer probably thinkin' of the way she is at school. She has to be serious there, she's the teacher."

"Even when she's here, she's not a whole lotta fun." Brianna rejoined the conversation.

"Josh says the girls really like her and are excited about her bein' their mother."

"Yeah, but only because then, we'll get a new teacher," Samantha explained.

"Samantha, what an awful thing to say! I'm sure their excitement has nothing to do with her no longer bein' the teacher. You like her as a teacher. At least, you used to! You couldn't quit talkin' about her."

"She's a nice teacher an' all, but after that first year, she got really strict," Brianna stubbornly rebutted.

"I hope Miss Taylor-Ryan will still let 'em come an' play in the creek," Samantha voiced, wistfully.

"Yeah. And will she still wanna come to our house for Christmases? Do you think she'll let 'em come for Christmas, Ma? It's only a few weeks away," Brianna pointed out.

"I'm sure they'll come. They've never missed a Christmas with us. Good grief, yer actin' as if she's an ogre! What has gotten into you? You liked her well enough before she got engaged to Uncle Josh."

"We kinda, uh, think that's the problem." Hailey looked sideways at her sisters. "We think that, uh, she…well, she's the, uh…sorta the reason Uncle Josh isn't around much."

"Nonsense, Hailey. They have a weddin' to plan, after all. They're bound to be a little busy."

Still, it gave Emily pause for thought. It did seem as though Joshua had made himself plenty scarce since announcing his engagement a few weeks ago.

"I want 'em to come for Christmas," Samantha wished aloud.

"I haven't had a chance to talk to Uncle Josh, but I'm sure they will. Like I said before, they haven't missed one yet."

"Yes, but they didn't come for Thanksgiving." Brianna, once again, had to point out the obvious.

"True." The memory brought back the hurt Emily had felt when Joshua sprang the news on her.

It had been a week before Thanksgiving and there had been a knock at the door. When Emily had answered it and found Joshua standing there, it should have been a sign that something was wrong. Emily didn't know when the last time was that Joshua had knocked on her door…other than the night of his engagement, but that had been for effect and the element of surprise.

"Hello, Emily," he had greeted quietly. Now *that* should have been her clue. And the fact that he'd used her full first name. He usually called her Em.

It was then that Emily had felt sick to her stomach. '*He has bad news,*' she thought.

Joshua had stepped in and, hat in hand, explained. "Katherine and I have decided to have Thanksgiving as a family."

"Alright," Emily hesitated, not sure where he was going.

'*That's not news,*' she thought. '*Somethin' is goin' on here, and I'm not gettin' it.*'

"Do you want to hold it at your house, then?" she asked, still unsure, but knowing she'd just asked a silly question.

That's when the blow came. Joshua explained. "No, I mean, just us…the girls and Katherine and I…sort of as a family. You know, to see what holidays will be like…in the future."

"In the future? Family?" Emily couldn't help dumbly repeating. "I thought we were your family." Emily wished she hadn't been so obtuse. She tried hiding her hurt and disappointment.

"Of course you are, Em! We'll still have holidays with you, too…sometimes. We think it'd be good to have just the six of us this year at Thanksgiving. That way, we can start our own traditions…as a family." There was that tag on the end again! 'As a family.' But he spoke of it as if he were unsure. As if the words were just as foreign in his mouth as they were for Emily to hear them.

Emily worked even harder at not being hurt and angry. They'd only celebrated every Thanksgiving together since becoming friends over thirteen years ago, but what did that matter now? Apparently it didn't!

Emily tried making her voice sound understanding. "If you think that's best."

At least she had already invited Keary over, so they wouldn't be totally alone on Thanksgiving.

"Mama? Mama!" Hailey brought Emily back to reality. "I said, I think the gravy's done."

Emily looked down at the pan she had been absently stirring. "Thank you…uh, you girls go wash up. And find Chris. It's time to eat."

Emily decided she needed to talk to Joshua about Christmas…without Katherine around.

"When are we gonna see you again?" Brianna asked Alexis during their dinner hour at school the next day.

"I don't know. We still go to Miss Taylor-Ryan's after school sometimes."

"Yeah, but Christmas break starts next week. Uncle Josh shouldn't be workin' much by then."

"No, but we're pretty busy. He's wantin' us to help plan the weddin'.'"

"Well, we all miss you, including Mama."

"We miss you all, too. I wish we could come over more...like old times."

There was a moment of silence, then it was broken by Brianna. "So, what does Miss Taylor-Ryan think of y'all helpin' with the weddin'?"

"She's alright. Sometimes she gets snippy, but Pa says she's only nervous, and all new brides are nervous."

"Isn't it gonna be strange callin' her 'Ma'?"

A peculiar look crossed into Alexis' eyes. "We aren't gonna call her 'Ma.'"

Brianna was flabbergasted. "You aren't? What on earth are ya gonna call her, then?"

Alexis answered awkwardly. "What we always call her outside school...Miss Katherine."

Brianna was really astonished now. "MISS KATHERINE?!"

"Shh!"

'*I wonder what Mama will make of this.*' Brianna tucked the tidbit of information away for later.

Another moment passed then Brianna piped up again. "Are you gonna join us for Christmas?"

Big tears welled up in Alexis' eyes then and Brianna was sorry she brought the subject up. It was obviously a sensitive topic for Alexis.

"I hope so. I really missed spending Thanksgiving with all of you."

"We missed you, too. Why didn't you tell Uncle Josh how you felt? We told Mama we didn't like all those suitors comin' over, and now she doesn't have any more come over. Except Mr. Somerville, but Mama says he isn't a suitor anymore, just a friend. He even came over for Thanksgiving. It was so much fun! We like him."

"We used to be able to talk to Pa like that but, now that he's engaged, he doesn't seem to hear us anymore."

"I hear that love can do that to a man," Brianna confided, solemnly. "They get all confounded or somethin', and their brains don't work right."

Alexis gave Brianna a funny look, but Miss Taylor-Ryan

came out, ringing the bell before Alexis could ask how Brianna came by the information.

"Speak of the devil," Alexis muttered.

Horrified at her friend's language, Brianna hissed, "Alexis! That's swearing!"

"No it isn't."

"Yes, I think it is."

"All I know is, she's changed, and so has Pa."

"You can't be serious!" Emily exclaimed when Brianna told her of her conversation with Alexis. The Tyler girls had always been like daughters to her and she didn't know if she could stand by and let them be so unhappy. On the other hand, was it any of her business anymore? "That is simply ridiculous."

"I told Alexis she should have told Uncle Josh how they felt about spending Thanksgiving without us. I told her it worked with us when we told you we didn't like all those callers comin' over. You listened to us. Maybe Uncle Josh will listen to reason."

Emily stopped her pacing and smiled at her daughter's 'grown up talk.'

Smilingly, Emily informed her daughter, "I didn't stop having suitors merely because you four requested it. I stopped because *I* wasn't in a place where I was ready for them. I am still your mother and make the ultimate decision. But, yes, I did take your feelings into consideration. And I'm glad all of you feel you can talk to me."

"You shoulda saw her, Ma," Brianna rallied. "Alexis looked real sad and pitiful. She really wants to spend Christmas with us. It sounds like they all do...well, all but Uncle Josh."

"That's still up to Uncle Josh." He surely wouldn't miss Christmas with them, would he? Not after missing Thanksgiving! Emily had sudden misgivings.

Emily *did* understand and respect their privacy, but this was a holiday, and enough was enough! It was past the point where it only affected her and her children...his own daughters were upset about it, too. She was all ready to make him see it her way, but had to remember that he was a grown man and could make his own decisions...even if they were bad ones, she couldn't help silently adding. Emily hated how it seemed to be affecting Madison, Alexis, Alyssa, and Kayla.

"Did you talk to any of the other three girls?" Emily asked.

"No, they were somewhere else at the time. I talked to her at dinnertime, but didn't want to bring it up again on the walk home. It seems that's the only time we really get to spend time with them is on the walk home. I didn't want to spoil the time with them. It seems we *never* get to see them or talk to them anymore."

Emily was trying harder and harder to fight the urge to have a little chat with Joshua.

Impulse won over the next day. Emily found herself marching down the lane to Joshua's house. She boldly walked in without knocking. Once he was married, she knew she wouldn't be so brazen. But that was always the way it had been at each other's houses.

"Josh!" she called.

It took a few moments, but she finally heard a faint reply. "In here." She followed the voice to the sitting room. Emily stood in the doorway until Joshua looked up from his writing table.

"Emily!" he seemed genuinely surprised, yet pleased, to see her.

"Expecting someone else?" She couldn't quite erase the haughtiness from her tone.

He hesitated, thrown off by her demeanor.

"No…" he answered uncertainly. Getting a little irritated at her unwarranted behavior, he curtly replied, "I'm only surprised because I thought I made our feelings about our privacy clear, that's all. I figured you'd be more thoughtful about it now that I'm engaged."

Thoroughly riled, Emily retorted, "Hush up, Josh! You and the girls…and *only* you five…are expected for supper one week from today, at our house. And be prepared to defend yourself about any decisions you've made concerning Christmas that might exclude us."

Emily couldn't remember the last time she'd been that forward with anyone! It felt kinda good. And at the same time, she felt a little ashamed.

Joshua wasn't sure how he ended up feeling like the naughty little boy, but Emily had certainly put him in his place. Or so it seemed. He couldn't remember Emily ever talking to him, or even Jacob, in such a manner! Deciding to be appeasing, he agreed, "We can come for supper...the five of us. As for Christmas, Katherine and I haven't finalized our plans yet."

"You have a week to do so."

Emily would've laughed at Joshua's startled expression, had she not been so upset. She rounded on him then.

"Do you know how your daughters feel? Do you know how they felt about Thanksgiving? Do you know how they feel about Christmas? Do you know how they feel about *anything*?" Emily had placed her fists on Joshua's writing table and was leaning forward into his face. Emily was suddenly aware she may have crossed a line. Stepping back, she held her breath and waited for Joshua's response.

Instead of rising to her ire, Joshua simply raised his eyebrows. Then he did something very irritating to Emily, he scooted his chair back. In a slightly mocking tone, he stated, "I sense you are upset about something," then grinned. And winked.

Absurdly, his bit of quick wit made Emily cool a little. Maybe she should've gotten off her high horse and simply explained herself. After all, she didn't want to come to blows with Joshua. Yet, that's what she was suddenly aware she'd been preparing for.

Straightening up, Emily decided to be rational. "Alright, Josh, look, I tried to be understanding about Thanksgiving. I would like you to try and understand our side of it now. It really affected Chris, Brianna, Samm, and Hailey. We're your family. We're all each other has. They missed you and the girls and so did I. I don't think you realize how it affected your own girls, too. You may wanna talk to them about it. And if you're remotely entertaining the notion of doing the same with Christmas, you may wanna talk to them and see how they feel about it first. We all miss you like crazy and it seems like it's been awhile since we've seen any of you."

"Thank you, Emily, for bringing this to my attention. I'm guessing you've heard about it second hand from one of yours from one of mine at school." Joshua was suddenly ready to be done with the uncomfortable conversation.

"Yes, Brianna was quite upset that Alexis was so broken up over it."

Joshua dropped his gaze a moment and it looked to Emily as if he was contemplating something. He seemed about to speak, but then closed his mouth. When he looked back at Emily, she could see pain in his expression. All he said, however, was "For what it's worth, we missed spending Thanksgiving with you, too." He seemed to add all too quickly, "We had a nice Thanksgiving... but it wasn't the same without the rest of our family."

Emily was touched. She had thought all along that he had preferred it this way, but it turned out he may not have enjoyed it as much as she thought. "Thank you for saying that, Josh." She was surprised at the amount of relief that flooded through her, relief she hadn't expected to feel. "We all missed you, especially Chris. You know he looks up to you. He misses Jacob a lot and he needs a man around he knows he can trust. He's way too young for the responsibility of being man of the house, yet that's what he's had to become." Unthinkingly, Emily's tone had become soft.

Joshua leaned back in his chair and folded his hands behind his head. Concern etched his face. "You know I've always thought of Chris as the son I never had."

Emily knew he'd said so before, but hearing Joshua reiterate it now meant a lot to her. Before she could get weepy, Emily said her good-byes, but at the doorway, Joshua's voice stopped her.

"I'm really sorry about hurting your feelings, Em."

Emily half-turned, stopped, then merely nodded, and let herself out.

Chapter 21: Supper Conversation

The rest of the week, excitement was building in the Matthews' home. Emily had told her children the good news of the anticipated visit from their friends. Much thought went into the preparation for the meal.

More than once during it all, Emily asked herself why she was going to so much trouble for one simple meal. She'd decided to make his favorite meal of fried chicken, mashed potatoes with thick cream gravy, green beans she had canned the previous summer, and fluffy buttermilk biscuits, washed down by milk. Following that, she'd planned on his favorite dessert, apple pie with plenty of black coffee. She tried to convince herself she merely wanted their visit to be nice, but knew there was more to it than that. She didn't want to explore the why for fear of what she'd discover.

Had she been brave enough to explore, she would have discovered jealousy. Dirty jealousy of Joshua's time being taken up with Katherine, as illogical as it seemed. In some ways, she felt Joshua was choosing Katherine over her. And, simply put, she was jealous they had each other and she was alone. In a manner of speaking, she was trying to win Joshua over. That was exactly why she decided she wouldn't explore the why and naively chose to believe that she was simply being nice...and that was all.

"Come on, Mama, the biscuits are done." Brianna was talking through her mother's bedroom door.

Emily, at present, was primping – primping! – for Joshua's arrival. Why...that was still beyond her.

"They'll be here any minute," Brianna pestered. "Should I go ahead and take the biscuits out of the oven?"

"Yes, yes, take them out – and set the table!" Emily hollered back. Then as an afterthought, "And y'all wash up – an' leave me be – I'm primpin'!" As soon as the words left her mouth, Emily turned pink. She heard footsteps fade away and fervently hoped Brianna hadn't heard the last part.

Turning to her reflection, Emily asked, "Why am I doin' this? Who cares what I look like? He certainly won't!" Nonetheless, she leaned forward and pinched her cheeks. "Ouch!" A sigh escaped. "That's what I get for vanity."

Emily critically surveyed her appearance. She had secured her hair so tightly, not a tendril even dare escape. In her eyes, her hair was her downfall. It was so wavy, it was almost untamable.

She had chosen a green dress to complement her eyes. It was a dress she kept for special occasions and now worried it would be obvious she was trying too hard. It was a dark green taffeta with a lighter green stripe. The cut of the dress slimmed her nicely, yet kept her features softly round. Besides the cloth covered buttons running from the waist to neck, the only other adornment was the ruffle at the throat.

Before she became too obsessed with her appearance, she hurried down to the kitchen. Presently, there was a knock on the door and a cheerful voice called out, "Hello! Anyone home?"

Someone informed the voice, "Mama's in the kitchen."

She knew who the voice belonged to, so long had she heard it. Emily looked up in time to see Joshua walk in. Unexpectedly, her heart gave a lurch. Nor did she expect her breath to get caught in her throat! He looked good...really good. And she was behaving quite irrationally. How many times had he entered this very house...this very kitchen?

'This is ridiculous! It's Josh, for heaven's sake!'

"Like what you see?" Joshua teased, his dark eyes dancing with merriment.

Great! He'd caught her staring.

Emily felt her cheeks flush. She brightly greeted, "Hello, Josh. Supper's about ready. I'll go call the children."

"Don't bother them. They're catching up; something you and I should be doing."

"Alright...how have you been? I suppose I wasn't exactly cordial the last time we talked." Gulp. That was rather forward. 'Emily, calm down!'

Joshua chuckled deep, a sound that Emily could never tire of hearing. "No, you certainly weren't. I gotta say, though, I don't exactly blame you. We did kinda drop our plans on you unexpectedly."

Emily glanced at Joshua sharply. "Oh, I don't know…I may have been a bit rough…sorry about that."

Joshua impulsively put his hand over Emily's, making her look at him again. Emily's stomach fluttered. "Let's try this again…how are you *really*, Em?"

Emily glanced at her hand, then into his eyes. Sucking in a silent breath to steady her nerves, she ventured, "Fine, can't complain."

What was she supposed to do? Tell him the truth? Confess her love and that she was jealous of Katherine? Tell him the whole sordid truth? She didn't think *that* was a good idea!

"Emily," Joshua insisted, "you can talk to me. Nothing's changed. I hope you know that. You can *always* talk to me."

Joshua went to sit at the small kitchen table as Emily put the finishing touches on the supper.

"I know," Emily forced herself to answer, trying to sound convincing. He was wrong. She couldn't possibly talk to him anymore, at least, not like they used to. Especially now. And she wondered how Katherine would feel about it if she did.

"Keary's been keeping me company." She tried to sound off hand. "He's becoming a dear friend. We've sorta picked up our friendship where it left off when Jacob and I left home."

Joshua couldn't explain it, but he suddenly felt disconcerted at the news. He didn't want Emily to find someone to replace him. At least, that's what it felt like she was doing. Truth be told, he had missed Emily and the children. He knew he had neglected them sorely. He knew it would be different, but he hadn't counted on how much. He wished Emily and Katherine could rekindle their friendship, then things could go back to the way they were…the way they *should* be in his opinion. And yet, he knew that Katherine was partly to blame for withdrawing from Emily, too.

Forcing a chuckle, Joshua protested, "I hope you aren't replacing me."

"Josh, I could never replace you." It came out more matter-of-fact than she had intended, almost cold. To cover her confused feelings, she turned to start carrying dishes to the dining room table.

Joshua got up to help, not at all sure now how the evening would go.

The conversation was kept light and informational. Most of it was catching up with one another. The inevitable eventually happened, as talk turned to Christmas.

"Are we gonna come here for Christmas, Papa?" Madison asked.

Joshua quickly glanced up. "I'm so sorry, Em. I forgot to ask Katherine about our plans. I know that was partly the reason you wanted us over – to discuss Christmas."

"I wanted all of you over because it's been forever since we've seen you; since it's felt like old times around here!" Emily protested, feeling twinges of hurt that the matter hadn't seemed important to Joshua. Of course she was being unreasonable. It wasn't as if that should or would be the first thing on Joshua's mind. However, Emily had to admit to herself that she was, indeed, disappointed. She gave a deep sigh. How she longed to be done caring about this man! It seemed to bring nothing but pain. Besides, it wouldn't matter in a couple of months, anyway. He'd be married, and she'd have to keep her distance. Emily didn't think she'd *want* to go near him, anyway, it'd be too painful. It seemed all she had done in the last year was try to avoid pain and she was tired of it.

Almost teasing, Emily suggested, "Then why don't you decide and let Katherine know your plans? You are the man in the relationship, are you not?"

It had occurred to Emily that Joshua seemed to be putting a lot of stock in what Katherine said these days and maybe he needed to make his own decisions. Especially concerning his own daughters.

"Emily, we don't do things like that. She's going to be my wife and needs to be part of the decision-making."

"Daddy, we *really* wanna come over here," Kayla pleaded. "Please, Daddy, we didn't get to for Thanksgiving."

Emily suddenly felt ashamed she'd put Joshua in this position with his daughters. He really shouldn't have to make a decision right then with all of them obviously hoping for a positive, in their eyes, outcome. But she couldn't help being irked that he seemed to blatantly disregard their feelings, and so, without thought, rallied, "It's their holiday, too, you know."

'*Stay out of it, you ninny! You're crossing a line!*' her mind screamed.

Too late, the dark look had come into Joshua's eyes. "I said," he growled quietly, "I will discuss it with Katherine." He eyed Emily, daring her to contradict him again.

Instead of voicing anything further, Emily wisely clamped her mouth shut. Quietly, she stewed. How could he do this to his girls? Did he care nothing for their feelings? What happened to the sensitive Joshua she used to know? Emily suddenly fervently wished Keary was there and she could discuss the matter with him. Perhaps, though, he was tired of hearing about Joshua. Since he was the only one who knew her secret, he was the only one she could talk to about Joshua.

Emily sat numb for the rest of the meal. She tuned everyone out, not feeling like contributing to the conversation anymore. Sitting there, she finally had to face the inevitable – her future would be without Joshua, even as a friend. As much as she thought she had prepared herself for it, she realized it had been wholly inadequate. In reality, she knew it would be inappropriate for them to have the close relationship they once enjoyed. He would be married; she still widowed. More than once, Emily had to choke back the tears that threatened. She promised herself a good cry once the house was quiet, later that night. Death was to be mourned, and she was mourning the death of a long friendship.

Pulling herself together again and again, she consoled herself with the fact that she still had Keary. Joshua was right, she supposed she was replacing him. Maybe she would marry Keary. They had discussed it – briefly. She had declined to discuss it further, being that her heart was somewhere else. Keary had no choice but to relent. Now, however, the prospect had a whole new appeal. They both enjoyed each other's company and he had said he loved her, despite her feelings for someone else.

A loud chortle brought Emily back to the present. Quickly grasping the flow of the conversation, Emily discovered they had, in fact, been discussing Keary.

"He's so funny! We really like him," Brianna apparently was ending her story.

Joshua gave a short laugh that Emily knew didn't ring true. "He seems like a nice enough chap."

"Oh, he is," Emily jumped in, a little too quickly.

"He's become a bit of a regular visitor, eh?" Joshua questioned lightly.

"Yeah," Hailey answered. "At least once a week."

"Well, I'm glad."

"He even came for Thanksgiving."

Emily inwardly groaned. *'Not this subject again!'*

"Oh?" Joshua raised his eyebrows.

"I thought you knew. Brianna told Alexis at school."

"No, I didn't know." He turned toward Emily. In a nearly scolding tone, he stated, "That's nice you weren't alone."

Emily was downright tired of the subject, so decided to simply get everything out in the open and be done with it. Abruptly, she countered with, "We wouldn't have been, had you joined us."

"You know I had my reasons."

"No, Josh, it was one reason...Katherine didn't *allow* you to."

'That was rather condescending, Em'. She bit her tongue, waiting for his response.

"Don't bring her into this."

"Why not? She *is* the reason, isn't she? You said so yourself that it was her idea to spend Thanksgiving without us."

The two momentarily forgot about the children who were still in the room, watching the heated conversation with wide eyes. The tension grew thick.

"It wasn't *without* you. It was us asserting our own family traditions."

"Really? And what did those turn out to be? Did you come up with any new traditions you'd be eager to share? You know, as a *family?*"

Joshua felt a little of his control slipping. Emily's words irritated him. He couldn't admit that, no, they hadn't come up with any traditions. Yes, he'd wished they could have been with the Matthews. That, while he wouldn't say it was miserable, it had been hard for him to enjoy the holiday without his other family present. Yet, he wouldn't allow himself to say any of those things because his pride got in the way. Joshua could not, *would* not give in to Emily. He couldn't let her think she could say what she pleased about his fiancée. Emily wasn't being fair to Katherine...he had to keep remembering that. Joshua tried giving Katherine the benefit of the doubt and chose to believe she'd had his family's best interest at heart. He chose to believe it was because Katherine had wanted to be with his girls without any other distractions.

Of course, Joshua said none of that. Instead, he simply said, "Emily, you are not being fair."

Emily could feel herself getting riled up, though she couldn't understand why she was feeling so passionately about any of it. So they didn't spend Thanksgiving together...big deal. It was only one holiday. In the spirit of the moment, however, Emily was caught. Immaturely, she lashed out with, "Neither are you! Do you *ever* think of your girls? Do you *ever* consider their feelings anymore? Alexis was in tears as she talked to Brianna!"

Not prepared to defend his actions against his own daughters, all he could think of was to knock Emily down a peg or two. Her words had hit too close to home.

"It's not their decision, *they* are the children, *I* am their father! It was mine, and Katherine's, decision to make. We will do what *we* feel best. *Without your permission!*"

Without thinking, Emily quickly shot back, "You don't care about us at all, do you? We are no longer family to you, are we? We no longer matter because it might upset your poor, precious Katherine!"

Joshua was incensed. "That is unfair, Emily, and you know it! I care about all of you, but Katherine's going to be my wife. I need to make her happy. Her happiness comes first, not yours! I think there's a deeper issue here, Emily, and I think it's jealousy. I think you're jealous! You're jealous of Katherine because she's taking your place as my best friend. You have to understand, things have got to change! They cannot remain the same once I'm married. I don't know why you thought they could! You have got to get a handle on that, but seem unwilling. Why, Emily? Why can't you understand that? Up until now, we've been family. I thought you, of all people, could understand why things can't remain the same! You're acting like a child! Why can't you simply be happy for me...as a friend?" He was torn. All he'd wanted was Emily's approval, but hadn't even had that from the very beginning with his relationship with Katherine. He didn't want to lose Emily's friendship. He knew it'd change once he married, but he was only just beginning to realize how much. He was sad about it. And he was mad that Emily couldn't be happy for him. He was upset that he felt he had to fight so hard for their friendship to remain intact.

Emily knew what he spoke was true. She was jealous, but he had missed the point as to why. And even though he didn't know her secret, it only proved to further upset her. She sputtered, "*I'm* acting like a child? We *used* to be family? Over these past few weeks, you've been like a stranger, Joshua! I feel like I hardly know you anymore! I want my friend back! The way you used to be. I *know* things will change, but instead of inviting me in, you're pushing me away! I'm *trying* to be happy for you, Joshua! But, it's so difficult when I'm in love with you!"

The room was silent. Emily's cheeks heated. '*Oh, no! Did I really say that out loud? It's out! My well-guarded secret is out! Josh, say something! He won't say something. What am I going to do now? Oh, Lord, please, please give me...words or...or something!*'

Emily sat very still, tears slipping down her cheeks unheeded. She suddenly remembered the children in the room. They had witnessed it, all of it. In an unsteady voice, she tried to undo the damage she had done. "I-I-uh, mean, that is, I love you, as in, *all* of you. Your whole family." She knew he saw right through her. This was Joshua, after all.

To her astonishment, she heard Christopher's loud whisper, "I knew it!" Emily's gaze flew to him as he exchanged a knowing glance with Alyssa, across the table from him.

Emily took a deep breath and calmly instructed, "I think you children should leave. Chris, light the lanterns and y'all walk the girls home."

Silently the room emptied of children as they filed out.

More breath than voice, Emily murmured, "Oh, dear." She couldn't look at Joshua, but felt his gaze on her. Finally, she said aloud, "I'm terribly sorry for embarrassing you, Josh. The words didn't come out quite as I intended." She knew it was a lie, but hoped desperately he'd buy it for the time being. She had never intended to have Joshua hear those words.

In true Joshua-form, he gently spoke, "Emily, I don't think I'm the one embarrassed here. Is there something else you want to say before I leave? This may be your last chance."

Emily slowly met his gaze. The inevitable had to happen. She had to let him go, but she didn't know how. Willing herself to keep steady eye contact, she relented. "You're right, Josh. I do love you and the girls as family, but with you, it's more. *I love you.*" Her voice broke. "As in, it-hurts-I-can-hardly-breathe-when-you're-around-I-am-warmed-from-head-to-toe-simply-by-gazing-on-you, love you." Swallowing hard, Emily forced herself to say what she needed to say. "And I can't be around you or Katherine anymore. It's too hard, and I'd be looking at you in the wrong way. I do wish you both the best, however." She managed to smiled a little. "In a way, I'm kinda glad this happened because I'm exhausted from trying to hide my feelings from you."

Joshua wasn't sure what he'd expected to hear Emily say. He was shocked to his very core. "What are you saying? We can't...be friends...anymore?"

Emily swallowed the lump in her throat, but choked on the words anyway. "That's what I'm saying. Please understand. The girls are still welcome here, of course. But, as for you and me and Katherine, it simply won't work. I'm sorry." And she deeply and truly was.

Too shocked to have a response, Joshua suddenly felt the need to leave. And he did. Abruptly.

Emily sat still, staring at the doorway he'd passed through. Shock hadn't quite set in, as she tried to convince herself it was for the best. Breaking off a thirteen-year-friendship hurt, but the reason had to be right, didn't it? She'd done the right thing, hadn't she? Yet, the way Joshua had left made her feel like something was hanging between them. Maybe it was her imagination. She'd never broken off a friendship before. Maybe that's how it was supposed to feel. Still, the feeling was unsettling and, try as she might, she never could quite shake it off.

As their mother was having her discussion with Joshua, Emily's children were having their own conversation on their way home.

"Can you believe Mama said that?" Hailey asked.

"I already knew it!" Christopher smugly interjected.

"How did you know?" Hailey chided.

"I simply noticed how she's been lookin' at Uncle Josh, and the way she acts when he's around."

"Like what?"

"Silly...kinda girly."

"That don't mean nothin'! But, wouldn't it be kinda funny if Mama 'n' Uncle Josh got married?" Samantha said, wistfully.

Brianna spoke up then, bursting Samantha's imaginary scenario. "That won't happen...he's marryin' Miss Taylor-Ryan."

Christopher sighed. "Yeah."

It was a somber group that eventually returned to their house. Just as they were about to reach their gate, they encountered a figure stepping out into the lane from their own door.

"Hey, Uncle Josh!" Christopher called.

Joshua seemingly picked up his pace as he passed. He merely mumbled a "Hey, Chris, girls," then continued on his way.

"That was strange," Hailey observed. "And I think he was crying!"

"What? No way!" Christopher countered.

"Yeah, I think he was," Brianna agreed.

"His voice did sound a bit strained," Samantha put in.

"Yours would, too, if you'd had a discussion like the one he and Ma surely had," Christopher reasoned.

"I think it was a little more than a simple discussion, Chris," Brianna corrected.

"Well, whatever it was, it wouldn't make a grown man cry!"

Joshua was lucky in not being able to hear the conversation after he had passed Emily's children. He had been embarrassed enough to see them while he was crying. He had seen them approaching and tried to quickly wipe his eyes before they came face-to-face. Yet, the tears simply sprang back into place.

Emily's seeming ease with which she had dismissed their friendship had hurt. No matter the reason. He knew her intentions were for the best, but he knew he'd miss her terribly. They'd been there for each other through everything, including the loss of their spouses. Joshua fought against different emotions, each one winning its way back into Joshua's heart. He felt despair and sadness over the loss of a friendship. He felt a little bit of anger at Emily for not trying to find another way to solve her problem, instead of throwing him out of her life. Surely she would have gotten over it...*will* get over it. Joshua merely chalked it up to Emily's jealousy over Katherine taking her place. Instead of being a true friend, and being understanding, Emily had acted irrationally, thinking she cared for him more than she really did. That was all, in Joshua's mind.

By the time Joshua reached this conclusion, he had reached home. His tears had been replaced by annoyed indignation.

She'd get over it, he knew it. She had to. She couldn't stay away from her best friend forever.

Emily looked forward to Keary's visit more than usual a couple of evenings later. She'd lost one friend and desperately needed to keep the only one she had left. Or, that's what it seemed like, anyway.

Unknowingly adopting Joshua's former habit of entering without knocking, Keary called out, "Em?" as he walked in the house.

"In here," Emily answered.

Keary entered the sitting room, looking around. "Are we sufficiently chaperoned?" he asked, eyeing Hailey in the corner.

"Mr. Somerville, I'm over here!" Hailey volunteered, giggling.

The youngster enjoyed this particular game. "Oh, there you are! I suppose it's safe for me to come in and have a visit with your mother, then?"

"I give my permission," she answered, in mock seriousness, another element to the game. Then, "I'm doin' my homework." And she sighed heavily. This was not a game.

"Be sure to leave the door open when you go into the living room. I need to discuss something with Mr. Somerville in confidence," Emily instructed, pointedly. Usually, she permitted the children to stay in the room with them when they visited, for propriety's sake and because the children adored him.

Hailey rose then and left the room, but making sure to keep the door to the two adjacent rooms wide open.

Emily smiled a greeting at her friend then.

"This is quite against the rules. It must be quite important," Keary teased.

"You should already know, Keary, that you are quite the exception to any rule. Besides, you know I only view you as a brother."

"Ouch!"

"Oh, stop," Emily laughed.

Sensing something different in Emily, Keary got down to the point. "What's this all about?"

Pricks of tears gathered in Emily's eyes. She wiped them away impatiently. "We had Josh and the girls over for supper a couple of nights ago," she began. She then proceeded to tell him of the events of the night. To her chagrin, she blushed when she got to the part about her confession. When she finally finished, Keary was quiet.

Emily broke the silence. "Say something! I've been waitin' all day to tell you and hear your take on it."

Keary simply answered, "I knew you loved him. I knew the day he came to announce his engagement."

"What? How could you know then? I don't think even *I* knew then!"

"The way you looked at him. The way you acted when he was around. You were so careful to act in the right way, like you had something to hide. Apparently, you did."

"That's why you never fought me on why we shouldn't marry," she surmised. "I have nothing to hide now."

"We could still marry. I know you don't love me in the same way I love you, but I'd take good care of you. You need someone to take care of you. You've been alone for far too long."

Emily pinked slightly. Trying to keep the mood light, she told Keary, "Don't make me have to get rid of another friend." In earnest, "Please don't make things awkward between us."

"I won't. Just know that the offer will always stand."

Changing the subject, she said instead, "I feel sad about

losing Josh but, what's more, I hate the way things were left. It doesn't feel real, somehow. It doesn't feel final. Maybe I'm worried things were left rather messy, so there are still loose ends. Simply put, I don't want there to be any hard feelings. I know that sounds ridiculous, given the circumstances."

"Oh, Em, how could there not be? You ended a very long friendship. You most likely really hurt the poor fellow."

"I know," Emily sighed. She hadn't wanted to hear that answer, so tried to defend, "It had to be done."

"Did it?"

"Yes! I can't be around him. Not with the way I feel. It would be inappropriate. Especially with the thoughts I was having."

Keary's interest was piqued then. "Inappropriate thoughts, huh?"

Emily rolled her eyes. "Nothing earth shattering. Just thoughts that a proper lady should *not* be having about an engaged man."

"Like?"

"Oh, stop it, Keary. I'm not gonna tell you anything."

After a few minutes' companionable silence, Keary asked, "Have you thought about going over there to clear the air?"

Flabbergasted, Emily protested. "I couldn't do that! I simply cannot see him! It's too late. I told him we couldn't be friends anymore."

"Even you have to admit, what you did was a little rash. Don't you think?"

"Telling him I love him? Of course! Calling off the friendship, I don't think so."

"At least *think* about going over there and talking to him. No arguments, just clearing the air."

After Keary left later that evening, she found that going over to see Joshua was all she could think abou

Chapter 22: Friendship On the Mend

Joshua haunted Emily's thoughts every day for the next month. She had finally come to the conclusion that perhaps she hadn't treated him fairly. It seemed she needed to make peace with him at least, even if it wasn't to restore the friendship. Maybe she'd sleep better at night knowing she had finally done the right thing. And one way she knew to make peace was through food. So, to the kitchen she went. She stuck to the task of making an apple pie to take to him so she wouldn't have time to think and, perhaps, talk herself out of it.

Finally the pie was ready. Pulling it out of the oven, she let it cool for all of a half hour, but then covered it and quickly left her house, intent on her mission. Already, she could feel the thoughts crowding her mind as they fought to be heard. The loudest one being, she shouldn't be doing this. Maybe she should simply let the matter rest and let time do its healing.

Sooner than she wanted to be, she was standing on the Tyler porch, shifting from one foot to the other. She hadn't knocked yet and realized that on their stoop wasn't the best place to be making up her mind. She was there; she needed to do it already! She told her brain to knock, but it wasn't communicating with her arm at the moment.

"Hello, Aunt Emily."

Emily spun around, almost dropping the pie. "H-Hello." Emily greeted Kayla.

"What're you doin'?"

Emily grasped for a response as she stared dumbly at Kayla.

"Been milkin' the cows." Kayla held up a pail full of milk.

"And I'm, um, here to talk to your father."

Kayla said, "Oh" in a knowing voice.

Finally Emily offered, "Here, let me open the door for you. Or, do you want me to take the milk in for you?"

Kayla spied the offering in Emily's hand. "It looks like your hands might be a little full, but follow me to the kitchen."

Emily idly wondered if Joshua had said anything to the girls about their friendship, or lack thereof.

Kayla led the way back to the kitchen then eagerly lifted the towel from the pie after Emily set it down.

"Mmm!" Kayla breathed in.

Smiling, Emily playfully slapped her hand away. "Git on outta here. That's fer yer pa...uh, father," she quickly amended.

Kayla stood and eyed Emily speculatively. "Aunt Em, are we still allowed to come over?"

Taken aback at the question, Emily replied, "Of course you are! Why do you ask?"

"Uh, cause Pa told us you and he weren't gonna be seein' each other anymore, on account of him gettin' married. We wondered if that meant us, too. Pa's been upset so we didn't want to ask him if that meant us, too."

Emily gave the girl a firm hug. "Of course not, darlin'. You girls are welcome anytime."

Kayla smiled in relief. "Boy am I glad you came by so I could ask you. You go wait in the sitting room and I'll go find Pa and send him in."

Emily laughed and playfully curtsied. "Well, yes, ma'am!"

Kayla ran to find her father. On a hunch, she knocked on his bedroom door. "Papa?" she called.

Unexpectedly, Joshua flung the door open and she nearly fell against him.

"Oopsy daisy, be careful now. What do you need, sweetheart?"

"Ummm, you have a visitor in the sitting room." Then she scampered away, in search of her sisters.

She went to each of their rooms, knocking out the code that meant there was serious business to discuss. They each snuck out the back door to their meeting place by the tree on the creek bank. In these situations, weather was not a factor, no matter that it was the middle of January.

Once they were gathered, Madison demanded, "What is it Kayla?"

"It's f-f-freezing out here! Make it quick." Alyssa's teeth chattered.

"Guess who's here?" Kayla asked with excitement in her

voice.

"This is not the time. We're gonna die from the cold. Just tell us!" Alyssa demanded.

"Aunt Emily!" Kayla squeaked.

A collective "what?" rose from the group.

Kayla responded. "We need to go back in and get on The Perch. I had her wait in the sitting room."

The Perch was on the stairwell, toward the middle, as it looked directly down on the sitting room, but was somewhat hidden from casual observers.

"Good idea, Kayla!" Alyssa enthused.

"Let's go," Madison urged.

Quietly they entered the house again, taking the back way upstairs and coming back down on the other side so they could see the sitting room. One drawback to their secret Perch, was that hearing conversation was a little hard. Each girl leaned forward as far as they dared, trying to catch any snippets of conversation they heard below.

Emily had entered the sitting room and waited anxiously for Kayla to return or for Joshua to come in. Much to her chagrin, she found herself fidgeting. She sat down in one chair for a few minutes, simply to rise, deciding to stand, then changing her mind and sitting again in another chair.

What will he say? How will he react? Doubts assailed her. More than once, she willed herself to fight the urge to flee.

Too soon, to her mind, she heard Joshua's heavy footsteps galloping down the stairs.

Joshua entered the room, curiosity piqued. Who would be visiting him that Kayla would dare put in the sitting room, of all places? She knew the living room was the suitable place for visitors, unless they were friends. Much as it pained him to admit, his friends, as of late, were few and far between. But, he didn't dwell on that, or he'd start thinking of Emily. He still wasn't sure how he felt about that whole mess.

Looking around, he froze when he saw the figure sitting in an overstuffed chair by the fireplace.

Emily had just decided to sit then, when she heard him enter the room. She flew to her feet.

Swallowing his discomfort, Joshua decided on the civil approach. "Hello, Mrs. Matthews."

Unexpectedly, Emily felt a stab in her heart.

'*Well, what did you expect?*' she chided herself. Instead, she reciprocated the greeting. "Hello, Mr. Tyler."

Formality seemed the best way. Formality and politeness, Joshua decided. "How was your Christmas?"

"Fine, fine…good…and how was yours?"

"Excellent."

'*Excellent,*' she mocked silently. '*As if he has to one up–*' the thought was interrupted. '*Stop being childish, Emily!*'

"Please, have a seat." Joshua indicated the chair Emily had vacated.

Taking deep breaths to calm herself, Emily sternly reminded herself why she was here. Having unkind thoughts wouldn't help. "Thank you." Emily graciously accepted the chair.

Joshua took the chair opposite so they sat face-to-face.

"Mrs. Matthews, what might I do for you?"

Emily composed herself and said, clearly and matter-of-factly, "Please forgive me." It had taken all of her mustered courage to utter those three words.

Taken off guard, Joshua unkindly grunted, "Huh?"

Her heart beating right out of her chest, she was sure, she tried to put into words what she was feeling. "I feel badly for the way things ended. In fact, I hate it! I did it all wrong. I take full responsibility. I am so very sorry."

Joshua seemed to light up and hope sprang in his eyes. "Do you mean it?"

"Yes! I can't stand having things left the way they were."

"So, we can be friends again?"

Emily's heart sank. "Oh, dear." She was doing it all wrong again. "No, Josh, we can't. I only meant to clear the air between us so there wouldn't be any hard feelings. My feelings haven't changed for you so, no, we can't be friends. I need your forgiveness for blurting it out the way I did. I wish I would've had the presence of mind to discuss it, rather than blast you with it all at once. I fear I've caused more undue hurt than was necessary."

Irritation crept into Joshua's voice. "Why bother coming

over at all then, Emily? I'm *not* going to accept this, no matter how nicely you put it!" Unconsciously he had used a more familiar name than the earlier 'Mrs. Matthews.'

Emily sent up a quick prayer to keep her resolve. She hated hurting him, but tried to keep the reasoning firm in her mind. She couldn't possibly be around him, especially when he was married. It upset her that Joshua was being so pig-headed and refused to even try to understand that!

Emily evened her breathing and tried lightening the mood. "I brought pie," she offered in a small voice. "It's apple and it's in the kitchen." Then she quickly grinned.

Disarmed for the moment, Joshua returned the smile. Still neither one spoke nor looked at each other. Emily played with her hands held in her lap and Joshua was seemingly entranced by the fire.

Emily racked her brain. Anything was better than this strained silence. Almost begging, she implored. "Please, say something."

"I'm not happy, Emily."

"I know. I didn't come here to try to make friends." She bit her lip to keep from laughing at the absurd irony of her words. "I wish you could *try* to understand, even if you don't agree."

"I have tried," Joshua bit out curtly. "I don't understand what my marrying has to do with any of this. You've always been my closest friend, you and Jacob. I consider you like a sister, closer than a sister. I am convinced that whatever feelings you claim you have for me will go away. They *have* to because I can't stand the thought of not having you as my friend, as my family." Joshua raked a hand through his hair in agitation.

Emily felt like crying out at the unfairness of it all. And she wanted to smack Joshua alongside of the head and hope he'd come to his senses. He'd said all the wrong words. You don't tell someone who loves you that they view you as a relation. It wasn't fair! Emily tried to speak rationally. "All I want to do is end this conversation without any more hurts caused, okay?"

Her emotions were raw and evident on her face. And she was weary of fighting a seemingly losing battle of ever trying to get Joshua to see any viewpoint but his own.

"I know you don't agree...I know you don't understand... and

I know you don't think anything needs to change. I've told you my piece. I've explained my part. I've let you go." Quickly she lifted up a prayer, *'Please, God, let that be true!'* "I simply couldn't leave things the way they were, that's why I came over. I hated seeing you leave like that."

"I am sorry about that, Emily. It's very clear you've made your choice. I will try to respect that. I'll work on understanding your motives. But please remember, I value your friendship...still do...always will. Since it seems I have no choice in the matter, I'll have to accept your decision." Joshua wouldn't look at her. "No hard feelings."

Silently, Emily started for the door. There was nothing left to say.

The following weeks found Joshua strangely empty. He couldn't explain it to himself, but things simply didn't feel right. When Emily had come to his house, he'd been thrilled. Until he realized what she was there for. Now, he was at an impasse as to what to do. He hid his feelings about it from Katherine, not wanting to upset her unnecessarily. She seemed absurdly happy, even with the little bit Joshua had told her. That Emily was distancing herself from them. Joshua supposed that would be a normal reaction for a woman in Katherine's position. He recognized a close friendship with a woman who wasn't his wife would make his future wife uneasy. But it bothered him nonetheless.

It was easier for Joshua to deceive himself into thinking Emily's feelings would go away, rather than face the truth...that Emily truly loved him and did what was best for all involved.

Coupled with those worries, Joshua began noticing Katherine's peculiar behavior. She seemed a bit distant lately and Joshua couldn't figure out why. Any time he brought it up, she'd refer to the wedding as being exhausting and that was all.

Through it all, the girls kept their distance. It had begun shortly after Emily's visit and Joshua put all of his strength into *not* examining the why behind it. He had enough troubles to deal with already. Besides, they were young, he reasoned, they'd come around. They'd have to. They'd have a step-mother in another few months and there was nothing they could do about it.

Madison let out a long sigh. The four girls were perched on her bed. They had much to discuss about the impending doom that was their father's wedding.

"I think I quite hate Miss Taylor-Ryan," Alyssa announced.

Alexis chimed in with her own complaints. "She sure is acting different since she got engaged. I don't like *that* Miss Taylor-Ryan at all!"

"Maybe she'll change once the weddin's over. I heard women act different when they're about to get married. They get all crazy or somethin'," Madison reasoned.

"I don't think she's gonna change," Kayla negated.

"You know who *should* marry Papa," Alexis decided.

The other three answered unanimously. "Aunt Emily."

The girls could wish with all their hearts that Emily would be their new step-mother but they all sorrowfully remembered the scene they had witnessed between their father and Emily from The Perch.

"They aren't even friends anymore," Kayla stated morosely.

"I know," Alexis whispered, upset.

"I wonder how it all came about. I'm still fuzzy on the why behind Aunt Emily's decision not to be friends."

A few minutes' silence reigned before Alexis broke in again with a small consolation. "At least I found out we are still welcome over there. They just won't be coming over here anymore...ever!"

Katherine stewed. She had been stewing since her engagement months ago. Why did she have such feelings of unease? And why did Joshua's girls suddenly seem to hate her? She'd done nothing wrong! She wasn't aware of any particular reason that warranted such feelings from them. It chafed at her. She got the feeling they were no longer thrilled with her and Joshua's upcoming nuptials. And, impertinently, they seemed to have no qualms about making their opinions known. It was highly rude and Joshua should not let them get away with it.

What Katherine didn't do was let herself dwell on the fact that the girls' seeming problem bothered her so much because it made her have to face her own discomfort with her doubts. Doubts she shouldn't have. Doubts that made no sense. No one knew about them, but if they did, she wouldn't even be able to explain them. It unnerved her and she second guessed everything she did, it seemed. Every emotion she felt. She couldn't even trust herself to have a rational thought. Unfortunately, that carried over into her job and she hated herself for it. She truly loved children, and had a special fondness for her soon-to-be step-daughters. But their misgivings only, irritatingly, mirrored her own.

She tried telling herself it was all because of Joshua's recent frustration. All she knew was that it had to do with Emily. Joshua had been fairly vague as to his conversation with her. After the day Emily had visited Joshua, he had started acting curt and was easily irritated. Katherine would've put it down to pre-wedding jitters had she not known of Emily's visit. Joshua simply told her Emily wouldn't be attending the wedding and had decided to cut them out of her life. He didn't give a reason why, so Katherine simply felt Emily was being immature. She only imagined it was because Emily was jealous that she couldn't have the close friendship she'd shared with Joshua, once upon a time. Since Joshua had firmly told Katherine it was best to give Emily distance, Katherine was left to make her own assumptions as to Emily's why. And the only explanation Joshua would give her for Emily's seemingly bizarre behavior was to tell her that Emily was having a hard time adjusting to him getting married. Miffed as she was, Katherine tried to be gracious toward Emily, in thought, anyway, but was coming up short. She supposed she needed to put it all out of her mind and focus on creating excitement she didn't feel about her upcoming wedding.

Sleep had cruelly been eluding Joshua since Emily had come. He couldn't seem to get her out of his head! She plagued him every waking moment; her sweet, smiling face...her flashing angry eyes...her clear, laughing voice...the many moods of Emily played over and over in his mind. He felt sick with guilt. She *was not* the one he should be thinking about. He *should* be plagued by images of his bride-to-be.

So far, every night since then, had been like the one he experienced now. He couldn't shut his mind off, thinking of Emily. He missed her. By sheer force of will, he replaced Emily's face with Katherine's. Yet, his mind rebelled again and again, switching it back to Emily.

When sweet slumber finally overtook him, he had the same dream. Not so much a dream as a memory. It was of the anniversary of Jacob's death and he was back in Emily's bedroom, comforting her. At the time, only as a friend…as a brother would do. Emily had clung to him out of sheer desperation to get a grip on her crumbling world. The dream, however, diverged a little from reality. In it, Emily clung to him out of her deep need to keep Joshua with her. And in the dream, she'd beg, "Please, Josh, don't go!"

As usual, when he got to that part, he woke up. The betrayal he felt toward Jacob was always immense. He took a tender memory of Jacob's wife truly needing him as a friend, and his dream warped it. It perplexed him because there was no reason for his mind to make up the emotions that his dream self felt. Upon waking, he didn't feel any differently toward Emily than he usually did.

Except this time. This time, upon waking, he discovered he had just cause to loathe himself even more and the sense of betrayal was even more acute. This time he felt something new, something different toward Emily. As he sat dazed, the truth sank in slowly. It seemingly seeped in, almost unnoticed, as if it had been a part of him all along. The truth didn't even surprise him. It almost came as a welcome relief. The only thing that stopped him from fully enjoying that moment was knowing that, with this new knowledge, he'd have to hurt someone else.

He whispered the truth, more so he could hear it out loud. "I love her." The words seemed to burn his lips even as they acted as a healing balm. Those three words were utter bliss and pain. Betrayal to one, but deep surrender to another.

Almost as soon as he figured it out, he tried lying to himself again, which is what he discovered he'd been doing all along. Muttering under his breath, he chanted, "I'm marrying Katherine…I'm marrying Katherine…"

As quickly as he'd almost have himself convinced that was what he was supposed to do, his mind would remind him, '*But you love* her.'

And he knew the *her* his mind betrayed him with was not Katherine but, in fact, Emily.

Emily was afraid she was obsessed. She watched Joshua in the fields, she looked for him to come down the lane on some errand that would take him by her house. Perhaps he'd need to go into town. Perhaps he'd need to visit a neighbor about something. Something…something…*anything* that might afford her a view. Maybe, just maybe, he'd need to see her about some important issue.

She often reminded herself that *she* had written Joshua off and, being a gentleman, he'd respected that. As well he should, she firmly retold herself. She had no claim to him anymore. He didn't belong to her. He never had. She had no right to him. *She needed to let him go!*

'*Stupid, stupid Emily,*' she often told herself. '*You're only hurting yourself. Let him go…*let him go*!*'

This internal struggle wasn't a daily battle. It was a minute-by-minute battle.

To no avail, Emily had already tried telling herself that maybe her feelings would simply go away. She *had* to believe they would, or she would be miserable. She'd already toyed with the idea of moving…far, far away. Yet, she didn't know where she'd go and, in the end, she convinced herself that was a silly idea, being that she'd surely get over this infatuation. That's what it was, after all. It had been only a couple of weeks. Or a month, at most. She'd give herself more time, and maybe, eventually, she may even be able to say hi to Joshua on occasion, if she happened to meet him in the lane or in town. And his lovely, wife, too. She knew the friendship, as it had been, was over, but there should be no reason she couldn't be civil.

With that new fixation in her head, Samantha came in the room and promptly broke her concentration on her new decision.

"Mama? Can I go next door?"

It was the first time any of her children had asked that since her fateful discussion with Joshua. Though she hadn't told them about it, the tension seemed to be there and they read it well. And she was sure there were many discussions about it at school between them all.

Emily realized she didn't have any idea what Joshua would think. He wouldn't mind, would he? Then Emily's eyes narrowed. She knew who might. Not today, but in the near future, there would be someone else who may not welcome any of her family into the Tyler home anymore.

Keeping her expression even, Emily managed to smoothly tell Samantha, "The walk over would be treacherous in this weather."

It was true. The wind had started blowing the night before, and hadn't let up all day. Then the torrents of rain had started in the early morning, and the rain now fell sideways out of the sky.

A sad smile played at Samantha's lips. "Okay."

Brightening, Emily suggested, "Tomorrow at school, why don't you ask the girls if they'd like to come over here?"

That seemed to do the trick, as Samantha's face beamed. "Okay." She skipped out of the room.

Chagrined that she had no idea how Joshua felt about her children or whether or not they were welcome in his home anymore, Emily decided she would waste no more tears on him. After all, what was done, was done. At least she wouldn't be betraying Jacob anymore. Shame colored her cheeks at the thought. If only he could see her now. Well, if he *could* see her now, then she wouldn't be in this predicament because he'd be here, with her. After all, she couldn't love two people at once, right? And she was still madly in love with her husband. So Joshua couldn't really be a factor after all, could he?

Even as she was thinking it and trying to deny it, she realized it was possible to love two people at once. The trouble only came in choosing, but she didn't have to choose. She'd loved Jacob more than anyone else in her world when he was alive. She still loved him even now. So there was no choice for her to make. She'd had Jacob, who'd loved her immensely. Katherine got Joshua. That was only fair. Emily didn't deserve to have two men love her and be completely devoted to her in her life.

Unbeknownst to her, she copied Joshua's chanting as a way

to convince herself of the truth as she knew it should be. "I *do not* love Joshua Tyler....I *do not* love Joshua Tyler..."

She tried conjuring up negative images of Joshua; Joshua in ire....Joshua filthy and dirty from the fields....Joshua looking at Katherine with love and adoration. Yet, the images were quickly replaced with a memory. A memory of the anniversary of Jacob's death. Guilt stabbed her, even as she remembered Joshua's arms, cradling her ever so gently as she washed her grief away in tears.

Katherine looked blankly back at the black board. She had simple sums up to teach the younger children. Yet, she couldn't seem to make $2 + 2$ equal 4.

Lately she hadn't been a very good teacher.

'*Lord,* please, *not now! Please help me gather my thoughts. I can't deal with these issues now.*'

Why was she thinking of Joshua now, in the middle of arithmetic? She knew why...she was about to marry a man who already had children. Choke. A man she couldn't share any firsts with. Double choke. It wouldn't be his first wedding...he wouldn't live in his very own first house....her first child wouldn't be his first child. The choking had stolen her breath. She couldn't breathe!

Katherine stood frozen at the front of the classroom, screaming to herself, '*Breathe, Katherine, breathe!*'

"Uh, Miss Taylor-Ryan?" Freckle-faced, red-headed Ansel Kendrick snapped Katherine's attention back to the present.

Ansel looked at her inquisitively. His blue eyes warily appraised her face.

"Yes, Ansel?"

"Are you alright?"

"Uh, yes, I'm fine." Katherine stumbled over the answer.

"You looked kinda far away, like I get when you rap my knuckles for daydreamin'. Should I get the ruler and rap your knuckles, Miss Taylor-Ryan?" Ansel asked in wide-eyed innocence. His devilish grin belied his seeming innocence.

Shocked, and desperately trying to keep up with the conversation, she was only able to gasp out, "Ansel!"

Slyly, Ansel boldly asked, "Were you thinkin' of your

mister?"

Katherine was fully aware now. She sharply scolded, "Mind your manners, Ansel. Children, finish your sums."

Ansel spoke up for his classmates then. "We did 'em already. We was waitin' on you. We've been waitin' forever!"

Katherine turned scarlet with that knowledge. A poor excuse for a teacher she was, indeed! "Very well. Take out your readers and do silent reading. Older students, help the younger if needed."

Katherine then escaped to her desk full of embarrassment and shame.

Emily was chagrined to learn that time wasn't making her separation from Joshua any easier. Rather, she viewed him as the forbidden fruit that Eve wasn't supposed to have. Of course, Eve gave in to temptation. That was why Emily had severed her ties. Joshua was too tempting. As any temptation, however, the harder she tried resisting it, the more tempting it became. Emily made huge efforts to put Joshua from her mind. She purposefully stayed inside as much as she could during the day so she may not catch glimpses of him as he worked so near. Even in the farthest field, he was way too near for her comfort. Yet, it was becoming too much. Too much effort. Too much burden. She desperately needed a walk to clear her head. Where could she go? A walk in the fields was out of the question. Yet, she needed to go somewhere...do something! Staying in the house wasn't helping anymore. So, Emily headed for the lane. Even if she walked past Joshua's house, she knew he wasn't home so wouldn't be tempted to stop. That's where her walk started; where it ended surprised her, for she hadn't really subconsciously decided to go anywhere. When she finally took account of her surroundings, she realized she had inadvertently gone around the Tyler's house and was walking through their field. The same field that eventually joined hers! Panic set in. What if he was near? What if he saw her? She hadn't meant to go there. In fact, it was very much the opposite of where she should've gone. She wouldn't lie and say she didn't *want* to go there. By the time she realized her dilemma, she was closer to her house than the Tylers', so it made more sense to simply go home. First, however, she had to cross the field.

Fervently she prayed it wasn't the field he was in, while at the same time, a tiny piece of herself acknowledged that's exactly what she wanted. Quickly, she worked on her escape. It was to no avail. As she got closer to home, she noticed some figures in the distance, one especially she recognized right away. Her heartbeats accelerated. Frozen, she seemed to be able to do nothing but stare.

Even under the ominously dark grey sky, he was hard at work. At church, in the view of the public, she couldn't simply stare at him as she wished. Here, on her own land, she had the liberty. It would cost her later, she knew. It was hard enough not thinking about him already, without seeing him in the flesh.

It was agony tearing her gaze away. She suddenly felt exposed standing in the open field and quickly averted her gaze. What if he had caught her? The distance *felt* safe, but if he had looked, surely he would know who she was. Who else would it have been?

With that disconcerting thought, she half-ran the rest of the way home.

Joshua thought he saw movement out of the corner of his eye. He turned his face slightly, but not noticeable enough for the figure to see. From a distance it would've simply looked as though he was checking something behind him, when in reality, he was double-checking to make sure his hunch was correct. The figure was Emily. When he noticed her wheel around and high-tail it home, he straightened up and watched her go, without fear of being observed.

Chapter 23: The Long Conversation

The knocking obviously had urgency behind it. The voice was familiar, but didn't explain the urgency. "Joshua! Joshua!" Katherine called.

Joshua was confused. It was unlike Katherine to come to his house unexpectedly. She was exceedingly bent on propriety. And calling out was most unladylike, not a practice Katherine had ever done as far as he could recall.

Joshua swung the door open and gently grabbed her wrist as gravity was propelling it down to land on the door again. He didn't want it landing in his face. "Hello, Katherine," he warmly greeted, releasing his hold.

Katherine smiled sheepishly. "Oops, sorry."

Her smile was beautiful and Joshua momentarily wondered why it was he couldn't marry her. All the reasons he'd built up to tell her had vanished. Of course, the main reason remained in place, but he didn't want to tell her that. That would be unnecessarily cruel.

"Do you want some tea?" he offered. It was the middle of February and the weather seemed to get colder.

Shivering slightly as Katherine stepped inside, she graciously accepted. "Yes, please."

Joshua led the way back to the kitchen. Once there, Katherine took over as if it were her own kitchen. The familiar act suddenly irked Joshua, but he hid it well.

"How was school?" he asked instead, thinking it a safe topic. Little did he know what had transpired there only hours before.

"It was fine," she answered airily. Too vague to satisfy Joshua. He knew something was wrong, but knew she'd get to it in her own time. One thing he'd learned about Katherine, it was that she wouldn't be rushed on anything.

They settled down with their tea at the small kitchen table by the window.

Katherine felt terrible. She needed to say what she'd come to say, yet, how could she hurt Joshua like this? He'd done nothing wrong. Everything that felt wrong was all on her. But, marriage was permanent. She didn't have a choice in the matter.

"Joshua," she began timidly, "I came for a reason today. I'm sure you already figured that out." She paused. "This is so out of character for me...to come here...un-chaperoned or, at least, not knowing if the children were around. Which they appear not to be." She was babbling, and she knew it. Trying to stall the inevitable. Her stomach clenched. She looked at Joshua's expectant, yet confused face, and felt sick. Warily, she tried putting what she needed to say into words. "Joshua, I...well, that is, I...um, I need your help with something."

'*Chicken*' she scolded herself.

"Yes?" Joshua was thoroughly confused now. And her obvious stalling was getting on his nerves.

"Yes, um, well, that is, uh..." she trailed off. Where did she expect to go with that? How could she tie her question in with what she needed to say? *Why* did she ask that in the first place?

'*Come on, Katherine, think!*'

Coming up with nothing, she started the question again. "I need help with a problem I'm having...it's about the wedding."

"With what? Decorating? The food?" All the while, Joshua felt horrible for leading her on. Why act like he was concerned about the wedding when there wouldn't be one? He needed to tell her, but it seemed she had something to say first. Maybe whatever it was would help him lead into it.

"No, no, nothing like *that*. It's simply...I'm having... issues, er...alright, I'm just going to say it." Her words rushed out then before she had time to think. "I'm having a hard time accepting the fact that you've already been married. I know this sounds selfish and I'm *so* sorry. This is my first time getting married and I always thought that when I got married, it would be my husband's first time, too. With all of it. It'd be *our* first home, *our* first, er, child." Katherine blushed. Now she was being inappropriate. "Maybe I need to get through the feelings and let them go. I've tried doing it on my own, but they won't go away. Then I thought that maybe if I talked to you, you could help me. But, even as I'm telling you all this, I know that's something I want. I don't think I'm going to be happy marrying you."

There was silence.

There was a confusing array of emotions dizzying Joshua. He hated seeing Katherine like this, but had to commend her for coming forward and being honest. It was more than he could say for himself. He'd been a coward.

Guiltily, he was a little relieved and somewhat happy. He could finally and fully admit to himself that he loved Emily. That brought a sobering thought. Why *hadn't* he done this very thing with Katherine earlier? Why couldn't he tell her he didn't think they should marry? That hadn't been at all fair of him. Katherine was the better person in this. Should he explain? How much should he tell her? Saying *something* would surely ease her obvious sense of guilt.

"Katherine, I hold no ill feelings toward you. In truth, I should have come to you before now and acted like a man. I've had my doubts, too. I wasn't sure if you and I were really meant for each other, either."

Relief flooded through Katherine and Joshua could read it in her face.

"You have feelings for another," Katherine suddenly surmised.

Joshua was stricken. Suddenly repentant, he bent his head in shame. "Oh, Katherine, I'm so sorry. I hurt you."

"No, it's just the way you said *you and I*. It made me think you must have someone else in mind."

Joshua hadn't realized he'd put any emphasis on the words. "Yes, I do...did."

Katherine's face lit up then as comprehension dawned on her. "It's Emily! Oh, it makes sense now."

"Believe me, Katherine, I tried denying my feelings for her. I'm a coward and should have said something long ago."

Katherine only smiled and put a friendly hand on his arm. "I came here, remember? I'm the one calling it off."

"Right, only I feel it would be the proper thing if I were the one to blame for calling it off. It's the least I can do. No sense in besmirching your good name." Joshua smiled and was relieved they could part on friendly terms. "Katherine, you do deserve someone whom you can experience new beginnings with."

"Thank you for understanding, Joshua."

Katherine mused aloud then, "It's kinda funny in hindsight. I wonder why I didn't see it before. You and Emily." Smiling, she assured him. "You have my full blessing to pursue her in earnest."

Madison came in the room, saw who was there, and turned to go right back out.

"Uh, Madison, hold on." Joshua stopped his daughter in her tracks. "We have something to tell you." Slowly she turned around, expectantly. "Miss Taylor-Ryan and I have broken our engagement."

Madison's eyes lit up and a slow smile spread across her face. "Thank you," she whispered.

Joshua and Katherine exchanged puzzled glances, not completely sure who she was talking to.

Then she asked, "Can I tell the others?"

"Of course," Joshua allowed.

Madison fairly skipped from the room.

"It'll be all over the schoolyard by noon tomorrow," Katherine figured. "And then the news will worm its way into the homes of my students and the rumors will start that our engagement has been broken.

Joshua chuckled his agreement. "You're probably right. I'm sure the girls will be glad to have you back as just their teacher."

"Only until school lets out in June." She smiled. "Joshua, I'm going home. My father is getting old and can't write to me much anymore, so I worry about him. My brothers are each married and busy caring for their families, so they don't have a lot of extra time to look in on him. And, of course, my father's stubborn and won't go to live with either one, though they've offered time and again. He doesn't want to be a nuisance."

Katherine rose then to take her leave, and Joshua rose, too. "Best of luck in the future, Katherine."

"Thank you. Best of luck to you and Emily as well."

"Thank you. As far as Emily's concerned, we'll see."

"You're pretty tenacious when you want something, Joshua Tyler. I expect to hear an announcement by the time I leave in June."

Joshua walked Katherine to the door. As soon as the door closed behind her, his four girls tumbled down the stairs.

"Pa, is it true?" Kayla wanted to know.

"Did you and Miss Taylor-Ryan really break your engagement?" Alyssa questioned.

"Yes, it was a mutual decision," Joshua confirmed.

"Maybe that's why she was so mean lately. She just didn't want to marry Papa!" Madison exclaimed.

"Ouch!" Joshua pretended to be hurt.

"Sorry, Pa. I didn't mean it like *that.*"

Joshua smiled.

Alexis spoke up. "*Now* can you marry Aunt Emily?"

Joshua was caught a little off guard. He wasn't ready to think about that yet. It would be unseemly for him to break an engagement with one woman only to start pursuing another, despite the fact that he knew he definitely wanted her back in his life. But what if she was done? What if she never wanted to see him again? Worse yet, what if her feelings for him had subsided? No, he decided, he most assuredly would *not* think of Emily. At least, not yet. He needed the current scandal that would surely ensue to die down first. Instead, he answered, "Those kinds of things take time. I can't walk over there and merely propose marriage. Especially on the same day I have broken an engagement with Miss Taylor-Ryan. Besides, it's not common knowledge yet."

"We'll take care of that. Don't you worry, Pa," Alexis reassured.

"I suppose there's no hope of me breaking the news to Aunt Emily myself?" Joshua asked, hopeful.

"I don't know." Alexis was doubtful. "It would depend on when. It'll be all over town by Sunday."

Joshua was thoughtful. "You're probably right."

"Unless you went over right now," Alexis hinted.

"No, not now."

"Why not?"

"Because it's almost supper time, for starters, and it's dark and I'd hardly know what I'd say." His giddiness was catching up to him so that he was blabbing like a woman!

"Just tell her you love her and can marry her now."

That was exactly what he wanted to do!

"It's really not that simple, darlin'. I'll let you know when I've talked to her, though, okay?"

The girls' disappointment was obvious. Yet, Joshua had to smile at their persistence. Joshua had other matters on his mind now. Like how *would* he break the news to Emily? Especially since she probably wouldn't let him step one foot near her house. Besides, would she even care now? Did she still love him? Had she talked herself out of that? Had this time apart been what she needed to convince herself she didn't really love him after all? Could anyone even talk themselves out of love?

Taking the cowardly way, yet again, Joshua thought maybe it'd be best if she simply heard it through the gossips. If she found out and wanted to ask him, she could. Joshua loathed himself then for being such a coward. He couldn't find the courage to tell her, though. He was afraid of what she might say now that she'd had ample time to think about it. Would she have finally come to the realization that he wasn't good enough for her? That she deserved far better than what he had to offer?

Emily sat stunned. Brianna had told her shocking news and Emily wasn't sure she could wrap her head around it. Brianna's voice played back through her uncomprehending brain. "Rumors are going around at school. Miss Taylor-Ryan and Uncle Josh aren't engaged anymore. They say the two had a big argument and now they hate each other."

Emily dumbly played through the conversation again. She had admonished Brianna. "You shouldn't listen to…nor repeat… gossip, Brianna."

"Maybe you should talk to Uncle Josh and see if it's true," Brianna had innocently suggested.

"It isn't any of my business."

"Maybe it is now."

"What?" Emily had been shocked.

"Now you can woo him."

"Brianna Emily Matthews! First of all, *women* DO NOT woo men! Furthermore, what makes you *think* I would want to concern myself with him?"

"You love him, Mama."

"Only as a human being that God created."

Brianna raised her eyebrows, but wisely said no more.

It turned out that Alexis had been the one who had been all too eager to spread the news of her father's broken engagement.

Emily couldn't deny that she felt a certain lightness after hearing the news. She didn't allow herself the thought that maybe it wasn't true. Yet, as Sunday approached, she had sudden doubts. Maybe that's all it was. Rumors. Maybe she'd walk into church only to be greeted by the happy couple.

They approached the church and Emily took her time getting down and hitching the horses. Slowly, she shuffled her feet into the building. Covertly, she looked around for any sign of Joshua or Katherine. There. She spotted Joshua in his regular pew. She tried to be subtle as she looked around for Katherine. The lady herself walked up to Emily then.

"Hello, Emily. I suppose you heard the news."

Emily swallowed, hoping to wet her dry throat. "Uh, yeah," she answered uncertainly.

With a knowing wink, Katherine said, "I suppose you're pretty glad Joshua is available again."

Emily could tell by Katherine's tone that it wasn't meant in malice. She genuinely seemed to want to see Emily and Joshua together. A little sad, knowing it wouldn't happen, Emily simply responded, "I suppose I should be…." She let her voice trail off, suddenly feeling the need to cry. "If you'll excuse me Katherine, I think services are about to start."

Emily willed her eyes to stay down as she took her place with her family in their regular pew. It was right behind Joshua's. Through the sermon, she tried pretending he wasn't there but felt her eyes go to him regularly. After the services, her eyes flashed through the crowd, but to no avail. It was then she felt a hand on her arm. A flash of hope flew through her as she turned, but it was only another neighbor, Yetta Fabian.

"My, but rumors are flyin' about concernin' your handsome neighbor." Yetta's voice was full of meaning.

Did everyone know her secret? How well she had thought she kept it hidden!

"Have you had a chance to talk to Mr. Tyler about his broken engagement? You might wanna find out the real story. I've heard 'em all, I think. My favorite is that Miss Taylor-Ryan had a beau back home and Mr. Tyler found out and flew into a rage! Of course, if you really see them together, you can tell there are no bad feelin's. They act like a couple of real friends."

Emily had always liked the woman and intimated to her now, "I'm kinda curious, I suppose."

'*More than kinda*,' she added to herself.

After a few more minutes of polite exchange, Yetta excused herself.

Emily felt suddenly peeved. Why hadn't Joshua been over yet to explain? The truth sank in fast and hard. Even though they could be friends again, he probably didn't want to be. Dully, she noted that she didn't blame him, really. Would she want to be friends with herself if she had done what she did to Joshua? The answer: probably not.

Joshua kicked himself all through the next week. He saw Emily at church, yet didn't even go over to say hi. He may not have told her everything right then, but he could've at least let her know he'd broken his engagement with Katherine. And it would've been to her face. By now, she most certainly would have heard all kinds of things second-hand through the gossip mill.

"Pa, you've gotta talk to Aunt Emily. Hailey seems to think she'd be glad to have a visit from you," Kayla pleaded. "Hailey says Aunt Emily seems cross and she thinks it's 'cause you didn't even talk to her at church and let her know about Miss Taylor-Ryan." Kayla had informed him of her opinion earlier that day when the girls had gotten home from school.

That had really pricked Joshua's conscience. He never should have let it go so long without telling Emily. He should have gone over that day and told her. Uncomfortable with his thoughts, he tried putting it back on Emily. If she really wanted to reconcile, then shouldn't she have come over after hearing the rumors to get the truth? Surely she'd heard them all by now. And she couldn't possibly believe them. Wouldn't she *want* to know the truth? Or didn't she care?

Joshua sighed inwardly. He knew deep down that Emily cared. How to breach the gap that they had created for themselves was beyond him. He was the man and should take the first step. Yet, matters of the heart still scared him.

Thoughts of Joshua clawed at Emily. She didn't know how much more of his silence she could take. Why hadn't he come by? Why hadn't *he* told her the news yet? Surely this was something he'd want to share in person…right?

On the other hand, she wrestled with herself, she'd been the one to break the friendship. Shouldn't she be the one to go over and make amends? But, would he want to be around her? Her feelings for him hadn't changed. She still loved him. Would he want to be friends knowing that? Should she put herself in that kind of a relationship, even knowing it may be best if he was out of her life? Of course, for purely selfish reasons, she wanted him back in her life. He may be uncomfortable being around her knowing what he knew now. And she couldn't seem to get rid of her tiny stabs of guilt any time she thought about Joshua in that way. Even now that he was free. Now all she could think about was Jacob. How could she betray him by loving another?

Joshua's courting Katherine had made her so uncomfortable and ill at ease. Now she knew why. Now she knew that was when she had fallen in love with Joshua. Again, she couldn't come to terms with it. Jacob had only been gone six months when that happened! How could she have fallen for Joshua so soon? Surely it hadn't been complete love yet. Maybe just infatuation. But, maybe, in a way, that was worse!

Stepping into the hall, Emily heard whispers. She saw the Tyler girls and hers. "What are you up to?" she asked suspiciously.

"Oh, nothing," Brianna answered…innocently enough.

"Hm." Emily wasn't quite convinced. "Don't get into any trouble now, ya hear?"

"Yes, ma'am" was chorused back by the group.

Emily went back to sit down and listen for a few minutes. She heard, "Come on, let's go!" fiercely whispered by Kayla.

Emily vaguely wondered what they were up to, but decided they were probably just being girls.

"We are all ninnies," Alyssa moaned. "We almost got

caught."

"Mama woulda suspected somethin' anyway. And she obviously heard us." Brianna tried to reason.

"It wasn't a very good plan in the first place."

The seven girls had been spying on Emily, trying to gauge her mood. If she was less cross than usual, as of late, they were going to try and devise a reason to get Joshua out of the fields and into the house and, hopefully, Emily's arms. They wanted their parents to fall in love so badly they'd decided to take matters into their own hands.

"What we need is a *really* good plan. We need to think of a way to get them together, but make it look like a coincidence."

"That's stupid and would never work! They are never in the same place at the same time!"

"That's why *we* would need to plan it all out and set up an 'accidental' meeting."

"The only place they go that's the same is church."

"Yes, but that's probably not the best place. They hardly notice each other there."

"That's not true. I know Pa looks for Aunt Emily. But, he doesn't think anyone notices him doing it."

"Mama does the same thing!" Brianna exclaimed.

Alexis spoke up then. "That settles it. We'll just have to get them to notice one another this Sunday at church and somehow end up walking together or bumping into one another. Maybe we could arrange it so Pa parks the wagon next to yours."

"That won't work. He knows what it looks like," Alyssa opposed again. "He almost goes out of his way to avoid Aunt Emily, even though he keeps an eye out for her."

"They avoid each other like the plague. Church is the one place they *know* the other will be. It has to be someplace where their guards will be down." Brianna was thinking hard now.

"Does anyone have any better ideas?" Madison queried.

There was silence.

Alexis spoke again. "I think we should *try* something this Sunday. It's only two days away and if it doesn't work, we'll know what not to do next time, okay?"

"Yeah, like *not* try it at church," Kayla sarcastically broke in.

"I'll watch Uncle Josh. When it looks like you're headed to

your wagon, I'll say I'm really sick. Mama will leave then, too. I'll watch where you are and I'll head in that direction," Brianna suggested.

"You're a terrible liar, Brianna," Madison complained. "I'll do it. I'll tell Pa I feel sick and head towards you."

"This is a really dumb plan and will never work," Samantha inserted.

Yet, those in the group knew that when Madison decided on something, it was hard to sway her. So, they knew that, like it or not, they were going with her plan come Sunday.

Though it was well into March, the temperature gave no indication in rising. Emily shivered in her pew at church, despite the roaring fire in the middle of the aisle, trying to spread its warmth amongst the members of the small church.

Out of habit, Emily started her search for Joshua. *'It's no use lookin,'* she chided herself, *'he doesn't even notice you're here. And that's your fault, you know.'*

Irritated with herself, Emily snapped her attention forward and waited for services to start.

If she had continued to let her gaze wander, she would have seen Joshua come through the door, eyes searching for her. They found her and he could hardly rip his eyes away as he started down the aisle to his pew. It was a wonder she didn't feel the hole being bored into the back of her head.

Emily willed herself not to look up as Joshua took his seat.

As soon as the service came to a close, Emily was headed out the door.

Noticing this, Madison suddenly turned to her father. Clutching her stomach, she moaned, "Pa, I don't feel so good. Can we go home…now? My stomach feels awful!"

Joshua had been preoccupied watching Emily practically run for the door. "O-okay," he answered offhand.

He started hustling his family up the aisle, taking the course Emily had moments before.

Stepping outside, he continued walking forward, even as he

looked back to check on Madison. His intent was to ask her how she felt, but he ran into something in the process that stopped the words in his mouth. Shocked, he turned to see what he had hit, flailing his arms as he did so, only to find himself face to face with Emily. He had accidentally struck her in the face. "A thousand apologies, Mrs. Matthews! I'm so sorry!" He was flustered and embarrassed and prayed for a hole to swallow him up.

Emily had managed to muddle through her reticule and came up with a handkerchief, which she promptly put to her bleeding nose.

Joshua was flabbergasted and at a complete loss as what to do. "Are you okay? Should I take you to Doc Allison's? Should I take you home?"

Flustered herself, Emily blurted, "It's fine, Josh! I'm fine, uh, Mr. Tyler. It's just a little bloody nose. It's not broken. You're quite strong." Emily's cheeks immediately flamed at the forward compliment. "Uh, er, come along, children. We are headed home."

Joshua offered, "I'll follow you" in a tone that brooked no argument.

Emily warily took the handkerchief away from her nose and tested to see if the flow had stopped. It was slowing, at least. "Al-Alright." She knew Joshua would anyway, with her consent or without it.

Seven girls covertly cast worried glances at each other. This wasn't exactly how they'd imagined their plan would end up. As dumb of an idea they had thought it before, they were all convinced of that now...even Madison.

All the way home, Emily was extremely conscious of Joshua's eyes on their wagon. The thought made her squirm, and yet, at the same time, her stomach was doing flip-flops and her heart was racing.

"We need a new plan," Brianna decided aloud.

The group of girls were together again for another planning session, as they called them.

"Something way better than Sunday. That was horrible!" Alyssa moaned.

"I didn't think he'd literally bump into her!" Madison protested. "Is Aunt Em okay?"

"Yeah," Samantha assured, "at least, she didn't say anything more about it after we got home. I *guess* that's a good sign. She hasn't complained of any pain."

"Are you a doctor now, Samantha?" Madison whined at her.

"No arguing," Kayla interfered.

"Papa didn't say *anything* all the way home!" Madison informed the group.

"Obviously we need to try a different approach."

"Like?"

"Well....hmmmm....is Uncle Josh planning on going to town anytime soon?" Hailey asked.

"Probably. He's like anyone else. Usually goes into town on Saturdays for supplies and such," Kayla answered.

"That should be easy enough then. That's when Mama goes."

"That's when half the citizens of Lorraine go! The other half already live smack dab in the middle of town!"

"Then it should be easy."

"Maybe gettin' them to run into each other isn't the best plan, no matter where it takes place. Maybe we shouldn't come up with anymore plans. If it's meant to be, it's meant to be."

"Would you listen to yourself? How will that work? They won't even speak to each other! We need to make sure that changes. It won't if it's left up to those two."

"We could set up a meeting place for us to see each other then let the others know where Mama and Uncle Josh are," suggested Samantha. "Then they could merely *see* each other and we'd come up and start talking, then they'd have to stay. Eventually they'd have to talk, otherwise that'd be plain rude."

Hailey rolled her eyes. "I think we are way over-thinking this. I say, let 'em be. It's no use. We should give up. If they knew what we were doing, we'd be in big trouble anyway."

"We should at least go to town the same day and see what happens," Samantha insisted.

It was put to a vote and Hailey was outnumbered.

Since Alexis and Alyssa's birthday was coming up,

Samantha didn't have to invent an excuse to ask if they were going to town on Saturday.

"What did you girls have in mind to get them?" Emily asked as they browsed the general store.

From time to time, Mr. Vantrice got little knickknacks and baubles of interest in his store.

"I'm thinking peppermint sticks," Hailey answered.

"But only Alexis likes peppermint sticks," Brianna reminded her.

"Oh, yeah. Alyssa likes lemon drops."

The three kept their eyes wide open for any sign of the Tylers. In all truth, Alexis and Alyssa had already informed them of what they wanted. That way, Brianna, Samantha, and Hailey could make the hasty purchases as soon as Uncle Joshua came into the store. Now, the three girls merely bid their time until the Tylers made their appearance. It was the best plan the seven girls could come up with on such short notice. None of them knew why, but it seemed time was running out. It seemed as if they didn't get Emily and Joshua together now, it would never happen. That was not a future any of them looked forward to.

"Are you ready?" Emily surprised the three coming up behind them. They were browsing, each one with a specific item in mind. They memorized where it was so they could snatch it at a moment's notice.

"Um, we haven't quite decided," Hailey lied, feeling horrible. Her job was to get the bracelet that Alexis told her she wanted and had spied in the window the week before. It happened to be displayed in the window, right next to the counter.

"How about those peppermint sticks? You said one of them liked peppermint sticks," Emily offered. She wanted to be on her way home. Saturday was typically the day most folks from outside of town came in to do their shopping. She was thinking of someone in particular and didn't want to risk running into him. She couldn't even bear to think his name.

Trying to distract their mother, Samantha grabbed her item from a shelf. Coming up to Emily, she said, "Smell this perfume! I think Alyssa would really like it."

Out of the corner of her eye, Brianna saw who they'd been waiting for. She subtly moved the group toward the counter to make their purchases, meaningfully catching Hailey's eye.

Hailey dashed to the window and grabbed the bracelet, bringing it to the counter.

"I'd like a peppermint stick and a lemon stick, please," Brianna ordered.

Emily didn't know what had caused her daughters' sudden haste, but she was glad.

Then the bell over the door tinkled. The three girls turned around to see the Tylers entering.

With mock secrecy, Brianna hid the bag with their purchases behind her back. "Alexis! Alyssa! You can't see this."

Alexis and Alyssa threw themselves into the charade and followed the girls out the door, loudly protesting. "Let me see!" "What's in the bag?"

It had all happened so quickly, Emily didn't realize her girls had all abandoned her until she heard Joshua's deep voice. "Hello, Mrs. Matthews."

She nodded, willing the blush to leave her cheeks. Blushing was so inconvenient! "Mr. Tyler," she nodded.

She willed her feet to move, but they were not bending to her will at the moment. The silence was awkward and she felt the sudden need to fill it, making a complete ninny of herself in the process. "We were, uh, just purchasing some, um, presents. For the girls. Your girls, Alexis and Alyssa. Their birthday is coming up, you know."

Joshua looked at her with laughter in his eyes. His reply was smooth, however. "Yes, I know."

Mentally Emily kicked herself. *'Of course he knows when his own daughters' birthday is! He* is *their father after all!'* Emily wanted to hide under a rock. Making a quick exit seemed like the best option. She mumbled an excuse. "I, uh, better go join the girls. They're, uh, waiting…outside…for me."

Joshua was half blocking the door, and Emily had to squeeze around him to get outside. If she had known better, she would've thought he'd planned it that way. Anything to make it more uncomfortable for her, she was sure. She deserved it, anyway.

Joshua rather enjoyed her squeezing by. He'd wanted to move out of her way, desperately, but his feet had seemed rooted to the spot. He couldn't move. In fact, all of his senses seemed to be slowed or stopped when he was near her. When Joshua had seen Emily standing at the counter, he thought that perhaps this was his chance to finally talk to her. Yet, all he did was stand there like an idiot while she talked on. It did satisfy him a little that she seemed to be tongue-tied as well. But at least she *said* something! No doubt she was thinking what a dolt he was. And Joshua's heart sank.

As Emily joined her girls outside, she resisted the wild urge to turn around and throw herself in Joshua's arms.

'Good grief, Emily! Get a hold of yourself!'

"Hello, girls!" she greeted brightly, trying to erase the pain of embarrassment she'd just been the victim of.

"Hello, Aunt Em. Is Papa still inside?" Kayla asked.

"Yes, dear, I believe he is." She willed herself *not* to turn around and look.

"See y'all later!" Madison parted with her sisters in tow.

If Emily had watched them retreat to the interior of the store, she would have seen Joshua watching her.

All the way home, Emily reminded herself that the encounter at the store was exactly why she needed to distance herself from Joshua. She should probably make him quit. She couldn't have him work for her anymore. Simply thinking about him made curious tingles shoot up and down her spine and her stomach do flip-flops. It was much worse when she was actually in the man's presence.

Straightening herself, she decided, *'I am too old for such nonsense.'* Maybe she should move…somewhere…anywhere but here. It was getting downright painful to see Joshua and the town simply wasn't big enough to help her keep her distance. Even if she did make him quit.

Their mother's demeanor puzzled the girls. They thought her spirits would be a little uplifted on the ride home. Yet, she was acting quite melancholy. They exchanged wary glances. Maybe they shouldn't try to set Uncle Joshua and their mother up anymore.

If Joshua'd had a hard time getting Emily out of his head before, it was nearly impossible now. Since Saturday, he'd been thinking about her constantly. It also hadn't helped that the following day had been Sunday, so that was a given that he'd see her at church. And now, it was Tuesday and he was in the middle of one of her fields and couldn't keep his mind on his work. As hard a worker as he was...something he took pride in...he was doing himself no justice that day. He needed Emily back in his life. Permanently. Why couldn't he simply tell her all about the broken engagement? Everyone else knew. Certainly she knew, but he was wise enough to realize that she needed to hear it from his lips. Of course, he foolishly kept convincing himself he wouldn't know what to say or how to begin. Coward again, he thought he should wait for her to come to him.

Instead, he longed to see her...even if it was only a glimpse...day after day. And night after night, she was in his dreams.

Chapter 24: A Timid Question

Three long weeks is all it took for Joshua to finally find his courage. It was a Wednesday and he had spent it like all the other days in between…pining after Emily. He finished in the fields and headed for her house before he could turn coward again. As it was well into April, the daylight was staying out a little later, so he didn't think about the lateness of the hour. Only that he needed to see Emily, talk to her, and he needed to do it now. Before he turned back into the coward…again.

"I'm sorry for barging in like this." Joshua quickly apologized after Emily had answered the door. He was surprised he wasn't more tongue-tied, but he figured it must be his adrenaline kicking in.

A little miffed that she was completely off guard, Emily curtly replied, "It better be important. This is utterly indecent, as you can see!" Flustered, Emily was having a hard time controlling her emotions with Joshua around. As it was, she was upset with him for not talking to her since his broken engagement. He'd never come to explain. Yet, she was still hopelessly in love with him which, she supposed, made it worse. Her emotions were that much stronger around him. She couldn't form a coherent thought. Mostly, she figured, she wanted to keep away from him. To make it easier on herself, she supposed. Having him so near was unnerving her.

"I'm sorry it's so late. I didn't stop to think of the time. But what I have to say is important." His words spilled out.

"It better be," she muttered.

They were in the kitchen now. Emily could think better in the kitchen, with something to do. She put the kettle on for tea.

Joshua began hesitantly. "Emily, I, I should have cleared something up…long ago. I know you don't listen to gossip, generally, but I'm sure you've realized by now that it was true, at least, the core of it was…is…true. Katherine and I broke our engagement. It was a mutual decision. That's it. No secret lovers, no heated arguments. We talked and decided to go our own, separate, ways. She did mention going back home to care for her aging father. That's all. I wanted you to know."

Emily had her back to Joshua when he began speaking. As he explained, she stiffened in response, holding very still so she might catch all of his words. Beautiful words to her ears. Of course, she wouldn't let him see that they had brought tears to her eyes. She kept her back to him. After he finished, she processed the information. For reasons unclear, when he said there had been no secret loves, her heart sank. Just a little. She realized it must have been her false hope all along. Had she really dared to dream he'd eventually feel the same way toward her? Obviously he hadn't.

Slowly, she turned around. All evidence of emotion carefully concealed.

Startled at her blank face, Joshua idly wondered what he had said wrong.

Emily woodenly moved to the table with two cups of steaming tea. She set one in front of Joshua before taking a seat. She laid one hand on the table, while the other grabbed her cup of tea. Trying to gather her thoughts, she took a sip.

Joshua used the opportunity to grab her free hand. He held it and it seemed to burn her skin. She didn't want him touching her when all of this was going to end so badly. He didn't love her and his touching her was sending mixed messages that her brain couldn't comprehend. Finally, she struggled to free her hand. When he didn't let go easily, Emily looked up to meet his gaze. She hadn't looked him in the face, so hadn't realized he'd been staring at her.

"Emily, I need to know that you understand."

Befuddled, Emily answered slowly. "Yes…I believe I do…you are no longer engaged."

His eyes still held hers and she couldn't seem to look away. "And I'm happy," he stated.

Emily swallowed. "And you're happy," she repeated.

Joshua let go of her hand and used both of his hands to cup her face. He looked into her soul and whispered, "And I love you."

Emily started to repeat it. "And you love–" She stopped and replaced it with a gasp.

For a breath all was quiet, then Joshua whispered, "And you love me?"

Swallowing hard and blinking back tears, Emily affirmed, "And I love you."

Emily sat, dumbfounded. Was she dreaming now? She didn't want to wake up! Or had God really allowed her dream of this reality to come true? Dazedly, a smile crept onto her face. Still whispering, she inquired, "Mr. Tyler, would you mind saying that again? Maybe giving me a pinch? I believe I may be dreaming."

Keeping his voice low, Joshua repeated, "I love you, Emily Sarah Matthews." He leaned farther forward as a huge grin lit up his face.

Emily was shaken to her core. An odd feeling overcame her then. A feeling she had never expected in this situation. She felt a little guilty. Now that confessions were made aloud, she felt almost irreverent to Jacob's memory. This was ridiculous! Surely enough time had gone by *now* for her to love another. Suddenly it seemed that Joshua speaking aloud his own feelings, making it real, affected her conscience. Emily quickly tried pushing the disturbing feeling away.

"May I court you properly, Mrs. Matthews?" Joshua mercifully interrupted her thoughts.

Except hearing the name stung a bit. Not hurtful. Only guilt.

Emily pasted a smile to her face, not wanting to spoil the moment. "I believe that can be arranged."

It seemed Joshua wanted to reminisce. "Emily, I think I've loved you since the day I found you in your bedroom." He frowned. "Is that too irreverent, being what that day represented, and all?" He continued softly, "You were in pieces and so vulnerable. As I comforted you, I had this feeling of rightness wash over me. Like that was where I belonged...forever. And I don't believe in this sort of thing, but it was almost as if Jacob was giving me his blessing. I was just too stupid to realize it at the time."

Heavy guilt this time shot through Emily. So, this was her price. She must live with guilt while being happy with Joshua because of her infidelity to Jacob's memory. She should have known she didn't deserve so much happiness for one lifetime. Jacob had been the ideal husband that no one could measure up to and she knew she was the luckiest woman alive to have had him for her own. And now, she had another wonderful man who loved her, and she didn't deserve him. She didn't deserve more of the same kind of happiness. Joshua was so different from Jacob in many ways, yet so much the same in others. Maybe this wasn't a good idea. Maybe the guilt was her warning that she shouldn't try to have all this happiness. Why should she deserve it, after all? She wasn't a saint, she wasn't anyone special. Just Emily.

Joshua brought her back to him. "Do you remember the first time you knew you loved me?"

Emily did blush at that. "Yes," she scarcely whispered. Clearing her throat, she spoke a little louder, hoping to drown out the torturous thoughts. "It was that first day you started courting Katherine. That was probably one of the hardest days of my life. I could hardly stand watching you two together. And then you got closer, and it was downright painful." Her attempt at teasing was feeble, at best. Her heart wasn't in this conversation with Joshua anymore.

'*You need to tell him. You need to tell him now that you can't do this.*' Yet, she couldn't bring herself to do it. She couldn't hurt him, but she knew that in the near future it would be inevitable. Not this night, however. Not this beautiful night when he confessed the words she'd been waiting so long to hear. Hoping to hear and fearing she would never hear. Courageously, she told him, "Maybe you should leave now. It is late and you shouldn't be here. Especially in light of your, er, recent confession." She smiled more genuinely this time, not that he had noticed the falsity of her smile before.

He seemed reluctant to go, but complied.

Joshua sensed Emily's hesitation, so determined to take things slow with her. They had even decided to wait to tell their children, "when the time was right," as Emily had put it. Joshua didn't think that was too fair, considering they knew the children had been wanting the two to fall in love for quite some time. Yet, he agreed to Emily's decision.

Joshua took to slipping little notes under the kitchen door on his way out to the fields for Emily to find later. Since he couldn't shout it from the rooftops yet that he was in love, he would make sure Emily knew his feelings and never forgot them. He was hoping that the act might also dispel whatever misgivings Emily was obviously having. For now, however, it was enough to know that he loved Emily and she loved him.

Emily, on the other hand, was driven to distraction. She couldn't seem to get her simple daily tasks done. Prayer was her constant companion, yet she was still at a loss as what to do. Give up the man she loved, she could not. Give up the memory of her late husband, she could not. Confusion was another constant in her life. Just because they loved each other didn't mean they had to act on it, did it? She tried to reason that simply knowing the one loved the other was enough and that's all it would come to. Deep down, however, she knew that wouldn't be enough for Joshua. It wasn't fair to him. Why all the questions *now*? Why hadn't they plagued her before? Perhaps because Joshua hadn't confessed his love before? Perhaps because he hadn't been free to love her before? Perhaps because now it all seemed too real? Before, she could merely dream about being in love again and having it returned. Now that it was a reality, she had to face the consequences, since she felt she was being terribly disloyal to Jacob.

Emily knew a decision needed to be made. The only decision she knew was to break it to Joshua gently. She wouldn't have all day to mope around and be restless with the children home all day. School would be out for the summer in another six weeks! As it was, it was hard enough hiding her feelings the hours they were at home already.

In getting nothing accomplished, Emily found she had nothing but time on her hands. She needed someone to talk to. Someone whose opinion she respected, whose advice she could take to heart, and who would criticize her in love, if need be. Gazing out the window that faced farther up the lane, she spotted her answer.

"Why, Emily, won't you come in? What a nice surprise!"

Yetta Fabian opened her door wide to admit her neighbor.

Emily suddenly felt awkward. She shouldn't have simply dropped in like this. "I'm sorry, Yetta, maybe you're busy...?" Emily had a sudden impulse to wish Yetta was too busy to sit and talk. Maybe she didn't want to open up about Joshua. Yet, she knew the whole town was already aware of Joshua's broken engagement and others had speculated about Joshua and Emily all along, apparently. Although, that had been a new development that Emily hadn't been aware of.

"Not at all, Emily. I'll go get us some tea and we'll have a nice visit. You still have a couple hours yet until the children arrive home from school?"

"Yes." It was all she could muster, her emotions in a swirl.

Soon, the two ladies were sipping tea and munching cookies while they resorted to small talk.

Yetta, usually no nonsense, finally asked pointedly, "I'm supposing there was a reason for your visit?" She wasn't harsh, she was simply asking the obvious question.

Emily gulped hard. "Uh, yes, ma'am." She felt like a naughty little girl who had been caught at doing something wrong.

"Alright, go ahead. I'm listening."

Emily smiled ruefully. "Truthfully, I don't know if I need advice or simply a listening ear."

Yetta nodded, putting down her teacup, patiently waiting.

Emily tried organizing her muddled thoughts. "Well, it's like this..." and then her words took off from her mouth, she being barely conscious of what she was saying. They seemed to spill out of her of their own accord. She then ended with, "I feel so disloyal to Jacob. How can I even *think* about being in love with someone else?"

"Why do you suppose you feel that way?" Yetta finally asked after Emily stopped talking. She wanted to be sure Emily was finished before she broke in.

"I don't know!" Emily wailed. "That's part of the problem!"

Gently, Yetta explained. "Emily, just because you love Josh, it doesn't mean you loved Jacob any less. I'm supposin' you love Josh in a different way than you loved Jacob. And that's okay. But, honey, Jacob's gone."

"Then why does it *feel* so wrong?"

"Is it pure?"

"What?"

"The love you feel for Joshua. Is it pure? You aren't mistaking lust for love? And you love him for who he is?"

"Yes!"

"Then what could be wrong about it? Have you considered this could be from God? Maybe God wanted you to fall in love with Josh, and he with you, and that's all there is to it. He knew you'd need someone to care for you. He knew you'd be lonely without Jacob. But, what's more, He knew you'd need someone to *love* and someone to *love you.* God made us, Em, and God knows what we need. Even before we do. And always, *always* He knows what we need, even if we didn't realize we needed it in the first place. If your love for Joshua is pure, it's from God. That's what the Bible says. God *is* love; that means He *has* to be part of love, any kind of love. He designed it."

Emily awkwardly stated, "It's kinda hard to imagine God part of, er, *romantic* love."

Yetta laughed outright. "Love is love, pure and simple. Sure, there may be different kinds, but it all stems from the same place. We couldn't love one another, even romantically, as you put it, if it didn't start with God."

"If this were from God, then why do I have such misgivings?"

"You know, Em, the devil's pretty weak, when you think about it. Unless he can feed on people. Feed on their doubts, their fears, and make them believe the worst. He's so good at it, people generally believe him and then he has a foothold in their lives and it only gets worse from there. He doesn't want anything that his ultimate enemy, God, wants so he'll do *anything* he can to make people believe that his way is better than God's. So, why on earth would the devil want you happy? He knows you're worried about your loyalty to Jacob, so he's going to use that to make you doubt and second guess yourself."

Emily sat quietly for some time. Yetta knew she was struggling and gently broke into her thoughts. "Emily, my advice is, *talk to him.* Joshua is not an unreasonable man. If you explain what you're feeling, I bet he'll understand. Maybe he's even having the same thoughts. Think about it, you were his best friend's wife! How could he not feel a little of what you're feeling already?"

Emily swallowed the sudden lump in her throat. "I know I need to. I'm just a little afraid of what he'll say."

Yetta shook her head. "The devil, Emily, don't let him get to you. Don't let him ruin something wonderful that God created."

One thing Emily did allow herself to take pleasure in was the familiar Sunday dinners. Occasionally, Joshua even invited them all to his house. As time wore on, Emily knew she was being severely unfair to Joshua. She should have talked to him long ago about their relationship.

After her talk with Yetta, she had felt better, but hadn't acted on the good advice. Soon, she felt herself slipping back into her old habit of doubting. It didn't seem fair to love Joshua and Jacob. And she could never forget Jacob. She'd never stop loving him.

One Sunday after dinner, she found herself with a perfect opportunity. The dishes had been cleared, the kitchen tidied, and the children seemed to have disappeared.

'*It's now or never, Emily. Do it quick before you lose your nerve!*'

Emily found Joshua in the living room. Clearing her throat as she entered, she sat down across the room from him. "Josh, I need to talk to you."

Not one given to unnecessary alarm, he patiently waited for her to continue.

"I want to start off by assuring you that I love you. *So* much. But, I love Jacob, too, still, and I don't think that will ever go away. I'm struggling with how to fit both of you into my life."

Emily stopped, willing the next words to come. The words she had to say, but didn't know if she wanted to hear the answer to. Pressing on, she forced out, "If you don't think you can handle that, then I need to know now. I don't want to find out when it might be too late."

Joshua wanted to wrap Emily in his arms right then and whisper that he would love her no matter what. That he accepted her the way she was. That she wouldn't be the woman he fell in love with if she still didn't have a piece of her heart belonging to

Jacob, his best friend. He knew he couldn't do the former, but he could do the latter in assuring her.

"Emily, I don't *ever* expect you to forget Jacob or to put me in his place. In fact, I don't want you to. Honestly, I'm a little worried about following in his footsteps." Joshua faltered. He had the dreaded sense he may have said too much. Of course Emily wouldn't be ready to talk about it, but he knew he'd marry her someday. Whenever she was ready. But he would have Emily as his wife. It was the only way he could see them ending up. Quickly trying to cover his tracks, he went on. "To have your love is something I'm honored with. I promise to try my hardest not to take it for granted."

Relieved that Joshua was the man she'd counted on him to be, Emily questioned, "Then you'll be patient with me as I sort this all out?"

Joshua smiled and replied, "I only have forever."

Up until that point, Emily had insisted they not tell the children anything. But, as the months passed, Emily felt they shouldn't keep it from them anymore. Whatever happened between her and Joshua, she felt certain they would only be furthering their relationship, not deterring from it. It didn't feel all that strange anymore to visualize that one day they may marry. In fact, she rather looked forward to it. Joshua had alluded to that fact a few times, but didn't press.

Another Sunday meal had passed. It seemed that was the only time they really saw each other anyway. He was busy during the week and now that another summer was coming to a close, Emily had to help the children prepare for school. It would be Brianna and Madison's last year.

Joshua and Emily quietly sipped their coffee. It wasn't an awkward silence, as they had fallen into a comfortable pattern after the Sunday meals.

Finally, Emily put her coffee cup down and asked hesitantly, "Do you think it's time to tell the children?"

Joshua tried to hide his shock, but wasn't completely successful.

"What was that look for?" Emily wanted to know.

"Nothing. Nothing at all."

Inwardly, he was elated! Emily wanting to tell the children was surely a sign that some of her doubts were slowly ebbing away. He'd been praying for this sort of sign for quite some time. Ever since Emily had first hesitantly brought up her doubts. Trying to be calm and casual, Joshua affirmed, "That's a good idea. They should know. If you really feel ready to tell them."

Emily had made it clear from the beginning, they were not courting. Right now, she simply wanted them to get back on familiar footing with their friendship. Joshua hoped this meant that they could start officially courting. Courting could only lead to one thing...a proposal which, in turn, led to marriage.

'Don't get ahead of yourself,' Joshua strongly cautioned himself.

"So, what exactly are we telling them? We aren't courting...yet." Joshua smiled mischievously.

"We will tell them that we have feelings for each other that could change things over the next several months. We aren't courting...yet" Emily winked at Joshua, "but they should be prepared for that when it happens."

Joshua was happy to hear that part. The rest seemed a bit much to Joshua, but he wasn't going to stir up any trouble if it meant Emily had time to do things her way and could come to terms with her doubts. One thing was for certain, she was trying to allay her fears and so far, she was doing a pretty good job of it.

Chapter 25: A Family Discussion

Emily felt she needed time to prepare for the upcoming talk she and Joshua had decided to have with their children. To make it easier, and because it also made more sense, they were going to sit all eight of them down together and explain.

It transpired that the day they chose was also the end of the summer picnic the town of Lorraine always had the last Saturday of August.

For some reason, Emily simply couldn't get into the festivities. With all of her heart, she knew what she wanted. She wanted Joshua. She wanted a secure future with him and their children. She wanted to be married to him and love him forever. And she wanted her worries about being unfaithful to Jacob to go away. One thing she had come to realize was that, deep down, she knew she was only being disloyal to herself by letting her thoughts take over. There was no reasonable explanation of the way she felt. Logically she knew she couldn't be betraying someone who was no longer alive. The Bible even said it was alright to remarry if one's spouse died. Her stupid worries were plaguing her, robbing her of the joy this day should bring.

Joshua, on the other hand, was enjoying himself immensely. More so, it was because of what he knew would transpire later. He was proud of Emily for forging ahead. They had talked about it only a few times. Sometimes it seemed she resented him saying anything at all. The fact remained that he *was* proud of her, even if she didn't want to hear it. He prayed for her constantly and was left with a peace, knowing all would turn out for the best in the end.

Later, as eight expectant faces stared back at the two of them, Joshua knew it'd be up to him to keep the atmosphere upbeat. It would help Emily relax and hopefully the children wouldn't sense any of her hesitation. He knew Emily was taking a big step by getting them involved. It showed she was committed, even if she couldn't see the end result. He'd already had to bite his tongue just before they'd enter the room to tell Emily, once again, how proud he was of her. Now wasn't the time to make her uncomfortable.

Emily was grateful for Joshua's strength as they walked into the room. He immediately took over the conversation. She felt too weak, and a bit cowardly, to continue.

"I'm thinkin' ya probably already have an inkling as to what we wanted to talk to you about," Joshua began.

"I think so," Christopher answered for the group without hesitation.

Emily raised her eyebrows, but said not a word. '*Oh, really?*' she inwardly queried.

"Well, it seems you an' Uncle Josh are friends again," Samantha supplied helpfully. "But we kinda gathered that when we started havin' Sunday dinners again."

Joshua tried to put it as succinctly as possible. "All we are trying to do right now is to move on...eventually, that may lead us to something, er, a little more serious in our relationship. We wanted to forewarn you in case that happened."

"We knew it!" Alyssa uttered fiercely to herself before realizing she had spoken aloud. She clamped her mouth shut.

Emily gave her a questioning look. Then she and Joshua exchanged smirks.

Joshua ended the conversation by encouraging, "If any of you have any questions or problems you want to discuss, you can talk to either one of us. We can come together in a few weeks and discuss any potential problems with the, er, arrangement."

Joshua knew there wouldn't be any problems with the children but, Emily, on the other hand, had her misgivings. He knew it was linked to her own insecurities and he determined he'd be that much more patient with her.

Emily's daily phrase became, '*Time heals all wounds.*' She's not sure it did much to alleviate her feelings, but it helped her to feel that she was doing *something* to help. God had started to feel distant. Rather, she didn't try to pursue Him much. She had a feeling it had to do with the fact that she was throwing something wonderful back in His face and so felt immensely guilty. As usual. Guilt seemed to be her companion lately.

She felt as if she were telling God, by her actions, that Him giving Joshua to her wasn't good enough for her. It was! She tried telling God that, but her guilt kept getting in the way and she wasn't sure how to get rid of it. Through it all, Joshua never wavered in his loyalty to her. Joshua was her one saving grace. Joshua was her rock.

What was she doing here now? Was she really about to discuss her love life with her children? It was necessary to help her know she was doing the right thing if she knew how they felt about it all. So, four expectant faces stared back at her, waiting for her to speak.

"I'm guessing nothing has really surprised you lately. I suspect you all were waiting, probably hoping, something like this would happen. Yet, I need to hear it from you. I need to know that I have your blessing in this, so to speak. Those are the wrong words, but I'm hoping you understand what I'm trying to say."

Happy glances were exchanged, but it was Brianna who spoke up. "Mama, we are all really happy for you and Uncle Josh." In a more subdued tone, she added, "That is, if you're happy."

Emily then noticed Christopher's face. He wasn't smiling and was sitting a little away from the group. Not enough that it was too noticeable, but enough that Emily made a mental note of it.

As her daughters chatted happily, Christopher remained silent until Emily tried drawing him into the conversation. "What do you think of all this, Chris?"

He said only, "It all seems fine to me."

Emily tried not to let it bother her, but vowed to talk with him later. Perhaps he didn't want to say anything in front of his sisters.

Later as they were filing out to get ready for bed, Emily called him aside. Once the room was clear, she gestured for him to sit down.

Bluntly she questioned, "What's going on?"

Christopher wouldn't meet her gaze and mumbled, "Nothing."

Emily tried again. "Come on, Chris. I know something's bothering you. I need to know what it is so we can fix it. You know you can talk to me about it, whatever it is."

Sullenly, Christopher asked, "Are you gonna marry Uncle Josh?"

"It's a possibility, Chris. But, keep in mind, he hasn't even asked me yet."

Christopher made a face she couldn't decipher. Instead of asking about it, though, she asked instead, "Don't you want us to get married? Your sisters seem excited enough about it."

The cold "No" he uttered surprised Emily.

"May I ask why?"

"I don't need a Pa and neither do the girls. We're doin' just fine on our own. We have been for almost two years."

"Chris, that wouldn't be the only reason I'd marry him. I love him and–"

"What about Pa? Don't you love him anymore? Or are you forgetting all about him?"

Stunned, Emily felt like she'd been slapped in the face. How had he guessed her misgivings so completely? Emily struggled for a response as she willed the sudden tears to stay at bay. He couldn't know how much his statement had hurt and how on point he'd been with his statement, mirroring her own doubts. Haltingly Emily explained, "I am who I am today *because* of him. I will *never* stop loving him nor will I ever forget about him!"

Emily could tell by the look on his face that he wasn't satisfied about something. Venturing a guess, she said, "And if you're worried about Uncle Josh tryin' to take his place...well, he would never do that. You know Uncle Josh and you know that would be the last thing on his mind."

"May I leave now?" Christopher asked quietly.

Nodding her assent, Emily sadly watched him walk out of the room.

Joshua was having the complete opposite reaction from his daughters. They were all excited.

Alyssa even got up the nerve to ask him, "What took so long?"

"We all knew you were in love with Aunt Emily," Alexis informed him.

Joshua grinned. "You know us old folks. We're slow to catch on."

Joshua wondered if he should issue the warning he'd been struggling with telling them. Finally, he cautioned, "Don't push her too hard, okay? She's still getting used to all this. Uncle Jacob has been gone almost two years, but she's still adjusting to that. We aren't officially courting or anything, so don't make a big deal out of this, okay?"

Hesitantly, Kayla asked, "Daddy, does Aunt Emily love you?"

Joshua's answer was immediate and emphatic, "Yes, she does."

"Why doesn't she want you to court her, then?"

Wearily, Joshua wished he hadn't said anything. Had it really been necessary to warn them after all? Sighing, he admitted, yes, it was. They could be a little exuberant when they were excited about something and he didn't want any pressure on Emily. Finally he answered, "It's complicated, Alyssa."

"What does it have to do with Uncle Jacob?" Madison inquired.

Momentarily caught off guard, Joshua was at a loss for words. He didn't want to betray Emily's confidence, so answered carefully. "It's been a long time since Emily has had to court anyone...she needs to get used to the idea in her own way and in her own time...she wasn't much older than you when she got engaged."

Meaning it as an explanation, it still gave him pause when he stopped to think about that fact. Saying it aloud made him realize how grown up Madison was becoming. By the end of the year, she'd be fifteen. That wasn't far away. And it was true, Emily had been only seventeen when she'd gotten engaged to Jacob.

Trying to shake off the image that in two years, his little Madison, the strong one, the stubborn one, the most independent one, could very well be getting married and leaving home. He took that moment to roughly tell the girls they needed to retire to bed, his voice raw with emotion he could barely conceal.

Thankfully John Carlisle was away at university and another young man would have the chance to catch her eye.

Ruefully, he reminded himself he had plenty of time to worry about that later.

Emily worried not only about her guilt, but about how long she was making Joshua wait. She knew that if she'd agree to it today, he'd marry her in a heartbeat. To make matters worse, hers weren't the only feelings to be considered now. How would Joshua take it, knowing Christopher didn't approve? And it didn't help any that Christopher's problems mirrored her own doubts.

Once again, she feebly attempted prayer. *'Lord, I sure could use your help here. Why do I keep going down this same road over and over and making the same wrong turns? I'm so weary of this. What do I need to do? Jacob has been gone almost two years,* two years! *So why can't I let him go already?'*

Emily knew she *had* to stop looking back. Only forward. She knew Jacob couldn't share in her future. Was she okay with that? Was she willing to let Joshua into hers? And what did that entail, anyway? Did Joshua have any particular way he envisioned their future? One of them should!

All through the night, Emily tossed and turned, sleeping only in fits and starts. Just before dawn, she gave up trying to sleep. What she needed, she decided, was a good, brisk stroll. And being that Joshua would be along soon to start work in the fields, she made a spontaneous decision to talk things over with him. After all, if they were eventually going to share a life together, they'd need to be open with one another.

The thought of sharing her life with someone else brought the inevitable stab of guilt. Frustrated with herself, she scolded the empty room aloud. "I can't live in the past! I have a man who loves me *now* and I love him! Why can't I be happy without the guilt marring it?"

The walk to the fields helped immensely in blowing off her pent up anger at herself. It had also calmed her somewhat.

Joshua had caught a glimpse of Emily coming, huffing really, and he stopped his work to wait for her to reach him.

"Hello, beautiful lady," Joshua greeted.

Emily blushed and ducked her head. She hadn't quite expected such a greeting. A small hole, still gaping, pierced her.

'That's the sort of thing Jacob would have said to me.' Mentally shaking herself, she rebuked, *'Stop it! Stop comparing Josh to Jacob! It isn't fair and you know it!'*

Emily began quietly. "Josh, I'm sorry, but I don't know if this is going to work."

Dread overcame Joshua. Slowly, he asked, "To what, exactly, are you referring?"

"Well…" she stopped, fighting back tears of hopelessness. "Chris is having a hard time adjusting." Immediately Emily felt horrible for using him as a reason. Yes, it was one that needed considering, but she needed to own up to her own fears, as well. Not that they were anything new to Joshua.

Sensing her hesitation, Joshua knew there was more, but he needed to proceed with caution. "Is that all?"

Emily felt her eyes being drawn to his. Knowing this was the time for her honesty, she decided to speak. "I'm also having a hard time…" she let her voice trail off. Resignedly, she tried again. "I love you, I hope you know that. But, I still love him, too. And I'm not willing to leave him completely in my past. I see him everyday in my children. I simply can't forget him." Irritated with herself, Emily found tears slipping down her cheeks. Maybe she was getting ready for the rejection that she was afraid would come next. Quickly, she looked away and missed the clenching of Joshua's jaw.

'Am I not good enough for you?' he wanted to shout. *'I'm trying to be patient, but I'm not a saint! I don't have endless supplies of patience!'* It had been several weeks since speaking with the children and even more months before that of them simply getting back to the familiar relationship they'd shared before everything changed.

When Emily didn't get a response, Emily dared a glance up at Joshua's hard face. He was staring down at her with narrowed eyes. Quickly she tried to explain. "I need more time. I'm sure I'll come around." She attempted a small smile. Hesitantly, she reached a hand up and ran it down his cheek then let it drop when it didn't seem to garner a reaction.

Unknowingly, Emily had caused quite a reaction. The touch had sent a shock through Joshua's entire body. The caress was sweet and all too brief. Joshua decided then to do whatever it took to ensure he could experience such tenderness every day of his life. He knew his life without Emily would be empty. He'd already had a taste of that and didn't wish to repeat it.

Managing to clear his voice, Joshua assured, "I'll wait, Emily...as long as you need."

Joshua and Emily did eventually sit down with their combined children to discuss anything that needed discussing. Christopher had slowly been coming around, Emily had told Joshua. So they thought they might as well clear the air, if there was anything that needed clearing. Yet, to Joshua's disappointment, Emily had not mentioned anything about being ready for official courtship.

Again, Joshua took the lead. "Are there any questions? Anything you need clarified or would like to discuss?"

He tried not to look pointedly at Christopher. He knew Christopher still had some uneasiness about the whole thing.

All seven girls, sitting close together, simply whispered and gushed to one another.

Trying not to roll his eyes, Joshua teased, "That's eternally helpful, girls. Thank you."

It was clear that he'd be getting nothing out of Christopher this way. He was also at the age where he didn't feel the need to express his feelings, so Joshua didn't press. Instead, he thought of another alternative. "Chris, want me to make the rounds with you?"

Joshua knew it was something Jacob used to do with Christopher that had fallen now to Christopher's responsibilities. Joshua hoped Christopher was willing to get help this time.

Christopher gave Joshua what appeared to be a slightly scornful look. At a sharp glance from his mother, he reluctantly agreed.

Joshua kept to small talk. "Weather's been mighty warm lately."

Christopher kept his answers short. "Yep."

"Nice night."

At that, Christopher gave a cursory glance up. "Uh-huh."

They entered the barn silently after that. The silence

continued as they checked and fed the animals.

"Thanks for letting me help you."

Christopher's reply was a grunt.

Joshua thought that maybe a firmer tone would elicit more of a response. "An actual answer is required when addressing your elders, Christopher."

Christopher's head shot up then. "Yes, sir," he amended somewhat sullenly.

Joshua wearily decided he needed to address Christopher's issues head on. "I know you aren't happy about the turn of events between your mother and me. If you have concerns, though, you need to voice them. Care to give me a clue as to what's going on in that head of yours? I know you have your reservations and I'd like to hear 'em."

Christopher took awhile to answer, as he tried to collect his thoughts.

'*I want my Pa back,*' was on the tip of his tongue, but he knew it was futile to go there.

Finally he was able to look Joshua in the eye. With unintended menace, he declared, "You ain't my pa!"

Although Joshua had expected that type of response, it still hurt to hear it. Instead he answered, "I know that, Chris, and I wouldn't ever try to take his place."

"You wanna marry my ma, don'cha?" Christopher spat.

"Yes—"

"Then you'll be tryin' to take his place!"

"No, Chris, I won't. I would never expect you to call me Pa or nothin'. We can remain friends, if that's all you want. I respected your pa a great deal and would never assume to take his place. He was my best friend and I am honored your mother would even consider givin' me the privilege of marryin' her."

Christopher refused to listen. "I wish things could stay the way they are." And he stalked out of the barn.

Joshua watched him go, then sighed. He hoped Christopher would come around, but he knew the key was Emily. The sooner she showed she was ready, the sooner he was sure Christopher would see that and hopefully be more accepting.

Patience and gentleness were apparently something God must've thought Joshua needed more abundantly. He got to experience a lot of practice in both areas regarding Emily over the following weeks. While not a constant companion, frustration was frequent. Partly, he had unreasonable expectations. He'd expected Emily to try harder to overcome her doubts. He'd expected her to be as excited over the prospect of them sharing their lives together as he was. He'd expected that she'd have gotten over her loss in much the same way he'd gotten over his. He'd expected her to all but come running to him with open arms. In reality, he knew he was being unfair. He had no right to place such expectations on her. Yet, it seemed to him, that she didn't seem to *want* to move on, much less *try*. Of course, this line of thinking only brought guilt.

He was genuinely worried about Emily. As much as he *wanted* her to move on, he knew she also *needed* to move on, if only for her own sanity. It wasn't good to hang on as tightly as she seemed to be. He did understand her unwillingness to let go. It was a hard process, but it had been over two years. So, in the midst of his patience and gentleness lessons, he was starting to get a little worn out. If he'd seen *some* sign from Emily that she was coming around, he felt he could bear it a little better. As it was, he was afraid it was all for naught. If Emily had simply told him so and walked away, he could bear it. It would be hard, but he'd be able to pick himself up and walk away. But she constantly asked him to stay, to be patient, to give her a little more time. Sometimes, he wondered if she simply liked stringing him along. Those unfair thoughts always caught up with him and brought shame. First and foremost, he was her friend. Maybe he should try and be satisfied with that before expecting anything else.

'*Help me, God! You know I love her or I couldn't bear this. But, please let something happen soon. Not because I want it, but because it's not good for her to hang on to Jacob so fiercely and for so long. She has to realize she isn't being disloyal to anyone but herself by not letting him go.*'

In perspective, Joshua knew Emily loved him, too. That also helped him forge ahead and work past his frustrations. He could see it in her eyes…the way she looked at him…in her smile…in her body language, the way she lightly touched his hand or brushed past him when she walked by…in the very way she opened up to him and entrusted him with every thought that was in her head. Emily definitely had her way of making him feel special. Why it wasn't enough for him, he couldn't fathom. All he knew was, it wasn't. She wasn't his wife. He wasn't her husband. Until she spoke the word to make it so, he felt her keeping him back, just a little.

The one and only thing she asked of him was patience. That's all it came down to. One word that took a lot of effort. Emily probably didn't even realize what she was doing. Perhaps it was time to enlighten her. If for no other reason than to get a discussion going about their future. Maybe she could give Joshua some idea on how long she was planning on keeping him in suspense.

Obsessed Emily was not. At least, that's what she kept telling herself. No matter that she kept going out to the fields at some point during the day, simply to watch Joshua. In a strange way, it made her feel secure. Like he wasn't going anywhere.

The thought made her slightly uncomfortable. Selfishly, she didn't want him to go anywhere, of course. Yet, was she being fair in making him wait for her to be ready? Was it fair to keep him with her, in a sense, when he quite possibly could've found someone else to share his life with?

It didn't matter to Emily that he *wanted* to be with her. That he loved her. She could only concentrate on her own selfishness and how guilty it made her feel. She talked about Jacob a lot to Joshua. He seemed to enjoy reminiscing with her but, lately that was all she seemed able to talk about. She was sure there were times Joshua would've liked to change the subject to them and their future. As a gentleman, he didn't venture down that path, but she knew she owed him that much. It wasn't that she didn't want to talk about it. In fact, she very much did, but in so doing, would she completely forget about Jacob? She was terrified of that prospect. Besides, she had found it oddly comforting talking about Jacob. It was healing talking about him, and if that's what it took for her to be able to finally move on, she'd take it. Although Joshua may not realize it, she was eager to begin a future with him.

Thinking of him always brought an unconscious smile. He was so patient, especially lately. She knew it couldn't be easy for him to wait for her. She knew she was being unfair in expecting it, yet he didn't press her. He didn't force her to make any quick decisions. She never had to question his feelings for her. She knew them absolutely.

One look at him, and Emily would resolve to do better by him. And then he'd lend his listening ear with such compassion, that she'd find herself bringing Jacob up again and incapable of talking of anything else. Emily knew she needed to apologize and talk to Joshua about it. It couldn't be encouraging for him to always hear of her dead husband.

As if on cue, Emily heard Jacob's voice in her head and what he'd be telling her if he were with her. "You've got to live life, Emily. Embrace it! Remember...take the good with the bad."

Emily frowned slightly. If Jacob was here, she'd have argued with him. Life had seemed so turned upside down lately. At the same time, she knew it was she that was making it so. Somehow, she needed to be the one to fix it and make it right side up again.

Puffing her cheeks, she determined she'd find a way to make it so.

Chapter 26: Second Thoughts

Emily finally determined what she would do, but she wasn't happy about it. It seemed the only solution that made sense and wouldn't hurt anyone but herself. Her heart had been slowly breaking as she came up with her plan, but had thoroughly convinced herself it was for the best of all concerned. After days of contemplation, she decided she simply needed to walk out to the fields, find Joshua, and get it over with.

Joshua looked off in the distance at the purposeful figure of Emily headed toward him. For some reason, his stomach clenched as he realized that whatever she had in mind would not be welcome news. He could tell by the determined, almost fierce look on her face.

Even before she reached him, she was calling out, "Josh, we've gotta talk!"

Joshua drew his hand across his brow. The Indian summer heat was getting a little old to work in, but he reminded himself that the cooler weather had to be just around the corner.

Emily came up then and noticed he'd been plucking ears of corn. "I'll help you with these if you promise to just listen and not interrupt."

She took Joshua's silence for agreement. She concentrated wholeheartedly on the corn and wouldn't look at him as she began. "I can't continue to allow you to wait for me. I love you but I also love Jacob and I can't seem to get over him. It isn't fair to you to be involved in any kind of romantic relationship, no matter the context, before I am completely ready to move on from Jacob. Unfortunately, I can't help the way I feel, nor can I do anything to change it. I'm not sure it's best, but we could always go back to the way things were. It's either that or nothing."

Fear had shot through Joshua the moment Emily had started talking. He tried grasping all she said, but he couldn't shake the feeling of dread. How could he go back to the way things were? Not when he loved her this much! Maybe that was exactly *why* he'd have to.

Emily had kept surprisingly composed and she was proud of herself. Her tone had been matter-of-fact and in doing that, she'd been able to deliver her speech without so much as a catch in her throat. And as long as she didn't think on it, she'd be fine.

Joshua had noticed Emily's rather stoic delivery of what she had clearly rehearsed to say. Disappointment washed through him at this realization. Perhaps this was simply Emily's way of letting him down gently. Yet, he had detected...something, some edge of, bitterness, maybe, to her words. Shock was slowly catching up with his system. It had been so sudden, the last thing Joshua had expected. He'd been patient, hadn't he? That's all she had asked! Confusion swept through him. Why? Why now? Why did she not love him anymore? Could she turn it off that quickly? She had said she loved him, but then how could she seem so cold, so distant? Joshua was suddenly aware of silence. He knew he should say something.

Emily waited expectantly. She wasn't sure if Joshua intended to say anything or not. It would be helpful, but what was there left for him to say? Did she really expect him to simply give in and agree? Of course, that's exactly what she hoped wouldn't happen. She wanted him to fight for her. But she also acknowledged that wouldn't be fair to put him in such a position. Dread was a pit in her stomach.

Grasping for what to say, Joshua numbly repeated her words. "Back to the way things were...that or nothing." The words weren't sinking in.

Emily finally looked him in the eyes. Joshua noted that her beautiful green eyes were full of guilt and regret.

Joshua rallied. "Emily, I don't want to go back to the way things were. I don't think that's even possible...for me, at least."

Emily felt drained and completely exhausted. She suddenly didn't want to go through this conversation anymore. She felt weary of it all. "I'm sorry, but that's the way it has to be."

"Can we at least talk about this?" Joshua looked around then sat down right where he was, on the hard earth.

Reluctantly, she sat down beside him and for the umpteenth time, she wondered, '*What is wrong with me that I can't simply accept this situation?*' Yet, at the same time, she longed to simply lay her head on his shoulder, close her eyes, and rest. Instead, she turned her head and rested it on her knees, looking at Joshua, trying to find the words she'd rehearsed. Taking a deep breath, she said, "I know I've been unfair to you. You're probably sick of hearing about Jacob. And try as I might, I can't seem to separate the two of you. I find myself comparing you to him and it's incredibly unfair. I don't know why I do it, I just do." She'd rambled a bit, she knew, but she hoped she got her point across. "And I realize that if it weren't for my interfering in the first place, you'd probably still be with Katherine. You'd be married to her by now, in fact. You can't even begin to comprehend how sorry I am and how awful I feel about that. And I'm scared, Joshua. I'm really scared that I'd been able to fall in love with you so soon after Jacob. Six months! What kind of normal person does that? I love my husband! And I can't bear to have you loving me more than I am able to love you."

Joshua longed to tell her it didn't matter. He had won her over and, as far as he was concerned, he'd use the rest of his life to make her as happy as Jacob had. He was no fool. He knew he could never measure up to Jacob. Jacob had been a good man and Joshua knew he wasn't worthy of taking his place. But he could still love Emily with everything he had and he knew she'd still deserve more. He wanted to tell her all of that, but he refrained. He knew that wasn't what she wanted, or needed, to hear at the moment.

Frustrated, Emily felt tears begin to gather. "I honestly don't know what's wrong with me. You've been so patient and understanding. I want you in my life, but I can't figure out where you fit!" She squeezed her eyes shut to stem the flow, and turned her head away so Joshua couldn't see.

Joshua looked at her and could only see beauty, despite the hurt and pain she was feeling. He wanted, more than anything, to fix it, but knew she'd end up resenting him if he tried to interfere. This was something she had to work out on her own. He fought the incredible urge to gather her close and wipe her tears.

Turning back, Emily knew she needed to finish what she had come out to say. He needed to understand that she was trying. "At first, I compared you to Jacob. Where you are weak, he was so strong. I've come to realize that there were areas where Jacob was weak and you are the strong one." The admittance cost her dearly and she felt the tears threaten again. "And it feels like such betrayal to him to even think that!"

Strangely, her confession stirred deep emotions in him. He understood what it had cost her to say that. To admit to finding weakness in someone she so dearly loved. And he was worried about her. She needed to move on. It wasn't healthy for her to stay in the state she was in, but he clearly couldn't and wouldn't be the one to push her. He'd tried waiting and being patient and she was most certainly worth waiting for. What bothered him was the debilitating thought that she would never be ready. He could wait as long as she needed, but he also needed to know that his patience would pay off someday and they could further their relationship. He needed to know she was willing to try. Right now, here was an Emily that had seemed to give up. Obviously, at this moment, she was incapable of moving on and, if that were so, she'd never be ready for him. Apparently he had to be the one to sacrifice and let her go. Yet, he heard himself making one last plea for his case. Gently, so the words wouldn't hold a sting, he told her. "Em, you have to let him go. You need to move on with your life. He isn't here anymore to judge what you are doing. Frankly, I think he'd be upset with how much you are hanging on to him. In fact, I don't think you really loved me when you think you did. I think that, yes, you experienced jealousy when I first started courting Katherine, but only because you were jealous of her new place in my life. As if she were replacing you. I honestly think you fell in love with me later. So don't let that torment you anymore." Joshua held his breath waiting for her response. All that he got was a quick spark of hope that flashed in her eyes, then was gone. After a few moments, he realized that was the only reaction he'd get, so he continued. "You can't keep reopening the guilt because of how you feel. The feelings you have for me are natural. There is nothing wrong with them, or you!" Without his consent, his tone became embarrassingly pleading, "Please, for me, please move on. I'll help you, if you want, but you've got to *want* to." Impatience, frustration, and desperation all surfaced then and he forced himself to be quiet or he might find himself doing or saying something that would only make things worse.

Slowly, so she wouldn't be startled, he scooted closer to

Emily and gently cradled her head to his chest. They sat that way for quite awhile. It helped him calm down and try to put things into perspective. All that mattered was Emily and he tried to keep that in the forefront of his mind. He knew she didn't do it to purposefully hurt him. It was hard to remember that sometimes but, sitting as they were, helped him to keep his focus where it needed to be.

Finally Emily said, in a quiet voice he almost missed, "I'm scared. I don't want to forget him."

Joshua's resolve to keep things in perspective rose at that. Confidently, Joshua answered her. "You won't forget. I'll help you remember. I don't want to forget him either." Joshua turned her face to his, "We'll help each other remember." He knew she'd need a lot of help, but he was more than willing to give it. He would need to be patient a little longer.

Joshua gave everything he possibly could and it wasn't without much prayer and begging God to help him go on. Sometimes he wondered if he had any more to give, but there was God, doling out just enough to get him through. Emily was making an honest effort to move on, and he did what he could to help her. Yet, there were times it almost seemed as if Emily resented his presence. It seemed she resented his help. It seemed, sometimes, she resented *him*. He tried not to be discouraged, but it was hard. Daily reminders were essential now, as to why he even bothered. He loved her. He loved her. He loved her. He loved her.

They had their little spats and, afterward, Joshua would always vow to keep his tongue in check. Then, she'd do or say something that irked him to no end, and he'd find himself saying what was really on his mind and she'd have her own biting come-back. Neither wanted to admit that sometimes something the other one said was something they, themselves, needed to hear.

Joshua grew more determined, but wondered where it would all end. Was what they were working towards, what he felt he was literally fighting for, worth it? Or should they give up now and go their separate ways? He wasn't one hundred percent sure of what Emily felt anymore, but he knew that if he let her go, he'd never get over her. There would be no one else for him. It was Emily or no one. If he gave her up, he'd undoubtedly be missing a bigger part of himself.

Emily could feel the thick tension between them. They carried on as normally as possible. One thing Emily really hated was Joshua's hovering. It felt as if Joshua was constantly there trying to figure things out, that she, quite frankly, didn't need help figuring. Some things she needed to do on her own. The seemingly constant bickering was getting on her nerves. Truth be told, she didn't see how any of this could come out favorably for either of them.

'I wish he'd leave me in peace! I could sort things out a lot better on my own!'

In reality, she was more fed up with herself than Joshua. She knew that if Joshua gave up and left, a real possibility, she'd have lost her reason to keep trying to move forward. She'd be lost without Joshua. She could admit that...some days. Once again, he was proving to be her rock. If he left, she was afraid she'd revert to the awful depression she'd experienced last year, the year after Jacob's death. So why couldn't she leave Jacob where he needed to be? A tender part of her past.

She knew Joshua had been right. She needed to move on. And she was desperately trying! Her frustration came when she'd think she was making one step forward, only to have the ugly guilt rear its head and pull her back under. Emily knew Jacob through and through and knew beyond a shadow of a doubt, that if he saw what she was doing, he wouldn't like it. He'd tell her to stop letting the guilt eat her alive and enjoy her life. If it meant marrying Joshua, then he'd tell her to do it. Jacob deeply respected Joshua. They'd been more like brothers than mere friends. Emily knew Jacob would approve. So it was her own stubbornness that wasn't allowing anything more with Joshua and she didn't know why she was fighting it so much. Especially since she had fought so hard for Joshua in the first place.

Over the next few months, the tension grew and so did her resentment. When she had originally gone out to talk to Joshua in the fields, she'd done it with the intent to end their relationship, tenuous as it was. Even returning it to where it had been would've proven a challenge.

Looking back, Emily was irritated with the way Joshua had responded. He tried fixing it, as usual. Instead of accepting the fact that it needed to end and totally discounting her intentions, he dug in his heels and got his own way. Every time she thought about it, she could feel herself getting worked up. She'd try to stop her thoughts, but they kept lingering on that conversation until she was quite angry! How dare he try and *save* her? There was nothing to save! He didn't seem to want to accept that. If she said it was over, it was over! But not according to Joshua, it would seem. In the back of her mind, it registered how absurd these thoughts were, but it never stopped the inner ranting. It would take her a good hour or more to work the argument from all the angles in her favor, then she'd decide, once again, that Joshua was interfering. As much as she was scared of losing him, she was also scared of letting him get too close. That would surely result in her completely forgetting about Jacob. And although her arguments were mostly unfounded, Emily, over time, felt a stubbornness settling over her. In her logical moments, she honestly couldn't fathom why she had to make Joshua see her view on things, but it became extremely important to her. Eventually, she came to her senses long enough to realize they needed to sit down and have a serious talk. The tension, the arguments, the hovering, all needed to stop or she feared what would happen.

One Sunday after dinner, Emily realized Joshua was missing. After a search, she found him on her porch, sitting in the rocking chair staring, unseeingly, into the distance. He didn't seem to notice her approach.

The sun was barely starting to dip behind the trees. The oppressive heat seemed to be dwindling, leaving the evenings balmy, but pleasant. Autumn had arrived, but the temperatures hadn't reflected it yet.

Emily stood by the door, slightly behind Joshua, hesitating.

The rocking stopped. Without turning, Joshua questioned, "Emily?"

Emily answered simply, "Yes, it's me."

Emily took a seat on the bench opposite the rocker. She could tell Joshua had been brooding. "Josh, you have to stop this," she began softly. "Whatever it is that's compelling you, needs to stop. Protectiveness, maybe, a need to save me....whatever it is needs to stop. We need to take a step back and decide where we are headed."

'*Please, God, not away from each other,*' she added silently. And then her usual rebuttal. '*But how can it lead anywhere else when you won't let Jacob go?*'

Joshua closed his eyes then and gritted his teeth. He tensed, waiting for the onslaught he knew was coming. Too harshly, he demanded, "Emily, if you don't love me anymore, say it!"

Emily reeled back as if she'd physically experienced the sting. Could he honestly not see that she did? Vehemently, she objected. "I *do* love you, Josh! That's the problem! I can't stop loving you and yet, I can't love two men anymore." And then she delivered a blow she didn't even know she had the strength to deliver. "And Jacob wins. Jacob will always win. That's what I've been trying to tell you!"

The carefully composed façade Joshua had kept up for the last four months came crumbling down. Bitterness that he'd kept in check oozed into his voice. "Stop it, Emily! Stop hiding behind Jacob. You're right, you can't love two men. At least, not in the present. Why are you choosing a dead man who can't love you back? I'm here *now*! *I* love you, Emily! Why can't you see that?"

At first, Emily was stunned into silence. Then she was angry. "How *dare* you accuse me of *hiding* behind Jacob? If I didn't love you, why would I be struggling with this? Why would it matter to me that I still love Jacob and can't love you fully? Why would I feel such guilt; to the point of anguish; that I can't love you back the way you deserve, if you didn't matter to me?"

"Good question, Em," Joshua pointed out sarcastically. "Why *can't* you love me? Am I not good enough for you? Do I not love you enough or in the right way? Nope. That's not it at all. It's because *I'm not Jacob*, pure and simple!"

Though not shouting, their voices were definitely loud enough to carry.

"You are being unfair, Josh, and you know it! I don't want to be disloyal to Jacob. You can't even fathom how hard and how long I have been struggling with this!" She rolled her eyes in exasperation. "We've been through this already."

"How well I know that!" Joshua spat. "I also know that as long as you keep comparing us, I'm always the one who will come up short. I have no hope with you, do I? The fact that I am so madly, give-my-own-life-for-you in love with you, doesn't seem to matter. It sickens me, Emily. And pardon me for being selfish, but I think I deserve a little effort on your part if this is going to have a fair chance of working. I've been here for you, done more for you than anyone else and all I'm asking is for a fair chance to prove myself to you. It would seem you're not interested."

The truth had been spoken and Emily knew it, but she stubbornly refused to give in to it, much preferring her own version of reality at the moment. After all, it would damage her pride to admit Joshua was right. Steadfastly, she held onto her version of the truth. Emphasizing each word, she tried to make herself clear to Joshua and convince herself she was right. "I. Don't. Want. To. Be. Disloyal. To. Jacob."

Joshua volleyed back, "Who do you have to be disloyal to? He's dead!" The truth spoken aloud sounded unnecessarily harsh.

Emily felt as if the wind had been knocked out of her and Joshua was struck silent. He couldn't believe he had uttered such cruelty.

Emily found herself with something to consider, nonetheless. Who *did* she have to be loyal to? All this time, she rallied for Jacob, but really, why did she feel she had to remain faithful to him? He had been gone two years. While he was alive, she had been a true wife and loved him fiercely. Everything seemed to finally click into place. He was gone. She was no longer bound to him, but she realized she *wanted* to be. It made her feel better, somehow, to think she was doing right by him, even after his death. He was her first love and no one could replace him. And then she thought of something Joshua told her and she finally listened to him, in that moment. Joshua didn't want to *replace* Jacob. She'd been so stupid! She didn't know how many times he had reiterated just that. And had done so in a patient and loving way, only to have her slap him in the face with it. Embarrassment and shame caused her to retreat a step, though. She wouldn't fully admit just how wrongly she'd been treating Joshua.

While these thoughts took shape in Emily's head, Joshua got to watch the emotions play out on her face. For a fleeting moment,

Joshua thought that maybe Emily had come around.

In the end, Emily's pride got in the way and she hissed, "We are through!" before stalking inside.

Emily felt restless. She and Joshua had retreated back to the pattern they were stuck in when Joshua was engaged. They didn't speak, didn't see each other, they avoided each other publicly. And they were both miserable. They didn't have any excuse for their behavior this time. Simply stubborn pride on both parts.

Samantha noticed it first and rallied her siblings into action. Actually, it was more like a plea. She approached Christopher first, knowing he'd had issues in the past with their mother and Uncle Joshua having any kind of romantic relationship. She figured he was ecstatic about the recent turn of events and knew she'd have to do some fast talking to convince him their ma was miserable. Samantha wasn't disappointed in his reaction. "Come on, Chris, you know Mama isn't happy without Uncle Josh. She needs him as much, if not more than, he needs her."

"Judging from their little quarrel the other night, she was none too happy *with* him, either."

"That's because Mama's worried about bein' disloyal to Pa. Pretty silly, if you ask me."

"Well, no one's askin' you, and it ain't silly to me. She *is* bein' disloyal to Pa!"

"No she isn't! How can she be? She's a widow. She's free to marry again and she wants to marry Uncle Josh, she's just havin' a hard time realizin' it, is all. He's a good man and they *should* get married."

"You're a silly girl, Samm."

"You know part of the reason she's hesitant is 'cause of you. She knows you're upset by all of this."

"Good! At least she's not bein' selfish about it like Uncle Josh was with Miss Taylor-Ryan."

"No, but *you* are, Chris. You *know* Mama's happy with Uncle Josh. I think it'd help her move on if we can show her we agree with her decision to marry Uncle Josh!" Men were such an exasperation! Samm decided. No wonder Mama was always having outs with Uncle Josh!

"But I *don't* agree!"

Exasperation colored her words. "Christopher Jacob Matthews, you're such a *man*!" Then she did something she hadn't done since she was a little girl. She stamped her foot and marched out of the room.

Emily was downright miserable without Joshua, though she wouldn't allow herself to admit it. She also wouldn't allow herself to finally admit that Joshua had been right. She preferred wallowing in self-pity at the moment. If anyone were to ask her directly if she was happy with her decision, she'd say yes and thoroughly convince herself that was the truth.

Until she could finally admit to herself the fact that she had treated Joshua and the love he offered in a most abominable way. Over time, Emily's despair turned into simple resignation. Her life, by her own doing, was empty now because of her stubborn pride barring Joshua. In her mind, it was now too late to do anything about it. Sheer will forced her to pick up and move on. Without realizing it, the one act Joshua begged of her to do was finally happening, and she was doing it now for no one but herself.

Joshua couldn't remember the last time a woman had affected him so strongly. Katherine hadn't even had the power to do it. Completely opposite to what Emily was doing, Joshua felt his life was at a standstill. Convincing himself he and Emily weren't meant to be wasn't working too well for him. He tried allaying those thoughts with the fact that he deserved better from Emily. *She* needed to show him that she truly cared for him and *wanted* to be with him. All he was asking for was a little effort.

Sighing, Joshua willfully determined to shut all thoughts of Emily from his mind. It would hopefully help him heal quicker and he hoped it would work soon. Yet, the energy he wasted on that was futile. He knew he'd wait for Emily. Even if she never chose him again, he'd wait for the rest of his life for her. He loved her too much to simply let her go, even if that's what she chose to do.

A small, secret place inside of him, hoped that the distance they'd forced upon themselves would eventually make Emily realize she needed him as much as he needed her. Maybe she would come to the realization that she could love him fully after all.

Chastisement set in for awhile, as he realized the distancing maybe should have taken place a lot sooner. He'd been too impatient, too eager, for Emily to think along those lines before. But, if he had, maybe they wouldn't be going through what they were now.

He couldn't shake the small part of him that worried Emily would never be ready. What would he do then? He'd be miserable, he knew.

He felt enough time had passed that if Emily had discovered she couldn't be happy without him, she'd have been to see him already. He argued with himself almost endlessly on that point. Of course, he could always go see her, but then he'd be doing exactly what had gotten them to this point in the first place. He'd drive her even farther away, if that was even possible.

She had called off their friendship when it had barely been salvageable and Joshua knew she'd have to be the one to reconcile. Any action from him would end in disaster; he was convinced of it. He knew he needed to simply let her be, but it was getting to be unbearable. If something didn't happen soon, he'd break.

Sundays were utterly unavoidable. Church was a must and if it weren't for their reverence for God, they would avoid church altogether merely for the sake of not having to run into one another at all. They were cordial enough, but it took quite a toll on each one as they tried to act cool and aloof toward the other.

Their all too brief encounters usually consisted of, "Hello, Mrs. Matthews." "Mr. Tyler." "Nice weather we're having." "How is your family?" And the like.

What Emily wouldn't give to spill her secret thoughts to Joshua once again. Unfortunately, they all consisted of him and would be embarrassing to share.

Surprisingly, she often found herself longing to tell Joshua she was wrong and she had firmly put Jacob where he now belonged, in her past. Occasionally, she'd think of Jacob, but it was always with great fondness and sweet memories, never yearning. Emily longed to tell Joshua that it was he whom she yearned for now.

And, as always, her pride got in the way before she could muster the courage to say anything.

Joshua waited in agony, week after week, for Emily to simply say the word. That he could finally court her. That he could, indeed, make her his to love and cherish forever. Alas, he went along with the niceties, grateful to have even that. He had to hold himself in great check so he wouldn't do anything rash.

One particular Sunday that all changed.

Emily found herself unable to concentrate on Reverend Chadrick's sermon. She kept glancing around, decidedly *not* looking in Joshua's direction. In a weak moment, however, she felt her eyes slide that way of their own accord. And, much to her surprise, she found Joshua's eyes staring back at her. Their gazes locked and Emily seemed unable to pull hers away. The feeling was quite unsettling. Then it was made worse by Joshua boldly winking at her. Only then did she look away, bright red with embarrassment.

Joshua thoroughly chastised himself for that one. What had made him wink at her? He'd made her embarrassed and quite possibly ruined any warm feelings she was having for him. And he was convinced they were there, otherwise, why had she looked his way? He'd read it in her eyes when she had looked at him. Her gaze was simply mesmerizing and he'd found he couldn't look away. Instead of doing something more mannerly, like smile, he'd winked! For the rest of the sermon, he kicked himself and gave up any hope of hearing anything Reverend Chadrick had to say.

Across the aisle, Emily sat in discomfort. She had taken to sitting across from where she used to so as to avoid anything untoward happening between she and Joshua. Something much like what had just transpired.

She didn't dare look back at Joshua, but she had much to ponder, borne from that moment. Was her insecurity of being rejected by Joshua enough to completely throw away any chance at all with him? She'd seen it in his eyes. He most definitely was *not* rejecting her. However inappropriate that wink was, it merely sealed the fact that his feelings for her hadn't gone away. That was really her only fear now. Did he truly still care for her? No, did he truly still *love* her?

Samantha had caught the exchange between her mother and Uncle Joshua. She watched Emily now as she battled some internal struggle.

'*This is ridiculous!,*' Samantha thought. '*She needs Uncle Josh as much as he needs her...maybe more. I've gotta convince Chris to be happy for them to be together. None of us are happy now with Ma bein' so sad; he's surely sensed that by now.*'

Growing in a maturity she didn't realize, Samantha could be very perceptive for a girl of only eleven.

Samantha realized her mother needed some reassurances from them, her children, as well, before she could be completely certain about her future with Uncle Joshua. She determined then that she'd do whatever it took to see her mother happy again. Even if it meant she had to hogtie Christopher!

Chapter 27: A Heart To Heart

Samantha made good on her promise to herself to corner her brother and make him see reason. His poor attitude had gone on long enough, she decided.

Their house was entirely too quiet without the Tylers coming over to liven things up. She mostly blamed Christopher.

Christopher still wanted to become a veterinarian and, since he wouldn't be able to attend school anymore, come fall, he would spend all of his free time studying various books on animals. He planned on apprenticing with Dr. George Allison since doctoring people was the closest thing he could find to doctoring animals.

Knowing this, Samantha easily found him in the library. She tip-toed up the stairs, so as not to disturb him.

The library was a smallish room, made so merely because there were four doors leading off of the room, making it naturally square. In front of the one floor-to-ceiling bookcase that housed all of their books, was where Christopher now reclined in one of the two overstuffed chairs.

Samantha cleared her throat audibly and Christopher put down his book, eyeing her.

"What do you want?" he asked, annoyed.

All business, Samantha decided to get right to the point. "You need to stop your brooding over Uncle Josh and Mama. She needs him and I'm going to do whatever it takes to make *her* happy. I don't care if you don't like it. It's going to happen."

Samantha steeled herself for Christopher's tirade that was sure to come.

Instead, he surprised her. He sighed and laid his book down on his lap. "I know Ma isn't happy and that it has to do with Uncle Josh." His voice was resigned.

Samantha was shocked, then she found her voice. "You really mean it? You think so, too? What made you change your mind?"

Christopher confessed, "I've been watching them the past

few weeks at church or whenever they happen to meet. It came to me quite suddenly, actually, that they do need each other. I suppose it's better than Ma bein' miserable all the time; if she can be happy with Uncle Josh."

"Then I'm goin' to tell Ma that it's alright to marry Uncle Josh and that *none* of us mind anymore!"

"Er, okay, but, Samm, I don't think Ma would appreciate you *tellin'* her what to do."

Sheepishly, Samantha smiled. "Well, I wouldn't *tell* her to marry Uncle Josh. Just kinda let her know that if she wants to, we're fine with it now. *All* of us." She couldn't help adding the emphasis.

"Samm," Christopher warned, "maybe it'd be best if you simply told her we're happy with whatever makes her happy….end of story. No hinting."

Christopher was still a little wary about Uncle Joshua becoming a permanent fixture in their household. But, he hadn't been lying when he'd said he wanted his Ma to be happy.

Samantha rolled her eyes and sweetly responded, "Whatever you say, big brother." But she couldn't deny her newfound excitement.

Samantha nervously wiped her sweaty palms on her nightdress for the fourth time. Standing outside her mother's bedroom door, she finally, timidly, knocked. She'd heard movement, so knew her mother was still awake.

"Mama?" she called softly.

She heard a faint, "Come in" from beyond the door.

Hesitantly Samantha opened the door.

Emily was in front of her vanity, brushing her long golden waves, which she always referred to as a ball of fluff.

"Mama, can I talk to you?"

Putting the brush down and turning to face her daughter, Emily responded, "Absolutely, darlin', what is it?"

Samantha paused then, wondering how to begin. "Well…" she bit her lip.

Emily smiled encouragingly, sensing Samantha's hesitation. "It's alright. Just tell me…or ask me…whatever you want."

Tentatively, Samantha began. "Chris and I had a talk."

Confused, Emily answered, "Alright..." drawing out the word. "What did you talk about?"

"You" Samantha hastily said. Then she started biting her lip again. She wasn't sure how to continue on, but decided to add, "And Uncle Josh."

Emily looked at her brush and began fiddling with the bristles. Acting nonchalant was taking all of her concentration. Managing to keep her voice steady, she simply wondered aloud, "Is that right?"

Samantha suddenly felt courageous. "Mama, he, er, Chris, wants you to be happy. No matter what. Even if it means marrying Uncle Josh." More lip biting. She held her breath, waiting for her mother's rebuff. Surely her mother would rebuke her for talking about such things with her older brother.

Emily was elated it seemed Christopher was finally coming around. Yet, it reminded her that there was no need for it now. Fighting to keep the emotion out of her voice, Emily offered, "That's nice, dear." Unconsciously, she frowned.

Samantha noticed the tight frown. "What's wrong, Mama?"

Emily smiled sadly. "It's futile now. It doesn't matter that Chris has finally come around. Of course, I'm glad he finally did, but it seems it's too late for any of it."

Puzzled, Samantha frowned, too, unknowingly mirroring her mother. "Why?"

"It's complicated, darlin'."

The next words out of Samantha's mouth utterly shocked Emily. "I don't think you should worry about Pa so much anymore. He'd want you to be happy, like we do."

Taken aback, Emily choked out, "What do you mean?"

Samantha answered frankly. "Pa would be happy you're moving on, especially if it meant marrying his best friend. Really, who else would be better than Pa's best friend?"

"What brought all this on, Samm?"

Samantha shrugged carelessly. "I think of Pa a lot and ask God to ask Pa what he thinks sometimes, especially when you're so sad. I'm pretty sure that's what Pa's tellin' God to tell me. Pa loved all of us very much and he always used to say he only wanted us to be happy. Sure, he was usually talkin' to us, but I think if he knew he was gonna die, he'd have included you in that, too."

With a shock, Emily realized the wisdom in her daughter's words. It made perfect sense when put that way. And it touched her that Samantha had been praying for her. It took an eleven-year-old to finally make her understand. And it was so stupidly simple. And too late. It'd been months of guilt, anxiety, and now, a broken relationship to finally understand something her young daughter had grasped all along. She'd been so focused on who Jacob was in relation to herself, she simply overlooked who Jacob *was*, as a person. He was kind...caring...*unselfish*; unlike herself...helpful...hardworking...the list could go on. Of course *Jacob* wouldn't want her being so hard on herself for loving Joshua. *Jacob* would want her happy. Deep down, Emily had known the whole time it was all her that was holding herself back from Joshua, but she hadn't wanted to admit it.

Coming back to reality hurt, though. It was too late, she reminded herself. She hadn't found this out sooner and now she had another kind of guilt to live with. Loss. It was her fault she'd lost Joshua.

Emily's silence worried Samantha. "Mama?"

"You're right, Samm," Emily acknowledged. "He only wanted our happiness."

In a small voice, Samantha reiterated, "You can be happy with Uncle Josh now," though a little hesitantly this time.

Emily stood up and caught Samantha in a warm embrace and murmured, "Thank you, darlin'. I really appreciate it, but I'm afraid it's too late."

Stepping back, Emily blinked back tears that threatened.

"Can't you give him another chance?"

"I think the question is will he give me another chance? And I don't think he will. I was pretty awful."

Samantha, adamant now, that her mother be happy, answered desperately, "I think so! He has to!"

Emily smiled sadly. If only it were that simple.

Samantha's plan was a little risky, she had to admit. She almost couldn't believe she was going through with it! Her rank among her siblings had always been the goody-two-shoes. Sadly, she reflected she would no longer be *that* anymore. She had told not a soul what she was doing. They would all be horrified, especially her Ma, but it was something she felt she *had* to do. She was determined to do.

Sneaking out had been easy enough. Everyone was occupied with their own activities. It wasn't that she couldn't trust them to keep the secret, if she asked, but she knew they'd probably try to talk her out of it.

Finally, she was clear of any detection and decided to run toward her object of interest...Joshua in the fields.

Breathless, she approached him. Under her breath, she muttered, "Here goes" just as Joshua spotted her.

"Hello, Samm," Joshua greeted her. Noticing her solemn face, he asked, "Is there some trouble?"

Samantha was tongue-tied at the enormity of what she was about to do. Mistaking her silence as a bad omen, Joshua demanded, "Is it Em...er, yer Ma?"

Triumph lit up Samantha's face. "So you *do* care for her!"

"Of course I care," he assured, not understanding. "Why wouldn't I?"

"And you care *about* her?"

Joshua answered slowly, clearly lost. "Uh, yes, I do. What's this all about, Samm?"

"Good, because she thinks you don't."

Joshua faltered. "Excuse me?"

Samantha clarified. "She thinks you don't care about her and she's afraid she's lost you forever. That's why I came out here...to find out if it's true."

"Um, Samm, I think this subject would be better discussed between her and I."

"Her and me" Samantha automatically corrected, not paying attention.

"Huh?"

"I think the proper grammar is 'her and me.'"

Unsure as to where exactly the conversation was headed, Joshua conceded. "Uh...okay."

"You're wrong, you know."

Irritated, Joshua stated, "Samm, I really don't care if it's 'her and me' or 'she and I'–"

Samantha interrupted, "No, I mean, you're wrong about discussing it with her. You can't. She won't talk to you. She feels it's her fault you two aren't going to get married now."

"What! Well, that's not true. I mean, no, we aren't getting married, but I hadn't even asked, I mean, it's not her–" abruptly he stopped and asked instead, "Should I go right now and straighten things out?"

"Maybe. *My* plan is for you to woo her."

"*Woo* her?" Joshua was incredulous.

"Yes, woo her. Start over. Like nothin' ever happened. Kinda like strangers."

"Strangers?"

"Alright, maybe not *strangers*. Friendly people...who like each other."

Joshua chuckled then. "You're incorrigible, young lady, you know that?"

Growing serious, Samantha solemnly told him, "I think she needs another chance. I know she'd appreciate one. She didn't say so out loud, but...."

Joshua asked skeptically, "What exactly *did* she say, Samm?"

Samantha briefly filled him in on her latest conversation with Emily. "She truly believes she's lost you, Uncle Josh. You *have* to tell her she hasn't! She's really miserable."

Joshua was touched that Samantha would come and talk to him on her mother's behalf, simply to make sure Emily was given the chance at happiness she deserved.

"You can't tell Mama or anyone that I came and talked to you. It'd ruin everything and I do believe it'd upset Mama."

Joshua solemnly promised he wouldn't breathe a word. He welcomed the opportunity to woo Emily Matthews.

Emily pondered her conversation with Samantha a lot. She worried she'd revealed too much to the young girl, being that she'd kept it locked inside so long. What had spurred Samantha to come and talk? Ironically, a subject that should have made her uncomfortable to talk to her eleven-year-old daughter about was oddly comforting. At least now she knew all of her children were alright with her relationship with Joshua…or, what *could* have been a relationship with Joshua.

If only she could go back to the way things were before…she wasn't even going to venture down that line of thinking, it would only reinforce her already broken heart. It was her own fault and she was getting what she deserved. Probably, she'd never find love. Probably, she'd die an old widow. Probably, she'd be one of those old women who lived with a lot of cats. Once her children got married and moved away, they'd have their own lives and didn't need to concern themselves with her anymore.

Resolutely, she pushed such depressing thoughts out of her mind. Really, what did she have to whine about? She had precious children and had had the blessing of having a wonderful man for a husband. Her life was blessed and she didn't have the right to ask for more. She needed to learn to be grateful for what she had.

"It's better to have loved and lost than to never have loved at all," she quoted to herself.

Emily presently found herself alone in the house. It was a rare occurrence. Either one or more of the children were constantly coming in or out, not to mention Christopher's odd hours he was keeping as of late. More often than not, when Dr. Allison got called out, he would send someone to fetch Christopher so he'd have assistance.

Reveling in the present quiet, she had plenty of time to think and reflect on what went wrong and what she could do. Although she wasn't exactly certain she deserved Joshua, even if she could work things out. And anyway, didn't he deserve better? She loved him and she should be able to let him go if for no other reason than that. Yet, she couldn't ever remember being in so much turmoil over one person! He was driving her crazy…of course, he didn't know that. She was sure the twisting pain inside, the churning stomach, the emptiness, was God's punishment. She had tried taking more than she deserved. She tried satisfying her earthly desires, the yearning of her heart.

Deep down, she knew that wasn't true, of course. God didn't work like that.

Emily was ashamed of herself. How could she allow one person to have so much control of her life? Why couldn't she simply let go? The empty feeling was awful. The hole she felt in her life that Joshua had filled was awful. The feeling that she had been torn apart from the inside out was awful. The memories of the two of them together were awful.

Even though it had been over two years since she had felt Joshua's arms around her and even though the circumstances were completely innocent, Emily found she missed them. She wanted that feeling back. She wanted that feeling for herself.

Two years! She realized this with astonishment. Had she really spent the last two years mourning Jacob? Letting guilt keep her from fully living her life? Making herself miserable because she couldn't let Jacob go? Why did she have such a hard time letting those go that she needed to and not embracing the ones that she was free to? What had she done to herself? Where was her life headed now?

Ever since his conversation with Samantha, Joshua couldn't stop thinking about Emily. Yet, he had no idea how to remedy the situation they were in. Most assuredly, he wouldn't do anything that might put undue pressure on her. Time was one thing he could, and would, give her. Despite Samantha's best intentions, he wouldn't be wooing Emily. Besides, if his and Samantha's conversation did get back to Emily sometime in the future, he didn't want her to think he'd only started wooing because of that conversation.

Samantha couldn't know it, but prior to their talk, he'd been working on getting his courage up to approach Emily. They badly needed to sit down and hash things out, but he was an admitted coward when it came to her. He could stand rejection by almost anyone with almost anything, but Emily. If she rejected him, he didn't know if he could stand it. The current rejection was hard enough. He'd been miserable without Emily. He wanted her, needed her, in his life. He *was not* going to let her go easily. Not without a fight, anyway. He only needed to plan out his strategy. One that she would have to fight awfully hard to untangle herself from. Samantha's conversation made it seem suddenly possible to get Emily back and he was bound and determined to do so!

Samantha sincerely hoped and fervently prayed that her talk with Joshua did some good. She knew her mother wouldn't approach Joshua, but she hoped Joshua would take the initiative now. She was convinced now more than ever that they needed each other. Even if it meant that she would have to concoct a way for it to happen. Talking with Joshua had boosted her confidence that something would happen. That was all she knew to do for now, but her mind furiously worked at another possible scenario if nothing came of this one.

Samantha dearly loved her Uncle Joshua as part of their family. The only thing keeping him and the cousins from joining their family was her ma. It made sense to Samantha to have them become a part of their family. Uncle Joshua had always been close to her pa, so it made natural sense. In all honesty, she couldn't understand why her mother hadn't come to the same conclusion. Over the past couple of years since her father died, nothing had seemed natural. The Tylers and Matthews had done everything together until Jacob's death. Then things had changed.

Her siblings, she was sure, felt much the same way. They had all grown up with the Tylers next door and Joshua had always been the closest thing to an uncle any of them had. In her mind, things would eventually take the natural course…if only her mother would cooperate!

Chapter 28: Pursuits

Emily had felt it necessary to lie down for a nap. She hoped she wasn't reverting back to the depression she had gone through after Jacob's death.

When she awoke, it was to a dark room. How long she had slept, she didn't know. Feeling disoriented, she pulled back the curtain by her bed and looked out. The sun was just disappearing behind the line of trees. She guessed it was around eight o'clock. She had slept nearly four hours! What would she do now when it was time to go to bed?

Groaning, she felt guilt settling over her. In her depression before, there were times she'd slept the morning away, not rising until well past noon. Other days, she'd take naps after lunch and not rise until it was time to prepare supper. Of course, there had also been days like this one when she wouldn't rise until the evening, leaving her children completely on their own for supper. That had brought on the most guilt. Why was she starting this vicious cycle again? Was she really so distraught over Joshua? It was ridiculous! He was only one person!

Quickly, Emily got up and freshened up as best she could. As she opened her bedroom door, delicious smells assailed her. That didn't make sense. Supper would've been hours ago. The times she had missed making supper, her children had assured her they had fended quite well for themselves and had even set some aside for her. As touched as she would be, she'd still feel the guilt of leaving them to fend for themselves.

Curiosity compelled her down the stairs and caused her to gauge the sounds coming from the kitchen. Nothing out of the ordinary, it seemed. As she passed through the doorway into the kitchen, she stopped and gaped at the sight that met her.

The man at the table smiled easily as he looked at her and simply noted, "You're finally awake!"

"What are you doing here?" Emily asked, astonished. She was suddenly very conscious of her unkempt appearance. She had merely pulled a brush through her hair but hadn't bothered to pin it back up and her dress was badly wrinkled, not to mention the pillow creases that surely graced her face.

"Making you a late supper," he explained cheerfully.

Emily didn't know what she was feeling. She was still shocked at seeing him there, in her kitchen, when she hadn't spoken to him beyond public civilities, in months!

"Come sit down," Joshua invited.

One thing was for certain, Emily didn't feel prepared for this. Especially not looking the way she did. And definitely not in the state she was in, so uncertain. It felt even more strange being invited by him to sit at her kitchen table.

Suddenly on her guard, Emily stepped all the way into the room, but didn't sit. She didn't think she could handle this. Why was he doing this? Why was he being so nice to her after the way she'd treated him? Taking a deep breath, she managed to choke out, "Thank you kindly, but you may leave." She absurdly wanted to cry.

Hurt surprise registered briefly in Joshua's eyes, before he hid it away. Calmly, he told her, "I will serve you your supper first."

Not quite sure where her unexpected ire came from, Emily answered curtly. "I'm not incapable of serving myself." Where her hostility came from, she wasn't quite sure. Upon further examination, she would have realized it was her discomfiture of being treated more kindly than she deserved by a man she so desperately wanted.

Indignantly, Emily tried wiping away the tears that were pooling in her eyes. She had already resigned herself to moving on without Joshua. Him showing up hadn't helped her resolve.

Inwardly, she was screaming. '*What are you doing? This is your chance! He's obviously trying to make amends or... something, why aren't you being gracious about this?*'

Keenly Joshua watched Emily. He hadn't been sure what to expect when he had arrived a few hours earlier. Certainly not that she'd be sleeping and that, according to her children whom he briefly saw, it was something she had been doing quite frequently as of late. This had alarmed him, being that it seemed like the same behavior she had exhibited after Jacob's death. In that moment he realized she needed taking care of. And he wanted to be the one to do it.

Emily couldn't help it anymore and suddenly felt herself giving in to the tears, right in the middle of her kitchen, of all places!

Noticing her shaking shoulders and the fact that Emily had buried her face in her hands, Joshua gently guided Emily into a chair. He sat down in a chair by hers and faced her, trying to get to the root of her tears. Lightly, he tried prying her hands from her face. Softly, he spoke. "Em."

Giving up trying to hold any pretenses, Emily let her hands drop and stared back. Her eyes were dull, lifeless; she had given up.

That was all it took to frighten Joshua. "Emily!" he gasped. He searched her face for some sign of the woman inside. Unconsciously, he cupped her face in his hands.

Emily flatly requested, "Kindly remove your hands from my face."

In that moment, he spied a spark of fear, before Emily's eyes became hollow again.

As soon as he complied to her request, she stood up and, as calmly as she could muster, walked from the room, all the while silently pleading with herself to stay. Alas, she couldn't. It was too much to be near him and she had given him way too much control to influence her emotions. The distance had been better.

Dumbfounded, Joshua watched her leave the kitchen. He knew better than to follow her. She obviously still needed time and lots of space. This was something much worse than he'd feared. Not the rejection, but the utter shell of a woman Emily had become. It would have been hard having her reject him, but he would've eventually gotten over it, knowing she was moving on with her life. This Emily was not even trying to move on with her life. He definitely should've come sooner. He shouldn't have let her push him away in the first place. He was now more determined than ever not to let her shut him out.

Emily had definitely been shaken up seeing Joshua in her kitchen. An odd assortment of emotions had assailed her.

Emotions that didn't seem to belong together. Confusion, hope, anger, suspicion, happiness, irritation…and fear. She certainly did not understand that one. Although, she knew that if she examined it, it would most likely come from the place inside that wanted to push Joshua away instead of making the complete transformation of moving on and allowing herself to love him fully. It was enough to convince her that Joshua most certainly needed to stay away from her. She had already convinced herself that she could give Joshua up. She didn't need him upsetting the delicate balance of her following through with her decision and succumbing to her yearning to let Joshua back in her life.

Joshua knew Emily's children were worried about her. They had each told him so when he had come over the other night. Resolving to help Emily, Joshua decided he would need to periodically check on her. He felt responsible for her, and not only because she was Jacob's widow. Joshua truly felt protective of Emily and he needed to see her restored to her old self. Even if it meant she wouldn't choose him in the end.

Making his presence as subtle as possible for Emily's sake, Joshua came over at least once a week, if not more, and simply made himself at home. Sometimes, he didn't see Emily at all, sometimes he'd see her in a hallway or passing through a room, but he didn't ever approach her. His purpose in being there was more so for the children. When he had proposed his idea to them, they were very accepting. They told him Emily was reverting back to the way she had been when their father had passed away and none of them could stand seeing her go through that again, especially not alone.

He'd made some progress in the weeks since he'd started coming. At first, Emily simply pretended he wasn't there. After she apparently realized he was becoming a regular fixture, she started glancing in his direction. Joshua couldn't be certain if it was out of curiosity, or if she was assuring herself he was still there.

Some days, Emily was annoyed by his presence, yet it seemed to be helping the children, in some mysterious way. Resigned, she let him be. As the weeks went by, however, she felt an odd sense of relief. At least, she supposed she'd classify it as that. It was comforting she had to admit, having Joshua around. His presence started having an almost soothing effect on the entire household. An added benefit was that his girls came with him. She had missed them terribly, more so than she had realized.

Over time, Emily had found she wasn't sleeping as much during the day as she had been. That led to her almost anticipating when Joshua would come. Eventually, she had even taken to preparing the meals while Joshua was there. He had always taken that responsibility on himself when he was there.

One Saturday, she found she could speak a little to Joshua. She started out by softly inviting, "Josh, lunch is almost ready if you're hungry."

Startled that she'd spoken to him, Joshua turned in his chair. He'd been trying to be inconspicuous, so had been reading. Holding up the book, he told her, "Thank you, Em. I'll be in right after finishing this chapter."

After she left, Joshua found he couldn't concentrate enough to finish his chapter. Joy filled him at the progress that had been made. Anticipation made him look forward to seeing what else time might help heal.

After that incident Joshua, cautiously at first, started greeting Emily and occasionally said a word or two to her.

He idly wondered if he could get away with actual small talk. Upon arriving one day, he found the house was quiet. Sometimes he'd let himself in. Usually, the children would see him, however, and let him in.

After letting himself in, he found Emily in the sewing room. He was pleasantly surprised, for he feared she'd be sleeping, despite the fact that it was five o'clock. Peeking his head into the room, he greeted, "Hello, Em."

Emily's heart rate quickened as it always did when he was near. Taken off guard, she pricked her finger and gasped, pressing her finger to her lips.

"Are you alright?" Joshua asked, concerned.

Emily looked at him and muttered, "Ow," but went back to her task at hand.

Grinning, Joshua sat down in a chair to watch her sew and hopefully make small talk. He idly picked at a thread on his shirt. "Glad I caught you awake today. Usually you're sleepin' when I get here."

Emily simply murmured, "Uh, huh." Her stomach was doing little flip-flops and she had to concentrate extra hard on her task.

"Do you need anything done around here? I might as well make myself useful. I woulda asked sooner, but you're usually–"

Emily cut him off. "No. Chris usually takes care of," she waved her hand dismissively, "whatever needs doin'."

Joshua needed to pluck up his courage if he was going to seize the opportunity and ask Emily what he'd been wanting to ask her for quite awhile. "Well, then, Em, will you go riding with me?" he asked in a rush.

Emily tried hiding her confusion. She pretended to be extremely focused so didn't look up as she repeated, "Riding?"

"Yes. I could stop by and pick you up. We can take a ride to the outskirts of town."

Joshua hoped she'd catch the significance. Riding on the outskirts of town was a popular courting ritual in Lorraine.

Emily grasped his meaning as heat crept into her cheeks. "You mean, courting?"

Joshua took a hard look at her and knew he needed to proceed with caution. Backing off, he amended, "Er...no, never mind. Let's just go horseback riding together...as friends. That's all."

Sighing, Emily had her answer ready. "I don't think that'd be a good idea–"

"Why not?" he interrupted, more exasperated than he intended. "You need to get out of the house sometime. I'm worried about you."

Oops! He hadn't meant to say that. He was trying not to get too personal with her yet.

"Let me finish!" she huffed. "I don't think it would be a good idea because I've neglected my children for so long, I feel I need to stay with them."

Trying very hard to mask the sudden bitterness he felt, Joshua pointed out, "They're hardly young children. Hailey's ten next month."

"I said no," she answered decidedly.

Didn't he understand what he was asking of her? Didn't he realize she didn't deserve him? It was torture having him here!

Abruptly, she left the room, calling over her shoulder, "Go home, Josh!"

Reluctantly, Emily admitted she liked having Joshua there. It was only torture when he talked to her. She much preferred his quiet presence to his talking one. His presence made her feel secure, something she hadn't felt since Jacob's death. It was selfish of her to allow Joshua to continue coming. As long as Joshua continued coming over, Emily feared he'd get his hopes up. She feared she'd give in to her desires and let him court her. It was better, for the long run, if she spoke up sooner rather than later, but she found she always seemed to lose her nerve when she should be speaking up.

And yet, she had to admit, that she'd found her sleeping habits were much improved since Joshua's coming.

No, she resolved, she had to make Joshua stop coming in order to be fair to both of them.

Of course, Emily's resolve lasted all of thirty minutes and the next time Joshua came, she didn't talk to him about leaving. He made her feel so relaxed. Sometimes she'd even start a conversation with him and they'd chat like old times.

Joshua was very careful in making sure Emily always started the conversation, but he still said his greetings and let her lead to how far the conversation, if any, would go.

On one such occasion, Emily was feeling so at ease, she blurted out, "Josh, would you still like to take me riding?" Instead of being embarrassed by the forward request, she merely laughed and amended, "I'm sorry, that was forward."

Joshua couldn't help but grin. Here was a glimpse of his old Emily. "I'd love to take you riding."

The traditional route for courters was on the very outskirts of Lorraine. There was a small path, barely wide enough for a wagon to get down, that was lined on both sides with trees, flowers, and other natural scenery. No one knew how the path came about, but looked too natural to be manmade.

Their drive was a pleasant one and occasionally Joshua would stop as he and Emily would watch a bird take flight from a tree branch or an occasional deer would take a drink from the lazy stream. All the while, they chatted and laughed about things of no consequence.

Emily couldn't remember feeling this carefree since Jacob died. And felt guilty for it. She was mad at herself for feeling that way. She thought she'd gotten over that. Determined to have an enjoyable time, she cast those thoughts aside. Yet, by the time Joshua dropped her off, she could sense the guilt come flooding back. Wearily, she didn't try to fight it. She was getting tired of fighting it and finally decided she should simply let it come. What was the point? She knew she was never going to allow herself to be happy with Joshua without some kind of guilt assailing her about Jacob.

When Joshua took Emily home, he could sense the marked change in her. He fervently wished there were some way he could help her move on. But it wasn't looking promising....

Chapter 29: A Secret

Samantha watched her mother carefully the following day. The way Emily carried herself and the way she acted around the house let Samantha know *something* had happened on her drive with Uncle Joshua. A feeling of frustration passed through her. Why couldn't her mother just be happy already? Pa was in heaven. Most assuredly he was happy! He wouldn't mind if Mama got married again. Especially if it was to Uncle Joshua. Pa had loved Uncle Joshua! Samantha sighed in exasperation and plotted her next strategy. Sometimes parents never learned!

Emily did not get a lot of sleep the previous night and awoke with the sun. She ambled downstairs, determined not to fall back into her old habits of leaving the children to fend for themselves. Wearily, she fixed breakfast and tried to appear as normal as possible.

School had started a few weeks before so that had helped in setting a routine she could follow without having to engage her mind in thinking too much. Simply put, she functioned by rote. It was because of this, she hadn't given much thought to the date until Christopher came cheerfully into the kitchen, whistling. He stopped abruptly when he saw her.

"Ma, why are you up so early?"

Confused, Emily asked, "What do you mean?"

"It's Saturday. Usually you're just gettin' up when I leave to go to Doc Allison's on Saturdays. Yet, here you are, lookin' all fresh and perty and makin' breakfast."

Mentally, Emily tried counting back the days. "Hmmm…"she pondered aloud, "yesterday was Friday, the…"

"25th," Christopher supplied, not sure if he should have.

Fighting control, Emily calmly asked, "So today is September 26th?"

Christopher gave her a sharp glance. He wasn't so sure it

was a good idea for her to remember the date. It always seemed to bring a great sadness upon her. Matter-of-factly, he told her, "Yes, today is Saturday, September 26th."

Three years! It had been three years, and here she was, still trying to hold onto him. Emily didn't know why the thought made her panic, but it did. Part of her felt sick over the realization that the three years since her husband had died had passed quickly. Some parts more so than others.

Time heals all wounds was something she believed in less and less. Or maybe she needed more time... Three years! A long time for some things. A short time for others. She wasn't sure which category grieving over her husband belonged in.

Concerned, Christopher offered, "You want me to stay home?"

Shaking her head, Emily opposed. "No, go ahead to Doc Allison's. You seem to be learning a lot from him." Changing the subject, that was good.

Christopher smiled. "Yeah, I am."

"You could take over his practice someday and expand it to include animals as well as people," Emily lightly teased.

"That's what I intend to do," he laughed back. And then Christopher was gone.

Emily smiled after him. Such ambitions the young had. Hopefully Christopher never had to experience any of the heartache she herself had gone through.

Sighing, Emily sat down and relived the past.

Emily noticed how strangely quiet the house had been all day. She simply figured the children were enjoying the last of the Indian summer days down by the creek.

She thought she had spotted the Tylers headed down there, too, when she had gone out to hang the wash. And because of that sighting only was the reason why she inexplicably thought about Joshua for the rest of the day...at least, that's what she told herself.

As she went through the mundane chores, Emily hadn't realized how late it had gotten until she heard the door slam. Glancing out a window, she noticed it was already dusk.

Samantha scampered into the house, calling, "Mama!"

"In here," Emily called.

Samantha peeked her head around the doorway. "Have you started supper yet?"

"I will shortly."

"No need, Mama, but you only have three-quarters of an hour to freshen up, then I have to come back and get you. There's a surprise outside."

Emily narrowed her eyes suspiciously. "What are you up to?" When she had made trips back and forth outside for the laundry, she hadn't noticed anything out of the ordinary. Not that she'd been looking, but she definitely would have noticed if something was off.

Innocently, Samantha simply said, "You'll see, but you need to freshen up and I'll come get you." Then Samantha scampered back outside.

Joshua had been back and forth from his own land to the Matthews'. He worked some in their fields, and worked some around his own property doing chores he'd put off for far too long. Especially since the cold weather would be setting in before too long.

Earlier, he had seen the Matthews come over, including Christopher, which made him curious. Usually, Christopher spent all day Saturday with Doc Allison. Joshua didn't dwell much on it, however, because their presence had brought to mind thoughts of their mother, not that he'd needed anything to prompt them lately.

Later in the day, right after dusk settled down, Joshua was finally ready to call it a day. As he entered the house, he smelled cooking, but it was too faint to be recent. Yet, lunch had been hours ago and it had been stew. This smelled like...chicken?

As he trudged upstairs to change he quickly forgot about the oddity. He pulled a fresh shirt over his head and pulled on clean trousers. Donning his worn slippers, he grabbed a book and headed for the living room, ready to relax.

He had just settled himself down and found the place he had previously left off when Alexis came in.

Using her sweetest voice, Alexis requested, "Daddy, you need to come with me please." Looking down, she noticed his feet. "Uh, get some boots on first, though, but hurry!"

A little alarmed, Joshua asked, "Is somethin' wrong?"

Slyly, she answered, "Not in the way you think."

His curiosity piqued, he ran back upstairs to trade his slippers for his boots and followed Alexis outside.

Emily dutifully followed Samantha all the way to the creek. Despite her protests and questions, Samantha had remained, for the most part, silent.

Up ahead, Emily saw something glowing. As she got closer, she realized a huge area had been decorated in candles. They were discreetly, and creatively, placed. On the ground, in the center of the soft lighting, a large quilt had been laid out with a picnic basket neatly set on a corner.

The candles had been stolen from all over both houses or there wouldn't have been enough for this special night. The Tylers hadn't mentioned most of theirs had been left over from their Pa's proposal to Miss Taylor-Ryan. In light of the current situation, they felt it prudent not to mention that fact, either.

Catching movement to her left, Emily swung her head in that direction. Christopher, Brianna, and Hailey stepped out of the shadows. "We decided to intervene," was all Christopher said.

"Intervene?" Emily puzzled aloud.

Hailey spoke up then. "Yes, we, along with the cousins, cooked supper and put it in a picnic basket so the two of you could enjoy some time alone."

"The...you..." Emily mouthed. With a sinking feeling, she knew what was going on. She wasn't in the mood for this, yet she couldn't spoil the children's plans and obvious effort. Panic choked her and she couldn't say any more.

Brianna noticed Emily's hesitation. "If you're mad, it was all Samm's idea."

"Hey!" Samantha protested. Then they heard voices.

Suddenly, Emily was left alone and Joshua was walking into the light.

Smiling slightly, Joshua said, "I was told to go on in. I'm presuming we are now alone and on our own."

Recognizing Joshua was as uncomfortable as she was, she

decided to play along and keep things light. "Some children we have, huh?"

"I hear it was all Samm's idea."

"Poor Samm. She gets blamed, but if it turns out alright, they'll all want the glory."

Grasping at his chance, Joshua impulsively asked, "Will it?"

Momentarily confused, Emily hadn't grasped what she had said. "Will what?"

"Will it turn out alright?" Smiling mischievously, Joshua added, "I don't want poor Samm to get into trouble."

Slightly embarrassed, Emily was able to laugh at herself. Ruefully she admitted, "Oh, Samm'll be okay. It's not as if we're in a torture chamber or something."

"Wouldn't know it with the way you've been acting lately." The words had slipped out! He winced. *'Way to go, Tyler!'*

Flame lit Emily's face. "*What* did you just say?!"

"I think you heard me," retorted Joshua. *'Be quiet, you fool! Those are the wrong words! Take them back, take them back!'*

This was starting off very badly. All the work and effort the children had put into it was going to be wasted because of his big mouth. Honestly, Joshua didn't want to argue. That was all they seemed to do, though. He was man enough to admit that he'd started this one and he was determined to finish it. It was time Emily took him seriously.

In anger, Emily grabbed the picnic basket. "I'm hungry and I'm eating. You can be civil and join me, or I'm leaving."

Joshua got himself in hand and quietly apologized. "I'm sorry, Em. That was way out of line."

"Yes, it was and I didn't deserve that." She would not be giving Mr. Tyler an inch.

"No, you don't." Joshua grabbed a piece of chicken and thoughtfully chewed. "What shall we do then?"

"Do?"

"About us."

Emily stilled. "I didn't realize there was any action required."

Joshua rolled his eyes in unconcealed exasperation. "You have got to be joshin' me," then winked at her and gave a great laugh.

Without thinking, Emily reached over and punched his arm

teasingly and smiled. "Knock it off. It sounded like you were actually tryin' to be serious before your corny little joke."

Joshua grinned. "Come on, it was a little funny. Joshin'...my name's Josh..."

It was Emily's turn to roll her eyes then.

Joshua couldn't stop grinning. "Well, at least it got you to smile and the tension's broken. Now we can get down to serious matters."

Sighing, Emily protested. "Not now, okay? Not tonight."

"Why not?"

"You need to disentangle yourself from me." There, she'd said it. She could let him off the hook. "I'm not being fair to you. You deserve someone who appreciates what you're tryin' to do." *'Oh, that sounds real grateful, Em!'* Suddenly tongue-tied, Emily quickly amended. "Not that I don't appreciate the effort you've put in...I mean, that is to say...." She stopped and took a deep breath. "I simply can't." Emily was horrified to find her throat thickening with tears. Enough tears! It seemed that was all she did anymore, was cry! She took a quick bite of chicken, hoping to dispel the unwanted sensation. "It's not right for me to love you nor is it fair for you to love me."

Joshua softened his voice and protested huskily. "I don't remember ever being told life was fair, Emily. And in case my opinion matters on the subject, I don't much care whether *you* think it's fair or not. I love you and you can't do anything to change that. Take my love, take my heart, they are yours. Even if you don't, they will always belong to you."

Tremulously, Emily protested. "That would be too greedy and much more than I deserve."

"Please, Em, open your heart to me."

Thick with held back tears, her voice shook. "I already have." A mere whisper. "And I can't seem to let you go."

"I don't want you to!"

Feebly, Emily tried again, "It isn't fair."

"Fair to whom, Emily? I can't stand this distance between us anymore. Please marry me and we can be done with it. I can't stand being apart from you. I physically ache when I can't touch you or look at you. When we don't speak, I'm pierced right through the heart. It makes me crazy! Please make me a sane man again and marry me!" His tone had taken on an urgent note that he fervently hoped she'd hear. He wanted her to know how desperately he wanted her, *needed* her.

Emily's dam of tears broke. They spilled down her cheeks unbidden. They were falling too fast for her to brush away. Protests rose to her lips, but she couldn't give voice to them.

Joshua knew he had finally broken through. He waited patiently for her tears to subside, all the while aching to gather her in his arms like he had done two years ago. It wouldn't be welcome, he knew.

Finally, Emily was able to control herself again. Risking a look at Joshua, she knew what she needed to do. It had been a long time coming, but she couldn't lie to herself anymore. Whispering, she answered. "Yes, Josh, I'll marry you. I want to be your wife. You're the only one who will make me whole again."

Hesitantly, Joshua reached out and gently gathered her in his arms and whispered, "You have made me extremely happy, Mrs. Matthews." And then he froze. He had meant it as a tease, but using her formal name resounded in his ears. He looked down into Emily's face sure he'd spoiled their perfect moment.

Emily didn't look upset. In fact, she looked quite happy as she thoughtfully asked, "Do you know what day it is?"

He knew, alright, but was hoping it wouldn't detract from their moment. Taking a deep breath, he answered clearly, "September 26th."

Suddenly she asked warily, "Do you mind?" Emily was afraid of the answer, but had to ask anyway.

"Mind what?"

"We just got engaged on the anniversary of his..." she let her sentence go unfinished.

"Well, it *is* my birthday." He grinned. Slowly, Joshua formed his answer to Emily's question. "In an odd way, it seems almost...fitting. It's as if we have his blessing."

Emily hugged Joshua fiercely then and secured her mouth to his in their first sweet kiss.

Chapter 30: In Addition

One year later, Joshua found himself pacing in front of the staircase as he waited. It was agonizing waiting for news of his wife. Doctor Allison was with her now, doing whatever he could to help Emily. Joshua was so worried he could scarcely form a prayer for his wife of little less than a year. The only refrain he could grab onto was, '*What time I am afraid, I will trust in Thee.*' In Joshua's heart, he hoped for a miracle. He could feel God's presence, but Joshua felt as though his world was spinning out of control.

Joshua and Emily had been married six short weeks after their engagement. They'd had a simple ceremony following Sunday services in early November.

Six weeks they had lived in wedded bliss and then Emily got sick. Nearly everyday she lost most everything she ate. She ached everywhere in her body, it had seemed. Emily couldn't remember ever feeling that miserable.

After three weeks of no improvement, and finally ruling out influenza, Doc Allison was called upon.

The memory of what he'd told Joshua and Emily brought tears to Joshua's eyes even now. Earlier that day, Emily's pain had become nearly unbearable, bringing her to her knees on more than one occasion before Joshua had a neighbor fetch Doc Allison. He simply couldn't bring himself to leave her for that one task, and Christopher had been called out earlier in the day to attend an emergency with the doctor.

Time stood still for Joshua. He raked his hands through his already mussed hair for the umpteenth time in frustration. He was helpless. There was nothing he could do for his wife.

He heard the wails again as Emily fought whatever pain wracked her body. Could the doctor not give her something to ease her discomfort?

Christopher came down the stairs then and headed for the

kitchen again. Joshua followed him, peppering him with questions. "How is she? Might I go see her? Couldn't I be there to make the end more bearable?" The last he asked with tears in his eyes.

Christopher could scarcely meet his eyes. "I really need to boil more water so Doc Allison can keep his instruments clean."

"Instruments? Why does he need his instruments? Chris, what is going on?"

With the pot of hot water in his hands, Christopher side-stepped Joshua. "Please, Josh, I've gotta get back upstairs to help the doc." He simply had to ignore Joshua's questions or he'd break. Watching his mother with the doctor had been nearly unbearable.

As Joshua watched Christopher carry the water upstairs, a sense of futility hung over him.

More hours went by. What was taking so long? Joshua had to fight the urge, several times, to run upstairs and burst through their bedroom door and demand answers. Instead, he resigned himself to a pattern of pacing in front of the staircase or sitting on the stairs while he impatiently waited, prepared to jump the minute anyone came down bearing news, whatever it may be.

He could hear the desperate wails of his wife and yearned to know what was happening.

Unbidden thoughts came to keep him company. Was this morning the last time he'd be able to see her? Why had he been kept out? Why couldn't he have been allowed in? If only someone would *tell* him something! He did much better when he had information, even if it was negative. At least he would know.

Joshua became earnest in his prayer, begging God to spare Emily. He couldn't bear it if Emily was taken from him so soon. He felt exhausted and told himself he needed to calm down. He kept trying to convince himself that everything would be okay.

Finally, he heard a footfall above him as it descended the stairs. He leapt up the stairs, three at a time.

"How is she?" he breathlessly asked with tears in his voice. He needed to know, yet didn't know if he was prepared.

Doc Allison, followed by a haggard Christopher, merely

answered, "You can go in and see for yourself, Mr. Tyler."

Almost knocking the doctor and Christopher out of the way, he finished leaping up the stairs, calming himself only as he stood outside the door and knocked.

Emily's weak voice answered, "Come in."

Hesitantly, he stepped around the door as he opened it and entered the darkened room. It was lit only by two lamps, one on his side of the bed and one on Emily's.

"Emily?" he called softly as he moved toward the bed. It seemed to swallow her up. Carefully Joshua sat on the edge of the bed so as not to jostle her.

Weakly, Emily struggled to sit up a little higher against the pillows as she managed a bundle in her arms. She frailly placed it in Joshua's arms. All she could muster was a whisper. "Meet your son, Josh." And she managed a frail smile.

Joshua took the small, sleeping form of his son and looked into Emily's joyous eyes. They weren't her usual clear green, being that she was weak and fragile, but they were happy, despite showing signs of her exhaustion.

"A son," Joshua marveled, speaking around the lump in his throat. He marveled at the tiny features of his son that mirrored his own. It amazed him that he could tell so soon that his son was a miniature of himself.

Smug satisfaction colored Emily's words. "He looks just like you."

Joshua felt the same awe he had with all of his daughters, only this time felt very like the first time, when Madison had been born. For this time, there was a marked difference. This time, he had a son! His own flesh and blood son! He let his happy tears fall unmarked.

After a time of letting him enjoy his son, Emily leaned forward and husband and wife shared a gentle kiss. Then she leaned down and kissed the forehead of their son.

"Thank you," Joshua whispered. He grabbed Emily's hand then and kissed it.

"How are you feeling?" he finally asked, concerned.

Emily softly laughed. "Elated, I gave you a son." She couldn't stop her grin.

Joshua smiled and kissed her brow, smoothing back what he

could of her unruly hair. "Other than that."

"Doc said it may take me longer to heal this time than before because of my age and the amount of time it has been since having Hailey. It's been eleven years, after all!" Giggling at a memory, Emily asked, "Remember what you did when we first found out I was pregnant?"

"I laughed."

Joshua remembered well the events that led up to that day.

After Emily had become so sick, it was all Joshua could think about. He'd spent his days caring for her and praying it would all go away.

Emily was sicker than she had ever been and attributed her lack of a monthly course to the fact that she had been so ill. It hadn't occurred to her she might be pregnant. All she could comprehend was that her body simply wasn't acting properly for some reason. By the time she was alarmed enough to call on Doc Allison, the pains had begun. She'd felt pain *everywhere* it seemed; her back, her stomach, her legs…everywhere ached. After Doc's initial examination, he told her his suspicions. While she literally cried with relief, Joshua had broken into laughter. He still maintained it was out of utter relief, not that he found her pregnancy so amusing. In truth, he'd laughed both out of relief and genuine joy that they would share a child together.

The glad tidings were accompanied by words of warning, however. Emily would have a difficult pregnancy because of her age and how long it had been since her last one. Her body wasn't used to it and it could be even more strenuous than a first pregnancy. Her age alone was a problem Doc Allison took very seriously. She would have a higher risk of complications arising. Bed rest was ordered, and lots of it. She could only get up if necessary and could do nothing even remotely strenuous.

The remaining thirty-four weeks of her pregnancy were difficult and spent, dutifully, in bed. The sickness and pain never let up, worrying not only Joshua and the doctor, but Christopher as well. He'd had enough experience and knowledge in medicine by then to realize the danger his mother was in. He constantly worried she'd lose the baby, or worse, they'd lose them both.

Ironically, because of that, he fussed over her the most. Between him and Joshua, Emily was spitting mad, but too weak by then to argue.

Then the day of reckoning had come. Emily had awakened with strong cramps around midnight and breathed through them, sometimes dozing, until four o'clock in the morning. That was when she'd realized they weren't merely cramps, they were contractions. She woke Joshua then, who galloped up the road to ask Herbert Fabian to ride into town and fetch Doc Allison so he could stay with Emily.

Christopher had dreaded the day his mother would go into labor. Although it mostly had to do with the worry he'd been feeling about her, but also because he would be extremely uncomfortable in seeing his mother in such an intimate setting.

He need not have worried, for Doc Allison proved to be a sensitive man and had kept Christopher busy with things other than dealing with his mother directly.

As Emily's labor had progressed, Doc Allison had been impressed by Christopher's courage. Despite his obvious discomfort with the situation, Christopher had taken charge when needed and gave Emily directions when the situation warranted. He also stepped in to encourage her as her strength waned. Through it all, he had been able to act as a professional doctor rather than the scared seventeen-year-old boy he would've liked to revert to.

Emily and Christopher both had an even stronger bond after going through that together. And Christopher had to admit it was an experience he'd never forget as he got to watch his little brother come into the world. He had got to be the one to cut the baby's umbilical cord. And the doc had done a good job in being discreet as to how Emily was covered.

Later, Doc Allison had given Christopher due praise. "You did a superb job, Chris. You should be proud of yourself."

Christopher beamed. "I am, sir! Thank you, sir."

Doc Allison started up the stairs again to check on Emily and make sure she was getting the rest she needed. He knocked on the door and then opened it slowly. "I need to check on my patient before heading home."

"Come on in, doc," Joshua invited.

"Your cheeks are getting some color back in them. That's a good sign. Are you hungry? It'd be a good idea to let you have some broth or something light for now."

Surprised, Emily realized she did, indeed, feel hungry. "Food sounds good."

Doc Allison chuckled. "Another good sign. On my way out, I'll let one of your daughters know. Now, let me check this wee lad as well. Does he have a name yet?"

Emily and Joshua shared a secret look as Emily answered. "Isaac Joshua."

Joshua still had Isaac firmly in his arms, but reluctantly handed him over to the doctor to be examined.

As the doctor looked him over, neither Joshua nor Emily could take their eyes off of their infant son. He had a full head of slightly curling brown hair already. After he was done, Doc Allison wrapped the baby back up and handed him over to Emily.

As Emily snuggled him in her arms, Isaac cracked open an eye. "Josh, look, his eyes are dark brown, just like yours! I can't believe he looks exactly like you, only in miniature form!"

As Doc Allison quietly left the room, he glanced back and smiled at the sight of Emily and Joshua marveling over their son.

Doc Allison was in the kitchen when Joshua came downstairs. "Doc? I wanted to know if you have any specific instructions regarding Emily. I know the whole pregnancy and birth were hard on her and I don't want her having any complications."

Doc Allison turned from speaking with Samantha about giving her mother something to eat. "Let her get rest, lots of rest. She should stay strictly in bed for the next two weeks at least. After that, she should still be careful in what she does and shouldn't push herself too hard."

Joshua nodded in affirmation then firmly shook the doctor's hand. "Thank you, doc...for everything." Relief and gratitude colored his voice.

"You're welcome, Mr. Tyler. You have a right fine son and a very brave woman."

Joshua walked the doctor to the door and saw him out. Not

being willing to leave Emily any more than necessary now, Joshua bounded back up the stairs to his wife and baby boy. He couldn't seem to get enough of staring at Isaac.

Emily gently handed him over to Joshua, then caught Joshua's eye and held it. They both grinned like children at each other and Joshua bent to softly kiss her lips. Isaac decided to use that moment to wiggle a little in Joshua's arms, pulling them apart. Joshua chuckled deep in his throat.

"I think he's vying for attention."

Emily took baby Isaac and set him to feeding.

As he watched her, Joshua grew thoughtful and mused, "I've always wanted a son, and then I got to marry you and have Chris as my son and I felt truly blessed to finally have a son. Never would I have imagined that I'd also gain my own flesh and blood son from you, too. Do you realize how blessed I am because of you, Em?" Joshua looked at his wife with adoration.

Emily smiled up at him through tears. She truly felt the blessings as well. "Thank you, Josh," Emily whispered softly.

Their quiet was interrupted then.

"Can we meet him yet?" demanded an impatient Alyssa, knocking on the bedroom door.

"Yeah, Chris told us all about him and how cute he is. Please! Let us in!" Another voice, Kayla's, insisted.

Joshua came to the door then. Opening it, he admonished, "Alright, but you have to promise not to stay long."

Seven female voices chorused, "We promise!" as they stumbled over each other into the sacred room.

Later that night, after the house had quieted down and everyone was in bed, Joshua wearily settled in beside his wife. He marveled at the miracles the Lord had brought that day. Not only Isaac, but Emily as well. *'Thank you, Father, for watching over Emily during her labor. And thank you for Isaac. I don't deserve any of it, but for some reason, you chose to bless me with it and I'm humbled.'*

Gently, he cradled the sleeping Emily in his arms and anticipated their future together.

ABOUT THE AUTHOR

Corinna M. Dominy lives in a small town in Oregon with her husband and four children. When she isn't homeschooling, refereeing, chauffeuring, cleaning up after, cheering on, supporting, and encouraging her husband or children, she manages to squeeze in time for her other passion...writing.

22088388R00177

Made in the USA
Charleston, SC
10 September 2013